A DESPERATE RESCUE

When I found myself moving toward the line of wagons Rion and Vallant were right with me. Some of the men were still fighting to stay on their feet, struggling to keep awake despite the sedative being put into them. They were the only ones still between us and our Blendingmates.

Three of those guardsmen refused to fall over. They were big men, taller and huskier than those around them, and when they saw us coming toward them they drew long, ugly-looking knives and one led the other two in attacking us.

If you've never . . . . scream-ing, wild-look . . . . at a shamblin . . . . to un-derstand h . . . . .

BETRAYALS

Book Four of THE BLENDING

2216 7230

SHARON GREEN

AVON BOOKS, INC.
1350 Avenue of the Americas
New York, New York 10019

Copyright © 1999 by Sharon Green
Cover art by Tom Canty
Visit our website at www.AvonBooks.com/Eos
Library of Congress Catalog Card Number: 98-93291
ISBN: 0-380-78810-1

First Avon Eos Printing: February 1999

AVON EOS TRADEMARK REG. U.S. PAT. OFF. AND IN OTHER COUNTRIES, MARCA REGISTRADA, HECHO EN U.S.A.

Printed in the U.S.A.

WCD 10 9 8 7 6 5 4 3 2 1

For Bob Rosenberg . . . more than just a good friend.
You were always there for me, Bobby, and I'll
never forget.

I believe I'm beginning to do more than simply enjoy this writing project. When I'm very tired ordinary despair becomes intense, and then I begin to doubt that we'll ever find a way out of the swamp our lives have become. Doubting is so much easier than hoping and believing, not to mention being completely free of disappointment. That's probably why I do it so often. . . .

But be that as it may, remembering the problems we've already coped with and solved has helped to soothe me. For that reason I eagerly continue this tale, taking it up again at one of the worst points we encountered. How innocent we all were then, to believe that we'd protected ourselves from treachery and betrayal. We actually had no true idea of what the words meant, but we certainly did learn.

It occurs to me that it might be best if I reminded whoever reads this about where that point was, and then I'll take up the narrative again. I know that the others were upset, but for Rion and me it seemed like the end of everything. . . .

ONE

Lorand awoke—to a certain extent. His head ached in a way that he'd never felt before, the pain so intense that he wished he were unconscious again. And there was nothing he could do to stop the pain. Even if he'd been able to work around it—and the blurriness covering his mind—he couldn't seem to figure out where the power was. . . .

"Look, he's tryin' t'wake up!" someone said, sounding alarmed. "He ain't 'sposta try t' wake up!"

"So what if he does?" another voice countered, male like the first voice. "They got him so doped up that he won't even know what day it is. When you feed him later, you'll probably have to keep shaking him to remind him what he's about. But you better not let him start wasting away, or they'll skin you alive."

"Why?" the first voice demanded, a heavy whine to it. "I heared he's prob'ly all kindsa damaged like, 'cause a th' way he got yanked outta that Blendin'. Gettin' yanked out's 'sposta damage 'em real bad, so why'd they still want 'im? An' if he ain't damaged, how'm I 'sposta handle a High?"

"Why do you insist on worrying about things that are none of your business?" the second voice asked, sounding angrily impatient. "Even if he's left with no more than Middle talent, they'll still want to find that out for themselves. They'll be able to use him even like that, but if his talent level remains intact, he'll be much more valuable. They'll dose him with Puredan to make him docile, and then they'll use him until they burn him out. You, personally, have noth-

2

ing to fear, because they'll transport him to where the army is before they let him come back to himself. Are you satisfied now?''

''Yeah, yeah sure,'' the first voice muttered, and then there was silence again. But it wasn't silent inside Lorand's head, where fear joined the unending pain. He had no idea what the men were talking about, and couldn't even remember what had happened to him. He lay on something hard in a place with a terrible stench, but he didn't know where the place was. He was supposed to have been doing something, but he couldn't remember what that something was.

All he knew was that someone was going to try to burn out his mind.

A long moan escaped Lorand's lips as he tried to free himself from whatever held him down, but it suddenly came to him that he wasn't chained or even tied. Something insubstantial held him in its grip, but its lack of substance did nothing to limit it. It held him tightly, like the arms of a very strong woman. . . .

A woman. Hadn't there been a woman in his life somewhere? The memory of her hid just out of reach, teasing him with hints and suggestions. Had she been like that, a woman who teased? He'd always wanted to meet a woman who would tease him lovingly and gently. . . .

Gently. That word didn't fit anywhere in his world. He'd tried gently to open his eyes, but they'd refused to work. He'd wanted his head to pound more gently, but he couldn't make it happen. Nothing was working right. . . .

Working . . . was he working? Had he had an accident? Someone really should have come by to tell him what was going on, it would only have been common decency. Now . . .

Now he wished he knew where he was . . . and what had happened . . . and who he was, anyway . . . ?

Jovvi felt as though she floated in a heavy sea, she herself heavier than usual. Everything around and about her was heavy, even the air almost too thick to breathe. It was a strain to draw that air into her lungs, and struggling to do it made her head hurt more. But it also seemed to thin the

sea a bit, enough so that she could just touch the outer
world. . . .

"Well, well, aren't you the adventurous one," a male
voice murmured very near to her, and then a hand smoothed
her hair. "You're actually trying to wake up, even though
it isn't time for you to do that. First we'll find a place to
make you nice and comfortable, then we'll wait for the first
transport group that's formed, and then you'll take a nice
long trip. You'll like that, won't you?"

Jovvi could almost understand the words being spoken to
her, but trying harder was out of the question. Even lying
wherever she lay was almost too much of an effort, so anything beyond that . . . except for taking a deeper breath . . .

"Now, now, just settle down," the voice said, again almost clearly enough to be understood. "I understand that
you're probably disappointed, but the lord who is Seated
High in your aspect decided that he doesn't want you after
all. To look at you, one might easily consider him mad, but
then one would have to pause in thought. If a man of his
strength doesn't even care to dally with you for a short
while, you must be dangerous indeed. I am a man possessed
of sufficient courage for all things, yet my sense of discretion usually surpasses the other. They'll make good use of
your talents—whatever they may now be—in the place
where you're awaited, and I'll find a less adventurous—and
adventuresome—woman to do my own dallying with. Rest
now, for when you get where they mean to send you, there
will be no rest short of death—or burnout, whichever comes
first."

Jovvi thought she heard the word "burnout," and agitation began to build inside her. That word . . . it meant something beyond the ordinary, beyond what most words mean.
She had to . . . do something she hadn't gotten around to . . .
had to remember something specific . . . find someone important . . .

Opening her eyes proved to be impossible, as was any
sort of movement. And that hand, smoothing her hair . . . it
made her want to rest for a while, to sleep until the sea
rolled out and she wasn't so heavy any longer . . . Heavy . . .
sleep . . .

*   *   *

"Yes, my darling, that's right," Rion heard, a woman speaking softly and encouragingly. "Try to wake up just a bit, my darling, so that you'll understand what I have to say."

Rion fought to open his eyes, but at first his vision was too blurred to make anything out. Blinking helped to solve the problem to some extent, but it was still necessary to focus. He finally did so, using the face which swam before him as an anchor, and once success was his he immediately wished he'd failed.

"No, no, darling, don't frown so," Mother chided, just as she always used to do. "It will put lines into your face and make you look older, and then people will think *I'm* older. We certainly can't have that, now can we?"

Rion tried to speak, to tell her just exactly what she would and would not have, but his tongue refused to operate properly. And his head ached so abominably that he winced at the concept of trying to form words into a sentence.

"Of course we can't," she continued with a smile and a pat on his cheek, just as though he'd agreed with her. "Now that you're back beside me again, we won't allow anything into our lives that isn't perfect. No, don't try to speak, you won't be able to do that for some time yet. I'm going to keep you drugged for a bit, you see, to make sure you aren't able to keep yourself from being permanently damaged."

Permanently damaged . . . the words chilled him, even though he had no idea what they meant. Nothing could have happened . . . he didn't remember anything happening . . . but where had that headache come from . . . ?

"Don't you worry about that now, darling," Mother went on, chatting happily. "The physician tells me that you're probably permanently damaged anyway, but there's a chance the damage can be minimized if you're able to work against it. But we don't want it minimized, not when that might let you imagine you can escape me again. You can't, you know, because you're mine and always will be. But please don't think you'll be given an allowance again, I'd hate for you to be disappointed. From now on Mother will control everything, and you'll be her loving, devoted, talentless boy."

Rion fought against it, but the tears rolled down his face

anyway. He couldn't even remember what had happened, but he still felt a vast sense of inconsolable loss. It wasn't even possible for him to move, and that seemed to please Mother enormously.

"That's right, my darling, you have a good cry," she said, the expression on her face making him ill. "Cry all you need to and then you'll sleep, and when you awake everything will be the way it was before. Except that I'll never again allow you to leave my side. But then—there won't be any reason for you to leave, will there, my darling?"

Rion let his eyes close again, which did nothing to stop his tears. It seemed as though the crying came from a very small boy inside him . . . while a grown man tried to rage and fight. But that grown man had no strength . . . and the mists of sleep were closing in again . . . and couldn't be avoided even though they would trap him forever. . . .

I think I became aware of my heart beating first, which struck me as being odd. A person is rarely aware of her own heartbeat, unless fright causes it to quicken or to nearly stop dead. My own heartbeat was more than ordinarily rapid, but I didn't know why. . . .

"I said, lovely child, can you hear me?" a man's voice came, the words answering my previous question. The thud of my heart grew even louder, as I recognized the voice. It belonged to a man whose name I didn't even know, but the vague, unformed memory of his intentions was very unsettling.

"Your muscles have tightened a bit, so I presume you can hear every word despite your lack of verbal response," the man went on. "That suits me well enough for the moment, as I shall speak and you need only listen. Later, of course, you'll also be expected to obey. If you fail to do so, you'll be made to produce a verbal response other than speaking."

He chuckled at that, a sound which made my blood run cold, but for no reason easily understood. Who was this man, and what did he want of me?

"To begin with, I should explain that the pain I'm told you probably feel is the result of your having been damaged," he said. "It's highly unlikely that you'll ever be what you once were, but please don't feel relief just yet. My interest in you remains as high as it was, for you're still perfectly able to serve my purpose."

What purpose? I wanted to say, but the lethargy all through me didn't allow it. I had no idea what he was talking about, but for some reason it still frightened me.

"Now, I mean to keep you quietly sedated for a time," he said, "but not for too long a time. I find I'm truly eager to begin with you, and as soon as the Puredan is brought to me I'll have you drink it. After that you'll no longer need to be sedated, and we'll be able to begin."

He chuckled again. "There's something rather amusing that you should hear. Your father and some crony of his attempted to claim you, actually challenging *my* right to possess you. I put them off until tomorrow, but only to give myself time to prepare something really special for them. It will be the highlight of my dinner party tomorrow night, and I mean to let *you* be present to watch. No, don't try to thank me, I've already decided on how I mean to be thanked."

His chuckling really bothered me, especially since I could almost remember something about my father and some friend of his. That memory was just as disturbing, even without any details. I didn't want to hear about any of it, and the best way to escape was in sleep. I felt sleepy anyway . . . sleepy and frightened . . . sleepy and miserable . . . sleepy and very lonely . . .

". . . know what they could do to me for this?" a thin and trembling male voice demanded. "They could end my career, and then where would I be? Please ask for something else, my dear, I beg of you."

"But there isn't anything else that I want," a female voice responded, one that Vallant seemed to recognize. "You owe me more than one favor, love, and if you don't pay up I'll just have to collect in another way. Would you prefer if I did that?"

"No!" the male voice almost shrieked, and then it quieted again. "No, I would not prefer that other way. You leave me no choice but to do exactly as you wish."

"Stop making it sound like the end of the world," the woman chided with a laugh. "No one will be doing anything with him until it's time to send him on his trip, so he might as well do his waiting here. I have this perfectly lovely little box prepared for him, made out of steel so that nothing will be able to harm him. When he learns to beg properly I'll let him out for a while, but I won't forget to put him back again. That should satisfy your feelings of anxiety, shouldn't it?"

"Perhaps," the male voice allowed grudgingly while Vallant's insides began to twist and burn. He couldn't quite remember why he felt like that, but it had something to do with part of what the woman had said. And his head hurt, for some reason he also couldn't remember. What was going on here—and where in the name of chaos was "here"?

"Oh, he'll be fine," the woman said with more laughter. "I'm just going to put him to work for a while, and then you can have him back. I'm sure he thought he'd seen the last of me, but a person's power isn't always linked only to her career position. When I decide I want something, I never rest until I get it."

"Well, now you have *him*," the male voice said, still sounding extremely unhappy. "Just be sure you don't lose or damage him, or we'll both regret it. If I'm blamed for anything, I'll make certain that you're right there beside me."

"Worrier, worrier," the woman laughed, then went on to reassure the man again in different words. Vallant tried to listen, hoping to find out where he was and what was happening, but everything both inside him and out began to lurch. Not sick-making lurch but sleepy lurch . . . as though he were being rocked in the arms of someone who needed badly for him to be there . . . even though he couldn't be there . . . wherever there was . . . sleepy lurch, back and forth, back and forth . . . out but not in . . . please, please, never *in* . . .

Two

The mists of confusion rolled out very slowly, like a tide receding inch by inch from the shore. The first thing I noticed was that it seemed to be midmorning, and the second was that I sat in a chair. The chair stood in a bedchamber a good deal larger than my own, the rest of the furniture and decorations speaking clearly of how much gold had been used to accomplish the look of understated opulence. Rose and gold combined with white and green and brown—none of the colors overdone, all of them perfectly balanced . . . Yes, a small fortune had been spent on that room.

I found myself wondering where it might be, but even as the question formed I already knew the answer: that noble I hadn't had much time to worry about; he'd made good on his threat, and had claimed me for his own purposes.

The ability for normal motion had also begun to return to my body, which let me put a shaky hand to my head. That awful man wanted children with stronger Fire talent than his noble women could give them, and so he'd chosen me in order to get what he wanted. I had some vague memory of him mentioning something about sedatives and Puredan. Once he'd given me the Puredan, he'd said, the sedative would no longer be necessary. . . .

It took two attempts, but I finally managed to get to my feet in order to walk around a bit. The fear growing inside my middle made me want to run, but simply walking straight was still something of a chore. That sedative must still be hanging on in some way, so getting rid of it was a priority. Not to mention figuring out what in the world could have happened . . .

I stopped not far from the wall of curtained windows, feeling the frown which creased my forehead. My last solid memory was of being part of my Blending, facing the last of the noble Blendings. It was the final competition, and we were just about to win. I knew that with as much certainty as our Blending entity had, knew we were stronger than the nobles, and then—nothing. Everything had stopped and gone black, but not for any reason easily seen.

"You're a fool," I whispered to myself, hating the way my voice shook even then. "The reason you lost is perfectly obvious: the nobles cheated. They were about to lose and they knew it, so they *cheated*."

A small amount of anger flared at that, the amount so small because of the size of the fear filling me. I fought to keep the fear from turning into terror, struggled to think calmly rather than fall to pieces, but wasn't having much success. No one had to tell me that my Blendingmates were nowhere near, that I'd been separated from them and now stood alone. I had no one to depend on but myself, and in the past myself hadn't proven to be very reliable.

The ice around my heart grew a bit thicker with that realization, so I continued on toward the windows. It was possible to see bright sunshine beyond the sheer white curtains, but nothing else. If there were terrace doors, for instance, stepping outside would help—especially if it were possible to simply walk away. I *needed* to be away from there, even though I had no idea where I would go. . . .

Brushing one of the curtains aside brought immediate disappointment. Not only was that room on the second floor of its house, a very fine filligreed grill had been put over all the windows. Sunlight came in, and it was even possible to see out easily, but the grill was of metal and didn't appear removable. No one would have been able to get through it, not even a child.

The word "child" made me sick to my stomach, so I turned away from the useless windows. The lethargy which had held me so tightly had receded quite a lot, but some of it persisted in tingeing my thoughts and motions with vagueness—which was an additional worry. That noble had spoken about giving me Puredan; would he come by with it as soon as the sedative wore off completely? Just how soon would that be, and was there any way I might avoid it?

Questions of that sort kept me pacing back and forth across the room for a while. At one point, when I passed a full-length mirror in a dark wood, intricately carved, frame, I noticed something else. I no longer wore the white robe we'd all had on for the competitions. Instead I wore a beautiful, obviously expensive dress of rose and gold which seemed to match the room. I had no memory of having put on that dress, so someone else must have put me in it. Another thing to add to the list causing agitation. . . .

I had just reached the vicinity of my chair again when I heard a sound at the door. Someone seemed to be unlocking it, and it came to me that I hadn't even tried that door. Obviously it *had* been locked, but what if it hadn't been? It made me ill to realize that I seemed to be in the midst of meekly accepting what had been done . . . and what *would* be done . . . Then the door opened, and my illness increased.

"Good morning, child," that noble said, smiling as he entered and closed the door behind him. He also examined me with his eyes as he walked closer, but happily he stopped more than five feet away.

"You needn't look so stricken," he said with amusement as my heart thudded painfully hard. "I've merely stopped in to say that business matters demand my time, and therefore I won't be returning until almost dinnertime. I'll see you then, of course, as I mean to keep my promise. You will share the amusement I've arranged, and then you will be permitted to thank me for the privilege."

"What amusement?" I forced myself to ask, again hating the way my voice trembled. "And if you're waiting for me to thank you for anything at all, you can expect to have a very long wait ahead of you."

"A show of spirit? How delightful." His chuckle did seem delighted, as though we were playing some sort of game. "In another woman that show would be quite unacceptable, but in you I find it rather enchanting. As for the amusement, I refer to the dinner entertainment I've arranged which will revolve about your father. He means to come here tonight to demand your return, obviously mistaking me for one of the peasants like himself whom he's accustomed to dealing with. I mean to teach him better.''

"But of course he's just like you," I said, the words popping out before I could stop them. "The two of you could be twins, aside from whatever meaningless title you have. And your title *is* meaningless, since you let it be given to you rather than insisting on working to earn it. They made you less than a whole man, and you allowed it."

"The delight has suddenly gone out of your conversation," he grated in return, his expression having turned hard with anger glittering behind his gaze. "With that in mind, I tell you now that you're never to speak to me in such a way again. You, of course, will obey, as you've been given no choice in the matter. Just as you will never exercise your talent again."

"What are you talking about?" I asked in a whisper, a terrible chill suddenly clutching at my insides. "You can't keep me from using my talent, no one can. . . ."

"I imagine that you're now in the process of reaching for the power, and are discovering that touching it is quite impossible," he replied, vindictive satisfaction appearing in his dark eyes. "Denying you whatever might be left of your talent was the first thing I did after the Puredan was given you, and commanding obedience was the second. You will learn just how obedient you must be tonight after dinner, when I take full pleasure from you. And now I really must go."

He performed a small, sardonic bow before turning and heading for the door, but I barely noticed. I stood in deep shock with my fists to my head, trying frantically to reach to the power just as I'd done all my life. The action was as natural as walking or speaking, and it felt as though I were paralyzed or struck mute! Not only couldn't I reach the power, it wasn't even possible to locate it!

I stumbled to the chair I'd returned to awareness in, collapsing into it as the sound of the door being locked again came as though from a great distance off. Heavy shock had wrapped me in numbness, so that even knowing I'd already been given the Puredan became no more than a secondary consideration. I'd been cut off completely from my talent, and would never be allowed to exercise it again.

That was the time I learned just how deeply into depression it was possible to fall, which was the point where the desire to die outweighed the urge to live. The monster who held me captive meant to keep me as a pitiful cripple, unable to deny his least whim and wish, unable to defend myself against his depraved intentions. To someone else, the matter stated in such a way might have seemed melodramatic; to me, it seemed the end of the world.

I sat unmoving in the chair for a timeless time, my mind almost empty of thought, and then there was sound at the door again. A moment later it opened, and two women entered. The younger was a girl carrying a tray with covered dishes and a tea pitcher, and the elder seemed a higher-level servant. I paid very little attention to the pair as the girl set down the tray on a table and left again, but the elder woman apparently disliked my extreme distraction.

"That tray contains your lunch, which you should be quite hungry for by now," she announced from where she stood, only two paces into the room. "Lord Lanir was quite clear concerning his wish to see you properly nourished, so you will go to the tray and eat. The command, of course, is to be considered his."

The woman's voice had been harsh with the tone of one used to being obeyed, and I actually stirred a bit in automatic response. My parents had certainly trained me well, and the unconscious response seemed to satisfy the woman. She gave a brusque nod and turned to leave, shutting and locking the door behind herself. But by that time I'd fallen back into apathy, so even the stirring quieted. I had no appetite, and probably would never have one ever again.

I sat staring and unmoving for another rather long stretch of time, but then an odd thought crept into my head. That noble, apparently named Lord Lanir, had said I'd already been given the Puredan as well as his orders. If that were so I would have no choice but to obey him, and yet there I sat, having nothing to do with the meal he wanted me to eat. That woman had clearly expected me to obey the secondhand orders, but I hadn't. Could she simply have been mistaken to expect something like that?

A moment of thought convinced me that her being mistaken was unlikely. Her noble employer must have told her what to expect, and the miserable man was certainly in a position to know. That meant I *should* have obeyed, and yet I hadn't. But not obeying orders given you while you're under the influence of Puredan is impossible . . .

"You fool!" I said to myself aloud, suddenly feeling extremely stupid. "When we freed ourselves from the first orders given us under Puredan, didn't we specify that we were never to obey such orders again? None of us knew if the trick would work, but it looks like it did . . . !"

Excitement rose in me so quickly that it probably would have knocked me over if I'd been standing. I'd forgotten all about that business of telling ourselves not to obey, and it made an enormous difference. If one of the man's commands hadn't worked, the other shouldn't have worked either. I *wasn't* permanently cut off from my talent, even if I hadn't been able to detect the power at all. . . .

With that thought I'd automatically reached out again, the way someone newly paralyzed probably tried without thinking to stand and walk. The only difference was that this time I detected a glimmer of something, a distant hint of the great ocean of power usually right there beyond my mental fingertips. The ocean was still there, only not quite as close as it should be and not as easily reached. But that was better than not being able to detect anything. . . .

Worry sent me up on my feet and pacing again, the darker emotion dimming the excitement I felt. I was now in a much better position than I'd been in earlier, but what had that Lord Lanir said about my talent? Something concerning "whatever ability" I might "have left"? He obviously knew something that I didn't, and it remained to be seen how true his beliefs were.

After pacing back and forth for a while, I finally decided that I needed a cup of tea. I went to the tray and poured the cup, but didn't so much as glance at whatever food lay under the plate covers. I might be free of needing to obey the monster who held me in capture, but without my talent I would certainly be helpless to defend myself against him. If a distant touch were all I ever found it possible to accomplish, I would still prefer to be dead.

Another stretch of time passed as I paced slowly and sipped tea, and the next change occurred so abruptly that I nearly dropped the teacup. One moment I walked and worried, and the next I was again so firmly touching the power that I staggered dizzily. Before this latest insanity began I hadn't been able to release the power except when I fell asleep, and now I seemed to be back to that exact same state again.

"So why wasn't I able to reach it sooner?" I asked aloud in a murmur, feeling the strength of personality that being in touch with the power always brought. "And why did that fool think my talent would be less than it was?"

Asking that second question aloud was indulging in a bit of bravado, as I felt quite clearly that I wasn't completely back to the way I'd been. There was still something of a ... drag, of sorts, slowing down my reactions and limiting my access to the power. That didn't necessarily mean I would *remain* less than I'd been, but—

"Oh, for pity's sake," I muttered, beginning to be really disgusted with myself. "That sedative the noble mentioned ... If it was hilsom powder, it's no wonder I'm coming back so slowly."

I'd heard of hilsom powder, of course, but never having used it myself meant I'd known nothing of the details concerning it until Lorand had explained its main purpose and effects. Hilsom powder was used for the most part by physicians, and not just to sedate certain patients, but also to separate them from the power. Even Low talents can cause a good deal of havoc if they're hysterical, or insane, or even just delirious from a fever. Hilsom powder denies them the use of their talent while they're sedated, and returns their ability slowly over a period of time.

"So that means all I should have to do is wait," I murmured, feeling a good deal better. "Once I've regained every bit of my strength, I'll simply walk out of here. Anyone who tries to stop me will find out the hard way why Fire is the guardian talent in a Blending—"

My words broke off rather abruptly, the silence caused by a sudden, deeper understanding of what I faced. Once I left that house, I not only had nowhere to go, I had no idea how I would locate the others. And I *had* to locate them, no other course of action was possible. They needed my help—assuming I found it possible to first help myself—

and whatever I did would have to be done alone.

Depression tried to fill me again, but the strength flowing into me from the power left no room for debilitating emotions. It was impossible to deny that I would have to act alone, but that would hardly be the first time. It might turn out to be the hardest time, but that would hold true only if I failed to make a decent plan. That, then, was my first objective: to make a plan rather than simply to act and run. Running blindly is often worse than not running at all.

So I returned to the tray with the intention of refilling my teacup, and ended up sitting down to the meal. I'd suddenly noticed that I was quite hungry after all, and it was necessary to remember that I'd been commanded to eat. Giving those people the least hint that I wasn't quite as helpless as they imagined would be stupid, and my Blendingmates and I had already committed enough stupidities.

By the time I finished the food—which I had to rewarm only a little—more of the fog was gone from my mind and I had a tentative plan. It had come to me that the others and I needed to know what had been done to us, to make certain it was never done a second time. I was sure Lanir knew the details, and it should be possible to get him to brag about his knowledge. He might even know what had been done with the others, and if so, then *I* would know. I promised myself that, in the grimmest tone I could ever remember using.

I sat back in the chair with my teacup, trying not to dwell on the most disturbing part of my plan—which revolved around the fact that I couldn't afford to leave the house until after that dinner party. I would have been happiest if I could have walked out immediately, but that Lord Lanir wasn't here to be questioned, and I really didn't want anyone sending guardsmen after me right away. They'd probably be sent eventually, but the longer I had to find a place to go, the better off I would be.

So I sipped tea and wondered what had been planned for my father as a reception. Seeing him again was another thing I would have been happy to miss, especially if he brought Odrin Hallasser with him. It was difficult to believe that anyone would actually try to challenge a noble's claim to anything, so my father had to be more than desperate. I might have pitied someone else in the same situation, but my father had brought his problems on himself. He'd deliberately made his bed without considering anyone else, and now he could lie in it without interference.

But I still would have been happier if I didn't have to see him pull the covers up. . . .

THREE

Rion sat in the chair the servant had helped him to, feeling more lightheaded than he could ever remember being. It almost felt as though he floated in midair, and his thoughts were much too vague. But that didn't mean he had no idea about where he was or what was happening to him. That he knew all too well, and if not for whatever drug had been given him, he would have been drowning in despair.

"Ah, good morning, my darling," Mother's voice came, and then she appeared to take the chair opposite his. "Did you sleep well? Did you enjoy your breakfast? . . . I know you're able to reply, Clarion, and I would advise you to do so at once. I'm sure you've learned better than to make Mother angry."

"In point of fact, I've learned a good deal more than that," Rion responded, forced to speak slowly and with difficulty. "The most important lesson is that your anger is meaningless, so you may do as you please in that regard. I assure you that it will all be the same to me."

"That, of course, will be the first fallacy you unlearn," she countered, no longer as pleased as she'd been. "You will quickly remember how uncomfortable my anger can make you, and also, if necessary, that it can become painful. I *will* have my darling boy back, just as he was before he left to be ruined.''

"You seem to think that ignoring the truth will make it go away," Rion observed, wishing it were possible to throw off the lethargy holding him in place. "Your former 'darling boy' has ceased to exist, and the man he has become detests you and all you stand for. If not for whatever I've been drugged with, I would walk from this house without a single backward glance.''

"To do what?" Mother challenged with a sound of ridicule. "You haven't a single copper of your own, and you're completely incapable of *earning* anything to support yourself. You would be reduced to begging in the streets, and everyone who saw you would laugh. Do you *want* to be laughed at? As a child, you hated when it happened. . . .''

"Do you mean when you arranged for it to happen?" Rion said, taking advantage of the way her voice had trailed off in an effort to humiliate him without words. "Yes, Mother, I *have* finally figured out that all my difficulties with people were caused by you. It left me no one but you to turn to for companionship, which was precisely the result you were after.''

"You don't *need* anyone's companionship but mine," she grated, once again less than pleased. "But that doesn't mean I caused those incidents. It's painful to say this to you, my dear, but your . . . clumsiness and lack of personality precipitated those discomfitures. You simply weren't able to cope, and all *I* did was sympathize and support you. If that's the sort of thing you wish to blame me for, please feel free to do so. A loving mother is always willing to be of whatever help she can be.''

"I find it difficult to believe that at one time I would have been swayed by that sort of nonsense," Rion remarked, ignoring the nobly suffering expression on her face. "This drug allows me nothing in the way of strong emotions, of course, but even beyond that your claims are patently absurd. Someone who is incapable is incapable *all* the time, not simply when one particular person is about. Tell me what has become of my friends.''

"I forbid you to mention low, vulgar peasants in my presence again," she said coldly with a gesture of dismissal. "If it had been up to me, those who ruined my darling boy would have suffered a good deal more than they shall ... And I *will* have my darling back again, even if I must use something other than persuasion to see it done."

"If you're waiting for me to ask what that something is, you're being absurd again," Rion said, trying to find the energy to at least think about struggling against the drug. "Your threats will never frighten me again, so you'd best resign yourself to not having your own way this time."

"Indeed?" she said, the sleekness enough to have made Rion extremely uneasy had he been free of the drug. "But I always have my own way, unless some vindictive sneak exercises his greater power behind my back. If I'd known Embisson Ruhl was behind your having been stolen away from me ... but no matter. I've already taken steps to even the score with him. He'll have as much pain as I had at your loss ... But we were discussing methods other than gentle persuasion for gaining what I refuse to do without."

This time Rion said nothing, principally to underscore his lack of interest. He truly felt that being dead would be preferable to remaining a prisoner for as long as his mother lived, something *she* needed to understand and believe.

"The physician told me something rather interesting," Mother continued in the purr that showed she was at her most vindictive. "The sedative you're being given is called hilsom powder, and I was warned not to keep you on it too long. Another day or two will be enough to be certain that your Air magic talent is ruined beyond repair, but then you must be taken off it or there could be ... mind damage. Are you able to appreciate what that means?"

"Mind damage," Rion echoed, a faint chill actually touching him. "My talent ... ruined? What are you saying?"

"Oh, my darling, don't you remember?" the vile woman said with what he used to consider full concern. "Being forced out of that Blending hurt you, and I've decided against allowing you to make any effort to repair the harm. Your talent encouraged you to disobey me, so now it must be forfeit. There will be no discussion on that particular point, but your mind is another matter. In order to keep it as it is, you must give me your solemn oath that you'll do as I wish. If not . . ."

She let the words trail off suggestively again, increasing the chill that refused to let Rion banish it. If he didn't obey her, he would be left in a state that was worse than death. But his talent, his ability! *That* she meant to take, and how could he face life without it?

"My poor darling, I can see how terribly confused you are," she said as she rose from her chair and came close to pat his cheek. "I'll let you think about your answer for a short while, but only for a *short* while. I've been thinking about it as well, and I'm nearly to the point of deciding that I might actually prefer you . . . altered. You'd be much more like the way you once were, and I really do miss that. I sincerely hope that your decision comes before I make my own, and now I must see to some business. We'll speak again later, darling."

She smoothed his hair before heading out of the room, leaving Rion to sit numbly in silent shock. What she'd said . . . He now knew that he would not only have to give his word to obey her, but that she would also require him to beg for the opportunity to do so. He would be forced to abase himself completely, and then might even be refused! And in any event, she'd already made up her mind to maim him . . .

Some part deep inside Rion wanted to weep like a brokenhearted child, but the rest of him had passed beyond the comfort and release of tears. His Blendingmates would be made to suffer, and he sat helpless and unable to help them. It was even beyond him to help himself, which brought self-hatred and even rage. The only blessing was that Naran couldn't see him now, and that she, at least, was safe. . . .

But what of the others? And in the name of the Highest Aspect—what was *he* to do?

"Oh, yes . . . ! That's marvelous . . . ! Why didn't I ever try this before . . . ?"

Vallant became aware of the woman's voice first, and then, after a long moment, he realized what she was in the midst of. His first thought after that was of Tamrissa, and he smiled to think how far she'd come. But then he opened his eyes, and shock tried to touch him when he saw Eltrina Razas instead of the woman he loved.

"Don't be a fool, dear boy," the woman laughed as her body tightened around him. "We're through when *I* say we're through, and that time hasn't come yet. Who would have believed that a *sedative* used at less than full strength would produce results like this? It has something to do with lowering inhibitions, I'm told, as if I care *why* it works. All I care about is that it does, and that it isn't going to stop anytime soon."

Vallant had been trying to move himself out from beneath her, but she'd put her hands to his shoulders to hold him still. The effort should have been a joke, but his strength had apparently disappeared somewhere completely out of reach. He *hated* what was being done to him, but there didn't seem to be a way to stop it.

"You'd better start showing me something in the way of enthusiastic technique," the female noble panted as she continued to move up and down on him. "If you don't, I have a cozy little crate to put you in until the next time I use you. Do you really want to be put into a tiny, airless crate?"

Panic flared in Vallant, a panic intensified by the sudden memory that he'd already been put into something like that. He'd choked and tried to scream, but the drug holding him had been much stronger than it was now. He'd quickly passed out, but the next time he would be fully awake and aware . . .

"That's only a little better," the woman said, still sounding dissatisfied. "If you can't do better than that, I'll probably leave you in the crate for good."

"I—don't understand," Vallant hedged, fighting to sound confused rather than terrified. "What am I supposed to be doin'?"

"You're supposed to be giving me *pleasure*," she replied slowly and clearly, as though she spoke to an imbecile. "You do understand what pleasure is, don't you?"

"I can't seem to remember *anythin'*," Vallant responded, now striving for an air of bewilderment. "Who are you, and what are we doin' here?"

"Oh, that's marvelous," the woman snarled, her expression vengefully spiteful. "He said you would probably be damaged, but he didn't say you would be *stupid*! What good is my getting what I want, if you don't *know* I'm getting it?''

"Am I supposed to know you?" Vallant tried, sticking to the pretense of mindlessness. "What you're doin' feels wonderful, so just keep on doin' it. But . . . shouldn't I be doin' somethin', too?"

"Oh, this is impossible!" Eltrina snapped, suddenly moving herself off him. "Not only isn't he suffering, now he's giving me orders to keep pleasing him! For your information, *peasant*, I *give* the orders, I don't take them. And I hope your frustration level rises really high, because you're under orders not to give yourself any relief. I'll be back later—*after* I speak to that fool in charge of your sedation!"

With that she stormed away, and a moment later Vallant heard a door slam. By then he had managed to turn to the side, and now braced himself somewhat erect with his right elbow and arm. Moving like that had been a battle, as what he most wanted to do was lie *un*moving.

Lie unmoving in a rather small bed, he couldn't keep from noticing. In point of fact the entire room was small, and there didn't seem to be any windows. Vallant's heart began to beat faster, but the panic trying to flood him had to fight its way through whatever they'd drugged him with. The idea of being put in a tiny crate might bring him terror, but the drug allowed him to think of the room as "just" being small.

Only a few drops of sweat dotted his forehead as he lay back, no longer interested in examining his surroundings. The room appeared to be something on the order of servant's quarters, and except for a plain wooden chest and the bed he lay on, it was completely unfurnished. Aside from the lock on the door, which he'd heard being thrown after Eltrina slammed out. . . .

Despite the drug, Vallant had to fight for a time to keep the terror from taking him over completely. Locked in, drugged into helplessness . . . it was a wonder his mind hadn't already snapped. His bare body had gone rigid as he struggled to free himself enough to move, enough to crawl to the door, at least, and try to break it down. Anything to get free, to reach the outer air where he could breathe . . .

But moving proved to be impossible, and after a time his straining body was forced to admit it. Then he remembered what he'd been in the middle of before this insanity began, and he groaned aloud. He and the others had been taken somehow, cut down just as they were about to win the final competition. Jovvi, and Lorand, and Rion—and Tamrissa. He had no idea what had been done with the others, but that noble who had wanted Tamrissa . . . At this very moment he might be savaging her, and *he* could do nothing but lie unmoving in a bed!

That thought set Vallant to struggling even harder, but it was still no use. The sweat now poured down his face and covered his body, but the drug continued to resist being bested. He was trapped and helpless—and had nothing to look forward to but Eltrina's return and more humiliation. But despite all that he had to stay sane . . . and he didn't know if he could manage it. . . .

Four

"You seem to be adjusting quite nicely," the older woman said as she gave my gown a critical examination. "You look lovely, and Lord Lanir will be very pleased."

"Has he returned yet?" I asked as casually as possible, keeping my gaze on the mirror and my reflection. "He stopped by before he left, to say that he would be late getting back."

"It so happens he's dressing," she replied after something of a hesitation. "I realize that with tonight's dinner being rather special you have reason to ask, but in future

such curiosity will not be received at all well. Lord Lanir is
not here for *your* convenience, you are here for his.''

"How good of you to explain things to me so clearly,''
I responded in a murmur, struggling to hold my temper.
"You can be sure I won't ask that same question again.''

"It's pleasant to see a young girl showing proper manners,'' the woman replied in her stiff, formal way, obviously
missing the dryness I hadn't been able to keep out of my
tone. ''Be sure not to muss yourself while waiting to be
called to dinner. Best, I think, would be to stand in the
middle of the room.''

She added a nod to that bit of advice as though to underscore it, and then turned and left. The maid who had
helped me dress went with her, so I was finally able to turn
away from the mirror. I'd needed the help of my reflection
to keep my expression properly neutral, especially after seeing the gown which had been chosen for me. All pink-and-
white lace with flounces, a costume obviously designed for
a very young girl. I looked like a child in it, a helpless,
innocent child.

Anger growled high inside me again, but the worry I'd
been fencing with for hours had no trouble overwhelming
it. As soon as my relief at being able to touch the power
again faded just a little, I'd remembered I wasn't able to
release that touch if I cared to. That meant I could be found
out at any time by someone with Fire magic, even though
that someone would also have to be touching the power.
Surely there were any number of people who made a practice of touching the power on a regular basis . . .

As I sat down in a chair, I remembered ruefully how long
I'd spent that afternoon, waiting to be found out. My usual
self-confidence while touching the power had been badly
shaken, and it only reasserted itself after time had passed
and no one had come bursting in to shout and point a finger.
It became clear that either no one in the house with Fire
magic *was* touching the power, or, more likely, those touching it were Low talents and too far away to detect me.

I reached for the teacup I'd left standing on the small
table next to the chair, sipping the cold tea without making
any effort to rewarm it. It had occurred to me that my touching the power might be overlooked by Low talents, but ac-

tually using my ability would certainly make it another story. Drinking cold tea was a much more pleasant option— at least until Lanir came to get me. He was the Seated High in Fire magic; surely *he* would be able to tell that I touched the power. . . .

I finished the tea in a gulp and replaced the cup, having already made up my mind about what I would do if Lanir did find out. I'd have to forget about questioning him, of course, but I couldn't afford to let him interfere with my escape. He would have the chance to give up all claim to me and to find something to convince me that he spoke the truth, or he would find himself facing me in challenge. If he were at all like the Seated High in Earth magic, he would probably stand no chance against me. I believed that, I really did, but the wait and the uncertainty about what would happen had been combining to fray my nerves to shreds.

Time began to drag again the way it had done that afternoon, but I refused to let myself get up and pace. Nervous energy had been flowing into me as the hilsom powder lost more and more of its hold, and I'd expended quite a bit of that energy in pacing. Now, though, when I might soon need every scrap of strength I could find . . . Pacing was no longer a good idea, so I simply sat and fretted.

When the sound of the door being unlocked came, it was something of a surprise. I'd spent so long getting myself used to the idea of waiting . . . When the time for the need was abruptly over, I found myself on my feet without remembering the process of standing. If this was Lanir, things could start happening at any moment. The door opened and it *was* the noble, and—

"My dear child, how very lovely you look," he said, taking only a single step into the room, his gaze moving slowly over me. "I will be the envy of all my friends, though only a few of them are invited to dine with us tonight. Those few will have their own lovely companions with them rather than their wives, of course, to round out the company in a proper way. My own lady wife is currently at one of our country houses, so you need have no fear of being forced to endure an embarrassing confrontation. Come, let us repair to the dining room."

He held out his hand to me, and if I'd never seen stark

desire in a man's eyes before, I was certainly seeing it now. For my own part I felt weak with relief, as the man was completely closed to the power. Just the way all those people at the palace had been, including the Fire magic member of the Seated Blending. Was this . . . ignoring of one's talent something all nobles did for a particular reason? I spent only an instant wondering, and then I began to walk toward my . . . host.

By the time we reached the dining room, I'd regained control of myself. The house Lanir led me through was enormous, at least three times the size of mine by the look of all the rooms we passed. Lanir chatted on and on, happily telling me what a wonderful life I would have with him. I would be required to remain in that house at all times, of course, but would not be disturbed by anyone—even the children I bore. The infants would be given over into the care of wet nurses, and would be housed elsewhere.

"And the children will certainly have no rivals for my attention," he continued as we walked down a rather long hall on the ground floor. "After years of marriage my wife has proven barren, and my few companions were unable to produce offspring of more than Middle talent. None of the women was a High herself, of course, which certainly made the difference."

"What if the difference was you rather than them?" I asked in my most innocent tone, paying more attention to the artwork on the walls than to the man whose arm my hand rested on. "We both know *I'm* a High, but from the little I've seen, there's no such guarantee about *you*."

Out of the corner of my eye I saw him part his lips, probably to remind me what his position was. A flash of anger had caused the urge, but both anger and urge died together when he realized I might be right. He hadn't earned his marvelous position, and denying that particular truth would be useless.

"We'll be taking our meal in the small dining room," he said after a moment instead, obviously trying to maintain his good mood. "Afterward we'll socialize a short while just to be polite, but then we'll send our guests home and retire to your bedchamber. I'm quite looking forward to beginning the first of our . . . association."

He touched my hand briefly with that, the expression in his eyes matching the words, but this time I held my tongue. Only after I'd baited him had it come to me that his anger might have made him reach for the power, which meant I'd been a fool to say what I had. I really did need to learn to watch my words, at least while in the position of being surrounded by enemies.

A short way down the hall there were double doors standing open, and as we approached I could hear music being played and voices in conversation rising slightly above the music. When we turned into the room, I learned Lanir's definition of a "small" dining room: a table to the right, large enough to seat twelve people comfortably; a beautifully decorated sitting area to the left, with enough couches and chairs to accommodate more than twelve; and a dais at the back of the room, holding a six-piece orchestra. When we appeared, the people standing about talking—five men and five . . . girls rather than women—all turned from their conversation to us.

"Well, it's about time," one of the men announced with a sly smile, his greasy gaze moving over me. "I can see what kept you, Lanir, but canapés are no substitute for an actual meal."

"You could do with an interest beyond eating, Fasher," Lanir replied with a smug expression, pointing to the man's protruding belly. "If you keep putting things down your throat, you'll soon be unable to get close enough to a table to reach the food."

Everyone including the man Fasher laughed at that, all but one young girl who stared at me wide-eyed instead. She was a pretty little thing, but more importantly she was someone with a Low talent in Fire magic—who also happened to be touching the power. Her hand reached out tentatively to the man she stood beside, probably to tell him about what she could feel of my strength, so I quickly locked eyes with her and shook my head slightly. Her hand immediately returned to her side as she obeyed my silent command to say nothing, but that incident added itself to my list of worries. She'd agreed to be silent, but how long would that agreement last?

"I'm told that it was business rather than your lovely little toy which kept you," another of the men said to Lanir as the man beside me began to lead the group toward the beautifully set table. "Everyone seems to be in a dither about something, but no one is willing to discuss details."

"At the moment there's only one topic causing a dither, and you should know perfectly well what it is," Lanir replied, his good mood fading again. "Everything was arranged for Adriari's group to take over, and now we're faced with *those* five. Debate and argument are raging like runaway forest fires, with no one able to bring Water magic to bear to quiet any of it."

"What could there possibly be to argue about?" a third man asked as we reached the table and Lanir began to seat me to his left. "If they won the competitions—and they did—then they have to be Seated."

"You've never met Advisor Zolind, have you, Wirn?" Lanir replied as he moved a step to the chair at the head of the table and sat. "The man has more power than any other ten people you might name, and the rumor is that he absolutely opposes Seating this particular new Five. I say it's a rumor, because a full Advisory meeting has been called for tomorrow. It would have been held sooner, but two of the Advisors are away and won't be able to return until then. Zolind means to voice his opinions at that meeting, and then we'll have fact rather than rumor."

"How often has Advisor Zolind's opinion failed to find support with the others?" the fat Lord Fasher asked, his own amusement having disappeared. "It would be most annoying to have to wait through another round of competitions."

"If the rumors are true, that's probably what we have ahead of us," Lanir replied, reaching for the wineglass a servant had just filled. "I'm told that Zolind's wishes haven't been argued with in fifteen years, so he's unlikely to be refused this time. That, of course, is the basis for all the argument. Those who had made . . . accommodations with Adriari's group want the chance to do the same with another picked group, while those, like you, who dislike the interruption in business or the cost of another round of competitions, want the annoyance at an end."

"Why doesn't that first group simply make the same arrangements with the new Five?" Wirn asked, having taken the chair at the foot of the table, which unbalanced the seating. "It shouldn't be all that difficult to do it a second time."

"It's a matter of changed circumstance rather than difficulty," a third man put in, someone who had remained silent until now. "Adriari's group was *chosen*, which made them reasonably amenable. This new group can claim actually to have won, and only a very few people can prove otherwise. Their standing is, therefore, substantially higher, so buying their cooperation will probably be a good deal more expensive."

"Not to mention who the five people are," Lanir added with a nod of agreement. "Their fathers are each powerful and respected men, but for the most part the children are either throwaways or potentially too dangerous. If your child is a High talent, he or she had better be fully capable and completely under your control. If he or she isn't, it's safer to dispose of that child as quickly as possible."

The other men agreed with that, and began to discuss various people who had wisely rid themselves of potentially dangerous or embarrassing children. Lanir, having started the discussion, joined in with full enthusiasm while beginning on the soup we were all being served. I spent a brief moment wondering if he were actually as stupid as he seemed, then came to the conclusion that he was simply one of those who were completely insensitive. I was a lowborn woman who had no choice but to do exactly as he wished; why should *he* care if I realized that he meant either to enslave or dispose of any High talented children I might give him?

The creamed soup was excellent, which helped me do something with my mouth other than telling off the fool of a man to my right. It would have been different if I'd actually had to have the man's children, of course, but since I would be leaving that place in just a few hours, it wasn't difficult to keep quiet. Or not *too* difficult. Now that I knew one of the reasons the nobility had so few High talents, it would have been pleasant to point out the stupidity.

In another group my remaining silent might have been noticed, but in that one I simply blended in. None of the other women said even a single word, and the men ignored them as though they weren't there. Women in that group were obviously no more than decorations, no more than the "toys" one of the men had referred to earlier. That arrangement annoyed me as well, but it was something I didn't *want* to do something about. The girl with the Low talent in Fire magic . . .

That girl had been having trouble controlling her agitation as she was seated to Wirn's left. On her right was another of the women, and Wirn himself was too involved in the first discussion to be interrupted. That meant she had to keep her discovery to herself, stirring in her chair and looking everywhere but in *my* direction.

And then the discussion about children began, and a frown appeared on her face. She listened to what was being said, the frown changing slowly to a look of painful despair, and after a moment I could see the glint of tears in her eyes. I had no idea what it was that actually disturbed her, but could only hope that it wasn't what had suddenly come to me: the possibility that she'd already given Wirn at least one child. If that were the case, she now knew what that child's fate would be. . . .

Suddenly the girl looked up, and for the first time met my gaze. There were still tears visible in her eyes, but she forced a faint smile and shook her head in a deliberate way, clearly sending me a message. She had changed her mind about speaking to Wirn of her discovery, and might even have been wishing me well. She could have had no idea what I planned, of course, and was probably only hoping that I meant to use my strength in some way. Rather than pretending ignorance and innocence, I smiled and nodded before giving my attention back to the food. That poor girl had deserved to be given *some* sort of positive sign. . . .

The topic of conversation shifted again with the next course, which was a deliciously sweet paté with shredded radishes. Talk of new houses and the newest "in" places to build them had barely been started, when a servant appeared at Lanir's side. Lanir ignored him while completing a remark, and only then turned his head to the servant and nodded.

"There is a person here to see you, my lord," the servant announced with frigid dignity. "He claims to have an appointment, which is the only reason I agreed to disturb you. Shall I have him thrown out, or simply put somewhere to await your pleasure?''

"Neither," Lanir replied with sudden amusement. "I'd nearly forgotten he was coming, and how much I'd been looking forward to his appearance. Show him in, Bowes."

"At once, my lord," the servant acknowledged with a bow, then disappeared as silently as he'd arrived. I sat there quietly finishing my paté, pretending I didn't know who the caller was. It seemed my father had arrived, and I couldn't help thinking how well he would have fit into that group.

Lanir went back to his conversation about houses, a secret smile curving his lips. Whatever preparation he'd made for my father's visit were obviously going to remain his secret for a while, which suited me just as well. With the choice between Lanir and my father, I couldn't decide whose side to be on. I took a hot, buttered roll and bit into it, and with the last bite the servant Bowes reappeared, leading the visitor.

"Gentles, the *merchant* Storn Torgar," Bowes announced, stressing the word merchant as though it were something low and slimy and obscenely amusing. My father, used to being looked up to and admired, colored at the slur and ground his teeth a bit, but by the time he moved past the servant, he'd forced a charming smile onto his face.

"Lord Lanir, how good of you to receive me," he offered, his attitude saying he spoke to a near equal. "I apologize for interrupting your dinner, but the matter is rather urgent. As soon as we're in agreement, I'll be on my way again."

"Did I remember to tell you all that I had an amusement planned for us tonight?" Lanir said to his friends while completely ignoring his caller. "This peasant is the father of my lovely companion here—do you see the resemblance, with both of them being blond?—and he's had the nerve to challenge my claim to her. He said he's willing to negotiate for her return, so shall we ask what his offer is?"

"By all means," Wirn called with a laugh from the other end of the table. "I haven't had a really good laugh in quite some time."

"Yes, let's hear it," the fat-bellied Fasher agreed while

the other three men made similar comments. "The posturing of peasants has always been good for a chuckle."

"Do you hear that, Torgar?" Lanir said to my father, who had gone absolutely expressionless. "They're all on your side, so let's hear what sort of offer you're prepared to make."

"I expected to discuss the matter in private, just between gentlemen," my father replied, an edge to the voice he held completely without inflection. "As you seem to prefer a public negotiation instead, I can do nothing other than oblige you. The girl is my daughter so my claim to her supersedes yours, but I'm prepared to be reasonable. A thousand gold dins if I walk out of here with her right now."

I couldn't keep from blinking at that, obviously having had no real idea just *how* desperate my father was to get me back. I'd noticed that Odrin Hallasser hadn't come with him, which wasn't a good sign where my father was concerned. The horrible beast of a man must have ordered my father to retrieve me or else . . . For the first time I wondered what that "or else" might entail.

"Really, my good man, how can you say that?" Lanir drawled as his friends laughed. "The young lady hasn't even finished her dinner as yet. Do you really expect me to turn her out hungry?"

"All right, two thousand!" my father snapped, coloring again at the laughter. In his embarrassment he'd glanced at me where I sat unspeaking, the expression in his eyes suggesting that he expected to see *me* laughing as well. Under other circumstances I might have done just that, but having two men discuss the price for my purchase was something I found less than amusing.

"Well, now we have an offer of two thousand," Lanir said, again speaking mostly to his friends. "He really seems to dislike the idea of her having dinner, but I find myself curious. Tell me, peasant: just how high are you prepared to go in order to spirit her away from my board? Stop playing the merchant for a moment, and pretend to be a man. What is the absolutely highest figure you're prepared to offer?"

"You're right, we're wasting time here," my father returned tightly, his fair skin still flushed. "I tried to save us both the trouble of a court appearance and a public scandal, but some people aren't capable of understanding when they're done a favor. My final offer is five thousand gold dins. If that figure doesn't suit you, we can continue this discussion before a panel of judges.''

"Oooo, now the peasant is threatening me," Lanir said, his bad pretense of being frightened causing his friends to laugh even harder. "He offers a sum that only a child would find impressive, then expects me to believe that any court in this city would find in *his* favor rather than in mine. You're obviously a fool, peasant, so I really ought to be gentle with you. You've named *your* highest price, but haven't yet asked *me* to name one. Would you like to try that before you go storming off to court?''

"It's fairly obvious I'm still wasting my time, but why don't you go ahead and name your price. That way *I'll* get some amusement out of this as well.''

My father had spoken tightly, with repressed anger, but he probably couldn't have refused to listen even if he'd wanted to. Not only did he have the awareness of Odrin Hallasser riding him, refusing to listen to an offer went counter to everything he stood for.

"If it's amusement you're looking for, peasant, my offer should suit you perfectly," Lanir said, a glitter of cruel anticipation in his eyes. "In order for me to even consider what you're asking, you must first put forth your proposal in the proper manner. If you'll turn about, you'll see a box on that table to the right of the door. Go and put on what you find inside the box, and then we'll be able to continue this discussion.''

My father hesitated visibly, only glancing at the box rather than going straight to it. He also glanced at me where I sat turned sideways on my chair, but I was just as much in the dark as he. I hadn't even noticed that box, the sort which clothing often came in, so I had no idea what might be in it.

Someone else might have refused even to look, but it was a measure of my father's desperation that the end of his hesitation found him walking over to the box. It took only a moment to open it, and then he threw away the top and pulled out the box's contents to shake the item in an angry fist.

"The motley of a fool!" he snarled, so livid he was nearly beside himself. "And you expect me to put this on?"

"But of course," Lanir agreed blandly while everyone else laughed uproariously. "Didn't I say you were a fool? I simply want you to look like what you certainly are. You may change in the next room, and then you're to return."

Despite his anger, my father hesitated for the second time. The pressure on him to get me back was obviously enormous, otherwise he never would have thought twice about storming out. It was clear he found himself in the midst of actually considering going along with what he'd been told to do, but then his years of experience in dealing with people came to his rescue.

"You said you would 'consider listening' if I did things your way," he remembered aloud, speaking to a patiently waiting Lanir. "Nothing about accepting my offer, just an agreement to consider it. I really would be a fool if I went along with this, so you can save this outfit for yourself. Specifically for when you find out that there are others with influence in the courts beside yourself."

He threw the motley away without watching to see where it would land, and simply stalked out of the room. Lanir's friends were all still laughing, their companions dutifully giggling along with them, but Lanir shook his head with a sigh.

"I'm disappointed," he complained to everyone in general, all but pouting. "I expected him to actually get into that outfit before he realized the truth, but he found me out. Now I'll have to find someone else to wear it. Maybe that friend of his, the one who didn't come with him this time."

"You've probably been saved some effort, Lanir," Wirn consoled his friend while I tried to picture Odrin Hallasser wearing motley. "If he'd put that thing on and only then found out you had no intention of giving the girl up, he might have done something foolish like trying to attack you. From the way he behaved, I doubt he knows who you are."

"But he'll find out if he tries to go to court," Lanir responded happily as he reached for a roll. "He'll discover that *no* one is allowed to institute suit against me, not as long as I remain Seated High. Do you think he'll decide to wait until the next challenge, to see if I'm unSeated?''

General laughter greeted that question, showing they all knew that the outcome of challenges was carefully arranged in advance. Servants reappeared with steaming dishes holding the next course, so once again I was helped to keep from commenting. Assuming Lanir turned out to be reasonable later and I was able to leave without interference, I intended to see if it was possible to return at the time of the next challenge. The man deserved to lose his place publicly, and being defeated by a woman would add insult to injury.

I spent the rest of the meal dreaming about proper revenge, and once we retired to the sitting area I went back to that very pleasant pastime. Lanir had one of the servants put on the discarded motley, and then he and his friends made the man dance around the way court fools were supposed to have done when there were kings and their courts running the world. Men who were very proficient in their respective aspect were called knights, which is where the phrase, "knight in shining aspect" comes from. I'm not sure how "shining" they were, but today's Highs are supposed to be their equivalent.

After the lordly nobles finished with their amusement, Lanir gave his friends a final glass of wine and then sent them home. None of them seemed surprised at being all but thrown out, nor were they insulted. They left laughing and joking with one another, and then Lanir turned to *me*.

"Your behavior tonight was absolute perfection," he said, holding out his arm to me. "The time has now come for the part I've really been waiting for, so let's hurry back to your apartment."

I rose from the chair I'd been sitting in and went to take his arm, ignoring the part of me that wanted to tremble with dread. I'd have no trouble handling whatever came next, I *knew* I would have no trouble . . . I hoped . . .

FIVE

Kambil Arstin walked into the sitting room of the residence where the others had already gathered, looking around with a great deal of satisfaction. Bron, Homin, and Selendi sat together chatting, and Delin simply sat by himself and stared. Delin would have been devastated to know how . . . vacant he looked, but Kambil knew better than the others that Delin was no longer being allowed to know anything. His unthinking body wasn't even aware of where it was, let alone that it was only permitted to follow orders, not to consider them.

"Ah, Kambil, you're back," Bron said after looking up. "How did it go? Did you learn anything?"

"I certainly did, which means we'll be busy tonight," Kambil replied, heading for the everpresent tea service. If for some reason he had to stop drinking tea, he had no idea what he would do with himself in place of holding a cup and sipping from it.

"Does that mean we still aren't to be allowed into the palace?" Selendi asked. "They have a lot of nerve keeping us out after we won the competitions."

"Don't forget that we were helped to win, my sweet," Homin told her with a chuckle. "That means they think we owe them something. But I take it Zolind is still being difficult?"

"Advisor Zolind Maylock was undoubtedly born difficult," Kambil said over his shoulder as he added sugar to his tea. "He's called for a full meeting of all his brother

Advisors, insisting that it be held tomorrow. Once the meeting is in session he'll certainly insist that we be disqualified and that a new round of competitions be held next year, with the present Blending remaining Seated for the time. We can't afford to let that happen, so tonight we'll see to it that the man who was born difficult dies the same way.''

"Won't he be expecting us to try something like that?" Bron asked, watching as Kambil carried his teacup to a chair and sat. "I mean, we *are* a functioning Blending, after all. Only a fool would ignore that fact and discount us."

"Sometimes ignorance accounts for a good deal of foolishness," Kambil told him, pausing to sip his tea before continuing. "For instance, there's a guard contingent stationed around this house now. It was posted there supposedly to 'protect' us, but they also have orders to make sure we don't leave. The guardsman I passed on the way out was kind enough to tell me that, although he doesn't remember speaking to me and is prepared to swear that no one got by him. Zolind doesn't even really understand what we're capable of individually, so how can he possibly guard against us as a Blending?"

"He can't, so he's ours as soon as we reach him," Selendi said happily, tightening her grip on Homin's hand. "And since no one will remember that we left and then returned, he'll even have provided us with witnesses to support our innocence."

"A point which I find extremely amusing," Homin said with a faint smile, briefly raising Selendi's hand to his lips. "What I'd like to know, though, is how we'll cover ourselves where the Seated Blending is concerned. You said we would be ending them as well, and who else but us will be considered able to do that?"

"No one, which is why they won't be 'ended,' at least as far as the world is concerned." Kambil made no effort to hide his amusement, as the idea which had come to him still had the ability to tickle. "The Five will be seen to leave the palace without their guard, on the way out saying something to the effect that they'd done their duty and had no interest in hanging about any longer. People will have the impression that they mean to implement private plans, which ought to explain their complete disappearance. And they *will* disappear, in a way that no one will ever find them again.''

"Is that why you had me check on the abandoned quarry ten miles beyond the far side of the city?" Bron asked, sudden understanding coloring his expression. "I remember thinking that properly weighted bodies thrown into the water would never come to the surface again—at least until the water had turned them completely unrecognizable. Is that where you intend to put them?"

"As soon as all clothing and jewelry are stripped from them," Kambil confirmed with a nod. "That way no one will know who they are even if the bodies *are* found. I doubt there are as many as a dozen ordinary people in and around this city who know the Five by sight, and that's who would find them: ordinary people. Those who would be able to identify the bodies won't even hear about the incident— assuming the bodies are found at all."

"And even if they are, we'll have been Seated by then," Selendi said with the satisfaction they all obviously felt. "We'll also have made good progress in ridding ourselves of anyone who might be willing to use the discovery against us, so we'll be doubly protected. When are we going to begin, and what do you have planned for Zolind?"

"I have something rather . . . complex in mind for our friend Zolind, and we'll begin about an hour before dinnertime," Kambil replied, letting his own satisfaction show through. "He always has dinner guests, which means our little production will have an adequate audience. I'll tell you the plan, and then you can all criticize it for flaws."

"Not all of us, happily," Homin disagreed rather dryly. "Poor Delin over there won't be criticizing or complaining ever again, for which I'm extremely grateful. If you hadn't put him under your control, I'm convinced he would have soon begun to whine."

"What do you mean, 'would have'?" Bron countered with a snort. "If he wasn't whining about being left out of things, I've never heard the sound. This way we have his strength and talent in the Blending, but otherwise don't have to put up with his feebleminded insanity. So what are we going to be doing to Zolind?"

Kambil leaned forward and told them, all the while marveling at the artificial personalities he and his grandmother had imposed on the three. The idea of doing that had been Grammi's, and it had come as a mild surprise that she'd perfected the technique on Kambil's father, who was her son. She'd begun her practice on her own husband, and when she'd accidentally ruined his mind had had to arrange his death. A different accident had made the death of her daughter-in-law also necessary, but by the time she worked on her son, she knew all the trouble spots which had to be avoided.

And Kambil had found the technique ridiculously easy to work with when they'd done his three Blendingmates. Their dysfunctional personalities had been pushed aside and over-shadowed by calm, rational pseudo-egos, none of which could really be considered fully normal, but ones which were easily led and manipulated. The three subjects loved what they called their new selves, of course; what they had no idea about was the fact that they weren't permitted to do anything *but* love them.

Their ability to function in the group had been increased, though, so Kambil was serious about consulting their opin-ions. The four of them discussed Zolind's coming demise for quite some time, until Kambil announced that he'd ar-ranged for a late-afternoon bite to eat. The interim meal would hold them until they returned to the house, and then they would dine long and well.

They took Delin along to eat as well, of course, and Kam-bil found himself regretting all over again that it hadn't been possible to adjust the man the way the others had been ad-justed. He had to be kept in a sort of nonthinking limbo most of the time, and then had to be controlled carefully when his talent was needed. It was a lot of extra effort that should have been unnecessary—except for the deeply twisted thing Delin's mind had been turned into. Kambil was beginning to nurse almost as much resentment against Delin's father as Delin felt. . . .

But simple revenge would have to wait until more press-ing matters were attended to. Kambil sat back at the end of the meal to study his people, for the most part satisfied with what he'd accomplished. That excuse his father had been given about why *he'd* been put into a Blending . . . Despite the care Kambil usually took to keep from frightening those he came in contact with, someone had seen through the facade and had become frightened anyway. Whoever it was had to have a respectable amount of power, and so was a dangerous enemy. As soon as Zolind and the current Blending—and certain of the rest of the Advisors—were seen to, Kambil would make it his business to identify the person, and then he would give the man his thanks for almost having ruined his life.

Once the meal was over everyone separated to prepare for the outing, Delin being taken care of by two of the servants. Their group tended toward brightly colored clothing, which simply would not do for their current undertaking. Not being noticed was more easily accomplished when people had drabness to overlook, and Kambil's groupmates never questioned the need to make things easier for him. That was one definite benefit which made up for the bother of having to be in charge.

When all five of them had reassembled in the hall, Kambil switched Delin over to simply being under control, then he initiated the Blending. Their entity formed at once, of course, and proved to be almost completely stable despite Delin's . . . buried desire to rage, might it be called? Somewhere beneath all the control and passivity was the angrily terrified Delin personality, hating what had been and was being done to him.

But Delin had never been able to resist being taken advantage of, and now was no exception. After a moment his part of the entity settled down, and then their combined talents were able to search out and affect every member of the guard force around the residence. The guardsmen would continue to remain alert, but would see nothing of the five as they left and returned.

Then it became simply a matter of their walking out to the coach Kambil had arranged for earlier. The driver would be seen to later by the Blending, after Zolind and the Five were taken care of. Kambil had no idea how long their practiced group could remain Blended before its strength was completely drained, and now was not the time to experiment. After they were securely Seated there would be time enough; for now, he kept their Blending separated when there was no real need of it.

The drive to Zolind's estate was a long, boring one, as Zolind detested living close to the city. During the day it would have been difficult to hide the presence of their coach, but with darkness all around they simply had to avoid the lanterns which had been strung along the approach to the house. The arriving guests saw nothing that way, which was just as it was supposed to be.

Delin stirred uncomfortably where he sat on the floor of the coach, which told Kambil that the man's position needed to be shifted. The movement meant the man's body was in pain, and pain would detract from what he added to the Blending. For that reason Kambil had Selendi trade places with Delin, as she was the smallest of them despite her skirts. The exchange of places was made without argument, of course, and then they were able to Blend again.

The entity floated to the large house and inside, locating Zolind after a few minutes in the salon beside the large dining room. It was clear not all of the Advisor's guests had arrived yet, and that despite the fact that almost twenty people stood about sipping wine. Zolind himself drank only tea, but never insisted that his guests do the same. The conversation was much too desultory, however, so the entity touched one of the men immediately around Zolind with a suggestion.

"Someone asked me today why the Seating ceremony for the new Blending hasn't been announced yet," the portly man who had been touched announced casually. "Since I don't really know the answer myself, I couldn't tell them."

"The answer is quite simple," Zolind replied obediently, now completely under the control of the entity. "The time of the ceremony hasn't been announced because there will *be* no ceremony. I wanted Adriari and her people to be Seated, and these others are not an acceptable substitute. Tomorrow I will announce that at the Advisory meeting, and none of the others will dare to disagree with me."

"My dear fellow, you can't be serious," the portly man protested, again at the urging of the entity. "Adriari and her group are gone, and these others *have* won the competitions. You can't simply discount that just because they aren't the group you favored."

"I can do anything I please!" Zolind growled in a louder-than-normal voice, drawing the attention of everyone in the salon. Those immediately around him had remained silent, trying to disassociate themselves from the portly man who was so rash as to disagree with Zolind. The entity felt their disturbance clearly, and made no attempt to change it.

"I can do anything I please, including rejecting people I simply cannot stomach!" Zolind growled forcefully, glaring at the portly man. "That Delin Moord is one of them, and I've become convinced that Moord is the one responsible for Ollon's death. *Someone* has to be responsible, *someone* has to pay! Do you have any idea how much I miss—"

Zolind's words broke off as he obediently turned away from his guests, one hand covering his eyes to demonstrate his anguish. A roomful of glances were exchanged, making it plain that most of them were aware of Zolind's relationship with Ollon Kapmar. It was also clear that Zolind had never mentioned it aloud before, and more than a few of the observers were upset by Zolind's abrupt loss of self-control.

"You have our sympathy, of course, my friend, but you must be reasonable," the portly man was made to say gently after a moment. "If the winning Five isn't Seated, the commoner leaders will want to know why. Telling them that someone has to pay for Ollon's death won't satisfy them, not when there's no actual proof that it *was* this Moord fellow. And you *don't* have actual proof, do you?"

"I dislike the elder Moord, and I loathe his son!" Zolind was made to shout as he whirled back to face the fool who challenged him. "Have you somehow forgotten exactly who I am? I *want* someone to pay for Ollon's death, and therefore someone *will* pay! Are you too stupid to understand that?"

Zolind was now in a frenzy, his eyes opened wide as spittle sprayed from his mouth. Those closest to him had taken a pair of steps back, some retreating even farther. The portly man was made to look horrified as he joined everyone else in recoiling, and that was allowed to increase the Advisor's agitation. Zolind began to shout incoherently, his face reddening dangerously as he accused everyone in the room of being in collusion against him. Then the Advisor gasped and clutched at his chest, faltering a moment before collapsing to the floor.

The portly man led some of the others in rushing to Zolind, but it was already too late. The entity had caused the Advisor's heart to fail, killing the man almost instantly.

"He's dead!" the portly man announced in a shocked whisper as he struggled to straighten up. "He's dead, and I feel responsible!"

"You were insane for arguing with him, but it isn't your fault that he's dead," one of the other guests grudged, relieving the entity of the need to *cause* someone to say that. "Losing Ollon obviously unhinged him, and we're *all* quite fortunate that he died. If he'd lived, his madness would have caused untold harm before someone found the courage to oppose him."

"If they'd ever found it," the portly man agreed with a sigh. "Zolind's autocratic manner has never been easy to disagree with, but tonight I simply couldn't abide letting the matter go. There would have been all *sorts* of trouble if the new Five failed to be Seated simply because Zolind disliked one of them, but the other Advisors would never have been able to overrule him."

"People have said for years that Zolind had a collection of serious indiscretions to hold over their heads," someone else put in. "Anyone opposing him would have been promptly arrested . . . and now I wonder where that collection might have been kept."

Others joined the speculation as servants were called to attend to the body, and the most uniform emotion the group shared was an air of disappointment. The entity perceived that Zolind's guests disliked the idea of no longer being an intimate of so important a man, although "intimate" wasn't precisely the right word. Zolind had been really close to no one but Ollon Kapmar; the rest had been all but faceless company for a man who had disliked dining alone.

At that point the entity withdrew, and once it had returned to the coach Kambil dissolved the bond. He joined the others in taking a deep breath to celebrate their first success, then rapped on the coach roof to signal the driver to get them away from there. There was still one further chore to be done tonight, and then they would be able to return to the residence to eat and rest. Tomorrow . . . well, that remained to be seen, depending on whether or not the rest of the Advisors held their meeting, or attended the farewell ceremony for Zolind.

Kambil smiled into the darkness as the coach began to move. There was no need for their entity to attend a farewell ceremony, but the full Advisory meeting was another matter entirely. . . .

SIX

"I've been looking forward to this all day," Lanir said as he closed the bedchamber door behind us. "I felt tempted to taste your charms yesterday, but I dislike lack of response in a woman. I expected to have most of the day with you today, not realizing that I would be called away on business. Don't bother ringing for a maid. Helping you out of that gown will be my pleasure."

"First answer a question for me," I said, crossing most of the room before stopping and turning back to look at him. "My group was winning that final competition, and then suddenly we were unconscious. How did they do that?"

"Hilsom powder in your underclothes, which stayed undisturbed until the underclothes were shaken with Air magic, forced you out of touch with the power, and then Earth magic users helped the powder to put you to sleep," he answered easily enough as he followed me across the room. "That's what's usually done, although it's never been necessary in the final round before."

"And what became of my groupmates?" I asked, standing my ground as his arms began to circle me. "Were they *all* claimed by someone like you?"

"I have no idea what became of them, nor do I care," he replied, smiling down at me as his embrace slowly tightened. "And I believe you'll discover that there *is* no one else precisely like me. Raise your lips to mine."

"For what purpose?" I asked, flatly refusing to let my voice tremble. "I may be prepared to say goodbye to you and this vile place, but that doesn't necessarily call for a kiss."

"Are you trying to tease me?" he asked, his tone less than pleased. "If you are because you think I might enjoy it, allow me to assure you that you're wrong. Denial is not my idea of enjoyment, and can only bring you punishment. Although how the need for punishment can be possible after the orders you've been given . . ."

"Have you finally noticed that I'm not as obedient as I'm supposed to be?" I asked in what I hoped was a mocking tone. "It's certainly about time, as the touch of you against my body is making me ill. Release me this moment, or you'll surely wish you had."

"How dare you!" he began to demand in a growl, and then his expression abruptly changed. Fear flashed in his eyes as he suddenly touched the power, but his burst of understanding came too late. I'd already applied a tiny line of flames to his forearms under his sleeves, which made him flinch back with a scream even as he opened his own talent wide.

"What have you done?" he choked out in a strangled whisper, cradling his arms in trembling hands. "You're opened to the power, but that's not possible! And you're so—"

"Strong?" I suggested, speaking the word he hadn't. "I would ask why that frightens you—if I weren't able to tell that you have no more than Middle talent. Doesn't that mean your title has to be changed to Seated Middle? I can't wait to tell that joke to everyone in the city. . . ."

His scream interrupted before I could suggest the price of my silence, and then there were flames all around, trying to burn me to cinders. My defenses had automatically flared into being an instant before the attack, which in this case meant no more than simply keeping the ravening fire at a distance. Lanir just wasn't strong enough to overwhelm me, so I smiled faintly through the flickering evidence of his fear-filled anger.

"You can see that that isn't doing you a bit of good," I pointed out gently. "If you're wise you'll be reasonable about letting me go, but first you'll have to convince me that you intend to keep to any bargain we happen to make. I have no reason to trust you and every reason not to, so—"

"No!" the man screamed with fists clenched, insanity beginning to peer out of his eyes. "I *can't* let you go after insisting that I be allowed to claim you! I'll look like a fool, and I'll become a laughingstock! Better to be thought clumsy for having turned you to ash—!"

And then his eyes widened with his effort, an effort I understood only after a very long moment. The fool was ignoring his limits and trying to take in enough power to match *me*, which meant he really was insane. Middles weren't able to step past that natural block—

His third and last scream shook me so badly that I stumbled back, narrowly missing a collision with a table. Along with the scream had come the abrupt severing of Lanir's touch on the power, followed by the man's sitting down hard on the carpeted floor. By then he had stopped screaming, and I didn't need to see his blank, fixed stare to know what had happened. He'd forced himself past his natural stopping place, and had burned himself out for his trouble.

I turned away to find a chair to sit down in, needing a moment to pull myself together. The fact that Lanir had taken himself out of my way permanently didn't bother me, but the screaming he'd done did. How soon would people come rushing in to see what had happened? And when they came, would I be able to protect myself from them? I wasn't sure, not when I didn't know how many there would be and what they would be capable of. . . .

Trying to still the trembling of my hands occupied me for a few minutes, and then I began to wonder why no one had appeared yet. Surely *someone* had heard the screams, no matter *how* big that house was, so why hadn't they—The question died as the answer came so abruptly that I was suddenly enraged. No one had come after hearing the screams, because they thought *I* was the one doing the screaming. They must have been very used to their employer's way of enjoying himself. . . .

That realization calmed me completely, so familiar was it. My husband had run the same sort of household, and now Lanir would soon be in the same condition as my husband. That idea seemed so beautifully right that I turned in the chair to look at Lanir, seeing again the way he sat and stared and drooled. When they found him they would put him down, making no effort to preserve an empty husk. The man who had been was no longer housed in that body, so what was the sense in keeping it alive?

I went to the tea service then to discover that it had been refilled with fresh tea, so I helped myself and spent some time simply sitting and sipping. I had to wait until the household had settled down for the night before I could leave, so there was no rush to go and start and do. What I would eventually do was walk away into the night, even though I had no idea where I was or where I would go. Lanir had claimed not to know where my groupmates were, but I still had to find them. . . .

The part of me that never seemed to touch the power quailed at the idea of such an impossible task, but it wasn't really all that impossible. *Someone* had to know what had been done with the others of my group, so the first thing I had to do was find that someone. It occurred to me that I could ask Eltrina Razas, who might not be very interested in answering my questions. I would then have to *make* her interested, and there would be no losing her the way I'd lost Lanir—at least not until she answered my questions.

Thinking about Eltrina Razas became planning a way to reach her, which brought me to the subject of a coach or carriage. I'd have to hire one, of course, even if Lanir had his own stables and coach house. Women just didn't go driving all by themselves in that city, and doing it anyway would simply get me noticed. But I had no money . . .

After putting my cup down, I rose and walked over to Lanir where he still sat on the carpeting. The stain on his trousers—added to the terrible smell that seemed to be all around him—suggested he'd lost control of his bodily functions, but his wallet still lay securely around his waist and untouched by any effluvia. I bent carefully and unbuckled it, then carried it back to my chair. Since the former Seated High had brought me to a place I never wanted to be, he could just pay to have me driven away again.

His wallet contained a really fat purse, which in turn contained quite a bit of gold and silver. Discovering that sent me on a search of the room, to see if I might find any sort of handbag. The wardrobe was empty of everything, including the dress I'd worn earlier in the day, which I found rather confusing. If I'd been meant to live in that room, why would there be nothing of clothing for me?

The possibility I eventually came up with made me sneer in Lanir's direction. He could well have meant to keep me in a nightdress—or naked—to be certain that running away was impossible, possibly as women before me had done. That said quite a lot about him as a man, making him someone who held women with restraints rather than with kindness or enticements. Was there anyone—other than his cronies in the government—who would mourn his passing?

I thought it unlikely as I turned away from my search with nothing to show for the effort. There was no handbag and nothing to use in place of one, which meant that I would have to tie the purse to my underskirts after taking out a few silver dins. Showing gold would bring trouble of its own if the wrong people saw it, and I'd certainly have trouble enough without adding to it.

Anxiety to leave that place had begun to grow inside me, but I forced myself to have one final cup of tea before making the attempt. It had been at least two hours since Lanir had brought me back to that room, and by now all the servants should have retired. I'd find out soon enough if they hadn't, but that final cup of tea would lessen the chance of an unpleasant encounter.

When the time finally came to leave, I took one last glance around the bedchamber and then walked to the door. Lanir hadn't locked it, I'd noticed at the very beginning, but I'd still taken a small ring of keys from his wallet as well as the gold and silver. If the servants were all in bed, the house ought to be completely locked up. I had no intention of creeping heart-stoppingly all the way to the door, only to find it locked with something other than a slide bolt.

And I did end up virtually creeping through the dark halls,

my heart pounding heavily in my ears. I felt certain that no one in that house would have been able to stop me, but the idea of running into someone still caused my heart to pound and my mouth to go dry. Most of me wanted to run to get out of there, and only the knowledge that I'd certainly have a long distance to go before I found a coach or carriage kept me from wasting my physical strength.

The creeping did prove itself useful, though. I'd decided against using the front door unless I absolutely had to, so I was in the midst of searching for a side door when I came across two servants. They sat in a small room drinking tea, looking completely bored as they waited for something. The bell arrangements on the far wall suggested what they were waiting for: a summons from the lord of the house. I tiptoed past the partially open door and then hurried my search, not knowing whether they were simply on duty for the entire night—or awaiting a definite summons. If Lanir was expected to ring for them, how long would it be before they went to investigate his continued silence . . . ?

It was a lucky thing that I found the door I sought just around the next curve of that dimly lit back hall. If I hadn't I would have certainly retraced my steps to the front door, taking the chance that there would be a servant on duty near it. I'd heard that people with really big houses had servants assigned to front-door duty at night as well as during the day, just in case an emergency of some sort arose. I now needed more than ever to be out of that house, and the thought of being stopped brought me close to losing control.

The small side door had both a slide bolt *and* a key lock, making me glad that I'd taken Lanir's keys. It took much too long to get the door open—almost a full minute—but I still forced myself to take the time to relock it once I stood outside. If Lanir was discovered before I left the grounds, the search for me might be confined to the house if all doors were found to be still locked.

That line of logic wasn't a very strong one, but I clung to the hope of it as I made my way along the footpath which led away from that side door. It was very dark out and rather chilly in the lacy gown I still wore, but a bit of moonlight was available to help me move carefully along the footpath. Happily no one had added gravel to make it look better—

and be more treacherous and noisy, footing-wise—but I still couldn't move as fast as I wanted to. Falling and twisting an ankle—or worse—would have been the end of everything, so I simply had to go rather slowly.

Leaving the vicinity of the house didn't bring me that much closer to a main road or street. The footpath paralleled a long drive ranging off into the darkness, a drive which seemed to go on forever. I trudged along the footpath, wishing I could walk the hard-packed earth of the drive instead, but that would have made me much too visible. Being in that gown was bad enough, considering the tiny sequins sewn all over both the skirt and bodice. If lamps were brought close the sequins would certainly gleam the way they were meant to do, making me completely visible. I needed to be able to hide behind a large tree, and trees were closer to the footpath than to the drive.

Walking along like that gave me far too much time to think, as the thought uppermost in my mind was how far I would have to go before I would be able to find a coach or carriage. Many public stables had carriages for hire, but how many of them would be open at that time of night? And when I finally did reach the main road, which way should I go? Turning right when the proper direction was left could have me walking for the rest of the night without finding what I needed—

I stopped dead as my latest glance up from watching where I put my feet showed me something other than empty woods. A large, dark shadow stood about thirty feet ahead, motionless at the side of the drive. The outline of the shadow suggested that it was a coach, and once I'd noticed that I could also hear the faint jingle of horses in harness. I'd been wishing rather fervently for a coach, but not for a moment did I believe that some beneficial superbeing had heard my wish and granted it.

Fear tried to wrap its hands around my throat and middle, but anger rose too swiftly to let that happen. I hadn't come through everything just to walk into the waiting hands of another enemy, not when my touch on the power was as firm and sure as ever. Lanir hadn't had to face my flames, but whoever lay in wait to trap me certainly wouldn't be that fortunate. I hadn't even produced a small fire to light my way along the footpath, just to be certain that I had enough strength in case of something like *this*. . . .

I was actually half a thought away from kindling a fire that would consume the coach almost instantly, when I noticed the human figure which had appeared beside the vehicle. The figure was engaged in pacing back and forth along the drive, and even more importantly it was female. Some woman waited there, and one who was certainly not tall enough to be either Eltrina Razas or my mother. A small woman, then, and one whose fingers moved nervously about each other. . . .

Curiosity took me silently nearer, but I had to close half the distance between us before I finally recognized the woman. Shock touched me briefly along with confusion, but there was only one way to find out what was going on. I left the footpath and crossed to the drive, and when I reached it I called softly, "Naran!"

Naran Whist, Rion's ladylove, whirled around in what seemed to be fright. Her case of nerves was apparently twice or three times worse than mine, and when she saw me she raised her skirts and actually ran to meet me.

"Oh, Tamrissa, I knew you would escape from there!" she sobbed, throwing her arms around me. "I *did* know it, but when hour after hour passed and you didn't appear . . . I was nearly convinced that I'd missed you, and that made me frantic."

"Well, now I'm here so everything's all right," I soothed her, returning her hug. It felt so strange, *me* soothing someone else's fright . . . "But how did you find me? Even I don't know where I am."

"I can't explain how I found you, at least not yet," she said, releasing her hold on me as she visibly regained control of herself. "Among other things, we simply don't have the time. I also know where Rion and Vallant are, but they can't escape without help. They're still under the influence of a horrible drug that affects both their talent and their bodies. You're the only one who has gotten free, so you're the one who has to help them."

"Are you saying someone made me designated hero when I wasn't looking?" I asked, a bit overwhelmed by the thought that two big, strong men needed *my* help. "Well,

I'd already decided to find the others . . . But what about Jovvi and Lorand? If you found the rest of us . . .''

"I haven't been able to locate them yet," she replied with a headshake, her pretty face looking drawn in the faint moonlight. "I don't know *why* I haven't been able to because they're definitely still alive, but—Let's get into the coach, and I'll explain where Rion and Vallant are."

"Where did you get a coach?" I asked as I moved toward the vehicle with her. "And one that has a driver," I added as I saw the man on the box turn to glance at us. "Have you paid him enough to keep him quiet? When they begin to look for me, they may offer a reward for information."

"He'll be well paid, but he doesn't really need to be," Naran responded as she opened the coach door and gathered her skirts before beginning to climb in. "He's the driver of a very good friend of mine, and neither of them would give a noble the right time of day even for gold. Don't most of the people *you* know feel like that?"

"Before becoming a member of our group, the only people I'd ever heard talking about nobles were merchants like my father," I replied, ignoring the trouble my skirts tried to give as I followed her into the coach. "My father's associates always waxed really enthusiastic when it came to the nobility, but I don't know if that was because of all the gold they made dealing with them, or because they were *afraid* to say anything negative. Nobles will pay you if you tell them about people who say things against the nobility, you know."

"Yes, everyone knows that," Naran responded with a sigh, still settling herself just as I was doing. "But everyone also knows the ones who would go after that dirty silver, so nothing is ever said in front of them. Ah, we've begun to move. Next stop—Rion's mother's house."

"Do you mean she actually managed to get him back?" I asked with surprise, then waved away the foolish question. "No, forget I said that. The real surprise would be if she *hadn't* gotten him back. Poor Rion. He must be absolutely frantic."

"That's why we're going for him first," she said, heavy worry now clear in her voice. "If he thinks he has no way to escape her, he might well do something desperate. Vallant won't be *allowed* to do something desperate, not while that woman still wants to make use of him.''

''That woman,'' I echoed, staring at Naran through the darkness. ''You're not talking about Eltrina Razas, are you?''

''Who else?'' Naran asked with a sound of scorn. ''Rion told me all about her, including the fact that she usually stared at Vallant behind her hand, so to speak, whenever she came to the house. He's unlikely to be enjoying himself as her captive, but he shouldn't be actually suffering.''

I had to agree with that, but the entire situation made me boiling mad. When women were so often taken advantage of by men, it was unconscionable to think that there were women stupid enough to try to match that evil. If things happen which you don't like, you make an effort to end the practice—not to get your own licks in. Hurting someone else because *you've* been hurt—that makes sense only if you go after whoever hurt you, not some possibly innocent substitute. . . .

My thoughts were a bit on the jangled side as the coach moved through the night, but that was only to be expected. It was still rather hard to believe that Naran had actually been waiting for me to escape, and if I'd left that house sooner I would have been in the coach sooner. The only thing to wear in the way of shoes had been what I'd had on: the flimsy slippers which matched the lacy gown. My feet now ached from the walking I'd done over stones and twigs, the ache telling me just how grateful I ought to be that I hadn't had to *keep* walking.

But there were too many distractions attacking my emotions for gratitude to have much of a chance. Outraged indignation toward Rion's mother was the easiest to define, and I felt glad that I was the one who would get him out of her clutches. She was a vile beast, easily as bad as Lanir if not worse. Enslaving a relative stranger was somehow not quite as bad as doing the same to your own flesh and blood. . . .

I raised a hand to my head as I tried to fight off the rest of what I felt, but it was simply no use. I'd agreed that Vallant's rescue could wait until Rion was free, but that had been an intellectual decision rather than an emotional one.

The inner me wept over Vallant's absence, cried for the safety of his arms about me, ached over what might be happening to him right now. The outer me wanted to race to the Razas woman's house and set a tightening circle of flame about her that would end up meeting in the middle of where she stood, but I couldn't deny that Rion needed me more.

So first I would free Rion, and *then* I would go to the man who meant more to me than I'd ever be able to admit. . . .

SEVEN

Dinner had been a dismal affair and was long since over, but Rion continued to sit in the chair he'd been helped to in the sitting room. Mother had joined him for dinner, of course, but after she'd had him helped to the sitting room she'd gone off somewhere. It was the way things had been before he'd left for the testing, being abandoned to his own devices in complete solitude. Mother was obviously trying to reaccustom him to the life, but Rion felt that she had another purpose in mind as well. She'd given him a decision to make, and with nothing else to distract him he would have to consider that decision.

Rion put his head back and closed his eyes, more desolate than he'd ever imagined it was possible to be. The terror he'd felt—distantly, because of the drug—over losing his talent had turned into a throbbing pang of emptiness which refused to be assuaged. He'd asked himself many times during the last hours if keeping his mind would be all that desirable with both talent and freedom gone, but he hadn't been able to come to a firm decision. The idea of death didn't frighten him, but what if his damaged mind retained enough awareness to remember what he'd once been . . . ?

The ice forming around his insides couldn't be affected by the intake of hot tea, but Rion still opened his eyes and reached for his cup. Lifting it to his lips took something of an effort and most of his attention, and when he replaced the cup there was a servant standing not far from him.

"Would you like me to pour more tea for you, Lord Clarion?" the man, Ditras, asked. "It would be no trouble at all."

"Yes, thank you, Ditras," Rion responded, still taken by the surprise of an earlier discovery. All those servants he'd thought were laughing at him; since his return he'd been able to interpret their true feelings, which was, almost to a man or woman, pity. They'd known the truth of his situation long before he had, and had tried to offer unspoken sympathy and silent consolation. That he'd interpreted their actions as standoffish ridicule had been Mother's doing, of course, using passing comments to make him think the worst of those around him. She'd wanted to make sure that no one would find it possible to take her place with him. . . .

"Here I am, my darling, back with you as quickly as possible," Mother all but sang as she sailed into the room. "Among other things, I've been busy arranging to have your clothing brought from Haven Wraithside, so you'll no longer need to wear *those* rags. I can't imagine what you did with the clothing you took with you to that filthy hovel. When I sent servants there to fetch it back, they were able to find nothing but those awful white shirts and gray trousers. I think the servants in that place must have stolen your lovely things when they realized that you would not be returning."

"No one stole those things, Mother," Rion said with a faint smile as Ditras faded back and away from him. "I burned all those ridiculous costumes, since not even the neediest of peasants would have been willing to wear any of them. You always told me they were the height of fashion and I believed you—until I learned what true fashion was.

The only ones who wear those costumes are useless, mindless fops—something I don't happen to be.''

"What you *will* be is what you once were," Mother replied coldly, seating herself stiffly without taking her equally cold stare from his face. "You've now had time to consider the problem I put to you, just as I've had time to consider it. Is there anything you'd care to say to me before I tell you what decision I've come to?"

Rion felt his blood icing up to match the rest of his insides, wishing fervently that it could be possible to get up and pace. Mother's declaration about having made a decision wasn't good, since there was now no doubt that he would have to beg to be allowed to keep his mind intact. Most of him wanted to do just that, beg and grovel and do anything else necessary to save himself, but that new part of him . . . *It* refused to let him abase himself in any way, even if he paid for the lack with his wits and sanity.

"I'm waiting, Clarion," Mother prompted, a gleam now evident in her light eyes. "I can see that you *want* to be a good boy, but you must be much more open and clear about it. Tell Mother your decision now, and be certain you do it in the manner which will please her the most."

"Very well, Mother," Rion found himself saying, the words impossible to hold back. "You've asked to hear my decision, so here it is: I'm not *any* sort of boy, and you sound an absolute fool referring to yourself in the third person. Only someone of real importance should be spoken of in that way, which means you simply don't qualify. And to make my position perfectly clear, allow me to say that even your peasant ancestors would turn away from the sight of you in disgust."

"How *dare* you!" she hissed in a strangled voice, all the blood having drained from her face before it came rushing back to show her extreme outrage. "How dare you even *consider* speaking to me so, not to mention actually doing it! Have you decided that I'm joking, that I won't have you punished terribly for attempting to disobey me? If so, prepare yourself to be disillusioned. Ditras, send to the stablemen's quarters for Hafner to attend me at once! Lord Clarion requires another dose of his sedative, and afterward he will also require a beating."

His mother's expression had turned triumphant, which would have sickened Rion if he hadn't already felt so ill. Hafner was a giant of a man with incredible strength and the mind of a child, a longtime servant of Mother's who would do exactly as she commanded. Ditras had hesitated a very long moment before bowing his reluctant acquiescence to the order, during which time Rion had tried to struggle to his feet. His body felt as though it weighed ten times what it should, but he couldn't simply sit there and allow himself to be turned into a broken toy—

"I don't think sending for other people is a very good idea," a female voice said suddenly, a voice Rion had feared that he would never hear again. "I've always preferred small, cozy groups like this one, with no more than five people in them. No, don't get up. I won't be staying long enough to require courtesies."

"How did you get in here?" Mother demanded of Tamrissa after shooting to her feet, her back ruler-straight and her face registering shocked outrage. "I was assured I would never have to be dirtied by the presence of your sort again—! Rovelon, run and fetch the guard at once! And when you return you may pack your belongings and go without another copper in pay, in punishment for having admitted her in the first place!"

"But, my lady, I didn't!" Rovelon protested wildly, shrinking back as far from Tamrissa as it was possible to go. "I simply opened the door to a knock as I was supposed to do, and she . . . forced her way in over my protests! She also required me to lead her in here, and how was I supposed to refuse?"

"Perhaps I'm mistaken, but you do appear to be larger than the trollop," Mother returned acidly as she glared at the quivering man. "Take her by the hair if necessary, but remove her from my presence at once!"

"I hadn't realized how really stupid you are," Tamrissa commented to Mother as she stopped beside Rion to take his hand and touch his face. "Anyone else would have realized immediately that something other than physical size is involved here. Just be easy, Rion. We'll be gone from this place in another minute or two."

"You are *not* taking my son from me a second time!"

Mother shouted as Rion's heart leaped in happiness, the woman's face going even more red. "This time I'll see you sent to the deep mines, a place I *know* you'll never return from! Ditras, Rovelon—!"

"That's enough!" Tamrissa snapped as she straightened, and her return glare was accompanied by long tongues of flame burning the air between her and the two male servants. "Not only won't you two interfere, you'll come over here and help Lord Rion to the front door. If you try anything else, it will be the last thing you *ever* try. And as for *you* . . ."

Tamrissa turned to Mother with that, and Rion could see how the older woman had paled. She also fought not to cringe from the awful strength Tamrissa had displayed, but wasn't completely successful.

"As for you, you'll have the chance to call the guard once we've gone," Tamrissa continued, her voice implacable. "If you do, you'll find out just what 'vindictive' means. They won't really have a chance against me, and if I have to burn *them*, I'll come back to do the same to you. Even if I have to follow you halfway across the empire to do it. We . . . *trollops* are like that. Do you understand me?"

Mother nodded spasmodically, the fear in her eyes something Rion had never expected to see. For once in her life, Mother was being wise. She made no effort to call Tamrissa a liar, as anyone with eyes and the sense of a nit could see that the beautiful girl wasn't bluffing. If Mother forced Tamrissa to kill a group of guardsmen, Mother would pay for it with her own life.

"All right, it's time for us to leave," Tamrissa said briskly, looking back to the two servants. "Come over here and help this man."

Rovelon looked as though he were trying to turn invisible as he came forward reluctantly, but Ditras obeyed without hesitation—and with hooded satisfaction in his eyes. The two men helped Rion to his feet, where Rion paused to look at Mother one last time.

"You had best hope that I truly am maimed in my talent," he said in the coldest voice he was capable of, all the loathing he felt undoubtedly clear in his eyes. "If I'm not and we happen to meet again, I'll rid this world of your evil even if the act has to be paid for with my own life.''

Rion had the satisfaction of seeing her go chalk white, after which he paid attention to forcing his body into moving properly. Apparently she'd believed him, which would hopefully keep her from interfering in his life again. In point of fact he'd never be able to harm her, despite what she'd done—and had planned to do—to him. For too many years she'd been the heart and spirit and anchor of his life, and one doesn't easily get over that.

Nor was it easy to reach the front door. The house had never seemed so large before, and it felt as though he trudged miles before reaching his destination. Sweat stood out on his face and he leaned heavily on the two men assisting him, but the thought of stopping even for a brief rest never entered his mind. He was on the way to being free again, and that end was worth any price he might be required to pay.

''Don't worry, Rion, we're almost there,'' Tamrissa said from where she walked just ahead, turning to look at him with the worry she'd suggested *he* not have. ''The coach is right outside, so you'll be sitting down again soon. Are you all right?''

''Better than I've been in days, actually,'' Rion panted in answer, then he tried a grin. ''And allow me to say how lovely you look in that gown.''

''Oh, you,'' she half scolded with a relieved laugh. ''Just save your strength for walking.''

That seemed like an eminently sensible idea, so Rion complied without argument. When he and the men holding him up reached the door, Tamrissa had already opened it.

''Now take him to the coach and put him inside,'' she ordered, most of her attention on him rather than them. ''And I have to say that I don't understand how you men can work for a woman like that. Personally, I'd rather starve.''

''When a man has a family, he's forced to do any number of unpleasant things to see them fed,'' Ditras replied after a moment, making no effort to meet her gaze. ''I might well choose the same starvation, but I have no right to ask my family to.''

''No capable man willing to work will ever starve,'' Tamrissa returned, having gone ahead to open the coach door. "If you haven't looked for a job that doesn't turn your stomach, it isn't because of your family, it's because you don't believe in yourself. And the only one who can change *that* situation is you."

This time Ditras made no reply, but Rion was pleased to see that the man appeared to be thinking about what he'd heard. Chances were excellent that both he and Rovelon would now find themselves unemployed, as Mother would want no one around to remind her of her embarrassment. Not getting her own way had always been furiously embarrassing to Mother, even though it had rarely happened. . . .

Climbing into the coach was almost more than Rion could accomplish, but the delightful shock of seeing Naran awaiting him inside helped him to tap unsuspected reservoirs of strength. The servants pushed from behind and Naran took his hand and pulled, and the next moment he sat beside her on the coach seat with his arms about her. As he'd never thought to hold her like this again, the experience went far beyond mere pleasure.

"Thank you, gentlemen, and good luck to you," Rion heard Tamrissa say. He looked up in time to see her hand a coin to each of the servants, which put shocked expressions on their faces. Ditras recovered quickly enough to assist Tamrissa into the coach, then their driver had started them moving away from the house and back down the drive.

"I gave each of them a gold din," Tamrissa said with satisfaction as she settled herself on the seat opposite. "I'd originally meant to give them silver, but I have the feeling they'll be needing the gold."

"May I ask where you got the gold?" Rion put in, for the most part occupied with how wonderful it felt to be holding Naran again. "And for that matter, where did you two marvelous delights come from? I was certain I was very much on my own."

"I knew where Tamrissa was being held, so I simply took this coach there and waited for her to escape," Naran replied, snuggling even more closely to him. "I would have had no chance of freeing you all by myself, otherwise I would have come here first. Are you all right, my love? She didn't torment you completely beyond bearing, did she?"

"The situation was about to turn considerably worse," Rion replied with a smile, refusing to think about might-have-beens. "The thing disturbing me most, though, is the way my mother spoke about my talent being permanently damaged. She said it has to do with my having been pulled out of the Blending so abruptly, and the truth is I . . . can't reach the power no matter how hard I try. . . ."

Speaking the words had been very difficult for Rion, the fear being a good deal more manageable while those words remained *un*spoken. His talent was all he possessed in the world; without it he would be useless, less than a man and completely unworthy of the woman he loved so . . .

"You can't reach the power because of the hilsom powder," Tamrissa said quickly, reaching across to touch his hand in support. "I felt the same way at first, but when the powder wore off I was just as good as new. Your mother could have been lying to you the same way Lanir lied to me, or maybe they both *thought* they were telling the truth. With as little as people really know about Blendings, believing what might just be an opinion would be foolish."

"That makes a great deal of sense," Rion agreed, relief and hope flowing in to warm away fear and tragedy, but then he frowned. "You said 'Lanir' told you the same thing. Who is Lanir, and how was it that you were able to escape him?"

"Lord Lanir Porvin was the noble I told you about, the one who decided to claim me," Tamrissa said, looking more grimly pleased than disturbed. "He was Seated High in Fire magic, and was stupid enough to depend on the orders he gave me while I was under the influence of Puredan. After giving me the Puredan he let the hilsom powder wear off, thinking he was perfectly safe. When he discovered he wasn't, he pushed his Middle talent too far and burned himself out."

"Then the order *I* gave directing you not to obey any other orders worked!" Naran exclaimed, sounding equally as pleased. "None of us knew if it would, but now we've found out in the best way possible."

"We certainly have," Rion agreed, hugging her one-armed. "And if we look at it properly, you're directly responsible for helping me to regain my freedom. Not that Tamrissa isn't to be thanked as well. . . .''

"What I did needs no thanks," Tamrissa assured him with a light laugh just as Rion began to worry that he might have upset her. "If you only knew how much I enjoyed doing that to such a pompous, self-indulgent woman . . . But I'll admit that what's ahead will be even more enjoyable. That Eltrina Razas needs more than simple taking-down, and I'm just the woman to do it."

"Eltrina Razas," Rion echoed, touched by sudden understanding. "She succeeded in securing Vallant for her own purposes, then, and we're about to free him, I take it. What may I do to assist you?"

"You can stay with Naran and keep her from fretting herself into a skeleton from needing to wait," Tamrissa replied at once. "You can also let your system wash away the hilsom powder, so that when the guard comes after us, I won't have to hold them off alone."

"Do you really think they'll come after us?" Rion asked, abruptly more than a little disturbed. "Mother would never risk her precious hide, not even to get revenge, and I'm certain she believed what you said to her. Do you expect Lord Lanir's people to be the ones to send them?"

"Once Vallant is free, there will be three noble households involved," Tamrissa replied with a sigh. "Most people would have the good sense to accept their defeat and give up the game as a bad idea, but something tells me that one or more of these nobles won't do any such intelligent thing. We'll have to leave the city as soon as we possibly can, which means we now have the time to hear how Naran found *us*. Naran?''

"Actually, we *don't* have the time," Naran disagreed apologetically. "Eltrina Razas's house is only a short way up this road, and we shouldn't be deep in distracting conversation when we get there. Besides, you have to understand how many people I know . . . and how frantic I was when the five of you failed to come home . . . I couldn't just sit there and make you do it all by yourselves . . .''

"You're right, Naran, we can discuss it later," Tamrissa said hurriedly when Naran's voice grew uneven and her rate of breathing increased. "You ought to be told, though, how grateful *I* am that you didn't just sit there. If not for you, I'd probably still be trudging down Lanir's drive, wondering if I'd reach the road before dawn.''

Naran's agitation eased with that, especially since Rion had put his arms about her again. He would wait with her in the coach because that was all he was currently capable of doing, but the helplessness still rankled. And all he could do beyond that was hope he didn't nod off while they waited. . . .

EIGHT

Vallant had dozed any number of times during the last hours, but at least he'd been able to keep himself from falling deeply asleep. It was only a small way of fighting against the drug in his system, but it was still better than nothing. At one point a servant had appeared with a tray of food, and had tried to feed him. The food might very well have had more of the drug in it, so Vallant had pretended to be too confused and logy to eat it even with the servant's help. The servant had left again acting frustrated and annoyed, and Vallant had gone back to fighting the drug while feeling hungrier than ever.

Now there was the sound of the lock being thrown again, but Vallant hadn't regained enough control of himself to take advantage of it. He wanted to jump to his feet and fight his way out of that room and house, but simply opening his eyes to see who his visitor was seemed to be the most success he was able to claim.

"You're beginning to really annoy me," the Razas

woman announced when she stopped beside the bed to look down at him. "I've just been told that you didn't eat anything, but that won't be permitted to continue. When I give you back you have to be in good condition, so after I enjoy you—thoroughly this time!—you'll eat everything you're brought. Do you understand me?"

"Have we met?" Vallant asked innocently as he pretended to study her face. "I'm not havin' luck rememberin' things, like how I got to *this* place. And what was that you said we were goin' to do?"

"Not we, *I*," she corrected, looking more annoyed than ever. "*I'm* going to enjoy myself, and whether or not *you* have any pleasure is entirely irrelevant. And don't even *think* about asking me any questions. You can't seem to remember the answers from one minute to the next, which I'm now told happens at times with that sedative. As if the fool couldn't have mentioned that in the first place. Take that sheet off you."

As she spoke she opened her wrap and slipped out of it, then stood naked in a pose she must have considered arousing. Vallant couldn't imagine *any* situation in which he would find Eltrina Razas attractive or desirable, not to mention the fact that her presence made the room even smaller. Those two factors combined to add to the woman's displeasure when she lost patience and pulled the sheet off him herself.

"This is beginning to be a good deal less than amusing," she growled when she saw his lack of readiness, the look in her eyes close to fury. "I went to a great deal of trouble to have you even for this short amount of time, and early tomorrow morning they'll be coming to take you back. I *will* have my enjoyment of you before then, even if you have to spend most of the intervening hours in that tiny box I had prepared. Do you really want to be put into that tiny box?"

Vallant tried to keep the terror from touching him, but even the sedative in his system wasn't able to do that. The mere suggestion that he'd have to face the equivalent of being buried alive was enough to set his heart pounding and his sweat to turn cold, but it did something else as well.

"Ah, I see there's something you do remember," the Razas woman said with a laugh, reaching down to caress him. "We can just dispense with the rest, then, and concentrate on your only current value. Here I come!"

Her tone had changed to a playful one as she came down onto the bed to bestride him, but not to immediately impale herself. She leaned forward first to kiss his face and lick his lips, teasing his arousal with her womanhood. The humiliation was intensely painful for Vallant and so was the revulsion he felt, but nothing seemed able to displace the terror. If he protested in any way she would have him put into that box, and he simply couldn't bear the thought of it—

"How dare you just walk in here!" the woman suddenly snarled as she looked toward the door. Vallant had heard the door opening, but the sound hadn't done more than register vaguely in his awareness. "Get out this instant, and go and pack your things. You no longer have a—"

Her words broke off as she colored even more, and then Vallant saw rage explode in her eyes. The doorway was all the way back to the right and well out of his line of sight, so Vallant had no idea about what was happening until he heard the voice.

"I find it really amusing that all you so-called nobles tend to say the same thing," were the words spoken, very dryly. " 'How dare you, how dare you'—as though any normal person needs permission to interrupt you freaks during your perversions. That pile of clothing in the corner appears to be his, so move your oversize backside away from him while this servant dresses him."

"You have the nerve to come into *my* house and try to give orders?" the Razas woman spat in response, nevertheless rising quickly to her feet. "You're even more stupid than you are useless, you ignorant peasant, and it will be my pleasure to—"

Once again Razas's words broke off, this time with a small shriek as she stumbled back. She'd begun to stalk toward the door, but a heavy wall of flame had erupted into the air in front of her, driving her quickly back. At that point, Vallant could have wept. It *was* Tamrissa who had appeared, and she'd seen everything.

" 'Useless' isn't precisely the right term to apply to me,"

Tamrissa said, her words still very dry. "As you can see I do have one use, and I'm still extremely good at it. Have you ever seen someone of my strength burn something from the inside out? The trick is to keep the outside from going up until the inside is completely consumed, but it isn't nearly as hard as it sounds. For the second and last time, get out of the way so the servant can dress him."

"How far do you think you'll get once you leave here?" Razas demanded, nevertheless moving back to allow the husky male servant to reach the pile of clothing on the floor beside the chest. "I'll have the guard after you so fast that you'll think they appeared out of thin air! And when Lanir gets his hands on you again, you'll spend a long time regretting whatever trick you used to get away from him!"

"Lanir won't ever be getting his hands on anyone again," Tamrissa commented, faint amusement now in her voice. "You fools had a lot of nerve, letting him call himself the Seated *High*. Seated Middle was more like it, but he isn't even that any longer. And you really ought to understand: if you send guardsmen after me and force me to kill them, I'll consider myself honor bound to come back and do the same to you. Even if you run away and try to hide. I'll still find you, and then you'll learn the most efficient way to slow-roast meat."

Razas paled at that, and the hands of the nervous male servant dressing Vallant began to tremble even more. It wasn't possible to believe that Tamrissa wasn't serious, and both of her listeners knew it.

"But you can't take him," Razas whispered, her pasty complexion showing the fear which now touched her. "They'll be here to reclaim him tomorrow morning, and if I can't produce him—! I'll pay you gold. Name a price and it's yours."

"You can't afford me," Tamrissa commented dismissively. "And if his being gone will bring you grief, so much the better. What were they going to do with him?"

"Why should I know or care?" Razas countered, beginning to look frantic as she bent to retrieve her wrap and put it on. "But you can't let this happen to me, not to *me*. I've almost gotten the power I was always meant to have, so you simply can't interfere. I'll give you a thousand gold dins if you just go away, or I'll use that thousand to buy someone with Fire magic stronger than yours."

"For some reason you seem to be deliberately trying to miss the point," Tamrissa said, without the anger which could normally be expected. "There's no one left with Fire magic even *as strong* as mine, never mind stronger. Even the Blending we faced in the final competition couldn't match us, and I suspect that the same can be said of the Seated Five. None of your misnamed Highs and Adepts could do anything like—*this*, for instance."

Razas shrieked as the wrap she'd put on began to burn, then terror silenced her as well as freezing her in place. She stood trembling with her fists and eyes closed tight, and in a moment the wrap was completely consumed.

"There, you see?" Tamrissa asked lazily. "There's nothing left of your wrap but ash, and yet not the least bit of your skin was burned. That should show that I can reach you even if you try to hide in a tight knot of innocent servants, so remember what I said about summoning the guard. Now we'll be leaving, so help him up."

That last was to the servant who had finished dressing him, but not in the robe and sandals he'd worn during the competition. Someone had apparently retrieved the pants, shirt, and shoes he'd worn getting *to* the competition, and that was what he now wore. The servant pulled him up to sitting and then hoisted him to his feet, but even with his arm draped around the servant's neck and the servant's arm around his middle, Vallant discovered that he could barely stand, let alone walk.

"Give him all the help he needs," Tamrissa directed the servant, stepping aside to clear the doorway. "If it becomes necessary, carry him."

The servant nodded with a grunt and began to half drag him toward the door, and Vallant had never been so mortified in his entire life. Tamrissa was as beautiful and vital as ever, and there *he* was, being hauled along like a useless side of beef. How many times was he supposed to accept being humiliated in front of her without dying from the shame? He didn't know, but even one more time would have been too much. For that reason he gritted his teeth and *forced* himself to walk, if that dragging shuffle could be called walking. . . .

"I think it's best if you stay in this room until someone lets you out, Eltrina," Tamrissa said as Vallant was hurried toward the door. The last glimpse he'd had of Razas was the way she still stood rooted to the spot, her eyes now open and visibly filled with fear. "Your people will be told that you don't want to be disturbed, and I suggest that you make no effort to call for help. The longer you stay locked up and out of touch, the better off you'll be if the guard comes looking for us after all. It won't save your life, but it will certainly save you a great deal of pain."

Vallant heard a sobbing moan come from Razas, and then the servant maneuvered him out of the room and began to guide him up the hall. Behind him he heard the sound of the door being closed and locked, and then Tamrissa moved ahead to lead the way. The way she glanced at him said he wasn't doing well at all with moving on his own—as though he needed to be told. Vallant made sure to avoid her gaze, concentrating instead on trying to keep up with the servant.

By the time they reached the front hall of the house, Vallant was drenched in sweat and gasping. He'd dreaded the thought that there might be stairs to descend, but his prison had been located at the back of the house rather than on an upper floor. Tamrissa moved forward to open the front door, then followed once the servant had him outside.

"Give me a moment and I'll have the coach door open," she said, but the expected delay wasn't necessary. Naran leaned forward to open the coach door from the inside, and the servant grunted as he lifted Vallant bodily and put him inside on the empty bench seat. Rion shared the seat opposite with Naran, and to Vallant the man looked almost as bad off as himself. That thought cheered Vallant not at all, but it was useful to help him ignore the way he'd been treated like an infant.

"Here, take this for your trouble," Vallant heard Tamrissa say, and he turned his head in time to see her handing something to the servant. "I'll appreciate your telling the other servants not to disturb Eltrina, and then you'll be wise to pack your things and leave. Even if you go and release her at once instead, she'll never keep you around after you witnessed what was done to her.''

The servant's expression said he knew that Tamrissa was right, and his curt nod was one of full agreement. He headed back to the house with his fist wrapped tight around the coin he'd been given, and Tamrissa climbed into the coach and closed the door behind her before taking the seat beside Vallant.

"The least he could have done was help me into the coach,'' she muttered as she fought her skirts straight, her gaze already on his face. "Vallant, are you all right? You haven't said even a single word yet.''

"Where is this coach takin' us?'' Vallant obliged in a croak, looking through the window rather than at Tamrissa. "Somewhere where we can eat and sleep for a while, I hope.''

"We need to stop back at Tamrissa's house,'' Naran said, sounding faintly disturbed. "I packed some clothing for everyone, so all we have to do is pick it up. Along with any food we can find. After that we'll have to find some place to hide, at least until we locate Jovvi and Lorand. Once we do we'll get out of the city . . . Vallant, you haven't said yet whether or not you're all right.''

"He's probably no more 'all right' than I am,'' Rion said after a moment when it became clear that Vallant had no intention of replying. "That damnable drug has taken all my strength both physical and magical, but when it wears off I expect to be able to touch the power again and find myself unchanged. Mother insisted that being pulled out of the Blending so abruptly had caused me irreparable damage, Vallant, but I mean to prove her wrong and I expect you to join me in the endeavor.''

Once again Vallant felt the clutch of fear, this time in regard to his ability. He could vaguely remember someone saying the same thing about *him*, that his strength would never again be what it had been. Finding out they'd spoken the truth would surprise him very little, especially after the rest of what he'd gone through. . . .

"Vallant, isn't there anything else you can think of to say?'' Tamrissa asked after another short silence, her hand coming to his arm. "What I mean is, something to *me*?''

"Oh, yes, forgive me for forgettin'," Vallant forced out, still making sure not to look at her. "You have my thanks for gettin' me out of that place, since it's perfectly obvious I couldn't have gotten *myself* out. Now I think I need to rest a while."

It was perfectly true that Vallant needed rest desperately, but what he needed even more was an end to the way Tamrissa was certainly looking at him: with compassion and pity. Just two days ago he'd been a full, strong man in her eyes, and now . . . Now she would never see him the same. She'd witnessed his humiliation and shame, so from now on she'd remember that every time she looked at him. A weakling who had to be rescued by the woman he'd loved when he was whole, a woman he still loved but who now could do no more than pity him.

After a short hesitation her hand left his arm, and happily she said nothing more. Vallant continued to stare out the window, wishing with his entire being that he might be back and alone in that small, windowless room—so that he might weep like a child for all that he'd lost. . . .

NINE

It had grown very quiet in the coach, my own silence adding to the rest. It had also grown even chillier out, and for some reason I noticed it more now than I had after we'd gotten Rion away from his mother. But it was true that I felt tired, so maybe that accounted for it. . . .

Outside the coach the night was also quiet. Nothing but the creak of springs, the jingle of harness, and the clatter of the horses' hooves to be heard. I closed my eyes and embraced those small sounds, holding to them in an effort to ease the pain I foolishly felt. I'd told Jovvi that I expected my relationship with Vallant to end abruptly one day, and now, apparently, that day had come. I'd expected him to be as glad to see me as Rion had been to see Naran, but Rion had only been taken away from his mother. Vallant had been taken from Eltrina Razas, a female noble who really had an incredibly good figure, and it was impossible to deny that he'd been interested in her. . . .

Keeping my eyes closed also became impossible, the pictures my mind dredged up making it so. Vallant had been about to make love to Eltrina Razas, and I'd come bursting in to end the time. His annoyance was apparently so great that he couldn't even look at me, and that despite the fact that he *had* to know he couldn't have stayed. The way he'd "thanked" me for saving him . . . I'd wanted just a few soft words of greeting, a strong arm around my shoulders, possibly even a kiss.

But I'd gotten none of that, and there was no use in wishing I had. Wishing never came true, just the way hoping usually failed. For a short while I'd had someone to do my hoping *for* me, but it had become very clear that Vallant no longer wanted the job. It was up to me again to do it for myself, but I'd given up on the practice too long ago to take it up again now.

It took quite some time before I found it possible to force my thoughts onto another track, and the only thing which made it possible was our next destination. I had my own reasons for being glad that we were returning briefly to my house, as Jovvi had shared a very important secret with me.

I'd already spent three gold dins of what I'd taken from Lanir, and it was impossible to know how much more it would take before Jovvi and Lorand were also free. For that reason I'd decided to retrieve the cache of gold Jovvi had left in the house, the savings she'd intended to use to start her own courtesan's residence here in Gan Garee. Even if it turned out that I didn't need to use any of it, at least I'd have it to hand back to her when she was with us again.

I found that I had to work rather hard to cling to the belief that Jovvi and Lorand *would* be with us again. Not even knowing where they were made the thought too much like wishing or hoping, which had, as already mentioned, always turned out badly for me. I had to make certain that I believed instead, with all the stubbornness that touching the power brought stacked up behind the belief. . . .

When the coach finally turned into my drive, I was even more weary than I had been. Rion had fallen asleep quite some time ago, and so had Vallant Ro. They both sat slumped bonelessly, deeply into that lack of consciousness which I remembered all too well. Even Naran had kept nodding off, but the change in motion of the carriage awakened her, and she looked outside.

"I'm glad we're finally here," she said softly, obviously to keep from waking the men. "The servants all left the house late yesterday, before I left it myself. I'll get the bags I packed, and then we can go to my friend's house. She's bound to have *some* idea about where we can hide until we find the others."

"I'll go inside with you," I said, just as softly. "There are a few things of my own that I'd like to get, not to mention an additional change of clothing. I'm freezing in this ridiculous gown, and my feet still hurt. These slippers are for walking around indoors, not outside."

"But shouldn't you stay with the coach to guard Rion and Vallant?" she asked, sounding unsure. "I can understand your wanting to change, but what if someone comes by while we're inside?"

"The driver can stand guard for a few minutes," I said, shaking my head a little. "Just tell him to shout if there's any trouble, and I'll take care of it by looking out a window."

"That should work," she agreed with a shadowy smile. "I'll tell him before we go inside."

A pair of minutes later the coach pulled up by the front door, and Naran and I got out. The men continued to sleep soundly, so I went to the front door while Naran spoke to our driver. I'd expected the door to be locked and so it was, but that didn't mean I had to burn it down in order for us to get inside—or use the window Naran probably had to leave by. A large potted shrub stood to each side of the door, and under the soil of the one to the right was a door key. My late husband had put it there years earlier, to be certain he would always be able to get back into his own house. I'd seen him checking on it once and afterward had found out what it was, but I'd never removed it even after his death. Right now I was very glad I hadn't.

The key let us in through the door without any difficulty, and I produced a small flame to light our way upstairs. Naran came with me and helped me change into warmer, more practical clothes in record time, and then I went with her to fetch the bags she'd packed. On the way I stopped at the statuette in the hall, groped around a bit to find the purse, then removed it.

"This belongs to Jovvi, and when we find her she'll want it back," I said in answer to Naran's unspoken question. "I'm tempted to take some of this very expensive junk to sell, but I suspect it would be wasted effort. A legitimate buyer will want proof of ownership, and a larcenous one won't give us more than a fraction of the piece's worth."

"And lugging it around until we find someone to buy it will be too much of a bother," she agreed with a nod. "I have some gold so we ought to get by, but we'll need more clothing for Rion. He only had those gray trousers and white shirts left, and his mother's people took those. I packed extra clothing from Vallant's bedchamber, but had to take only the uniform from Lorand's. The rest of *his* clothing is almost as distinctive as Rion's was."

"Once we get the bags downstairs, let's check the kitchen," I suggested after nodding to what she'd said. "If they've left any food behind, we ought to take it with us."

This time it was her turn to nod, and then we took care of the first part of the plan. There were five bags, none of them terribly heavy, so we got them down to the front hall rather quickly. A glance outside showed everything to be quiet, so we went back to the kitchen and looked around. Everything was perfectly clean and orderly, and there wasn't a single crumb of food left. With no one around to keep the perishables cold that was understandable, but not finding even a single loaf of bread was somehow depressing.

When we returned to the front hall we picked up the bags again—Naran insisting on taking three of them—carried them out to the coach, then put them in the boot. While

Naran stowed them properly, I turned back to the house to relock the door. If it was at all possible, I meant to reclaim that house one day. Leaving it open to thieves and defenseless against invasion wasn't something I felt prepared to do. I took two steps back toward the house—then stopped short when the large figure of a man came forward out of the shadows to the left. I quickly put a ring of flame around him, freezing him in mid step, then just as quickly let the flames die. I knew the man, even though I hadn't expected ever to see him again.

"Popping up like that without warning can be dangerous, Dom Meerk," I said to the man who had been helping Lorand locate his friend Hat. "I'm afraid Lorand isn't here right now, and it's extremely unlikely that any of us will be back in the near future. If there was something you wanted to tell him, I'll do my best to pass on the message."

"I didn't mean to frighten you," he said as he came closer, somehow no longer sounding quite as low-class as he always had. "I know what you're capable of, so I was an idiot for not letting you know I was there . . . and I'm not here looking for Dom Coll. I found out that you'd gotten away from that noble who claimed you, so I waited here in the hopes that you would come back, even for just a few minutes."

"I seem to have missed something here," I said, shaking my head against the confusion. "How did you hear about something that happened only a few hours ago, and what happened to the way you used to speak? And while we're on the subject, why would you want to be here in the first place?"

"There are long stories behind the answers to each of those questions, and we don't have the time to go into them now," he replied, running a hand through shaggy hair. "What I *will* say, though, is that my former accent was part of my disguise, and that I'm a member of an organization dedicated to finding out the truth about what the nobility is doing. We've suspected for some time that they're using unfair and illegal means to keep themselves in power, but we haven't been able to prove it. You and the rest of your Blending will be able to prove it *for* us."

"And then what?" I asked with a sound of ridicule.

"You'll expose them? And what after that? If you expect them to hang their heads in shame and meekly hand over the reins of power, you're dreaming. They'll have their guardsmen arrest the lot of you, and while you're all being thrown into the Deep Caverns or sent to work in the mines, they'll have parties to laugh at your naïveté."

"If there were only a few of us, that's probably what *would* happen," he agreed with a faint smile. "In point of fact there are thousands of people in our organization, all of them having been questioned by Middle talents in Spirit or Earth magic before being accepted as members. And since a large number of our people happen to *be* guardsmen, we're not in as much danger of being arrested as you might think. But the same doesn't hold true for you and the others with you, so will you please let me take you to a place of safety? I promise to tell you everything once we get there."

"I think we ought to trust him," Naran said quietly when I hesitated. She'd come over to stand beside me when Meerk had appeared, and had heard everything he'd said. "I have the feeling that my friend—whose coach we're using—is one of his members, even though she's never said so."

"I know who you mean, and you're right, she is," Meerk said with a nod. "So is the man driving the coach, so if you like you can speak to him first. But whatever you do, you must do it quickly. I can't possibly be the only one who'll think of checking this house."

"All right, I'll take the chance," I agreed, forcing myself away from indecision. "I just hope for your sake that you're telling the truth."

"As justifiably nervous as you are, I don't dare do anything else," he said, looking soberly serious. "If you ladies will get into the coach now, we can be on our way."

"One more question," I said as Naran turned toward the coach. "Do you happen to know where Jovvi and Lorand are being kept? We haven't been able to locate them yet."

"You and the two men in the coach were easy to trace, but we haven't had the same luck with the rest," he admitted heavily. "I have everyone able to walk, hobble, or crawl out looking for them, so hopefully we'll know something soon. I promise we won't give up until we find them."

I nodded at that, the only thing I *could* do, then went and locked the door of the house before turning toward the coach myself. Meerk helped me inside, checked the boot to make sure everything was properly secured, then went to climb up on the box with the driver. When the coach began to move again, Naran and I exchanged a glance. She looked slightly less unsure than *I* felt, but we'd really had no choice. We needed a place to stay and we needed help in locating Jovvi and Lorand, and if Meerk had been telling the truth we'd found someone to supply both.

But I couldn't stop worrying about Lorand and Jovvi, and where they might be that no one could find them. If they were dead, Meerk's people would have no need to prove anything against the nobility. If Lorand and Jovvi were dead, I'd see to it that there weren't any members of the nobility left to be accused. . . .

TEN

"I think we're about to have some distinguished visitors," Kambil announced softly to the others. They currently relaxed in the main sitting room after sharing a late breakfast, which they'd indulged in after sleeping late. "Four carriages have just come up the drive, with three people in each carriage."

"An even dozen," Bron remarked with faint amusement. "Are they counting on finding safety in numbers, or are they trying to impress us?"

"I'd bet on the impressing," Selendi said as she rearranged her skirts. "If they were worried or afraid of us, they wouldn't have come themselves."

"And they wouldn't have canceled the full meeting Zolind called," Homin added. "Having found out that they no longer have a Seated Blending to work through must have upset them, so they've come to make their positions secure again."

"I think I'll ask why the rest of the Advisors haven't come with them," Kambil mused aloud. "I'm certain it's because the rest of the Advisors were under Zolind's control and therefore don't want us Seated, but I'd like to make sure. It would be a shame to do away with people we might be able to make use of instead."

The others chuckled, understanding exactly what he meant. Once they were Seated and had taken up residence in the palace, Zolind's most loyal supporters would be seen to one at a time until there were none of them left. And the empty seats would *not* be refilled, not until *they* decided on the replacements. Letting the Advisors themselves choose their own membership had brought a lot of deadwood to their ranks, so from now on Kambil and his Blending would take care of the matter.

"Gentles, I have the privilege to announce a number of members of the Advisory Board," a servant appeared to say, looking properly impressed as he bowed them into the room. Kambil rose to his feet to bow in supposed respect, making Delin do the same as the others followed suit of their own volition. It would be necessary to remember to make Delin move around a bit more than usual, just to keep their visitors from becoming suspicious.

"Well, I see that what we were told is quite true," the apparent leader of the twelve, Lord Velim Shoons, announced with the most hollow joviality Kambil had ever heard. "Our new Blending *is* still in their former residence rather than at the palace preparing for the Seating ceremony. We must discover the person or persons responsible for this affront to them, and have them properly punished."

The men who had arrived with Lord Velim murmured their supposedly full agreement, doing no better with the charade than their spokesman. Velim was beyond middle years and rather stout, just as most of his fellows were, with thinning blond hair streaked with gray. Kambil had never met the man personally before, but observation from a distance had shown him to be one of those who reacted rather than thought. It was said that Zolind had allowed Velim his seat on the board because the man was easy to manipulate, then had regretted the choice when Zolind's political opponents found manipulating the man just as easy.

"Lord Velim, this is a great honor," Kambil said with another bow, seeing the fool's chest swell over being recognized. "But I'm afraid I don't understand. We were told that returning to our residence was standard procedure, as arrangements had to be made for us at the palace. Wasn't that the truth?"

"Not entirely," Velim said with the broad smile of a man who suddenly believes he's found people he can control. "The five of you couldn't be expected to know any better, of course, but no real harm's been done. We're here to escort you to the palace personally, while the servants pack your things. The coaches should be here at any moment, so if you would be so good as to ready yourselves . . . ?"

The man's words actually ended in a half question, as though he'd already forgotten that he was supposed to be in control. Kambil exchanged happy glances with the others as they all assured the fool that they would be delighted to get ready to leave, and then they excused themselves in order to return to their bedchambers. In actual fact they could have walked out the door that moment, but it would never do to let the group of fools know their visit had been expected.

Kambil sent Delin to his own bedchamber while he, Kambil, went to get a coat, then he followed Delin to the latter's room. What to do with the man so completely under his control had been a disturbing question in Kambil's thoughts, and the decision he'd come to wasn't wholly satisfactory. Once at the palace they would each have their own wing, and Delin would have to be as active in his as the others were in their own. At least until the ceremony was over, that is, and they were Seated.

"Delin, old fellow, I have some good news for you," Kambil murmured as he faced the man standing empty-minded in the middle of the floor. "I'm going to bring part of you back for a while, as a joke on all those fools downstairs. You won't remember everything and you won't be entirely free of control, but a lot of you will still be back. What do you think of that, hey?"

"Kambil, what's happening?" Delin said suddenly with confusion, one hand going to his head. "What are we doing here in my bedchamber?"

"We're getting ready to be escorted to the palace," Kambil replied, putting concerned worry into his voice. "Don't you remember that we won the competitions, and now we're to be Seated as the new Five? I agreed to wait for you out in the hall while you got your coat, but when you didn't appear I came looking for you. You haven't had another blackout spell, have you?"

"No, no, of course not," Delin assured him hastily with a forced smile. "I've just been preoccupied lately, so I haven't been paying the closest attention. Who did you say was here to escort us to the palace?"

"Twelve of the Advisors, led by Lord Velim Shoons," Kambil supplied smoothly. "Don't you remember how they marched into the sitting room downstairs, all but holding out their hands with their Advisor's rings like talismans in front of them? Most of them are extremely nervous about being this close to us, but they came anyway because they believe their political positions depend on it."

"And they'll do anything necessary to maintain themselves in place," Delin said, nodding even as he sneered. "But as long as they're determined to see us Seated, we shouldn't be *too* critical, should we? Well, let's not keep them waiting."

He walked to the wardrobe where his coat hung and took it out, looking as though he hadn't a care in the world. Kambil, who felt his confusion and fright clearly, knew better, but certainly wasn't about to comment. A confused and frightened Delin would be a cautious Delin, asking no questions that would betray his weakness. Kambil would keep very close tabs on him to be sure he remained cautious, but for the rest of the time Delin would again be on his own.

They walked downstairs together, where their three groupmates waited with three of the Advisors. The other nine had returned to their carriages to wait, they were informed, mostly to keep the new Five from feeling outnumbered. They all chuckled dutifully at the joke, then went out to climb into their own coaches. Velim and the other two Advisors chose to ride in their carriage rather than join them in the coaches, to make sure they didn't "crowd" the Five. Kambil smiled and thanked them for their concern, making no mention of the fact that they'd lied through their teeth.

"Who did they think they were fooling?" Bron asked once he and Kambil and Delin were settled in one of the coaches. "They're obviously terrified of us, and probably wish they were anywhere but here."

"They have reason to be terrified of us," Delin murmured with very obvious satisfaction, gazing out of the window at the nearest Advisor-filled carriage. "Most of them won't survive our Seating by more than a few days. They were the ones who allowed their underlings to throw our lives away, putting us in a position where our own people would destroy us even if our opponents didn't. One doesn't forgive something like that, not until it's been fully revenged."

"Which it will be," Kambil said, exchanging a glance with Bron. It was annoying to have to put up with Delin's madness again, but it would only be for a short while. After that Delin would sit quietly in his apartments when he wasn't needed for the Blending, and his servants would be adjusted to the point of seeing nothing odd in his behavior. Until then the man could simply be agreed with, which would avoid awkward confrontations.

With one Advisor-filled carriage leading the way and the other two following the coaches, they really did make a procession of their trip to the palace. The gate guards came to attention as the vehicles passed, making no effort to stop any of them. They'd obviously been warned in advance of the arrival, as had the palace staff. Dozens of them lined the approach to the main entrance, the rest undoubtedly lined up near the areas of their various duties. It would have been unwieldy having the hundreds of servants all waiting in the same place to greet their new superiors; dozens made the approach crowded enough, leaving barely enough room for the carriages and coaches.

They left the coaches to the applause of their audience, too much of which Kambil found to be either simply for form's sake or actually hiding hostility. He hadn't realized that *that* many palace workers would be displeased and disillusioned, but maybe the reaction was due to their predecessors. As soon as possible he would walk about and get to know some of the servants involved, and in that way would find out if there was anything which needed the attention of the Blending.

The group of Advisors escorted them to the area where the Five's individual wings began, but not simply for form's sake.

"Those servants will introduce themselves later," Velim said with a vague wave meant to indicate the five separate groups of servants. "Before they show you around your new domains, though, we'd appreciate a few minutes of your time."

"Of course," Delin responded with distant superiority thinly covered by a charming smile. "In which of our wings would you prefer the meeting to be?"

"There's a sitting room right here, meant to be used for purposes such as this," Velim responded, indicating a doorway half a dozen steps short of the area of divergence. "We've arranged for tea and cakes to be provided, and if you desire anything else you need only ask for it."

"If we desire anything else, we certainly shall," Delin allowed regally, then led the way toward the sitting room. Kambil joined the others in following, happier now about having had to restore Delin. The man knew nothing about what they'd done since returning to the residence after the final competition, so whatever Velim wanted to "discuss" would come as a surprise to the man. Even though Kambil suspected he already knew what the Advisor had in mind. . . .

The "sitting room" turned out to be a good deal larger than ordinary, more like a conference room with easy chairs and no table than like anything else. Five of the chairs stood together in a row facing all the rest, and Delin headed directly for the set of five. Kambil let him seat himself in the center chair before sitting down beside him, then they all took a moment to tell the servants how they liked their tea. After another moment the small army of servants had brought their tea and left, and Velim cleared his throat.

"As I said earlier, we apologize for the unconscionable delay in bringing you here," he began, obviously trying not to sound tense and nervous. "To make up for the unintended slight, we've arranged for you to move directly into your various wings of the palace, and the Seating ceremony has been scheduled for tomorrow morning. Anyone of any importance will certainly be there, and two days after that we'll hold the public ceremony."

"Won't the current Seated Five be annoyed at having to share their wings?" Delin asked after sipping his tea. "And I do hate to be indelicate, but it's impossible to miss the fact that Advisor Zolind isn't among you. Does he intend to repair his absence now by coming to the ceremony tomorrow, or will he be 'regrettably detained' the way he clearly was today?"

"There is—ah—sad news where Lord Zolind is concerned," Velim replied after exchanging a glance with one of his brother Advisors. "Last night our good friend passed away, apparently from heart failure. His send-off cremation is tonight, which is why the Seating ceremony has been delayed until tomorrow."

"That's distressing news," Kambil said as the others exclaimed in shock, only Delin's surprise being real. "Advisor Zolind worked with us through most of the time of the competition, and we upheld our end of the bargain we made with him. I assume that your being here means you're prepared to uphold his end *for* him?"

"Ah—we'll have to discuss that agreement at another time," Velim hedged, suddenly and momentarily panic-stricken. He obviously knew nothing about a bargain, and Kambil could see that he wanted it to remain like that. If it hadn't been the perfect way to lever concessions from the Advisors, Kambil might have been willing to forget about the nonexistent bargain himself. As it was . . .

"You still haven't answered my question about the outgoing Five," Delin prompted, only partially recovered from the shock of learning about Zolind's death. "You seem to have given us freedom of their wings, which, I've been told, only *they* can give. Are we likely to have to defend ourselves from them, or does the invitation come from them rather than from you?"

"Neither, actually," Velim admitted after exchanging another glance with the same crony. "The fact is the previous

Five have already left, apparently being anxious to begin some new plans of their own. They seemed to have expected to be able to leave as soon as the competitions were over, and decided not to change their intentions just because your group wasn't immediately brought to the palace. They took only a very small amount of personal possessions with them, so don't be afraid that they stripped their wings. I'm sure they'll send for the rest of their possessions as soon as they're settled elsewhere. . . ."

"I dislike saying this, but I'm afraid I'm beginning to grow uneasy," Kambil announced slowly when Velim's voice trailed off. It was sight of Delin's now obvious shock which had caused the ending of the Advisor's maunderings, and Kambil had been waiting to take advantage of the moment.

"Surely you see why I *would* be uneasy," Kambil continued, projecting disturbance as he looked from one uncomfortable Advisor to another. "First you tell us that Advisor Zolind is gone, and now you say that the previous Five are gone as well. I have no idea what's happening here, but I'm afraid 'uneasy' was much too understated a choice of words. I hope everyone understands that we *will* defend ourselves if necessary?"

Many of the Advisors began to assure him immediately that that would not be necessary, including a brow-mopping Velim. The gist of the comments was that *nothing* was happening, nothing but a string of odd occurrences. Some of them even seemed to believe that, but most of them were frightened and worried. Kambil was delighted to see that, of course, but made sure not to let his expression reflect that delight.

"Well, I believe it's time for us to go," Velim said as he rose to his feet, the others quickly following his example. "Would you like us to escort you back out to the beginning of your respective wings?"

"Thank you, but I believe we'll remain here for a few moments longer," Kambil replied, showing a still-disturbed smile. "It will probably be best if my groupmates and I establish a loose link, to be certain we remain in touch with one another even after we separate. That way we can Blend instantly if it should become necessary . . ."

Kambil let his words trail off as his gaze moved among the twelve men, and most of them obliged by paling a bit before heading for the door. Even Velim found it impossible to do more than nod a bit before lumbering after his associates, and a moment after the door closed Kambil showed a much better smile.

"None of them made the least attempt to listen at the door, nor are any of the servants close enough to hear us," he told his groupmates. "Did you see how frightened they became at the idea of us linking? I got the distinct impression that their previous Blending never did anything like that, which explains part of their overall nervousness."

"And the rest of it is probably explained by the fact that we're all High talents," Bron said with faint amusement from Kambil's left. "It suddenly occurred to me that no other chosen Blending could have been the same, not when the Advisors intended to use them rather than serve them. We weren't supposed to survive, but now that we have and are also to be Seated, they have to find a way to deal with us."

"I really sympathize with those poor dears," Selendi said with a laugh from her place to Delin's immediate right. "They *have* to have a Seated Blending in order for them to continue to run the empire, but the only Blending available is one which is far too strong for them to control easily. I wonder what they'll do to try to force us to obey them—and who they'll use to make the attempt."

"We'll certainly find out after the ceremony tomorrow," Homin, equally amused, said from the seat beyond Selendi's. "We probably aren't supposed to know it, but in the past there's only been *one* ceremony. Saving our public Seating for another time probably means they intend to bargain with us, our complete cooperation in return for their allowing our Seating to become completely official. *I* wonder how they think they can keep it from happening."

"I'm sure they have *some* plan, which is why I let them know we can link," Kambil replied, sharing the general amusement. "They were probably counting on tackling us one at a time, but now they know that won't be possible."

"How can all of you find this *funny*?" Delin suddenly demanded, his inner thoughts in complete turmoil. "If we don't agree to their terms they won't let us be publicly Seated, but if we do we'll be completely powerless. And why haven't we linked yet the way you said we would?''

"Delin, we're not *going* to link," Kambil explained as he automatically calmed the fool's agitation. "If we do we'll be wasting our strength, especially since I intend to keep alert against any sort of attack. If someone tries something I'll initiate the Blending, which will protect us from anything they care to try. You *do* remember that we can Blend even when at a distance from one another?''

"And don't worry about our being powerless," Bron added when Delin nodded jerkily to Kambil's question. "They can threaten not to hold the public Seating ceremony, but they won't be able to follow through on the threat. The only official power the Advisory Board has is through the Seated Blending, and that remains true no matter how far they've gone past it *un*officially. If they keep us from being Seated, they'll just be cutting their own throats."

"Yes, of course, you're right," Delin said after Kambil touched him with complete belief. "I'd forgotten about that, and I appreciate your reminding me. So let's forget about those fools and go have a look at our new quarters."

With that he rose from his chair immediately and headed for the door, leaving Kambil to exchange glances with the others before they also rose to follow. Delin was back to thinking of himself as their leader, but it wouldn't be for long. And as long as they each had their own wings of the palace to live in, putting up with Delin would be a good deal easier.

Kambil smiled as his group of personal servants came forward to greet him and introduce themselves, and then he let them lead the way into his wing. After he had a look around he would find a comfortable spot for privacy, and then he would do some thinking. Any ultimata would not be presented by Velim, that was absolutely certain. They would be brought by the real powers on the Advisory Board, the men who were closest to the late Zolind and who hadn't shown themselves today.

He'd been planning to do away with those men, but now Kambil smiled again as he reconsidered his options. Some of them would certainly prove useful to him, and if he found it possible to take control of them, he'd have no need to deal with incompetent bunglers like Velim. In fact he'd be able to rid the Board of all its deadwood, which would be just as satisfying as ridding it of strong opposition. Yes, he'd definitely have to think about that . . .

Delin made himself comfortable with a cup of tea in the beautiful little study while a meal was being prepared for him, enjoying being alone after that tour. He'd never really stopped to think about it sooner, but the term "wing" actually meant what it suggested. There were thirty bedchambers in his wing, most of them part of actual apartments, and that didn't count servants' quarters. The kitchens were enormous, there were four dining rooms of varying sizes, and two gigantic ballrooms. There were also three libraries, four conference rooms of different sizes, and half a dozen small meeting rooms, none of which included *his* private suite.

The tea in his cup tasted better than any tea he'd ever had, especially since he'd taken the trouble to check it with his talent before drinking it. He'd do the same with the food they brought, and then he would enjoy it even more than the tea. He'd finally made it to where he belonged, to where he *deserved* to be, and he had no intention of denying himself a single moment of the pleasure.

Despite the fact that the Advisors would try to take it away from him. Delin's fist clenched in fury as he remembered that, also remembering how lightly his groupmates had taken the danger. Apparently they were too innocent to understand just how difficult the Advisors could make life for them, which was why it was a good thing *he* was their leader. He knew trouble when he saw it, and was also prepared to do something about it.

A smile finally turned Delin's lips, brought about by the discovery of the one feature of his wing that he'd taken the trouble to ask about: the section of his personal guard used for political assassinations. He'd discovered their existence by the merest accident, having thumbed through the private journal of the late husband of one of his group of older women. The man had found out about the assassins and had feared he'd become one of their victims because of the knowledge, and there the journal had abruptly ended.

Delin had asked the woman how her husband had died, and she'd told him the death was perfectly natural. She'd also told him that no one else had read the journal, and she'd even forgotten it was there. The slut was such a woolhead that when Delin took the journal with him, she'd never noticed. After reading it carefully Delin had destroyed it, making sure in that way that no one else would be able to discover what he had.

And now he stood in a position to make use of his knowledge. He'd spoken to the head of his guard only briefly, but certainly long enough to determine that there would be no hesitation on anyone's part in accepting his orders. They would do exactly as he told them to, and the orders he gave after he finished his meal would be a schedule for tomorrow, to be carried out after he and the others were Seated.

But tonight, tonight would be the sublime end to a lifetime of fear and misery. Delin's heart beat faster at the thought of it, excitement and delight causing his blood to rush about. Tonight he would have his parents brought to him secretly, gagged, of course, and he would sit and watch as they were slowly put to death. His mother, the slut, deserved death for never having protected him, but his father . . . as long as his father continued to live, Delin knew he would never find it possible to breathe freely.

Tonight would be marvelous, then, and afterward he'd have to think about seeing to Kambil. He was certain he'd meant to do something about the man sooner, and couldn't imagine why he hadn't. Ah well, tomorrow was another day, with any number of days coming after that. . . .

ELEVEN

It felt as though the coach ride lasted forever, and I couldn't keep from dozing for shorter and longer periods of time. Naran had fallen asleep not long after we left my old neighborhood, and Rion and Vallant Ro hadn't awakened at any point. I felt completely alone again, but touching the power made the loneliness slightly more bearable. It also helped that Meerk was there for us, assuming he'd been telling the complete truth. If only Jovvi or Lorand could have been there to confirm what Meerk had said . . .

I sighed over that, then impatiently reminded myself how useless wishing was. If Jovvi and Lorand weren't lost somewhere, we wouldn't have needed help from anyone. Naran had tried to say she knew they weren't dead, but thinking about it let me know the same thing with a good deal more certainty. I'd suddenly understood that I would be immediately aware of their death, and that no matter *where* our enemies had hidden them.

The comfort of that thought let me nod off again, but as soon as our rate of motion changed I awoke again. The coach had begun to slow, and the darkened neighborhood showed hulking warehouses standing silent all around. Some of them looked abandoned, while others were littered with debris showing how casually uncaring their users were. There was no pride of ownership visible—if the owners of warehouses ever did show pride. I'd never been anywhere near a neighborhood like that before, so I had no idea how such people thought.

88

The coach passed an intersection of streets at the slower pace, then slowed even more as we approached the middle of the block. Meerk, who had been riding on the box with the driver, dropped off the coach at a run, and not just to maintain his balance. He continued to run until he reached a wide door in one of the buildings, which he then drew open. I didn't know how really wide it was until the coach passed through with inches to spare, taking us into a dim, vast, lanternlit area. As the driver pulled his horses to a stop, I heard the wide door being closed behind us.

"Where are we?" Naran asked sleepily, straightening up in the seat. "Have we gotten there yet?"

"I'd say yes, we're there, but don't ask me where 'there' is," I responded, trying to see into the shadows of the immense building. "And people are starting to appear from somewhere, looking as sleepy as you sound."

"Have *you* gotten any sleep?" she asked softly as I watched Meerk approach one of the newcomers and begin to speak to him. "I know you're supposed to guard the rest of us, Tamrissa, but you can't do that if you're falling off your feet."

"Since I'm not currently on my feet, I don't think we have to worry about it," I commented, paying more attention to Meerk and the man he spoke with. The conversation was too low for me to hear, but they didn't seem to be exchanging any secret nods to indicate prearranged plans, nor were they looking particularly furtive. The man rubbed his eyes while listening to Meerk, nodded as he ran his hands through his hair, then turned to a group of other men while Meerk headed back to the coach.

"Paisin tells me there are quarters ready for you," Meerk said when he reached us, looking up first at me and then at Naran. "They'd given up expecting us anymore tonight, but the quarters are still available. There's also food in case you're hungry, but first we have to get the men and your luggage out of the coach. The driver needs to be out of here before the neighborhood starts to wake up, which happens extremely early."

"I thought the area was abandoned," I said, moving toward the door he'd opened and beginning to climb out of the coach. "Recently abandoned, possibly, but definitely no longer in use."

"None of it's abandoned, including this warehouse," he replied, helping me to the ground before turning to offer Naran the same assistance. "When the workday starts, our people will start with it. Wagons will come with shipments of produce to be unloaded, and later on empty wagons will come to pick up what was unloaded. No one knows that part of each shipment stays here to be used by our own people, but then it's no one's business but ours."

"Is everyone here part of your organization?" I asked, watching the man Meerk had called Paisin send people in different directions before starting to lead six big men toward us. "They all *seem* to know what's going on so I suppose they are, but what about the men who work here during the day? Surely some of *them* aren't members."

"We can't afford to have anyone around who isn't one of our own," Meerk said, his attention returned to me now that Naran had also left the coach. "From time to time we transfer people elsewhere, and then we 'hire' replacements for them. What we actually do is pretend to hire people we already know and have been waiting for, making it look as though there's a normal turnover in our workers. Dama Domon, Dama Whist, allow me to introduce my second-in-command here, Paisin Phile. You'll also meet the others, but tomorrow's soon enough."

"We're very relieved to see you ladies, and the gentlemen as well," Paisin Phile said politely. He was a tall, thin man who looked as though he were weak-willed or possibly waspish, but his even, friendly tone and the smile on his long face belied that. "We were afraid Alsin hadn't been able to locate you, and you were wandering around the city only two steps away from being found and arrested. We ought to be able to keep you safe here, at least for a while. If you'll excuse us for a minute?"

His request was just for formality's sake, as Meerk—Alsin—had already said the coach had to be on its way. Two of Paisin's men went to the boot for our bags, and the other four, working two at a time, got Rion and Vallant Ro out of their seats. Both men continued to sleep soundly, even while they were carried toward a flight of stairs.

"We have most of the upper floor fixed up for our own use," Alsin said, gesturing me along with him toward the stairs. Naran already followed close behind Rion's limp body, looking slightly less worried when a third man joined each group of two to help get the unconscious men up the steps.

"The front of the floor looks perfectly normal with crates and bales," Alsin continued, "but those crates and bales are just for show. Behind them is where our people stay when, for one reason or another, they can't go home. Sometimes, like tonight, they stay because there's work to be done."

"And what do you do when you're not rescuing people who are rightfully the next Seated Blending?" I asked, finding it easy to keep the bitterness out of my tone. I felt much too tired to be bitter, but possibly tomorrow I'd be able to manage it.

"What do you mean, rightfully the next Seated Blending?" he asked, staring at me with a frown. "You and the others lost the competition, but you're much too valuable in spite of that to let the nobles dispose of you. That's why we worked to keep track of you afterward—I'm babbling. Please tell me what you meant."

"I meant what I said," I replied with a shrug, stopping near the stairs to give the men doing the carrying a chance to get up them. "We were about to win the competition, we knew it beyond all doubt, and then suddenly we were unconscious. I asked Lanir about it before I left, and he admitted they'd put hilsom powder in our underclothes. When it became clear that we would win, they had some talents shake the underclothes so we'd breathe in the powder. Once it forced us loose from our abilities, Middles in Earth magic put us to sleep. That's why we dropped as though poleaxed, and that's why we stayed down."

When he heard that he growled under his breath, looking as though he would prefer to snarl.

"Excuse me for that," he said after a moment, his anger under slightly better control. "We were sure they couldn't possibly do anything underhanded with thousands of people watching, but they did it anyway. And the neutral judges were a waste of time, with their talk of needing to be circumspect and not arguing about what they were allowed access to! We can't be unreasonable, they always insist—! I should have remembered what happened at the challenge for Seated High in Earth magic. . . ."

"I can't see how you could have prevented what happened without you and your people being in power," I said, understanding his anger all too well. "They had everything their own way, but it won't be the same the next time we go up against them. Why were you able to trace me and Rion and Vallant, but not Jovvi and Lorand?"

"We had people watching the amphitheater, of course," he answered, only partially distracted from his irate regrets. "You and one of those men were taken away from it in private carriages, and the House insignia were perfectly clear. The other man was put into a wagon with nothing to show who it belonged to, but a female noble questioned the wagon driver rather closely, and my watcher recognized her. Which was a lucky thing, because no one was able to follow the wagon. Or wagons, since Dom Coll and the other lady were taken away in wagons of their own."

"Why wasn't anyone able to follow them?" I asked, aware of the frown I wore. "Most wagons don't move fast enough to suit anyone, since most people end up getting stuck behind them. It should even be possible to follow one on foot."

"Normally you would be right," he agreed with a nod filled with annoyance. "Following a wagon is effortless even if you don't want to follow it—except when a large number of guardsmen stop all traffic to let the carriages of nobles go first. The wagons had already gone past the line of guardsmen, and by the time my people were able to follow, there was no sign of them."

"I'm suddenly furious with myself," I said as an abrupt realization hit me. "If Eltrina Razas was able to have Vallant brought to her, she knows where he was taken. That means she might also know where the others were sent, and I made no effort to question her. Of all the stupid oversights . . ."

"No, you're wrong," he said, looking as though the same sort of revelation had struck him as well. "I'm the stupid one, because I was told when Dom Ro was brought to the Razas woman, and I made no effort to find out if the watchers followed the wagon back to where it had come from! Damn! It's too late to send for the men now, but first thing in the morning—!''

He turned and took the stairs two at a time, able to go all the way to the top and beyond because the men with their burdens had already disappeared. A glance back showed that our coach had also left, and the wide door was once again closed tight. That left nothing for me to do but raise my skirts and follow everyone upstairs, although I wouldn't have minded being carried myself. It been a long, tiring day, and was destined to be even longer.

By the time I reached the top of the wide staircase, the only one in sight was Alsin Meerk, striding back in my direction. All around were the shadowed outlines of the bales and crates he'd mentioned, looking faintly ominous in the dimness. At another time I might have felt nervous, at least until I saw Alsin Meerk's expression.

''Dama Domon, I'm so sorry!'' he apologized even before he reached me, embarrassed mortification riding him heavily. ''I didn't mean to abandon you like that, but finding out that we might not be at a dead end after all—! I usually have better manners than that, and I hope you'll forgive my thoughtlessness.''

''If you happen to have a hot cup of tea hidden up here somewhere, I'll probably be willing to forgive quite a lot of things,'' I returned, adding a smile in an effort to ease his very obvious discomfort. ''In fact, if you want the real truth, I'll settle for cold tea and then simply warm it myself.''

''No decent host would put an honored guest to the trouble of warming her own tea,'' he replied with a grin that softened his craggy features almost to the point of attractiveness. ''If you'll be so kind as to follow me, I'll show you to where you can sit and enjoy that cup of tea.''

His bow and gesture weren't entirely serious, but the courtliness wasn't a complete mockery either. I acknowledged his gesture with a matching nod before going along, wondering where all the comforts he'd mentioned were hidden. The vast floor looked completely filled with all the things warehouses are reputed to be filled with, leaving nothing but narrow aisles here and there among the looming shadows.

"Here we are," he said after leading me all the way to the right and in front of a larger than usual crate. "The 'merchandise' stored up here was carefully made by some of our members, and are works of art that can even stand up to close inspection. This entryway, however, isn't the same, so we keep it locked when it isn't in use."

As he spoke he pushed on the front face of the crate, and it swung silently inward. That made a doorway almost as wide as the one we'd come into the warehouse through, one which showed a good deal more light and warmth beyond it. Alsin gestured me forward with a smile, so I stepped in and looked around while he closed and locked the unusual door behind us.

From where I stood it was possible to see nothing but two long corridors, one stretching straight ahead on my right, and the second doing the same to the left. We stood in a fairly wide entrance area that was lit with lamps, more lamps spaced along the walls of both corridors. There was nothing in the way of decoration to be seen, and in fact the place looked as though it were made of crate facings.

"Your friends were taken that way," Alsin said, pointing up the corridor to the right. "I'll show you where they are on the way to that hot cup of tea, so you won't spend your time wondering."

I appreciated the thoughtfulness of that, once again finding myself surprised that this was the same man who had brought Hat to the residence and then had threatened Lorand. Remembering that, I had a sudden idea.

"You didn't just *happen* to get involved with Hat, did you?" I said, trying not to sound accusing. "You deliberately did something to make him beholden to you, just to gain access to *us*."

"The opportunity was much too good to pass up," he admitted, looking a bit shamefaced. "We don't often get access to those who test for High, and the reason for that is another story. When I came across that boy trying to drown his sorrows in drink while gambling away every copper he had, I believed his claim about having a friend who had certainly passed the test. No one else believed him, though, so I had no trouble becoming the one he lost his money to.

It was a good thing I did, too, because he was making every effort to cheat.''

"I can't say I'm surprised," I commented, glancing through the occasional doorways we passed on our left. Most of them were empty, but one held Paisin and a group of men seated around a table. We seemed to be in an area of conference rooms, and I wondered if Paisin was in the process of passing on whatever orders Alsin had given him.

"The boy wasn't a particularly nice person," Alsin agreed with a sigh. "He kept muttering things about how Dom Coll had stolen his rightful place, so when his debt to me mounted really high, I was able to order him to a place where he would see all the hopefuls pass by in their coaches on the way to their practicing. That was how he spotted Dom Coll, whom he immediately pointed out to me. I told him I knew the coach driver, which wasn't a lie, and was able to put him in contact with Dom Coll that way. I went along the second time to make a contact of my own, which worked out better than I could have hoped."

"Were you ever able to locate Hat after that farce of a challenge?" I asked, suddenly curious all over again. "Lorand said you weren't able to, but was that the truth?"

"I wish it weren't," he said, frustration clear in the words. "The boy disappeared completely, and I can't help feeling that if I'd located him I'd have some idea about where your missing friends are. I also can't shake the conviction that something is going on that none of us knows about, something the nobility is involved in that they don't *want* us to know about."

"Lanir said he had no idea where my friends were, but now I'm wondering if that was the truth," I admitted with a sigh. "It might have been possible to force him into telling me what he knew if I'd tried, but now it's much too late even if I wanted to go back to that house."

"He's dead, then?" Alsin asked after a very brief hesitation, obviously trying to be circumspect. "He was the Seated High in Fire magic, but you had no trouble besting him? That alone should be part of the proof we need ..."

"It won't really do you any good," I told him, my head-shake having caused his words to trail off. "Lanir wasn't dead when I left, just burned out. He was no more than a

fairly strong Middle, but he knew *I* was a High. He tried to
force himself past a Middle's natural stopping point in an
effort to match and defeat me, but ended up burning himself
out instead. We can't really say I bested him, because I
never had the chance to.''

"But you could have, couldn't you?" he persisted, looking as though he thought furiously. "That should be enough,
especially when they promote his first alternate and try to
protect the man the way they protected Porvin. A challenge
has to be held no later than one week after the man is
Seated, and if we spread the word it will be *very* well attended. We also have enough of our people in positions that
will let us enter our own candidate for the challenge, and
once their pet loses there won't be anything they can do
about it.''

"Personally, I'd hate to be that winning candidate," I
said, trying to be gentle about bringing him down to earth.
"Do I have to tell *you* what's most likely to happen to the
person? They'll be able to insist on seeing to the winner
themselves, away from all those witnesses in the audience.
At that point they'd be able to do anything to him, possibly
even causing a fatal 'accident' after neutralizing him with
hilsom powder. Do you really want to throw someone's life
away like that?''

"No, you're right of course," he admitted with a deep
sigh, his previous enthusiasm dying. "As long as they're
still completely in charge of things, someone put into their
hands would have no chance at all. It's just that it's now
become worse than ever, to accept having them running
things when I know for a fact that they don't deserve to.
And your friends should be in there.''

We'd turned a corner to the left, which, after a few steps,
led to a widening of the corridor. Rooms stood closer together in this area, but the doors also stood closed—except
for the one at the end, which didn't seem to have a door.
The room Alsin had pointed to was on the right, and I
opened the door quietly to peek inside.

A number of cots were arranged in a row, six to be precise, and Rion and Vallant Ro lay stretched out on two of
them. Naran lay on a third, but the cot had been pushed as
close to Rion's as possible, and she held his hand tightly

between both of her own. She looked at me and smiled when I put my head in, so I returned the smile and withdrew again.

"I'm sorry I didn't mention this sooner, but I'm afraid you're going to have to find someplace else to put Vallant Ro," I said once I'd closed the door again. "He can't abide small, closed-in spaces with no windows, and if he wakes up in there he'll suffer quite a lot. Is there anything you can do?"

"As a matter of fact, there is," Alsin agreed, nodding as though I'd said nothing unusual. "Dom Ro isn't the only man with a problem like that, and it made no sense to exclude a man from our ranks just because he has an unusual need. One of these rooms is built against a wide access-window, one that hasn't been used since another warehouse was put up really close to this one. The window faces a blank wall, but if necessary someone could climb out of it and shinny down the pulley rope, which was left for precisely that reason. I'll have him moved right away."

We'd been walking toward the room without a door as we talked, and now Alsin moved ahead to enter it first. When I followed I saw a large room containing a number of tables and chairs, with another doorless entry directly opposite the one I stood in. Although there was seating for more, the room only had three small groups of men, seated separately. Some of the men ate and some simply drank whatever was in their cups, and Alsin had walked over to one of the groups. After he spoke to the three men, they nodded and rose and left the room the way we'd just come in.

"They'll take him to the window dormitory right away," Alsin said as he returned to me. "And I always seem to be abandoning you, so I'd better make immediate amends. The tea you wanted is right over here, and it can be joined by a meal if you happen to be hungry."

"Thank you, but I'm not," I answered, letting him guide me to the left to a long counter against the wall. The counter held the largest tea service I'd ever seen, with what looked like fifty cups without saucers. "Are you really expecting that many people to be thirsty during the night, or is that arrangement simply preparation for the morning?"

"A bit of both," he replied with a smile as he reached

for one of the cups. "We occasionally have people coming and going at all hours here, so it's easier to keep things ready than to make them ready. Your tea, lady, and the sugar is right over there."

I accepted the cup he'd filled while giving him a nod of thanks, then put sugar into the tea while he poured a cup for himself. My fingertips told me that the tea could stand to be a bit hotter, so when he put his cup down near the sugar I warmed his tea as well as my own. One of the men sitting in the room gasped, and Alsin glanced at him questioningly until he picked up his cup again.

"Ah, now I understand why Gorliss was so surprised and impressed," Alsin said with a chuckle. "You warmed our tea, and since Gorliss is technically on watch, he's touching the power. I hadn't remembered that his aspect is Fire magic, but now there can't be any doubt. I think I'd better introduce you."

Just then the three men who had left abruptly returned, two of them carrying Vallant Ro's still-limp body. The third seemed to be in charge of leading the way, probably to open and close doors. We waited until they passed through the room, then Alsin led the way toward the table where the man Gorliss sat.

"There are no others in the dormitory room he's being taken to, so Dom Ro won't find himself crowded if he awakens early," Alsin murmured as we walked. "There are also special arrangements for food to be brought there, and if you like there's a place for you in the room as well."

"Thank you, but I prefer to stay with my other friends," I replied, not quite able to produce a smile. Then I raised my voice a bit to add, "It should amuse you that your friend Gorliss here seems to be a stronger Middle than the former Seated High in Fire magic. And you can tell him that he needn't hold to the power quite so tightly. I'm saving my strength for any nobles I happen to come across."

That produced chuckling in all the men, especially the one who had been staring at me so intensely. Alsin introduced me to everyone, and the man Gorliss shook his head ruefully.

"I apologize for reactin' like that, ma'am, but you're surely the strongest talent I ever did feel," he said. "There's some who tell me *I'm* a monster, but my strength compared to yours . . ."

He shook his head, and Alsin smiled in the same rueful way.

"I know just what you mean, Gorliss," he admitted. "I used to think *I* had all the strength there was, and then I watched her friend Dom Coll at work. He made me feel like a Low talent, and he wasn't even straining. When Dama Domon and the others finally get to take their proper place as the Seated Five, no one will have to wonder if they deserve to be there."

The men all agreed with that rather more strongly than I expected them to, and then Alsin excused us and led the way to a table a short distance away. He seated me before settling into his own chair, and then he smiled rather wearily.

"It's been a very long day, so I imagine you're glad to finally have the tea and chair you were promised," he said. "Personally, I'm not tired at all, and if necessary I could just keep on going for another—oh, two or three minutes at least. As long as I spend the time sitting down."

"I don't know if I'm quite that strong," I said with a smile I didn't have to force. "If I didn't need this tea to help me unwind, I'd probably already be asleep. Would you prefer to wait until tomorrow before telling me what your organization is all about?"

"I don't have to be awake to talk about the organization," he said after sipping at his tea. "I know our aims so well, I probably recite them in my sleep as it is. Do you have any idea how hard it is for people to make something of themselves in our society? I'm not talking about people with no ethics or conscience, because people like that always manage to prosper—at the expense of those around them. I'm talking about your average man or woman, ordinary, decent people."

"No, actually, I don't," I admitted, sipping at my own tea. "My parents are the sort you mentioned first, without ethics or conscience, and so are all their friends and acquaintances. Why is it so hard for decent people to get ahead?"

"The nobility is why," he responded, bitterness creeping

into his voice. "Everyone gets a basic education because the schools teach obedience as well as restraint in using one's talent, but in order to go beyond the basics, you have to have a 'sponsor.' The sponsor must be a member of the nobility, but you don't even get to see him. You simply make your payment to his agent, the higher the payment, the higher up on the list your name goes. After that you're allowed to pay through the nose for the education itself— and then just try to find a job where you can use what you learned."

"What about those who don't want a higher education?" I asked, only just beginning to understand how really sheltered I'd been. "There's nothing wrong with opening a shop or providing a service, and a lot of people seem to have done just that."

"No, a lot of people do it for various members of the nobility," Alsin corrected gently, leaning forward to put his forearms on the table. "Not one man or woman in ten owns his or her own business. What they do is buy a license from the noble in charge of their section of the city, then they pay three-quarters of what their business earns to its real owner. All expenses are paid out of their end, and they're allowed to live on whatever's left."

"That's outrageous," I stated, beginning to get angry. "No wonder they're all so rich without having to lift a finger. But why do people stand for it? Why don't they leave the city and move elsewhere so they can live better?"

"Where would you suggest they go?" he asked, smiling without amusement. "There isn't a single part of this empire that the nobles don't own, even if most of the time they live *here*. They have agents to represent them everywhere, so they don't *have* to be on the spot to collect their gold. We might as well have brands on our shoulders and steel collars welded closed around our necks. We're slaves to them in everything but name."

"It's not supposed to be like that," I said with a shake of my head, the agitation growing. "I know there was a time when the nobles didn't own everything, and we need to bring that time back again. What are you doing to make it happen?"

"One of the things we're *not* doing is racing around like

chickens with their heads cut off,'' he soothed, his amusement for some reason returned. ''There have been other organizations from time to time, but none of them were able to accomplish anything because they tried to attack the nobles themselves. We're out to show that the nobles are maintaining themselves in power by breaking the law. If we can do that, *then* we can take the individual nobles down without their being able to scream about lawless rebellion. And with the law on *our* side, most of the guard will have to support us.''

''I don't see things working out that way,'' I said with another shake of my head. ''Most people are content to live quietly even with things as they are, so you can't expect support from them. If you come forward—with just your supporters—claiming the nobles are breaking the law, those same nobles will laugh and tell you to take them to court and then they'll go about their business. That business will consist of delaying or outright squashing any charges being brought against them, in the meanwhile having you and your people quietly arrested. You can't bring charges in court if you don't come forward, and if you do come forward you'll never live long enough to see those charges pressed. You need to do something else entirely.''

''Like what?'' he asked, the amusement gone again. ''Recruit an army and depose the nobles by force? Not only does that go against everything we believe in, it just isn't possible. It takes experience and training to use the talents of an army effectively, and no one among us has that. It's been far too long since our empire *had* an army, so any veterans we might have recruited are long since dead.''

''How does the empire get along without an army?'' I asked in confusion. ''Especially since we're supposedly still expanding into what used to be other people's countries? No, never mind, the question isn't relevant. What *is* relevant is that your plans will never work. I'm sorry to have to tell you that, but I prefer to hurt your feelings rather than stand back and watch you die. Thank you for the tea. I think I'm ready to sleep now.''

He rose when I did, but he made no effort to come with me when I left the room. He'd looked furiously unhappy, but he obviously couldn't think of anything else to say in argument against what I'd told him. I suspected he knew as well as I did that his plan would never work, and had kept on with it only because no one had been able to think of anything better.

Opening the door quietly to the spartan communal bedchamber showed that Naran now slept as soundly as Rion. I slipped inside and closed the door again just as quietly, tiptoed to the door on the far side of the room in an effort to locate privacy facilities, and was glad to find them just behind the door. I used them quickly, then returned to the outer room where I chose a cot to lie down on. I was hardly used to sleeping in my clothes, but if Naran had been able to do it then I had the hope of being able to do the same.

Hope . . . I lay on my right side, the tiny pillow under my cheek, my gaze on Naran and Rion. Although both lay sound asleep, they nevertheless continued to hold hands. That was probably what being able to hope did for you, which was why I'd never have what they did between them. I could hope to fall asleep, but I'd never learn to hope for any situation which had the power to bring such incredible pain if it *didn't* succeed. *When* it didn't succeed . . .

I closed my eyes, but sleep was a very long time in coming.

TWELVE

Rion yawned and stretched, then got a good enough look at his surroundings to wonder where in blazes he was. The last thing he remembered was being at Mother's house. . . .

"No, that's not the last thing," he murmured when he

saw Tamrissa sound asleep just a few beds away. Memory now flooded back about the way he'd been rescued, and Naran had been there as well. He had a vague memory of traveling in a coach forever, and then of being carried. And Vallant had also been there . . .

Without stopping to think, Rion swung his legs off the thin, narrow bed and stood, pausing to stretch again before realizing that he'd done it all without help. That abomination he'd been fed had finally worn off, then, and what a relief it was. Hobbling about like an old man, needing the help of others to walk without falling—

Sudden worry caused Rion to stand unmoving. His mind seemed perfectly all right, but he'd abruptly remembered what Mother had said about his talent. He was supposed to have been permanently damaged, especially since he hadn't been free to fight against the damage. Well, he seemed to be free now, so it might be wisest to see if something positive could be done.

Rion first took a deep breath to brace himself against what he might find, and then he gingerly reached toward the power. There was a slight drag to his efforts at first, as though he needed to break through some sort of delicate barrier, and then his touch was full and sure. Strength flowed into him, both physical and talent-wise, and once again he was aware of everything to do with the air about him.

"It's all there, just as it was before the betrayal!" he whispered ecstatically, needing to say the words aloud to make them absolutely real and true. But he had no wish to waken Tamrissa from the sleep she so obviously needed, and he also wanted to find Naran. It would be nice to know where they were, and also what they'd be doing next.

A door at the far end of the narrow room opened on a privacy facility, so Rion made use of it before trying the other door. He also used the shaving gear near the basin to rid himself of stubble, and splashed water into his face to drive away the last mists of sleep. But finding a bath house would soon become an absolute, top-drawer priority. He'd never slept in his clothes before, and disliked the sweaty, rumpled sensation doing it had left behind.

The second door led into a corridor, and after closing the thing as silently as possible he followed the corridor to an archway at what appeared to be its end. As he approached he heard low conversation, and stepping inside showed him a room filled with tables and chairs and people eating. Hunger suddenly touched him as well, but Naran had seen him come in. He first wanted to give her the good news, and then he would find a plate to fill.

"Good morning, my love," Naran greeted him with a matchless smile once he was close enough, her lovely eyes shining. "I'm delighted to see you up and around again, and I apologize for not waiting until you awoke. When I opened my eyes I discovered that I was ravenous, and so had to come looking for something to eat."

"Apologies would be necessary only if you *hadn't* seen to yourself, my love," he returned, bending to exchange a quick kiss with her. "And I must say I agree with you. It's a very good morning indeed."

"Oh, Rion, you've completely returned to yourself!" she exclaimed delightedly, taking the hand he held out. "I knew you would, but there was confusion about when. Oh, excuse my terrible manners. This gentleman is Dom Paisin Phile, one of those who are so kindly helping us."

The tall, thin man sitting with Naran rose with a smile to offer his hand, and Rion took it while showing his own smile. It was marvelous to feel like a full man again, and also to be treated like one. . . .

"It's good to see you up and about, Dom Mardimil," the man Phile said warmly. "Please help yourself to something to break your fast, and then I'll leave you and Dama Whist alone."

"It's difficult to be alone in a room filled with so many people, Dom Phile," Rion responded easily. "Please stay where you are, and I'll return in a moment."

Phile nodded his thanks for and acceptance of the invitation, so Rion went to locate the food he'd been able to smell ever since he'd walked in. The long counter he found it on wasn't precisely a buffet, and the platters holding the food weren't warmers. But there was still a circle of warmth around the eggs, bacon, and fried potatoes, as well as around the lightly toasted bread. Those four things were the only offerings, but there was enough of each that Rion was able to help himself with a free hand.

After taking a dollop of butter and one pinch each of salt and pepper from the bowls holding them, Rion prepared a cup of tea then returned to the table where Naran and Phile sat. It was faintly amusing that at one time Rion would have been unable to touch any of the crudely arranged food, but Mother's prejudices happily no longer affected him.

"Dom Phile was just telling me what some of his people are doing now," Naran said when Rion sat with his plate and cup in front of him. "They haven't been able to locate Jovvi and Lorand either, but Dom Meerk feels they might pick up a clue from Vallant's situation. He was brought to that vile Eltrina Razas's house from somewhere, and the men who had been watching her house might just have followed the wagon which brought him when it returned to wherever it had come from."

"Unfortunately those men aren't here, or we would already know if one of them did follow the wagon back," Phile put in, his expression one of disturbance mixed with frustration and anxiety. "I sent people to search for them first thing this morning, as soon as the warehouse opened. We can't afford to have our men be seen coming and going from here at all hours unless there's an emergency, and your arrival during the wee hours was emergency enough for one day."

"When we do manage to locate them, at least I'll be able to assist Tamrissa in freeing them," Rion put in after swallowing. "I would have dearly loved being able to help with Vallant, even though Tamrissa had no need of my help. You have no idea how helpless one feels . . ." Rion shook his head, forcibly dismissing the memory, then added, "And speaking of Vallant, what became of him? He was neither in that sleeping room, nor, so far as I can see, is he in this room. Has he gone out of wherever this place happens to be?"

"We're in a secret section of a warehouse," Phile replied, then went on to describe the location of their surroundings before adding, "And Dom Ro was taken to a dormitory room with a window. I was told that Dama Domon mentioned how uncomfortable he would find it to be in *this* area with us, so Alsin—Dom Meerk—had him moved."

"I would appreciate directions to where he is," Rion said

with a nod after another bite. "Once I finish breakfasting, I mean to go and see how he's doing. I'm certain he'll be just as eager to help free Jovvi and Lorand as I am."

"And I'll go with you," Naran said with a smile. "I need to see both of you up and about for a time before I'll find it possible to wipe away the image of the two of you just lying there unmoving—Please excuse me while I go for another cup of tea."

Rion put a supporting hand to her arm for a moment before allowing her to hurry away, just to help convince her that he really was returned to himself. He hadn't fully understood just how frantic she must have been when none of them returned to the residence, but he was beginning to. Add to that the way he'd looked when Tamrissa had freed him . . . It was a wonder that his poor beloved hadn't broken down in hysterics. . . .

Naran was smiling easily again by the time she returned with a fresh cup of tea, giving Rion a better idea of the strength possessed by the woman he loved. He couldn't have been more proud of her, and he spent the rest of the meal gazing at her in wonder. How *he* had been so blessed as to gain her love was a mystery he would likely never solve, most especially now that he knew himself to be something other than a real noble. He was no more than a sham in that respect, but with Naran beside him he would forge a reality even stronger and more successful.

When Rion had finished, Phile offered to guide them to Vallant rather than simply supplying directions. Rion and Naran accepted the warmly given offer, then followed the man through the archway on the far side of the dining area. The place reminded Rion of that tavern he and the other men of the residence had had such a marvelous time in, the tavern where he'd first met Naran. No wonder he'd felt so immediately at home in the area, or rather, *not* at home . . .

Phile turned right up the corridor, then, after a short distance, right again. This latter corridor proved to be rather long, but at the end of it was a crossing corridor which held three doorways fairly close together. Phile stopped there and indicated the door farthest to the left.

"Dom Ro was put in there, as there were already men in the other two dormitories," he said. "We've learned that those who feel discomfort in windowless places also dislike being in the midst of crowds, and it's in all our best interests to have Dom Ro recover as quickly and completely as possible. If you should happen to need me, ask any of the men you see to come get me. I'll be doing my—'job'—in the warehouse.''

He left with a parting smile, providing Rion with a reason to admire his discretion. Another man might have hung about, having no idea that his presence might be an intrusion. It was pleasant to knock on the indicated door with no one but Naran beside him . . . just in case Vallant wasn't as fully returned to himself as he should be. . . .

Rion waited, then knocked a second time, but when he still received no answer he reached to the doorknob and quietly opened the door. His ability told him that someone was indeed in the room, and it was perfectly possible that Vallant hadn't yet awakened. If so, he and Naran would simply have to return a bit later. . . .

And the person in the room certainly did prove to be Vallant. The big ex–sea captain lay on his back on the narrow bed closest to the large window, a window which had been swung open almost completely. The blank side of a building stood no more than feet beyond the window, but a rope and pulley arrangement at the window's side said that reaching the street outside would be no more than slightly difficult. Rion knew that Vallant must appreciate the arrangement quite a bit, at the same time realizing that the man was awake.

"Vallant, are you all right?" Rion asked with quickly growing concern when the man on the bed made no effort to see who had come in. "It's Rion, and Naran is with me. Is there something we can do? Can we bring you food?"

"I've already eaten, thank you," Vallant replied in a distant, emotionless voice, his gaze unmoving from the opened window. "A fellow came by earlier, right after I awoke. He said the eatin' hall is much deeper inside the maze, and so he brought me a plate with everythin' available. Because he knew I would never be able to stand goin' to the eatin' hall myself . . .''

Rion exchanged a worried glance with Naran, but she seemed to be at as much of a loss as he. This wasn't the same Vallant Ro they'd known, speaking to them as though they weren't really there. Something was seriously wrong, and although Rion dreaded whatever he might learn, he still had to ask.

"Vallant, tell me what's troubling you," he urged in a gentle voice, stepping more fully into the room. "I want to help, but it's impossible for me to do so until I learn what I must help *with*. Are you still held in the grip of that hilsom powder?"

"No, that sedative wore off some time ago," came the response, still as distant and chilling with all trace of humanity gone. "I can get up and walk all by myself now, but I found that there's two things I *can't* do: go to the eatin' hall and have a meal there, and touch the power. I find it amusin' that I no longer even know where the power *is*, not to speak of touchin' it. If—people—thought I was useless and pitiful before, wait until they see me now . . ."

The lifeless words trailed off, but the silence came far too late to keep Rion from being touched by ice. Mother had threatened *him* with permanent damage, but it was Vallant who now had to face the life of a cripple. Rion felt like weeping for his brother's loss, but tears had proven themselves useless in really serious situations, which that one certainly was. He held to Naran instead as she clung to him, trying to think of what in the world it was possible to say. . . .

Vallant had to struggle awake, but once he got a grip on the condition he was able to retain that grip. In another moment he had his eyes open, and then he discovered that the more he did, the less he had to struggle. Sitting up led to stretching hard, and then he climbed to his feet.

"Better," he muttered as he looked around, running one hand through his hair. His enjoyment of the freedom wasn't yet complete, not when his muscles felt stiff and his mind fuzzy. It would obviously take a while before that drug he'd been given was completely gone from his system, but at least he could move around on his own while he waited for it to be gone. And the first place he meant to move to was the door in the wall opposite the line of cots. He needed privacy facilities rather badly, but if he'd needed help to use them . . .

But happily he needed no help, and when he emerged again he was able to look about a bit more thoroughly. The big open window at one end of the relatively small room had worked to calm his automatic unease, but when he opened the door leading out of the room his insides immediately knotted up. The corridors beyond the door were tiny and completely enclosed, and there was no telling where the next window or door to the outside might be found. Vallant felt a clutch of fear at the thought that he was trapped, and only the presence of the window in the room behind him kept him from falling into panic. Where in the name of chaos *was* this place, and what was he doing here?

"Hey, good morning," a voice said, and Vallant turned his head to the left to see a man emerging from the corridor a few feet away. "We thought you might be up and about by now, so I brought you some breakfast."

Vallant had already noticed the tray by then, and the aroma of the food had begun to take its turn knotting his stomach. He stepped back at the stranger's approach and managed something of a smile.

"You're the best-lookin' room maid I've seen in a long time," he commented, glancing around the sparsely furnished room again. "There's no table in here to eat at, but I don't mean to let *that* stop me. Just set that tray down on one of the cots, and I'll take it from there. And by the way— thank you for botherin'."

"No problem," the man returned amiably after putting down the tray. "My brother has your trouble, and when he's here he starts choking everywhere but in one of these dormitories. Walking down to the eating area is completely beyond him, since it's a bit like a maze that you walk through to get there. They finally moved my brother to another facility, and now he's a lot happier. And since I didn't know what you would like, I brought some of everything."

"Decent of you," Vallant said distractedly, suddenly not quite as hungry as he'd been. With half the nobility knowing about his problem, the matter hadn't precisely been a secret until now. But these people in whatever this place was . . . now it seemed that all of *them* knew as well, which somehow made the situation more than mildly humiliating.

"Well, go ahead and dig in," the man urged with a gesture of both hands. "We don't stand on ceremony here, not when we don't know if some emergency won't keep us from sitting down to our next meal on time. And we want you and your friends to be healthy and strong. We've needed something everyone can rally behind for a long time, and once we have all five of you rescued we'll have that something."

"You've found Jovvi and Lorand?" Vallant asked around a mouthful of eggs, hunger finally overcoming discomfort. "I remember now that they weren't with us."

"We may have found something that will lead us to them," the man replied, pacing around in a tight circle rather than sitting down. "Some of our people are looking into it now, and you can take my word that they'll do everything they can. We've sworn to find a way to bring the nobles down without bloodshed, and this has to be it."

"You expect to use their cheatin' with us to force them out of power," Vallant stated, staring at the man thoughtfully as he chewed. "Simply provin' they cheated won't do anythin' but make them laugh, not when there's no one around who can demand that they give up their place and make the demand stick. If they have to, they'll fight to keep what they have; anyone wantin' to take them down has to be just as willin' to fight."

"But that's not true at all," the man protested with a small laugh. "The nobles may be greedy pigs, but they aren't stupid. Trying to fight once everyone knows the truth about you is mindless, so they'll *have* to step down. They simply won't have any other choice."

"They'll have the choice of killin' the first five or ten or a hundred people talkin' against them," Vallant pointed out, knowing he probably wasted his breath. "After that the talk will stop, and everythin' will go back to the way it was. If you aren't willin' to fight to get and keep what's important to you, you probably won't get it in the first place."

"No, it's not going to be like that," the man insisted stubbornly, the words almost a litany. "We'll expose the nobles for the cheats they are, and then they'll be forced to step down. It's barbaric to think that people have to be *fight-*

ing all the time. . . . Look, I have work to do, so I'll come back for the tray later. Enjoy your meal.''

And with that he was gone, probably to keep from hearing Vallant ruin his dream again. The world had need of people who were incapable of fighting, to maintain whatever peace the fighters achieved. That was the way progress was maintained and improved upon, but as long as human beings were involved, peace was an unstable condition at best. There would always be someone coming along who wanted to take away whatever others had managed to earn, and only being ready, willing, and able to fight might keep that fight from happening. The nobles obviously knew that, considering the number of guardsmen they kept around themselves; a shame that man would never know the same. . . .

Vallant worked his way through most of the food on the tray, using the contents of the pitcher of tea to wash it all down. When he finished he felt a good deal better, more ready to face the world and what it brought. The stiffness in his body was almost gone, and most of the fuzziness in his mind. Now if he could just figure out a way to find Tamrissa and the others . . .

Thought of Tamrissa made Vallant pause, reminding him as it did of the night before. He'd been deeply and completely humiliated in front of her, and afterward he hadn't been able to face her. That pity he'd been certain she felt . . . could he have been mistaken and simply imagining things? He loved her so much that he never wanted to be anything but perfect in her eyes. . . .

Standing up and walking to the window gave Vallant a chance to think, and by the time he had a closer view of the building which stood so near this one he also had an answer. The questions of where Tamrissa had spent the night, who had told these people about his problem, and where the woman he loved might be right now—they said it all. If her own love hadn't turned to pity, she would have been there when he first opened his eyes.

He took a very deep breath, realizing he couldn't blame her. He was supposed to be the strength she relied on to bolster her sometimes less-than-adequate self-confidence, and he'd failed her. Not only hadn't he been able to rescue her from capture, she'd had the trouble of needing to rescue *him!* And look at him right now, wanting to go searching for his friends but too afraid to leave the room. He was patently useless, in everything but his talent—

Another memory froze Vallant where he stood, this time a memory of something said last night during the coach ride. It was Rion who'd mentioned it, telling the others that his mother had claimed he was permanently damaged. Tamrissa had said she'd been told something of the same, and he himself had a very vague memory of something the Razas woman might have said.

But that didn't necessarily mean anything, Vallant told himself with a forced laugh. Tamrissa hadn't been hurt at all, and Rion had insisted he would recover to spite his mother, if for no other reason. That should mean that he was all right as well, even though he'd as yet made no effort to touch the power. All he had to do was reach out . . .

In no time at all the sweat began to stand out on Vallant's brow, but that was the only evidence of his efforts. He'd fought to open himself to the power, fought to touch it, but finally had to admit to himself that he didn't even know where the power was. He'd been aware of the vastness of it for his entire life, and now all trace of it had disappeared. Gone, leaving him damaged forever . . .

Vallant groped his way to the nearest cot and slowly lay down on it, so deep in shock that the world seemed miles away. And hidden behind transparent cotton, which was for his own protection. He needed to be protected now, just as all thoroughly useless people needed to be. He had nothing left, and even from a distance of miles he was able to feel the edges of the excruciating pain brought by that knowledge.

He floated in nothingness for quite some time, then a sound came that was easy to ignore. A repetition of the sound still brought nothing in the way of reaction from him, but a time later there was a familiar voice, and the words spoken worked their way through to him.

"Vallant, are you all right?" the voice asked. "It's Rion, and Naran is with me. Is there something we can do? Can we bring you food?"

"I've already eaten, thank you," Vallant replied, feeling very far away. "A fellow came by earlier, right after I awoke. He said the eatin' hall is much deeper inside the maze, and so he brought me a plate with everythin' available. Because he knew I would never be able to stand goin' to the eatin' hall myself . . .''

There was silence for a time, and then the familiar voice came again.

"Vallant, tell me what's troubling you," it urged. "I want to help, but it's impossible for me to do so until I learn what I must help *with*. Are you still held in the grip of that hilsom powder?"

"No, that sedative wore off some time ago," Vallant replied, still untouched by anything said. "I can get up and walk all by myself now, but I found that there's two things I *can't* do: go to the eatin' hall and have a meal there, and touch the power. I find it amusin' that I no longer even know where the power *is*, not to speak of touchin' it. If—people— thought I was useless and pitiful before, wait until they see me now . . .''

After Vallant spoke the truth there was an even heavier silence than before, one which he appreciated. It gave him the chance to let his own words echo inside his head, forcing him to get used to them. Even though he didn't want to get used to them. They hurt so very much, but all the wishing in the world couldn't wish them into being a lie. Not that it really mattered anymore. . . .

"So here you all are," another familiar voice suddenly came. "I've been looking everywhere for you. Alsin has come back with an answer, so we have to leave here as soon as possible. Don't stare at me like that, Rion, I'm not being hysterical. Furious is what I am, that and worried sick. He told me that Jovvi and Lorand are no longer in the city. Those animals have sent them somewhere, and we have to follow and get them back."

And that was news so serious that it even came close to reaching Vallant.

THIRTEEN

Kambil walked into the conference room closest to the throne room, relieved that the Seating ceremony was over. The others felt just as relieved, although they weren't doing much in the way of talking. They'd agreed that morning to be as quiet and unobtrusive as possible, to lessen the chance that someone would notice Delin's lack of animation. It had been necessary to put Delin back under full control even before the ceremony . . .

A servant came forward to offer iced fruit drinks to the new Seated Five, and Kambil accepted the offer with a smile while concentrating on the sensation of the jeweled band about his brow to keep his anger from showing. He'd been a fool to turn Delin loose and then fail to watch the madman closely, but there had been so much else to do . . . Well, that was an excuse, and from now on there would be no further need for excuses.

"Dismiss the servants, please," a deep pleasant voice came, breaking into Kambil's thoughts. "There are important matters which we all need to talk about."

Kambil turned slowly to inspect Lord Ephaim Noll, the most influential Advisor on the Board now that Zolind was gone. The black-haired man was only just past his middle years, and fully as large as Kambil himself. The lack of fat showed that Noll took good care of himself, housing his extremely powerful personality in a matching body. There were those who had been fooled by the man's soft brown eyes into thinking him weak, but no one had ever made that same mistake twice.

"Certainly, Lord Ephaim," Kambil agreed just as pleasantly, gesturing the servants into leaving. "We were honored to have you and your brother Advisors attend the ceremony, and we were hoping you would take the time to speak to us. We'll certainly need guidance during the coming years, and yours will be the most valued."

"Nicely said," Noll commented with a faint smile once the last of the servants had closed the door behind herself. His four supporters, men with almost as much standing as he had, also looked amused. "At least you have the good sense to *pretend* to be normal when others are around."

"I'm afraid I don't understand," Kambil said after an appropriate hesitation, working to look perplexed. "Why would I have to *pretend* to be normal? As far as I know, that's what we all are."

"You can't possibly think I'm ignorant of what happened last night, boy," Noll said as he chose a chair and settled himself into it. "I happen to know that you and three members of your group made an unannounced visit to Moord's wing of the palace at a rather late hour, and there was a good deal of frenzied activity before the four of you left again. Would *you* like to begin speaking about exactly what happened, or would you prefer me to?"

Kambil found his own chair to sit in, pausing while the others took places near him. Noll's people were already seated, so Kambil was able to reply almost immediately.

"I really don't have any idea what you're talking about," he said mildly as he met Noll's gaze. It hadn't been difficult to tell that the man was bluffing about knowing details, which showed that Noll wasn't quite as formidable as his reputation suggested. Only a fool would try to bluff a High in Spirit magic. . . . "If you have details to supply, by all means go ahead and supply them."

"So you're going to brazen it out," Noll said while his mind sorted lightning fast through dozens of options and plans. "I usually admire a man with the stones to stand his ground no matter what happens, but there's a time for that sort of thing and a time to admit the truth. The man who learns to tell the difference is the man who succeeds in life.

Do you deny that Lord Ossim Moord and his lady wife were brought to the palace last night, but no one saw them leave—or has seen them since?''

"I, personally, never even saw them arrive," Kambil replied, having a better idea now of what Noll knew. "If you were here and saw the arrival yourself, I certainly won't argue with you. What I still don't understand is what point you're trying to make."

"Accusation," Noll corrected, all traces of amusement gone from his thoughts. "It's an accusation that I'm making, to wit, that Moord killed his parents just as he killed Elfini Weil and Ollon Kapmar. You can't deny it, so let's just get beyond it."

"You want to get beyond Lord Zolind's irrational and unsubstantiated hatred of Delin?" Kambil shrugged, keeping all traces of a smile from his face. "Very well, I'm willing to go along with that. Let the man's obsession be cremated with his body, and then we'll finally have an end to it. But as far as Delin's parents go, I'm afraid we'll have to insist that the subject not be brought up. Lord Ossim did unspeakable things to Delin as a child, and if anyone makes any accusations . . . Well, let's just say it's possible to get the names of those who joined Lord Ossim in his . . . pastimes."

"I'm told that those particular people—if there really were any to begin with—are almost all dead," Noll countered blandly, his expression showing nothing of the agitation in his mind. "Trying to threaten me won't get you anywhere, boy, not when you and your friends haven't been *publicly* Seated yet. There are still two days before that happens, and unless we come to a firm agreement right now, it just may not happen at all. Does that state it clearly enough to gain your full attention?"

"You may take it as a fact that you've had my full attention all along," Kambil said, pleased that they were finally getting down to the meat of the meeting. "And please believe that I never threaten, it's too much of a waste of time. What sort of agreement did you have in mind?"

"The sort you and the others should already be bound by," Noll told him bluntly, having settled into a more comfortable frame of mind. "Those who are permitted to call themselves the Seated Five have certain responsibilities toward those they spring from, notably the support of their people against rebels and troublemakers. Should some district of the empire decide to flex independence we don't want it to have, bringing them back into line will fall to you.''

"Oh, I see now," Kambil said with an amiable smile and nod. "Anytime one of you decides to tighten your grip around the peasants you control, you worry about whether or not it will be the final straw in their minds. We can appreciate that, most especially since revolution would be bad for the empire. I'm certain we can come to terms with those of you in such a position—once we discuss the details.''

"If you're referring to being paid, you'll have to make a certain accommodation," Noll said, loosening up even more because of the satisfaction flowing through him. "Some of us have already paid in gold, in advance, to Adriari and her group. Since we can't reasonably be expected to pay twice, you'll simply have to uphold those agreements without further compensation.''

"*Further* compensation?" Kambil echoed with brows raised, not about to let the man get away with that. "My dear Lord Ephaim, you and the others have our sincere sympathy, but we have nothing to do with Adriari's group. If gold was paid to them in advance, you should really make an effort to retrieve it from their estates. Was that all you wanted to talk about?''

"No," the man growled, satisfaction having quickly changed to anger. "Nor is that subject closed as yet. When a man pays for something, he should be able to count on getting it no matter what happens. Then he's less likely to look more closely into the reason why he was disaccommodated. But as I said, we'll go into that again tomorrow. The much more pressing subject must be seen to today.''

"And that is?" Kambil prompted, suddenly a good deal less pleased himself. Noll had hinted that he suspected Kambil's group of having had something to do with Adriari's defeat, and that was disturbing. Those five commoners Kambil and his group had faced in the final competition had been in the hands of the nobility at least for a short while before they'd been disposed of. If Noll had taken the trouble to question one or two of them and had found out they'd been sent the keying phrase which had freed them from the Pure-dan . . .

"The most pressing subject is your relationship with your Advisors," Noll replied, his thoughts rigidly inflexible on the matter. "There are quite a number of our group who are . . . uncomfortable with the idea of dealing with you, pri-marily because of the presence of Moord. We both know that Zolind wasn't imagining things about him, and none of my peers is willing to let the man run around unchecked. There will have to be guarantees on your part, guarantees we're able to rely on without hesitation."

"I'm willing to admit that Delin is a bit . . . unstable," Kambil granted cautiously, wondering what Noll was lead-ing up to. "For that reason I've had him put on sedatives of a sort, to keep him from becoming overexcited. You may have noticed how quiet he's been; you have my word that he'll continue to be just as quiet."

"That's not good enough," Noll stated, and again that rigidity was clear in his mind. "Those who are concerned want firmer guarantees than someone's word, so *we've* come up with a solution. Moord is to be put on Puredan, and so is the rest of your group. In that way we'll be able to be certain that any agreements we come to will be upheld at all times, and Moord's . . . proclivities will no longer be of concern."

"Oh, now I see," Kambil exclaimed, delighted to have reached the heart of the reason why the Advisors were there. "You and your cronies are afraid of us, because there haven't been true Highs Seated on the Fivefold Throne in a hundred years. You've decided to use the accusations against Delin as an excuse to get us completely under your control."

"Reasons don't count, only results do," Noll said bluntly, his mind grimly pleased that Kambil had made no effort to beat around the bush. "Either all five of you agree to taking the Puredan to relieve our minds, or the public Seating cer-emony will never be held. Your group will be declared dis-qualified, and a new round of competitions will be held next year. The peasants will like that, since they'll see it as another chance for five of their own to win. For that reason I'll need your response immediately. New competitions will take time to arrange.''

''And you see us simply stepping aside and allowing your plans to continue unopposed?'' Kambil inquired, really curious about the point. ''What do you imagine you might do if we refuse?''

''Imagination has very little to do with it,'' Noll responded dryly, a certain nervousness under tight control. ''We have the doses of Puredan with us, which you'll take before any of us leaves this room. If you refuse, or if we don't *live* to leave this room, your own lives won't stretch much beyond ours. You'll be killed one at a time, from a distance, without magic being anywhere involved. That's all I'm prepared to say until we've reached agreement.''

''Oh, I think you'll say more than that,'' Kambil disagreed pleasantly before reaching out to his Blendingmates with his mind. The Blending formed instantly, of course, and a heartbeat later the entity had control of the minds of all five of the Advisors. One of them actually managed to begin struggling, but his strong Middle talent was no match for true strength. The adjustments previously decided on were made by the entity, and then it was Kambil back alone in his mind again.

''Now tell me what arrangements you've made,'' Kambil said to Noll, who hadn't been able to resist the entity at all. ''And don't be shy about going into details.''

''Of course,'' Noll replied without hesitation. ''There are expert bowmen stationed in hidden places all around this area. Unless they receive orders to the contrary from the five of us, they'll pincushion your group at the first opportunity.''

''Bowmen,'' Kambil mused, once again finding himself surprised. ''That's the weapon developed by those savages our people discovered about fifty years ago, isn't it? The ones on that very large island who had degenerated into a society of untrained Lows and talentless cripples?''

''The weapon itself is called a bow, the people using it, bowmen,'' Noll corrected calmly. ''Aside from that, your observations were right. We don't need to call on the bowmen often, but when we do they're extremely efficient.''

"So I would imagine," Kambil agreed musingly. "Striking enemies down without giving them the least prior warning. I'll certainly have to keep the matter in mind, but at the moment we have other things to discuss. Right now you and your friends are completely under our control, but I sense that that won't hold true for very long. In two or three days you'll be able to throw off the effects, especially if something prevents you from returning here to have the control strengthened again. Tell me what you would do if you suddenly returned to yourself."

"I would immediately arrange for your assassination," Noll replied promptly—and predictably. "Your Five will either be under our complete control, or it will be dead. None of us is willing to take the chance of having it any other way."

"And we can't *pretend* to have taken the Puredan," Kambil said with a nod of understanding. "Most of your fellow cowards will insist on testing the matter, most likely in the most outrageous manner possible. Taking over five minds at a time isn't difficult, but handling all of you at the *same* time . . . No the risk simply isn't worth it. If we should happen to lose control at the wrong time, the results could be disastrous. We'll simply have to go with my alternative plan."

"You intend to give *us* the Puredan," Noll said, the words in no manner a question. "We considered that possibility a likely one."

"And so took precautions against it?" Kambil said, his brows high again. "What precautions are possible against Puredan?"

"None," Noll said, his mind still open and totally amenable. "The precautions are against the possibility of our being drugged, which will be investigated as soon as we leave this room. Puredan remains in a man's blood for some time, and strong Middle practitioners of Earth magic are waiting to see if they find those traces in *us*. If they do, your assassination will be arranged no matter what we say against it."

"Your preparations were thorough," Kambil remarked, gazing at the man. "And I myself walked in here thinking I might find you of use in some way. It saddens me to say now that that seems impossible; you're much too . . . inventive for my liking. Give me a moment to think.''

Everyone in the room sat agreeably silent, giving Kambil the opportunity to consider his options. Using Noll and his cronies as puppets must be forgotten about, therefore they couldn't be allowed to continue living. Their demise would be arranged easily enough, but there was still the matter of getting them safely out of the palace . . . safely where Kambil and his group were concerned, that is . . .

''I think I may have it,'' Kambil announced after a few moments. ''Tell me what chance of success the plan has, and make any suggestions to improve it which might come to you. In a short while the five of you will leave here, signaling your assassins with bows to stand down. The reason for that, you'll inform your associates, is that we've all taken the Puredan as demanded. But you won't be completely satisfied.''

''Why not?'' Noll asked, his mind poised to consider the question once all of it had been presented. ''If you've taken the Puredan, we should be delighted.''

''Not if we've only let you order us to never even consider turning on the Advisors,'' Kambil responded with a smile. ''The order will assure the safety of all of you, but it doesn't give you the control you want. You'll tell them that you agreed to the compromise, but only for now. In a little while you'll come back with second doses to give us— even if you have to force them on us—and we won't be able to refuse because we're bound not to harm any of you. Does that seem reasonable?''

''Very much so,'' Noll replied with a slow nod. ''It's my usual habit to get a light, preliminary hold on someone, which makes taking them over completely later no more than child's play. Allowing you to limit my demands now gives me more control later, so I would certainly go along with the compromise.''

''Excellent,'' Kambil said with full satisfaction, relaxing back in his chair. ''It's amazing how closely that parallels my own working methods. You and the others will hand over the doses of Puredan before you leave, as I've decided to see if I can make use of them. But before we get to that, I have additional orders for you and your friends here.''

"Certainly," Noll agreed at once—as though he'd be permitted to do anything else. "What orders do you have?"

"You five men have sadly reached the end of your lives, but most of you needn't worry about having to face violence. Only one of you will be attacked and killed, possibly by an irate and irrational commoner tenant. You'd know best which of you that would be most likely to happen to, so I leave it to your discretion to choose the proper member."

They nodded thoughtfully, making Kambil wish he might laugh uproariously. He could have been discussing which of them would be throwing the next party, and who it would be best, politically speaking, to invite.

"Another of you, also to be designated by your group, will die in his sleep of natural causes," Kambil continued. "That one will cause his own heart to stop at the stroke of midnight, a feat most of us are capable of. We only have to believe it's possible in order to do it."

"Using Earth magic is easier and more effective," Noll disagreed in a faintly reproving tone. "Allow *us* to see to the details, if you please."

"As you wish," Kambil agreed, suddenly *very* sorry that these men would not be available to help run the Empire. Their expertise and efficiency would be sorely missed. . . . "The other three of you will suddenly decide to take brief vacations, and will therefore leave Gan Garee at once. Two of you will go this afternoon, and the third will leave tonight. Before you go, make certain you assure everyone that you'll return for the public ceremony."

"But we won't be back for it," Noll said after nodding. "What will happen to us instead?"

"One of you will find a commoner girl to rape, first making sure that her father or husband is nearby and is the sort to kill any man caught doing something like that," Kambil responded. "Again you must choose the one whom others will be most likely to believe it of. The fourth will go boating somewhere bright and early tomorrow morning, and will make sure that the vessel is lost with all hands aboard."

"And the last?" Noll asked, looking as though he were taking mental notes. "What's to befall the last of us?"

"The last is to go off with his favorite mistress for two

days of dalliance, and is never to be seen again." Kambil's smile was filled with satisfaction, as the plans he'd come up with were really much too good to waste by not implementing them. "His mistress is to disappear with him, of course, giving people the impression that they ran off somewhere together and will eventually return. Instead they're to be dead, in a place and in a way that won't be quickly, if ever, discovered."

"We'll see to it," Noll said, brisk now that all instructions had been given. "If there's nothing else, we'll give you the vials of Puredan now."

"Don't forget about calling off those assassins," Homin put in, the only words he—or the others—had spoken. "We have too many plans for our future to want them cut short— the plans *or* the future."

"We're not permitted to forget," Noll informed him haughtily as he and his associates stood. "Possibly the point slipped your mind ... We'll be going now, boy, and I'll expect you to be a bit more reasonable the next time we meet."

"You may count on that, Lord Ephaim," Kambil said, accepting the vials that the five men had no idea they were handing over. "And thank you again for coming to the ceremony."

Noll grunted as he headed for the door, which one of the others opened for him. The five Advisors left looking only somewhat appeased, and once the door was closed again behind them, Kambil sighed.

"Well, that's over with," he said, looking at his three groupmates. "Let's have one more leisurely cup of fruit juice to give them and the others time to leave, and then we can go back to our apartments."

"I think we ought to make an effort to find out who Noll's spy is," Bron put in, rising to go to the pitcher of iced fruit juice. "*He* won't be using the spy again, but someone else might."

"I agree," Selendi said, holding her cup out so that Bron might refill it. "Converting the spy to someone who reports to *us* can save us some trouble later, but first we have that other chore to see to. Do we really have to do it ourselves?

Having a few of the servants do it would make my stomach a good deal happier.''

"Mine as well, but we can't take the chance," Kambil denied with another sigh. "If someone comes across *us* while we're dealing with it, we can handle the matter so there's no problem. Controlled servants won't have the same option, so we simply can't use them."

Homin grimaced at that and Bron shook his head, but neither of them made any more effort to argue than Selendi did. They knew Kambil was right, and that he really wished the matter might be otherwise. That ridiculous, mindless fool of a madman Delin . . .

Kambil lost all satisfaction as he remembered again what he and the others had found last night when they'd burst into Delin's private quarters. Kambil had known that *something* was going on, but the glee in Delin's mind hadn't really prepared him. He'd had his parents brought to him, both of them bound and gagged, and he'd been directing the efforts of two members of his private guard—

The picture evoked tried to turn Kambil's stomach, coming as it did from a time when the slow mutilation and torture had been going on for a while. Neither of Delin's parents had been dead, but healing them as far as possible and then turning them loose had been out of the question. They'd never be functioning human beings again, so they had to be disposed of. And Kambil had had to make Delin use his abilities to be certain they didn't die *yet*, when he and the others couldn't conveniently dispose of the bodies. The smell would have attracted unwanted attention no matter where they were hidden. . . .

So late this afternoon they would all take a ride in a pair of carriages, with one of Delin's victims hidden in each carriage. Kambil hadn't been able to destroy their minds, not with their bodies in such terrible, fragile shape . . . he would have to ride with and near them, feeling their agony and terror and insanity—

Kambil abruptly got to his feet, needing to pace a bit to fight down his rising gorge. If he didn't need Delin for the Blending . . . Well, the next time the madman needed to perform as though he were uncontrolled, it would be allowed only with his body and mind fully in the grip of Puredan.

There would *never* be another incident like the first. . . .

And now it would be necessary to find out who besides Noll had been told about Delin's parents coming to the palace. . . .

FOURTEEN

"What do you mean, Jovvi and Lorand have been sent out of the city?" Rion demanded of me, his expression terrible. "Where have they been sent, and how can we possibly follow to find them?"

"Alsin's people found out that they've been sent from the city in some sort of convoy," I replied, trying not to show how really agitated I felt. "Arrangements are being made to get a coach for us . . . Can we all sit down somewhere to talk about this? Alsin woke me with the news, and after splashing some water in my face I came looking for the rest of you. Right now I could really use a cup of tea."

"We'll go back to the eating area," Rion said, as though making up his mind about something. "The rest of us have already eaten, and Vallant said he needs a bit more rest. Once I have the entire story, I'll come back here and pass it on."

"All right," I agreed after almost no hesitation. Vallant had begun to sit up at hearing about what had happened to our groupmates, but then he'd stretched out again and closed his eyes. Without a single word of greeting for me, even a neutral one. I'd expected him to at least offer some of the tea in the pitcher standing on a tray left on one of the beds near the door. . . .

Rion seemed to be in something of a hurry to get back to the eating area, and I can't say I really minded. Naran was very quiet, which probably meant she'd noticed the way Vallant had been behaving. I wasn't certain that Rion had, although *something* seemed to be disturbing him badly. . . .

When we reached the eating area, Rion insisted that I take more than just tea. I really had very little appetite, but with the possibility of my talent being needed later, I agreed without argument. Rion and Naran sat quietly while I finished what was on my plate, so I took a swallow of tea and then began to tell them what I knew they were waiting to hear.

"Alsin's men *hadn't* followed the man who brought Vallant to Eltrina Razas's house, at least not at first," I said after describing what Alsin and I had discussed after we'd gotten to that warehouse. "Early this morning the man and his wagon came back, though, and the watchers were there and waiting. They said that Eltrina didn't come to the door, and her servant refused even to let the man into her house. The man shouted and screamed something about not being about to take the blame for not producing the 'segment' for transportation that morning, then he stormed off."

"What did he mean by 'segment'?" Naran asked with a frown. "I've never heard the word applied to people."

"Neither has any of the rest of us," I assured her. "The watchers followed the irate man, probably hoping they'd be able to find out, and learned something else instead: where Vallant was supposed to be taken. There was a large gathering of wagons and riders just outside the western approach to the city, and the irate man—now more frightened than irate—left his wagon and approached someone who seemed to be of the nobility as well as in charge. The resulting scene apparently wasn't very pretty."

"With the man needing to report Vallant's disappearance?" Rion said with a faint smile. "I would imagine not. I hope he put the blame where it belonged."

"The watchers said he tried to, but the other noble apparently lacked our bias against Eltrina," I replied with my own faint smile. "He said the man and Eltrina were equally responsible, he for having given her the 'segment,' she for refusing to give the 'segment' back."

"Give him back?" Naran interrupted to echo. "Didn't the man admit that Vallant was gone?"

"The watchers decided that he actually might not have known," I said, having asked the same question. "They couldn't hear everything Eltrina's servant said, but it's perfectly possible the man wasn't told about Vallant's being gone. At any rate, the noble decided not to waste everyone's time by pursuing the matter immediately, and ordered the man to have his other three segments transferred to the wagon they were assigned to so the convoy might leave on time."

"*Other* three segments?" Rion and Naran said nearly together, causing them to smile with brief amusement at each other. "Does that mean three other men?" Rion asked by himself.

"It meant two men and a woman," I answered after taking another sip of tea. "The watchers were at least as disturbed about that as we are, so when the unmoving bodies were taken out of the wagon and the man left, one of the watchers followed him. The other stayed to watch the wagon convoy, which left a short while later heading west. He also reported that the riders seemed to be mostly guardsmen."

"There to guard . . . *how* many unconscious bodies?" Rion asked, obviously a rhetorical question. "How many wagons were in the convoy?"

"The watcher reported seeing ten, all of them larger than the one driven by the man they'd followed," I said. "He followed the convoy until he was certain about which road they were taking, then he returned here."

"I hope the other found out more than that," Naran said, disturbance clear in her eyes. "So far it sounds like no more than guesswork about Jovvi and Lorand being with that convoy."

"Happily, the other watcher did do better," I agreed with a nod. "He followed the man in the wagon to a small constabulary post, the sort of place manned by only one or two workers. They're used for the temporary housing of prisoners arrested by guardsmen, in areas where the main lockup is too far away for the prisoners to be taken there easily. Alsin said he began to curse horribly when he heard that, because constabulary posts were just about the only places he and his friends hadn't thought to look."

"I don't blame him for being upset," Naran said with her brows high. "How could anyone expect them to use those posts to hide drugged captives? You *expect* a prison to have bars, so how are you supposed to know that the bars are official—so to speak."

"I guess you can't know," I said, not quite sure I understood what she'd said but having no time to question her about it. "When Alsin's second watcher reported back to him, Alsin took some men and went to pay a call on the wagon driver. He was alone when they entered the post, and the fact that they'd put on masks frightened him badly. He tried to use Water magic on them, but one of Alsin's men was stronger and so was able to stop him. Then he tried to frighten them in turn by telling them he was a member of the nobility."

"Even if he were telling the truth, it's highly unlikely that he has much standing, either politically *or* socially," Rion commented. "One of my mother's peers, for instance, would sooner die a bloody and painful death than be caught driving a *wagon*. And as for having a *job* somewhere rather than a career or business interests, even if it isn't really a job . . ." He shook his head. "No, he can't be of much importance at all."

"Alsin thought he was very important, since the man had certain information that we wanted," I replied with a type of smile I knew wasn't particularly nice. "He made the fool understand that he would die in quite a lot of pain if he didn't answer the questions put to him, then he listened to those answers with his Middle strength in Earth magic. Only someone with a stronger talent could have lied to Alsin and gotten away with it, and the man didn't qualify.

"But what he did do was assure Alsin that Jovvi and Lorand have to be in that convoy. All drugged Highs are sent out of the city in the same way, and the previous convoy left three days earlier. He knew in particular that our people are with this convoy, because the noble in charge had complained about having three members of the strongest challenging Blending so close to each other for so long. If something went wrong and they came back to themselves, they could end up being more trouble than all the rest combined.''

''I don't like that phrase, 'for so long,' '' Rion said with a frown. ''It suggests that they'll be separated once they reach wherever they're going, which won't be of help to *us*. And while we're discussing it, what *is* their destination?''

''The man didn't know, which supports your theory that he isn't a very important noble,'' I said. ''He usually has someone with him who feeds and cares for the captives, but picking them up in the first place and then transporting them to the convoy is much too important a task to trust to an underling—according to him, at any rate. Personally, I'd say they wanted to limit the knowledge of commoners, so they limited the participation of those who aren't their own.''

''And now we're going after the convoy,'' Naran said, actually looking eager at the idea of leaving our safe hiding place. ''How soon will we get started? And while we're waiting, is there any chance we can have the use of a bath house?''

''I asked those very same questions,'' I replied, more than aware of how . . . well used my clothes and body felt. ''Alsin said he'd be back with the coach as quickly as possible, probably within the hour, and this warehouse has no actual bath-house facilities. We'd have to go elsewhere, and that would be dangerous as well as time-consuming. We'll just have to wait until we reach an inn along the way.''

''I'm in need of a bath as well, but our clear priority is following those who hold Lorand and Jovvi captive,'' Rion said, looking more determined and . . . *dangerous* than I'd ever before seen him. ''If we all consider the problem, we should find it possible to free them before the convoy reaches its destination and our people are separated. Right now, however, there's something you must know about another of us.''

''Another of us?'' I echoed, wondering what he could be talking about. ''I don't understand. Who—''

''Yes, I mean Vallant,'' he confirmed when he saw my sudden grasp of what he'd said. ''I told you he still seemed to be tired, but that wasn't the truth. He told Naran and me that—that he was no longer able to touch the power. I believe he's still in shock over the discovery, and may well decide against accompanying us. We mustn't allow that.''

If he thought Vallant was in shock, he should have felt *my* mind. I sat staring at my teacup, not quite able to remember its purpose, mentally groping for something solid to anchor myself to. Those people had been right after all, and Vallant's ability to Blend with us was gone forever?

''If you'd heard him, your heart would have shattered the way mine did,'' Naran added in a rough whisper, holding to Rion's arm and obviously trying not to cry. ''He said that if certain people considered him pitiful and useless before, now they certainly would. Who do you think he was talking about?''

I shook my head, having no idea whom he could have meant. It was ridiculous to think that there could be someone around so blind that they would believe those things about Vallant, but that had nothing to do with *my* position. Yesterday Vallant had clearly and definitely ended things between us; now that he was almost a different man, would he change his mind? And remembering how his pushing me away had hurt, did I really *want* him to change his mind?

But those questions were personal, and there was another much more important one: would Rion and I be able to free the others all by ourselves? We certainly *had* to, but . . . could we?

FIFTEEN

''Tamrissa, can you suggest the proper way to deal with Vallant now?'' Rion asked as gently as possible, seeing how horribly upset the girl looked. ''If we commiserate, is that likely to make things better or worse? As Naran pointed out, our groupmate now feels pitiful and useless. If we offer sympathy, isn't that apt to make him feel even worse?''

"I really don't know," Tamrissa responded, sounding bewildered and almost as devastated as Vallant had. "I, personally, would probably hate having everyone around me oozing sympathy, but—I just don't know."

"I'm inclined to agree with Tamrissa," Naran said, obviously deliberately ignoring the other girl's shocked confusion. "If I were in Vallant's place I'd hate sympathy as well, especially since we don't know if his talent really is gone for good. Lorand isn't a trained physician, but I'll wager that if *he* works on Vallant, whatever is wrong will probably *stop* being wrong."

"Why, Naran, you're absolutely right," Tamrissa said, suddenly pulling away from the numbness which had held her. "Lorand *is* the best, so we've got to get him to Vallant as quickly as possible. As soon as Alsin returns with a coach, we'll have to catch up to that convoy as fast as we can."

"And do what to stop them?" Rion asked, hating to deflate her enthusiasm but realizing that it was necessary. "The answer to that question has to be carefully considered, as you and I will find it extremely difficult to handle the guardsmen you mentioned as well as the wagon drivers. Unless we kill them all, which we could probably accomplish. Was that what you intended for us to do?"

"I—no," Tamrissa said with a violent headshake after a very brief hesitation. "Possibly if there was no other way, but not without trying other things first. Most of those guardsmen probably have no idea what they're guarding, so killing them would be—wrong. And what about the rest of the poor victims in that convoy? Can we free Lorand and Jovvi, and simply leave the rest to their fate?"

"I hadn't even considered the point," Rion admitted ruefully. "Once put into words, however, there's no denying that we simply can't turn our backs on our own. But where did so many other High talents come from? We were told, were we not, that all testing and qualifying was done for the year?"

"Alsin asked the same question," Tamrissa said after taking a deep breath and a sip of her tea. "Apparently all *qual-*

ifying was done for the year, but testing is another matter entirely. There's a constant stream of potential Highs coming to Gan Garee, and at this time of year they're given a much less . . . stressful test than we were. If they fail, they're turned out and sent home as the Middles they are. But if they pass, they're drugged and put into a convoy and taken—somewhere."

"To keep the city as free of High talents as possible," Rion said with a nod. "If one attempts to think as our enemies might, it makes considerable sense. After all, what benefit would there be in having people walking about who have stronger talent than the current Seated Blending?"

"But not stronger than the *new* Seated Blending," Tamrissa pointed out with a thoughtful look. "When we faced them, there was no doubt that they were High talents even though they weren't as strong as our own Blending. Lanir and his friends weren't happy about having to deal with them, so I wonder what made the nobility change tactics and let *them* win instead of the Middles they'd been using until now?"

"I'd say *we* were what made them change tactics," Rion reminded her. "That first Blending we faced, the one which died because it was composed of no more than Middles—*that* was undoubtedly the Blending they meant to have Seated, and were forced to support the others simply because they were the only noble Blending remaining."

"Which means we were right to believe that that group was using us for their own ends," Tamrissa said in agreement. "We eliminated their most important rivals ourselves, and most of the rest of our common Blendings took care of the others. I wonder how long they'll be allowed to run around uncontrolled?"

"That all depends on how frightened the others are of them—and how well they've planned for the time after the competition." Rion shook his head, hating the feeling of ambivalence now touching him. "It's difficult to decide which group to pin my hopes of victory to: the group which used and betrayed us, or the people who betray everyone as a matter of course, but are now being forced to support that first group."

"I know exactly how you feel," Tamrissa agreed with a

smile which Naran echoed. "I can't—Wait, there's Alsin."

Rion turned to look toward the doorway behind him, and saw a large, rugged-appearing man striding toward them. An air of competence and authority surrounded him, and when he reached their table he nodded to them.

"We're all set," he announced without preamble. "The coach is in an alley two streets from here, and there's a wagon unloading downstairs right now that will take you to the coach without your being seen. The alley is actually a minor through street, so we'll be able to set off without the notice that backing out and turning around might bring. Are your belongings ready to be loaded?"

"As far as I know, none of us has unpacked anything," Tamrissa replied, looking to Naran and Rion himself for confirmation. "Their nods tell me I'm right, so that won't be a problem. What is, though, is Vallant. How is he supposed to walk through these corridors to *reach* the wagon downstairs? And even if he does, what about whatever you plan to do to disguise our presence in that wagon? Will he be able to stand it?"

"Since you'll be completely covered up, probably not," the man Alsin replied, now looking thoughtful. "Your friend will probably be best off going out through that window in his dormitory, using the pulley rope to reach the ground. Do you think he's up to it?"

"I'm sure he is," Rion put in at once when Tamrissa hesitated. "What's more, I've decided to join him in that. The ladies and our baggage can be taken out in the wagon, but Vallant and I will walk."

"I'll send someone to steady the rope for you, and then he'll guide you to the coach," Alsin agreed with a nod, eyeing Rion's clothing. "That outfit is plain enough so that no one ought to notice it, but if I recall correctly your friend is wearing the same white shirt and gray trousers. One of you ought to change the shirt at the very least, to keep you two from looking as though you're in uniform. If you agree I can supply a shirt from my own possessions, which I'm now on the way to pack."

"Does that mean you're going with us?" Tamrissa asked, looking surprised. "What about your family and your work here in the city?"

"My real work here in the city consists of trying to find a way to loosen the grip the nobles have around our throats," the man answered candidly. "Since the best way to accomplish that is to help *your* group, I certainly am going with you. And as far as a family goes, I don't have one. Would you like to come with me now, Dom Mardimil?"

"Certainly," Rion answered, rising to his feet after giving Naran's hand a parting kiss. "Vallant and I will see you ladies in just a little while."

Both Tamrissa and Naran nodded, so Rion followed Alsin out of the eating area. The direction they took was the one in which Vallant's room lay, but Rion's guide stopped at a door only half a corridor away from the eating area. Leading the way inside, Alsin went directly to a small, plain wardrobe and opened it, reached to the bottom of it, then turned with what he held.

"Try this on," he suggested, handing over the silver-blue shirt he'd chosen. "I've never quite found the occasion to wear it, so it can't be considered used. It should distract any observer from noticing that you and Dom Ro are wearing the same sort of trousers."

"Are there likely to be a large number of people riding or walking about looking for us?" Rion asked as he began to remove his own shirt. "Tamrissa and I each made an effort to discourage my mother from sending anyone in pursuit of me, but I'm not certain how successful we were. The noble who held Tamrissa should certainly have been found by now, and we were told that Vallant's absence has already been noted. How much of a pursuit does that make?"

"Less than you apparently think," Alsin replied as he busied himself with putting clothing and toilet articles in a large leather bag. "We've had observers at your mother's house and at Lord Lanir's, specifically to let us know when to expect the pursuit you mentioned, but so far there hasn't been any. As of an hour ago no one has left either place, nor have guardsmen been called *there*."

"But that doesn't hold true in Vallant's case," Rion said as he settled the new shirt on his frame. It fit much better than he'd been expecting it to, and the fabric was finer than the plain cotton he'd been wearing.

"Actually, there hasn't even been a flurry of activity connected with Dom Ro," Alsin replied, turning to look at Rion now that his packing was apparently done. "The man I questioned was convinced that Lady Eltrina had simply decided not to release Dom Ro, and that was what he'd reported to his superior. The superior decided to handle Lady Eltrina himself, so the man I questioned had dismissed the entire matter. And as far as that man himself is concerned . . . once he walks back to the city from where my men are now taking him, he may decide not to report the incident to save himself embarrassment."

"You should be warned that anger and vindictiveness may well overcome possible feelings of embarrassment," Rion said after tucking the shirt into his trousers. "All members of the nobility are constantly encouraged to report even the slightest indication of disrespect on the part of commoners, and being kidnapped after being threatened and questioned is a good deal more serious. But hopefully we'll be gone from the city by the time he returns and makes his report. And thank you for this shirt. I appreciate your parting with something this fine."

"Clothing is meant to be worn, not to lie about gathering dust," Alsin returned with a deprecating gesture. "I'll take the shirt you removed along with my own things, and return it to you once we're out of the city. If you know your way back to Dom Ro's dormitory, I'll go and find someone to hold the pulley rope and guide the two of you to the coach."

Rion assured him that he did indeed know the way to Vallant, so they left the room together and parted company. Alsin returned the way they'd come while Rion continued along the corridor, and a few moments later he reached the proper door. A knock brought no response, so Rion opened the door and went in.

"We'll be leaving here in a short while," Rion said to a Vallant who still lay on the cot by the window, pretending there was nothing wrong with the man. "Jovvi and Lorand are indeed being taken somewhere away from this city, and we're prepared to follow and free them."

"How will we do that?" Vallant asked slowly and with difficulty, obviously fighting to pull himself out of the depths. "And why would you need *me* along? I can't even face the idea of leavin' this window, never mind walkin' that corridor outside or doin' somethin' to help. I'm the one who *needs* help, but I'm not likely to get it."

"We won't be leaving this place by the corridor, but by that window you've become so attached to," Rion responded lightly, ignoring the rest of what had been said. "We'll slide down that rope, which, I'm told, is as easy as falling off a log. That analogy may prove to be a shade too accurate, but escaped criminals such as we are should be fearless. Simply because I've never done anything remotely like this before is no reason to picture myself broken and bloody on the ground below."

"It really isn't as hard as it sounds," Vallant offered, finally struggling to a sitting position as he stared at Rion. "But you don't have to do this, you know. *You* have no reason to use a window instead of leavin' the way you came."

"But of course I have a reason," Rion disagreed, walking to the window to watch for the one who would come to assist them. "My good friend has an adventure before him, and I wish to share that adventure. Never having been allowed such a thing before makes the undertaking even more special, and I eagerly look forward to it."

Vallant made no reply to that, but peripherally Rion was able to see a peculiar expression fleet across the man's face. Then Vallant had forced himself to his feet, to shake his head hard before running his hands through his hair.

"I could use some bathin'," he muttered as he rubbed his face. "Not to mention a shave. Just how soon are we leavin', and where are we goin'?"

"We're leaving as soon as someone arrives to hold the rope for us, and we're going to the coach which is waiting to take us west, after the convoy carrying Jovvi and Lorand. On the way, you might like to join us in trying to think of a way to rescue our groupmates without needing to kill every guardsman and driver and noble in the convoy. So far Tamrissa and I haven't been able to formulate such a plan."

"If Jovvi and Lorand were with us, we could put them all to sleep," Vallant said, moving heavily to join Rion at the window. "Or at least the rest of you could do that . . . Does Tamrissa know what's happened to me?"

"I broke it to her as gently as possible, but she was still shocked," Rion responded, turning his head to study Vallant. "Naran recalled your comment about being pitiful and helpless, but none of us was able to imagine who would regard you in such a way. I think that if Tamrissa hadn't been so shaken, she would have been furious at the idea of someone discounting you so easily."

"Really?" Vallant asked, blinking in obvious confusion. "She would have been furious? But that—that's not possible. I didn't get to rescue *her*, she had to rescue *me*. How could a woman feel anythin' but contempt for a man who has to be rescued?"

"Are you saying that both Naran and Tamrissa feel contempt for me as well?" Rion countered, refusing to look away from his brother's misery. "If so, I'm forced to disagree with you most strongly, as it's perfectly clear that they feel no such thing. All living beings need assistance at *one* time or another, and who better to give it than those who love you? And why would it be acceptable for you to do the rescuing, while Tamrissa's doing it is *un*acceptable?"

"You . . . weren't raised like most men are," Vallant groped, his confusion clearly having increased. "It's somethin' the rest of us were taught, that the man has to be the strong one . . . But if she doesn't despise me, why wasn't she here when I woke up? I'll bet Naran spent the night next to *you*."

"Yes, she did," Rion agreed at once. "But perhaps that was because I made no effort to cut her dead when I was helped into the coach. As I was there at the time, I can assure you that the same cannot be said for *your* behavior with Tamrissa."

"I . . . was feelin' raw and humiliated," Vallant said, rubbing his face with one hand again as he avoided Rion's gaze. "You have no idea what was bein' done to me when Tamrissa walked into the room . . . Was I really *that* hard on her?"

"I had the impression that you blamed her for having freed you," Rion told him frankly. "If she received the same impression, is it any wonder that she spent the night elsewhere than beside you?"

"No, no it isn't," Vallant admitted, now sounding and

looking totally defeated. "As usual, all the trouble is *my* fault—but maybe this time it's for the best. The last thing she needs is a cripple who was once a whole man."

"Why don't you let *her* decide what she does and doesn't need?" Rion returned, definitely becoming annoyed. "Making the decision for her is downright insulting, a foolish thing to do in any event. Doing it to someone with her strength and ability in Fire magic . . ."

Rion let the rest of the thought go unspoken, but Vallant clearly picked up on it anyway. The man's head came up as he remembered Tamrissa's temper, along with the fact that he was unable to protect himself with Water magic.

"And we've decided that Lorand can probably do something to cure your problem," Rion added casually, to give Vallant another point to occupy his thoughts. "If we ever manage to free him, that is . . ."

This second point struck home even more strongly, Rion was pleased to see. It should galvanize Vallant into making the effort to free himself from depression, and possibly even to repair his error with Tamrissa. And although Rion hadn't mentioned it, there would be no trouble at all with going down the rope. His Air magic would see to that, both for him as well as for Vallant. As long as no one saw them walking to the coach, their departure would be easy and uneventful.

But what in blazes were they going to do to free Jovvi and Lorand—not to mention the rest of the captives? And once freed, what in the world would they do with them all . . . ?

SIXTEEN

Eltrina Razas was more than simply annoyed. She paced back and forth in her husband's study, trying to figure out a way to report the outrage which had been committed without getting *herself* into hot water. Her appropriation of that Ro commoner hadn't precisely been proper, even though a man would have gotten away with it without the least effort. It simply wasn't fair, especially since she'd spent hours thinking and hadn't had a single idea. . . .

Suddenly there was a knock at the door, even though she'd specifically left orders not to be disturbed. Her first urge was to ignore the knock, but she was far too angry for that. She needed to blister *someone's* hide, and whichever servant had dared to disobey her would do nicely for the purpose. So she strode to the door and yanked it open, and—

"Your pardon, Lady Eltrina, but this gentleman insisted that you be disturbed despite your instructions," the servant said with visible disapproval. "Shall I summon others of the staff and have him put out forcibly?"

"Ah . . . no, Jomsin, it's all right, I'll see him," Eltrina managed to say after a moment. The caller was Lord Rimen Howser, a man who was soon to be made a High Lord. Everyone who was anyone at least knew *of* the man, only a certain lucky few actually knowing him personally. Once the shock had passed Eltrina could think of at least a dozen ways in which the man might be used to her benefit, so she wasn't about to let the opportunity slip out of her hands.

"Do come in, Lord Rimen," she purred, giving him her most attractive smile. "May I have the servant bring you something? Would you care to stay to lunch?"

"It's business which brings me here, Lady Eltrina," the man replied coolly as he entered the room and waved a hand. "Dismiss the servant, please, so that we can get straight to it."

Eltrina dismissed the servant with a nod, then turned to study Lord Rimen. The man was tall and slender and elegant, always dressed in the finest clothing, his dark hair curled in what was fast becoming the newest popular style. Aristocratic was the best descriptive word for him, especially when he walked to the middle of the room and turned to stare at her.

"The most important difference between men and women seems to be a sense of proper proportion," he said very flatly. "When a man avails himself of the use of one of the lower animals, he doesn't need to be told when continuing to keep the little thing becomes impolitic. Women, on the other hand, tend to *cling* . . . My men are waiting outside, and when I summon them you will *immediately* show them to where you've put *my* animal—whom you should never have appropriated in the first place."

"I—ah—you don't understand," Eltrina began to babble, not only in shock again but now frightened as well. "I *did* have the man, but I returned him some time ago. If he's been misplaced somehow, it's Dilis's fault, not *mine*. Dilis is such a fool, always doing something wrong and then blaming some perfectly innocent person—"

"Lady Eltrina!" Lord Rimen interrupted sharply. "I've already spoken with Lord Dilis, and I'm satisfied that he told me the truth. If you insist that he lied, I'll be forced to contact your husband to get his permission to question you under Puredan. This matter is much too important to let slide, as I also have my own instructions to carry out. Now tell me: where is the animal I'm searching for?"

"I don't know," Eltrina whispered in answer, too chilled by the threat to lie any longer. If *anyone* ever questioned her about *anything* under Puredan—! "I was all ready to return him to Dilis, but this—this—*woman* burst in here . . . And if men are so marvelous about doing things right, what was *she* doing running around loose and undrugged? The last I heard Lanir had claimed her, and—''

''Wait,'' Rimen interrupted again, now showing a cultured frown. ''Start from the beginning, and tell me who you're talking about. Are you saying another *animal* freed mine? That's quite preposterous.''

''Only if you're silly enough to call them animals,'' Eltrina countered, knowing she lost nothing of advantage by speaking the truth. ''They may be quite a bit less than we are, but they're still people—and one of them, from the Blending that nearly won the competition, came and took Ro with her. Perhaps *you* would be foolish enough to argue with a High practitioner in Fire magic, but I'm not quite that suicidal.''

''A High in Fire magic,'' Rimen repeated, clearly controlling the anger Eltrina was able to see in his whole manner. ''You're correct in saying that Lord Lanir was supposed to have her in his keeping . . . How do you know that she was no longer drugged? Did you simply take her word for it?''

''I don't believe in taking a peasant's word for things,'' Eltrina returned coldly. ''Most of them seem to lie as easily as they breathe. This one, however, didn't hesitate to show me the truth—by burning the clothing off me without raising even a single blister. I had no idea that that sort of thing was possible, and I was terrified. What choice did I have other than to let her take Ro?''

''You could have chosen not to appropriate him in the first place,'' Rimen countered, his tone flat again. ''Lord Dilis will face a stern reprimand for having let you take the animal, but you, as his social superior, will face far more. You abused your authority to the detriment of your peers, caring more for your own desires than for the well-being of your equals and superiors. The lapse will neither be overlooked nor forgotten.''

And with that he marched to the door and out, without a parting bow and not even waiting for a servant to precede him. Those points somehow upset Eltrina even more than the rest, and she stumbled to a chair and collapsed into it. It was going to be terrible, she knew it was, and it was all the fault of those peasants. If they were ever captured again . . .

When they were captured again, Eltrina corrected her thoughts with a growl. Her career was almost certainly ruined completely, but when those peasants were recaptured she would find *some* way to get even . . . no matter what had to be accomplished to do it. . . .

Lord Rimen Howser was furious, but sudden worry now worked to keep him from showing his temper. He'd expected his visit to the Razas woman to be short and productive, but now the previous single problem had grown into a multiple one. Stupid female, to bungle so badly and then try so lamely to lie about it. But that was to be expected when a man married so far beneath him, as her husband obviously had. Rimen would certainly have to have a word with the man. . . .

But first there were other, more important things to see to. The four animals Rimen used for menial work stirred in their wagon when he reappeared, but his going directly to his carriage quieted them again.

"Take me to the secondary house of Lord Lanir Porvin," Rimen said to his driver as he settled himself in the carriage. "You know where it is, I trust?"

The man nodded rather than answering in words, keeping silent just as he was supposed to. Rimen detested the sound of animal accents in speech, and therefore never let his animals speak unless *he* felt it to be absolutely necessary. The animals all went to great pains to obey him, of course, as they all knew that failure would result, not in dismissal, but in losing their tongues.

The trip to Lord Lanir's secondary house—meaning the place where he kept his toys—was tiresomely lengthy, forcing Rimen, as it did, to fret all the way. It was to be hoped that the Razas woman had lied to him about the female animal with Fire magic, but Rimen feared she hadn't. It was necessary to learn the truth before he reported to Lord Embisson, and not just part of the truth. After visiting Lord Lanir, Rimen meant to see Lady Hallina Mardimil, who had reclaimed her half-animal son. Surely *she*, despite her perverted sense of the proper, had managed to keep from having her property stolen.

When his carriage finally pulled up in front of Lord Lanir's house, Rimen overrode the urge to hurry and moved at his usual pace to the front door. A noble was a noble at all times, as his mother was fond of saying, and compromise with that idea wasn't to be considered. Rimen also knocked unhurriedly, but the door opened almost immediately.

"Lord Rimen Howser to see Lord Lanir," Rimen announced as he strolled inside. "Please tell Lord Lanir that I'm here."

"Your pardon, my lord, but Lord Lanir is unavailable," the servant responded in tones that were at least bearable. "He hasn't yet arisen, and the staff is forbidden to disturb him until he does."

"Even at this time of day?" Rimen said with a frown, his worry abruptly strengthening. "That's absolutely absurd, and at this point in time totally unacceptable. Show me to his apartment and *I'll* wake him."

"My lord, please, Lord Lanir isn't *in* his apartment," the servant protested, clearly suffering. "He—ah—spent the night elsewhere, and we're *absolutely* forbidden to disturb him there. But he should be down at any time now. If you would care to wait in the sitting room with refreshments . . ."

"Listen to me carefully, animal," Rimen said slowly after taking a firm grip on his temper. "The female Lord Lanir is supposed to be with has been reportedly seen elsewhere, which means something may have happened to Lord Lanir. Take me to the proper apartment at once."

The servant hesitated only a brief moment before nodding, then led the way to the stairs. Rimen followed, wishing for once that he could hasten his pace, but that would certainly lack dignity. He had to be content with allowing his normally long stride to do its best to keep up with the servant, who obviously hadn't any dignity to lose. The animal hurried in a most unseemly way, trying to do its best to lose Rimen.

And yet, when it came to entering the proper apartment, the animal returned to a state of hesitation. He hovered near the door as Rimen reached him, hanging back as his superior simply turned the knob and entered. It was a sitting room, of course, with the door to the bedchamber standing closed. As Rimen approached it he was able to hear a sound of some sort, proving *someone* was in there. That meant knocking was in order . . .

After the second unanswered knock, Rimen repeated his earlier intrusion and simply opened the door to walk in. The servant now hovered directly behind him again, and when Rimen stopped short the servant came within a hair of crashing into him. Then the animal saw what Rimen already had, and a gasp was torn from him.

"Oh, no!" the animal moaned as he wrung his hands, staring at the hunched-over form seated in a puddle of its own filth. "My Lord Lanir—What's wrong with him?"

"I'd say his mind was gone," Rimen muttered in answer after putting a handkerchief to his nose and mouth against the terrible stench in the room. The hulk of flesh that had once been a noble now made a humming sound of sorts, a single note moaned out without stop. The sight of it all threatened to make Rimen violently ill, so he simply turned and walked away from it. And there was certainly no sign of the female Lanir had claimed. . . .

Once back in his carriage, Rimen allowed himself to take two deep breaths before ordering his driver on to the Mardimil place. This time the ride was more settling than disturbing, so he had completely returned to himself by the time a servant opened Lady Hallina's door to him.

"Your pardon, my lord, but I'm afraid entrance is impossible," the servant said before Rimen could even open his mouth. "Lady Hallina has left for her house in Haven Wraithside, and won't be returning for some time. This house is now in the process of being closed down."

"How curious that Lady Hallina has left so abruptly," Rimen said, staring at the servant to let the animal know that he addressed a superior. "And Lady Hallina's son . . . did he accompany her on her precipitous departure?"

"I'm afraid, my lord, that all queries must be addressed to Lady Hallina," the animal had the nerve to respond. "If you like, a letter may be sent along with those members of the staff who will soon leave to rejoin her. Other than that—"

"Be silent and listen to me!" Rimen snapped, completely out of patience with all the disobedient animals he'd been coming across. "If Lady Hallina must be questioned on this matter, it will be done by Advisory agents! If you wish her to know that the ordeal was caused by *you*, so be it. If not, answer my question."

"Yes, my lord, at once," the animal replied, proper fear showing in his eyes. "The answer you seek is that no, Lord Clarion did not accompany her."

"And where else has he gone?" Rimen pressed, grimly satisfied to have his surmise vindicated. "Or has he remained here, in this house which is about to be closed?"

"Lord Clarion left . . . in the company of friends," the animal admitted, the words all but forced out of him. "What his destination was, no one on the staff can tell you."

"You've already told me quite enough," Rimen said with a curt nod before turning away. Lord Embisson needed to hear about what was happening, and that at once.

Once again Rimen was forced to endure a tedious ride, and when his carriage turned into Lord Embisson Ruhl's drive he felt a great deal of relief—until he saw the various vehicles which stood directly in front of the house. Visitors' carriages would normally be put around at the side of the house, out of the way and out of sight. And for what reason would an official guard coach be there among the others . . . ?

Rimen was given immediate access when he knocked, but it wasn't Lord Embisson who came forward to greet him. Lord Ophin, Embisson's second-eldest son, appeared behind the servant sent to apprise Lord Embisson of Rimen's arrival, and Ophin looked gravely concerned.

"Rimen, I'm glad you're here," Ophin said as he offered his hand. "I know how close you are to my father, so you need to know what's happened. Our physician is with him now, but I'm told it will be weeks or months before he's able to function normally again."

"Was there an accident?" Rimen asked with all the agitation he felt as he shook hands automatically. Lord Embisson had been going to sponsor *his* rise to the position of High Lord, but now . . .

"My father was viciously attacked and robbed," Ophin

stated, anger in his whole manner. "The miscreants had obviously studied him before striking, as one of them had Water magic ability superior to his own. They beat him physically as well as subjecting him to attack by both Earth and Fire magic, but luckily the assailants were Low talents. He's been very badly hurt, but the physician is confident of his recovery."

"At least there's that," Rimen said with relief. "And now I understand why there's a guard vehicle outside. Will they be able to find the animals who committed this outrage?"

"They swear they'll do their best, but it isn't very likely," Ophin replied with a sigh. "My father was able to tell us that his attackers were masked, so he won't even be able to give the guardsmen descriptions. They're waiting to talk to him anyway, as soon as the physician is through healing him as far as possible. Would you care for a cup of tea? You probably won't be able to visit with my father until tomorrow or the next day, but—"

"Visit!" Rimen interrupted to blurt, suddenly remembering that he wasn't there simply to visit. "No, I've come with extremely urgent news, but obviously your father can't be bothered with it. I think I'd better go directly to Lord Zolind, and let *him* decide who to put in charge of the problem."

"Surely you've heard," Ophin said, now regarding him strangely. "Lord Zolind's heart gave out, and he's dead. He was in the middle of a reception when it happened, and those who were there say he worked himself up into a rage just before it happened. What urgent news do you have?"

Rimen was far too stunned to answer Ophin's question. Lord *Zolind* was dead, the man they'd all expected to live forever? Zolind was to have been Rimen's ultimate patron, the man who could simply announce Rimen's advancement without anyone trying to oppose it. Now . . . for all the good Embisson would be able to do alone, he might as well have died, too. . . .

"I think you ought to sit down," Ophin said with ridiculous concern on his face. "You've obviously had one shock too many, and could probably even use a drink stronger than tea. Come into the study and I'll join you."

"No, thank you, but no," Rimen forced himself to say,

realizing that the rumors were true. Anyone who would offer a drink other than tea at *that* hour . . . "No, I'm afraid I haven't the time. It's urgently necessary to pass on what I've learned to someone with enough authority to do something about it. . . . Please give your father my good wishes, and tell him that I'll return when he's up to having visitors."

Ophin agreed with a shrug to deliver the message, then saw Rimen to the door. Once outside and back in his carriage, Rimen forced himself to calm down and do some rational thinking. He *had* to pass on what he knew, otherwise any unfavorable results accruing from the incidents would be made *his* responsibility and fault. That meant finding someone who would take immediate charge, someone too powerful to need a scapegoat if things went even more wrong.

Rimen all but pounded his brain, and in a moment he smiled as the obvious answer came. He knew just the man to speak to, the perfect person to shift the burden onto. With Zolind dead the man's power would be tremendously increased, and he would certainly appreciate being the first to learn about what had happened. Lanir might be mindless, Embisson beaten to pulp, and Zolind dead, but nothing was ever likely to harm Lord Advisor Ephaim Noll. . . .

SEVENTEEN

"His Excellency Bron, Lord of Fire, asks a moment of your time, sir," the servant said to Kambil. "Shall I tell him that you're otherwise engaged?"

"No, show him in," Kambil said, putting aside the book

he'd been reading. He'd had a marvelous lunch, had taken a refreshing nap, and was thoroughly enjoying the book he'd chosen to read. All that made for a wonderfully mellow mood, so there was no reason to turn Bron away. Now that the man had been properly adjusted, speaking with him was often actually pleasant. . . .

"Kambil, something's going on," Bron answered as soon as he walked in, his expression one of faint confusion mixed with annoyance. "Do you remember the meeting you asked me to attend, the one with Lord Velim and some of the people Velim wants us to make deals with? You said we needed to know what the average man was willing to offer in order to keep his tenants quiet and his income trouble-free."

"I remember that," Kambil agreed. "We also need to question Velim and some of his more pliable associates to find out what the Advisory Board is mixed up in. Lord Ephaim and *his* cohorts wouldn't have told us without coercion even if they'd lived, and we have to have *some* source of information. What did you learn from Velim?"

"Absolutely nothing, which is my entire point," Bron replied, dropping into a nearby chair. "Velim never appeared for the meeting, and never even sent word that he'd be delayed. As eager as he was to begin dealing with us, that made very little sense. I waited only a short while, and then I called in my guard commander. He told me he had men who were very good at discreet investigations, so I told him to send some to find out what Velim is up to."

"Which information should prove nicely valuable when we next decide to deal with the man," Kambil said with a nod of approval. "First, though, we'll have to let him squirm for a while. It would never do to let him know how much we need his information now that Lord Ephaim and the others will no longer be with us. What did your investigators learn?"

"Not nearly as much as they should have," Bron replied, leaning forward with his fingers locked between his knees. "Velim was supposed to meet the group he meant to bring to the meeting here, but he also never showed up at the dining parlor where they were all supposed to have lunch. The men looked for him at his house, but no one remembered seeing him after he retired last night. They looked for him when he missed breakfast, something he *never* does, but he was already gone from the house.''

"I don't think I like the sound of that," Kambil decided aloud, feeling the frown he'd grown. "Go back and have your investigators see what Velim's closest cronies are up to. If they're having a private meeting somewhere, we need to know about it. For some obscure reason they may have changed their minds about supporting us, and we can't let that continue."

"There's no need," Bron said, holding up one hand. "Those guardsmen really are good, because one of the first things they did after leaving Velim's house was to locate his closest associates. Or at least they called at the men's houses. The men themselves weren't available, and no one knew where they'd gone. Just like with Velim, none of them have been seen since last night."

"That I definitely don't like," Kambil said, rising to his feet in order to pace a bit. "If you decide to plot against someone, you don't do it at a time when everyone, including those you're plotting against, are almost certain to notice. Velim isn't the brightest flame ever to burn, but he's been an Advisor too long to be that sloppy. Something is definitely wrong, but what can it be?"

"I asked myself that same question," Bron replied, his thoughts as agitated as his adjustment allowed. "The only thing I came up with was something rather ridiculous: it sounded as though *we'd* arranged to remove those men, but without the careful thought which went into removing Lord Ephaim and his group. Their deaths and disappearances can't be linked to us at all, but with Velim's group . . . It seems as if someone wants people to believe that his group decided against supporting us, and because of that we made them disappear."

"You're right," Kambil decided, stopping to look at Bron. "When the disappearances become public knowledge, we'll be the first ones everyone looks at accusingly. They'll think that all those men agreed with Zolind, and weren't going to allow us to be publicly Seated. But who could be behind a move like that?"

"Maybe Lord Ephaim arranged it before he came to

speak with us," Bron suggested, nevertheless still looking doubtful. "It doesn't make much sense considering the Puredan he brought, but maybe he had a private argument with Velim's group."

"Velim and his people weren't powerful enough for Ephaim to worry about," Kambil disagreed with a head-shake. "If he'd wanted them to do something, he would have spoken to them privately and forced them into it. Eliminating Velim and the others would only mean having to deal with their replacements, some of whom might not be quite as pliable. No, eliminating those people is more the move of a fool, someone who acts without thinking—"

"What is it?" Bron asked when Kambil's words suddenly broke off. "Have you thought of someone who might be doing this to us?"

"To quote you, the idea is ridiculous," Kambil answered slowly, his insides beginning to twist. "It should really be impossible, but I have the most awful conviction . . . Let's take a walk and find out."

"Take a walk," Bron echoed as he rose to follow. "You can't mean you think *Delin's* behind the disappearances? Isn't he still completely under your control?"

"Now, certainly," Kambil agreed as he led the way out of his private apartments. "There was a day and a night when he wasn't, though, and we already know what he did with his night. Now I think we need to find out about the day."

Bron said nothing else aloud, but his thoughts and emotions began to take on the same shape and texture as Kambil's own: furious, with the urge to commit violence striding strongly to the forefront. That impossible fool of a madman . . .

Kambil sent servants to tell Homin and Selendi to meet them in Delin's wing, then he and Bron went directly there. The servants around Delin were pleasant and unconcerned, having been convinced that there was nothing odd about one of the Five doing nothing but eating and sleeping and exercising a bit all the time. Kambil had even gotten these servants to tell him who had been spying for Lord Ephaim, and the woman had also been adjusted. Now she spent her time on the alert for anyone else who might have outside employment.

"He looks as innocent as a babe," Bron growled, standing over the chaise an expressionless Delin was stretched out on. "Go ahead and ask him if he really is all that innocent."

"We'll wait until Homin and Selendi get here," Kambil responded, also staring down at a Delin who was oblivious to their presence. All rational—and irrational—thought had been denied him, which meant he simply existed in a world without meaning. He would eat when fed and would give a grunt when he needed to eliminate bodily wastes, but other than that the real world touched him not at all.

"What's happening?" Homin asked when he and Selendi arrived together. The two still spent quite a lot of time in each other's company, but Kambil had relaxed the part of their adjustment that demanded complete constancy. Selendi had been growing impatient on the inside, and Homin had become curious about the female servants who let it be known how available they were. The two had performed admirably well, and now deserved to reap some of the benefits which they'd earned.

Kambil explained why they were there, and once they understood what might have happened they became just as angry as Bron and Kambil himself. Now that all four of them were present to hear the answers, Kambil touched Delin's mind and released the necessary portion of it.

"How are you feeling, Delin?" Kambil asked, letting the man pull the threads of his memory together again. "Are the servants treating you as well as they should?"

"No," Delin mumbled crossly, his heavy frown showing how hard he struggled to reassemble his mind. "No one ever treats me as well as they should. . . ."

"Well, we'll certainly have to look into that, now won't we," Kambil said, carefully guiding the man's thought patterns. "But first we need to ask you something. The other day, when we first came here to the palace, you arranged for certain things to be done. Tell me what those things were."

"I arranged to have my parents brought to me," Delin replied, an incredibly ugly smile now twisting his features.

"It was something I used to dream about, something I waited my whole life to do. When they were brought in they were gagged, so my father couldn't simply order me to release them. I still can't keep from obeying him, you know. . . . But that quickly didn't matter, because the first thing I had done was—"

"Yes, I know about all that," Kambil interrupted, not about to stand there listening to a rehash of what had made him so ill. "What I'd like to know is if there was anything else you did, any other arrangements you might have made. . . ."

"Just the arrangements for the disappearance of those Advisors," Delin replied, showing no reaction to Bron's wordless growl and Homin's and Selendi's sounds of vexation. "They were fools who lacked the proper attitude toward us, so I had my assassination team cause them to vanish. No clues were left to show what happened to them, of course, so no one will ever know for certain."

"That . . . assassination team knows for certain, you complete fool," Bron said coldly, calmed again by the adjustment in his mind. "If any of them decide to sell the information . . ."

"They don't even have to," Selendi said with heavy disapproval. "Once everyone is certain those Advisors are gone, who else are they going to think is responsible but us? We're the only newcomers to high power, so we'll be the natural suspects."

"And once Ephaim and his people begin to have 'accidents' and 'incidents,' they'll all look at us twice as hard," Homin added. "Before there would have been no reason to suspect us, but now . . ."

"That isn't the worst of it," Kambil told them, needing to fight harder than ever before to keep from exploding. "If we intend to run this empire, the first thing we need is information about everything currently being done, and the second is to designate certain puppets for us to work through. With both Velim's and Ephaim's factions gone, most of the information we need is gone with them. The ciphers left on the Board won't know half of what we want, and no one will ever believe that one of *them* is running things."

"So what can we do?" Bron asked in disgust. "Aside from killing Delin, that is? Having new Advisors appointed to the Board won't help, not without knowing what we're appointing them to *do*."

"What about the Advisors' secretaries and assistants?" Homin asked. "My father's secretary always knows everything he's doing, sometimes even when he's not supposed to know. And if enough of the Advisors used their assistants to do what had to be done . . ."

"That's a good suggestion," Kambil said, getting a slightly better grip on his temper. "Once we're officially informed about Ephaim's group, we can get in touch with their secretaries and assistants. Until then we'll have to start an official investigation into Velim's group's disappearance, following up and making public what Bron's people have learned. But before we do *any* of that, the Blending has to look into this assassination-team business. I had no idea there was anything like it, and I want the details on it. Once I have those details, we can either adjust or eliminate the assassins who were involved."

"I suppose this is what we get for not letting our predecessors welcome us to the palace," Selendi said with a faint smile. "I wonder how Delin learned about it—and whether or not there's more we should know."

"Obviously I'm going to have to question Delin a good deal more thoroughly," Kambil said with a sigh of annoyance. "I suppose this happened because I was so delighted to be shut of him that I hadn't let myself realize it's much too soon to sit back and simply enjoy life. We're going to have to build a firm, able network to work through, starting as soon as we're told the terrible news about our Advisors."

"Which, hopefully, won't be too long in coming," Bron said, now sounding fretful. "I have this sudden feeling that things are happening which we ought to know about, but which we *don't* know about because of the large gaps caused in our lines of communication."

"I'm sure the word will reach us soon enough," Kambil said soothingly as he distastefully turned his attention back to Delin. "And I'm also sure that we'll find nothing of any importance that we've missed. After all, with everything else taken care of, what could there possibly be?"

The others made sounds of agreement, Bron reluctant but still in agreement. There *was* nothing that needed immediate attention, nothing but Delin and whatever secrets he continued to hold. And after he'd drained Delin dry, Kambil vowed to begin looking for a High talent in Earth magic to replace the madman with. But until he found that replacement, he would spend some time thinking of a way to punish the fool for what he'd thoughtlessly done to the rest of them. . . .

EIGHTEEN

Vallant wasn't the only one in the coach who sat without speaking until the last of Gan Garee was behind them. He and Rion had gotten to the coach first, after climbing down the rope outside the window. Vallant still felt annoyed over that descent, annoyed with himself for being so much clumsier than usual. If Rion and his Air magic hadn't been there, he probably would have gotten fully outdoors a lot more abruptly than he'd planned.

But Rion *had* been there, and had taken the trouble to disguise his help so that the man steadying the rope never noticed. Vallant was in his debt for that, and had tried to thank him once they reached the fancy, dark red coach waiting for them and were left alone by their guide. But Rion had refused to hear him, blandly insisting that he'd done nothing but help *himself*. . . .

Vallant rubbed his bristly face with his hand, fighting to keep the coach's smooth motion from rocking him to sleep. There were things he had to say to Tamrissa once Gan Garee was a bit farther behind them—and he had worked up his nerve a bit more. When she and Naran had been brought to the coach, she'd taken the seat beside him only, he was sure, because there was no other. He and Rion had been told to stay in the coach, and Naran, who had been helped in first, naturally sat beside the man she loved. Loved . . .

Tamrissa had barely glanced at him, and once those two men transferred the baggage to the coach's boot, one of them had joined the coach driver on the box and they'd started on their way. Now Tamrissa sat as close to the window on her side of the seat as possible, looking out and not saying a word. He'd have to be the one to start the conversation, but what could he possibly say? Their relationship was probably over, but if there was the least chance she *didn't* want it that way . . .

"I think it's time for cautious self-congratulations," Rion said suddenly, also looking out the window. "If I'm not mistaken, that posting house we just passed is considered the last of the city of Gan Garee. That's the way it's done on the road to Haven Wraithside, and the two posting houses appear just the same."

"I'm sure you're right, my love," Naran agreed with a serene smile. "While we were still in the city there was always the chance that we would be stopped, but now that chance is behind us. If pursuit does come from Gan Garee, it won't be able to catch up with us."

"But we might too easily catch up with the convoy," Rion said with a frown after taking her hand and distractedly kissing it. "Did Dom Meerk have anything to say about that, Tamrissa?"

"Alsin told me that the convoy had started out at a fairly good pace," Tamrissa replied after the smallest hesitation, as though she'd been pulled away from her thoughts. "If they have places to change their horses at regular intervals, they may have no trouble staying ahead of us."

"So we, ourselves, may end up pushing our horses or replacing them at similar intervals," Rion said with a nod. "We needn't worry about catching the convoy until we have a plan of action, which I assume we don't have as yet. I, at least, have thought of nothing, so I would be pleased to learn that one of you others has been struck by inspiration."

"Struck by a stick is more like it," Vallant forced himself to say when the ladies simply shook their heads. He shifted his body on the seat, a body which had begun to ache a bit. "And speakin' about sticks, I'm reminded of stones, which I deserve to have people throwin' at me. I still haven't really thanked all of you for gettin' me out of the Razas woman's house when you did. She repels me so badly that it was about to override the only thing she wanted from me, and when that happened I would have paid hard for the failure."

"It's odd, but you didn't *seem* repelled by her," Tamrissa commented without looking around, speaking before Rion could. "Do you suddenly find her so unattractive because she's no longer in reach?"

"It wasn't me findin' her attractive, it was the drug in me," Vallant countered, suddenly appalled to realize that he'd been considering the wrong emotion. It wasn't his humiliation that Tamrissa had been thinking about, it was her own jealousy.

"She told me all about that drug," Vallant continued as quickly as possible. "It tickled her that a *sedative* could be used to inflame a man, somethin' she hadn't known about before. When I tried to refuse to play, she threatened to lock me in a tiny crate. That left me with nothin' to do but to pretend I didn't remember her or understand what was goin' on. She didn't like that either, and was in the process of threatenin' again just before you walked in."

"Then I apologize for the comment I made," Tamrissa replied, still sounding distant as she continued to gaze out of the window. "Please feel free to go back to your conversation with Rion."

"But it isn't Rion I'm interested in talkin' to," Vallant said, wishing he could touch her. Normally he would have, but now something told him he'd be a fool to try. . . . "You're the one who needs to be apologized to more, to have explained to you that I couldn't help myself. First I couldn't stand the way I'd been humiliated in front of you, and then I thought I'd lost you because of losin' my ability. That would be harder than never bein' able to touch the power again. . . ."

Very briefly Vallant was ashamed of himself for trying to hold Tamrissa with pity, but considering what she meant to him the regret was extremely short-lived. He'd spoken the absolute truth when he said losing her would be worse than losing his ability, and when she suddenly turned to look at him he thought the plan had worked. But then he saw her expression, and her following words confirmed the dread abruptly gripping him.

"You're saying that you thought I'd turn my back on you because you've lost your ability," she accused, fury flaming in her beautiful eyes. "So now we know at last what you really think of me: that I'm a shallow, stupid woman who can't be relied on to act like a decent human being! And if you want my opinion on what was really bothering you, here it is: you couldn't stand the fact that you had to be rescued by *me*, a woman. If it had been Rion or Lorand showing up just in time, you never would have been so bent out of shape. Go ahead and deny it, I dare you!"

Vallant began to do just that, but his protests sounded hollow even to him. She'd hit on what really was the truth, but not for the reason she thought. He finally decided that the matter had to be explained, but before he was able to start he was abruptly interrupted.

"Oh, spare me!" she snapped, dismissing his excuses with a sharp wave of her hand. "Everything you've said boils down to the fact that *you* have to be the big hero, and you're far too selfish to share something that important with me. Well, it's time for me to admit that I'm just as selfish, but what *I* won't share is a relationship. Not with you, at any rate, so please do me the favor of not speaking to me again."

"Tamrissa, you're wrong," he tried, putting a hand to her arm as she deliberately looked back to the window. "That isn't at all what I—"

Vallant suddenly sucked his breath in sharply, the reaction caused by the brief but very intense heat touching his face. It hadn't precisely been painful, but he'd been left with the definite impression that it could easily have been just that. The hand he'd quickly pulled away from Tamrissa's arm moved to his face, where he gingerly examined what had been done.

"Now you no longer look like a derelict who needs to be hidden when we reach an inn," Tamrissa said, that same cold shoulder still pointed in his direction adding to the shock he felt. "I'm sure you've never had that kind of shave before, at least not one *that* close. If you ever touch me again, you'll find out what close can really mean."

Considering how smooth his face felt, there was nothing Vallant could think of to say. She'd obviously burned away his beard stubble without doing any damage to his skin, showing once again what it meant to be a High talent in Fire magic. He'd obviously done it good this time, getting her so angry that she'd had to do *something* to show it. Only a High in Water magic might have a chance to defend against her anger, and he no longer qualified. . . .

Vallant took a deep breath before sitting back, forcing himself to accept the fact that pushing Tamrissa's power-backed temper right now was a very bad idea. Rion and Naran looked even more shaken than he himself felt, and he didn't blame them. He'd caught a glimpse of the very intense fire Tamrissa had used, and colored circles still floated before his eyes. They must have had a much better view of the thing, and caution was now keeping them as silent as he.

But he refused to remain silent forever. No matter how dangerous it turned out to be, he was determined to find a way to make Tamrissa listen to him. It wasn't selfishness or male pride that had caused him to act the way he had, but being shamed in front of the woman who meant everything to him. The situation would have been better even if it had been Jovvi rescuing him, as long as it wasn't Tamrissa who had seen him so weak and helpless and humiliated. But it *had* been Tamrissa, and now she refused to hear and understand. . . .

Just as she'd refused all those times in the past. Vallant leaned back in his seat as he suddenly remembered that, the fact that Tamrissa never wanted to hear things from *his* point of view. It was as if his own feelings were unimportant next to hers, unimportant and decidedly secondary. And she never shared *those* with him either, those very important feelings of hers. She never asked him why he said or did something, and she never explained why *she* said and did things.

Maybe *that* was what they would have to talk about, whether or not his ability was ever restored. . . .

NINETEEN

The sun had almost set by the time our coach pulled into the front court of a rather large inn. The trip had been extremely silent, and there was no need to wonder why. A short while after our . . . discussion had ended, Vallant had actually fallen asleep. So much for his intense desire to "apologize" to me. . . .

I stirred a bit as the coach slowed, trying to work the aches out of my body so that I'd actually be able to walk. I hadn't realized how physically numbing and exhausting a trip like that could be, and Rion and Naran apparently felt the same. Not that they were even looking in my direction, either of them. My little explosion of temper seemed to have affected *them* a good deal more than it had the man it had been aimed at.

A twinge of conscience tried to take my attention, but I refused to let that happen. Vallant had brought that exhibition on himself by touching me, and I didn't regret having done it. Talk about adding insult to injury . . . No, Tamrissa, I don't think much of you as a person and I don't even care how you feel, but *I* want to put my hand on you so I will. We both know you won't dare do anything about it.

Well, I *had* dared, and as I got ready to leave the coach behind Rion and Naran, I made certain not to look at the man to my right, who was just beginning to awaken. Vallant Ro had nothing to say that I cared to hear, not anymore. If what I'd done didn't convince him of that, I felt perfectly ready to find another lesson that would.

159

"I was just telling the others that we'll spend the night here," Alsin said as he helped me down. "I sent one of my people to follow the convoy on horseback at a discreet distance, and then he's to meet us here, at the first inn beyond Gan Garee, to report. Not many people leaving the city early stop here since it's less than a full day's ride from the city, but those getting a late start and people coming from not very far away in the other direction are plentiful enough to keep it in business."

"As long as it has a bath house and a private room with a bed for me, I don't care if it's full or empty," I said, reaching up to massage my left shoulder. "This coach rides more smoothly than most, but tomorrow will be twice as bad as today so I'd like to get some real rest tonight."

"We'll get rooms and have something to eat, and then we'll use their bath house," Alsin said, putting a hand to my elbow to start me toward the inn. He'd first glanced back to see that Vallant Ro was finally with us, so there was no reason to continue standing there. "I've stayed at this inn a few times, so I know you'll be comfortable and will enjoy the food. Lidris will play servant to us, and after taking care of the horses he'll eat in the kitchen."

He obviously meant the coach driver, who was already moving the coach toward the stable area. The rest of us were heading for the inn's front door, Alsin busily brushing dust from his clothing. None of us was exactly neat and tidy, but riding on the box had added a layer of road dust to the man. He stopped brushing when he reached the door, opened it, and stood aside to let me enter first, then he strode forward to receive the host's friendly welcome.

Alsin really was known at the inn—under another name—and we were treated very well. Four rooms were assigned to us, and our baggage was taken upstairs by houseboys while we went into the dining room. The common area had only been partially filled, and there were even fewer people in the dining room. We all sat at a large table, and a serving girl began to bring out bread and soup. Dinner would be pork roast and yams, a mix of vegetables, and a choice of desserts.

The food was just as good as Alsin had said it would be, and we were sitting there considering dessert when a man walked into the room. Conversation had been rather desultory until then, but once the newcomer brought over a chair and sat down beside Alsin, that abruptly changed.

"Those people you're all interested in stopped to camp for the night a couple of hours ago," he said softly, speaking mostly to Alsin. "I had the impression that they leave the road early because their . . . cargo has to be cared for before the drivers and guardsmen can see to their own needs. I also had the impression that they'll be moving on again tomorrow rather early."

"Grath has Spirit magic," Alsin explained to us just as softly, then his attention returned to the man. "Were you able to find out what they use to keep their . . . cargo quiet? If it's hilsom powder, there may not be much left of them by the time they get to wherever they're going."

"I'm certain it isn't hilsom powder," Grath denied with a headshake. "They began to unload kegs with some sort of liquid, and no one waters down hilsom powder. It would lose its effectiveness, and would also have to be poured down the victim's throat. If you want to use the powder, you just hold it under the person's nose."

"That's true, so they only start out using the powder," Alsin said with a distracted nod. "After that they use something else, and it would help enormously to know exactly what. See if you can find out tomorrow, Grath, once you pick them up again. But don't take any chances trying to get a sample of the liquid. If it becomes necessary, I'll take your place following them. Once I get close enough, I ought to be able to identify the substance."

"You have Earth magic, then," Rion observed, having paid very close attention to what had been said. Then he looked at Grath and added, "Was it possible to learn which wagon or wagons our friends are in? If we have to choose between freeing just them or losing all the victims, we'll have to concentrate on them. Once they're returned to themselves, they can help us to see about the others."

"It wasn't possible to tell who was in which wagon," Grath said with another headshake. "They don't unload their cargo, I think, they just feed it, clean it up, and massage it a bit. Their mind-sets were like those of people who have to care for a large number of infants."

"I think that eventually we'll all have to get nearer to their campsite," I said when Rion sat back looking frustrated. "We're closer to Jovvi and Lorand than anyone else could possibly be, so maybe *we'll* be able to locate them. In the meantime, it won't hurt to think about a way to free *all* the prisoners, just in case we find that we can't reach unconscious people."

Everyone seemed to agree with that, including a still-silent Vallant Ro, so Grath pushed his chair back and stood.

"Tell Lidris to leave the coach where it can be seen from the road tomorrow night," he said to Alsin. "That way I won't have any trouble finding you, since there isn't a coach quite like it anywhere. I'm going to get a room, some food, and a quick bath, then I'm going to bed. Tomorrow is bound to start even earlier than I expect it to."

He nodded to us all then strode away, and Alsin took a deep breath which he let out slowly.

"I have no idea where Grath gets all that energy from, but talking to him when I'm tired makes me even more tired," he commented. "I, for one, am going to skip dessert, and go straight for a bath and then bed. May I call the serving girl for any of the rest of you?"

It turned out that no one was in the least interested in eating any more, so we went to our small but pleasant rooms to fetch clean clothing. It came as a surprise to find a cheap wrap and a pair of scuffs in the room, obviously supplied by the inn for the use of its guests. Not having much experience with inns, I had no idea whether or not that was usual. But that didn't mean I couldn't take advantage of the courtesy, which I did as quickly as I was able to get out of my clothes.

When I stepped out of the room again, I found Alsin waiting for me in the hall. He wore the same sort of wrap and scuffs, and when he saw me he grinned.

"It's fairly obvious they expected those things to be worn by someone my size rather than yours," he said, referring to how big the wrap and scuffs were on me. "But I have to admit that that's better than the reverse. I'd look incredibly foolish wearing a wrap made to fit someone your size."

"If I trip and kill myself in this thing, you may be forced to change your mind," I countered, nevertheless smiling at his amusement. "Which way is the bath house?"

"It's bath *houses*, plural, and they're attached to the back of the inn," he replied, beginning to lead the way to the stairs. "One for men and one for women, and a single hall leads to them both. If I ever build a house of my own, that's the arrangement I mean to have. Most people are scandalized at the thought of having a bath house connected to their residence, but once the weather turns cold I become less and less concerned with propriety."

"As a fellow lover of warm weather, I have to agree with that," I said as I made my careful way down the stairs. "I've always hated having to leave the warmth of the bath house for the cold of outdoors, but I've always been told that that's the only proper way to do it. My one consolation is that at least I don't have to face the cold while I'm damp."

"A definite benefit in having Fire magic," he said, looking ready to catch me if I happened to trip. "Not having the same myself, I'll just have to settle for the improper."

I had the feeling that Alsin Meerk would have chosen the improper no matter *what* the circumstance or situation, but I didn't say so. The man was going out of his way to help us; to offer what he might consider an insult wasn't my idea of a way to thank him.

Alsin led the way to a hall which ran to the back of the inn, where the wall held a sign showing a picture of someone washing and an arrow below pointing to the right. We turned right as directed, then turned left in obedience to a second sign, where we found the others waiting a short way down.

Naran looked just as silly in the wrap and scuffs as I did, but no one said anything as Alsin and I joined them. The first door had a sign projecting from the wall showing a picture of a featureless face with a high-piled hairdo, and a second sign, some feet down the hall, showed another featureless face sporting wide, sweeping mustaches. That was clear enough, so we separated to go into our own sections of the bath house.

"There haven't been many times in my life when I've so looked forward to taking a bath," Naran said once we were inside, flashing me a brief smile as she began to remove her wrap. "Although it feels odd not having to walk outside to reach it."

"Alsin was just saying how much he enjoys that oddness," I commented back as I also hurried to get out of the wrap and scuffs. "It's made me wonder why bath houses aren't attached to residences, rather than standing at a distance from them."

"Someone powerful and opinionated must have set the style, and now everyone follows along," Naran suggested as we approached the steps and began to descend into the water. "That's usually the reason something that doesn't make sense continues . . . Are you feeling any better now?"

"Some," I lied with a shrug as I spread my arms wide to embrace the marvelous water all around my body. "I should have apologized to you and Rion for that outburst, but I'm afraid I'm still not much in the mood for apologies. Maybe that will change once I've had a decent night's sleep."

"*Not* in clothes," she agreed fervently, then submerged to wet her hair. I did the same, and when we'd both come up and wiped our eyes, she looked at me with clear hesitation. "Tamrissa . . . will you mind if I say something to you?"

"That all depends on what you say," I pointed out, pushing back sopping wet hair. "But in case you were wondering, this is probably the best place to say something that might get a Fire magic user angry. It would probably take quite a bit of time and effort for me to burn away all this water—and I couldn't possibly do that until after I washed."

I smiled to show her I was only joking, but the smile wasn't a very successful one. Her own smile was full of sympathetic understanding, that and real concern.

"Then I guess I'd better take my chances while I can," she said, trying to share the joke. "It's . . . something I don't know if you've noticed, and that's why I'm mentioning it. That man, Alsin Meerk—he's more than just slightly interested in you."

"Really, Naran, you have to be imagining things," I said with a startled laugh, having expected her to talk about something else entirely. "Alsin is helping us in the hope that we'll eventually be able to help him in turn, and I know him from when he first contacted us through Lorand. All he's doing is being friendly.''

"Tamrissa, he truly isn't just being friendly,'' she said, soberly trying to convince me. "A man doesn't always have to devour you with his eyes or try to overwhelm you if he's strongly attracted. Some of them approach slowly and gently, in a cautious rather than a brash way. They're trying to find out if their advances will be welcome, and if Alsin Meerk decides that his *will* be—there's no doubt that it will cause quite a lot of trouble.''

"Why should it cause trouble?'' I asked, still trying to make myself believe her. Alsin wasn't behaving like any man I'd ever met before—aside from Lorand and Rion— but Naran knew men a good deal better than I did. Once again I wished Jovvi were there, if for no other reason than to give her opinion. . . .

"Yes, I know, it isn't likely to cause trouble for *you*,'' she responded wearily. "Not only is your talent incredibly strong, you've more than proven that you're willing to use it. What I meant was Vallant, and the fact that he isn't about to give you up without a struggle. I know he saw the way Alsin looked at you, and can't imagine what great good fortune kept him from saying something. The next time the same thing happens, that good fortune may not be present.''

"Vallant Ro doesn't have to worry about giving up something he doesn't have,'' I said, finding it impossible to keep the stiffness out of my voice. "Whatever was once between us is now over, and he'd better learn to accept that truth. A relationship isn't supposed to be there only when *he* wants it to be. . . . I'm sorry, Naran, but I'm really tired. I'm going to wash and go to bed, and we can talk again some other time.''

Only her sigh came as a response as I headed for the side of the bath, where small metal racks held jars of soap at ten-foot intervals all around the entire rim. I really did need to get some sleep, and then maybe *I'd* notice what Naran said everyone else could see. If it really was there to see . . . and anyone really did care . . . not that *I* cared if someone did . . .

At that point I forced myself to stop thinking. When you reach a time where the ludicrous comes forward without effort, you *have* to save thinking for another day.

TWENTY

Rion shifted just a little on the coach seat, needing desperately to move about a bit but reluctant to wake Naran. She'd fallen asleep against his shoulder not long after they'd eaten lunch, something he would have enjoyed managing himself. After nearly two and a half days of traveling in that coach and stopping only at odd-mile inns, the pursuit had become not only boring, but trying.

"I hope the place we'll be stayin' at tonight is better than the one we stopped at *last* night," Vallant said softly. Tamrissa had also fallen asleep, but Vallant seemed just as wide-awake as he. "Not only was the food barely edible, the room I slept in was only a bit larger than a wardrobe. If it hadn't had a window, I probably would have had to spend the night in the stable."

"I doubt if even the horses enjoyed being stabled there," Rion commented sourly with matching softness. "And tonight will most likely be worse rather than better, as odd-mile inns do tend to get worse the farther they are from Gan Garee. Leaving that first inn at lunchtime would have brought us to a prime-mile inn at sundown, and then a full day's travel could be begun the following day. Those who travel soon learn that that's best."

"I'm used to travelin', but not by coach," Vallant replied, doing a bit of cautious shifting of his own. "That's why I know all about ports, but nothin' about—odd-mile inns, did you call them? It's too bad that if we speed up we'll run

166

smack into that convoy, and if we slow down we'll be too far behind.''

"Hopefully we'll find it possible to do something soon about our inactivity," Rion said. "Alsin should rejoin us tonight, bringing with him some of the information that we need. After that . . . well, we can't simply continue to follow. If they reach their destination before we manage to free Jovvi and Lorand, there will be a lot more of them than one convoy of guardsmen."

"Yes, that's also the way I see it," Vallant agreed, looking no happier than Rion felt. "Tamrissa's friend Meerk claimed that that wasn't necessarily so, but he seems to be into wishful thinkin'. If we don't break them loose now, we may never have another chance."

"Tamrissa feels the same, so we had better all speak to Alsin tonight," Rion decided aloud. "I just wish we had a better plan than what we've come up with. I'll certainly have no trouble knocking out the sentries by temporarily depriving them of air to breathe, but then having to search wagon by wagon . . . Locating Jovvi and Lorand first would certainly make things easier, but the rest of the plan still seems to lack something."

"Control is what it lacks," Vallant supplied with a nod of agreement. "We won't really have control of the situation, and anythin' can happen to disrupt the rescue. That's been botherin' me as well."

"It's a prime example of being trapped in all directions," Rion said with an exasperated sigh. "If we had either Jovvi or Lorand to help, we'd have considerably more control. But those two are the ones we need the control *for* in order to rescue them. Annoying is much too mild a word."

"Speakin' of annoyin', it looks like we've reached the next inn," Vallant said, glancing out his window. "It also looks more like a run-down roadhouse, but there are torches burnin' in the courtyard and lamplight showin' in the windows. Without that it would be easy to think the place was abandoned."

"Torches rather than lanterns?" Rion said, shifting around to get his own look at the place. Naran stirred at the movement, but now it was all right. They would be stopping in just a few minutes . . . at the worst inn they'd so far come to. Rion hadn't protested over what they'd needed to put up with, and not only because of the travel schedule forced on them. Prime-mile inns would have travelers of considerably higher caliber, and his group was, after all, composed mainly of fugitives.

But this place really was the worst of the lot. As the coach slowed even more, it was possible to see in the torchlight that the inn probably hadn't been repainted in years. Although there were quite a number of horses tied to the right of the front door, showing that the place was well patronized by the locals. Transients would leave their vehicles and mounts to the left, near or in the stable.

The coach slowed to a complete stop, and by then both Naran and Tamrissa were awake again. For a short while Tamrissa had used Vallant's shoulder as Naran had used his, and Rion had been able to see that Vallant had treasured the time. But when she'd shifted away again, he'd made no more effort to stop her than he'd tried to speak to her after that first, disastrous occasion. Rion was certain that Vallant hadn't given up on their relationship, but wished he knew what the other man had in mind to repair the damage done.

Grath, the man whose place as a forward scout Alsin had taken, climbed down from the box where he'd ridden beside their driver. His movements seemed stiff and a bit awkward, and when he opened the coach door his first words matched quite well.

"If Alsin tries to take my horse again, I'll probably have to kill him," the man grumbled as he rubbed at his back. "Riding up top on this thing is enough to cripple you, and I don't understand how Lidris does it all the time."

"Ridin' inside isn't all that much better," Vallant said as he slowly left the coach. "I thought I'd gotten used to it durin' the past weeks, but I'm learnin' I was foolin' myself."

"We probably need more rest periods than the horses do." Rion added his agreement as he followed Vallant out of the coach, then he turned to assist the ladies. They looked logy from sleep as well as stiff, and the way they stared at the inn as they descended suggested that they were likely hoping the place was simply a bad dream.

"This progression downward keeps gaining intensity,"

Tamrissa said once she stood with the rest of them, her glance at the inn more than simply displeased. "I think it's time to do something about it before we find ourselves sharing our rooms with rats and a variety of wildlife."

"That's for you and Alsin to discuss," Grath said quickly with both hands raised. "I'm nothing but hired help around here, and happy to have it like that. Let's just be careful when we go inside. They're bound to notice us no matter what we do, but we don't want to give them anything . . . spectacular to remember."

Rion joined the others in nodding, understanding as well as they why such caution was necessary. It had so far been their good fortune that there was no sign of pursuit. There had been no uniformed guardsmen pounding along their trail and catching up to demand their whereabouts from those in whatever inn the fugitives currently stayed, but that good fortune wasn't likely to last. There *would* be pursuit, and the less those pursuers were able to learn when they came, the better off *their* group would be.

Grath led the way toward the inn while the driver Lidris moved the coach to where Alsin would be able to see it. Rion had wondered about that, the supposed need for Alsin or Grath to see the coach to know where they were, but he hadn't had the chance to ask about it. Considering their rate of travel, there was really only one choice of which inn they were at along that road. . . .

Grath entered the inn, then moved forward to look for the landlord while first Naran and Tamrissa and then Rion and Vallant followed. Quite a lot of noise came from the crowded common room to the left, as someone played a musical instrument and someone else seemed to be doing something to that music. With the left wall of the entry area cutting off sight of the far end of the common room it wasn't possible to tell what, but the whistling and clapping and shouting of the audience said it was something extremely enjoyable.

"Looks like Grath may be havin' trouble gettin' us rooms," Vallant murmured only loudly enough for Rion to hear him over the noise. "We may end up havin' to sleep in the coach, or maybe even goin' on to camp with the convoy."

Rion looked toward Grath where he stood talking to a boy who had appeared behind the registration counter. The boy kept shaking his head, obviously disagreeing with whatever Grath said, but Grath seemed unprepared to accept the denial. It was possible that they haggled over price, Rion realized, as the price of a room and meals had not been the same in every inn. Their sojourn was being paid for by the gold and silver Tamrissa had gotten from that Lord Lanir, and although there was still a surprising amount left, Grath might be trying to conserve their funds.

A burst of laughter and shouting and longer applause came from the common room, but Rion wasn't distracted from watching Grath's efforts to get them accommodations. To Rion's left, Vallant also watched the exchange closely, possibly thinking the same as Rion: that it might be wise of them to join Grath. Saving pennies was all well and good, but not at the expense of a place to sleep. And their last meal was too many hours behind them for Rion to enjoy the thought of a delay in sitting down to—

"Well, *h'llo* there, lovey," Rion half heard, and then there was a cry of protest in a woman's voice. Rion turned his head quickly to see that one of the roughly dressed men in the common room had come into the entrance area, and now had his arms wrapped about Tamrissa. The man was obviously drunk, as were his three friends, who stood in the entrance to the common room and laughed out their encouragement to their crony. Tamrissa, clearly mindful of the caution against doing something that people would remember, struggled futilely to escape the drunkard's embrace.

Caution or no, Rion was affronted enough to do something with his own talent to free Tamrissa, but wasn't given the chance. Even as Rion took in the situation, Vallant was already striding toward the coarse animal pawing Tamrissa. When he reached the pair Vallant broke the man's grip on the girl, pulled him away from her, then threw a fist into the drunk's face. With Vallant's entire body behind the blow, the burly drunkard stumbled backwards to fall to the floor at the feet of his friends.

The three men had stopped laughing when Vallant interfered with their friend's entertainment, and seemed about ready to come forward in the man's defense. For that reason

Rion quickly strode over to stand beside Vallant, and a heartbeat later Grath had also joined them. Together they stared at the three men, who now showed hesitation along with their drunken belligerence, and the confrontation held for several seconds. Then one of the three bent to help their fallen friend to his feet, and all four staggered back into the common room to seek safer entertainment.

"Nicely done, people," Grath said softly to all of them, including a quietly furious Tamrissa. "Most people don't go beyond the physical with those who have been drinking, since it's smarter not to set them off talent-wise. Are you all right, Dama Domon?"

"I'd be a good deal better if I could have taught that fool how big a mistake he nearly made," Tamrissa replied in a growl. "I really hate having to do things this way."

"Are you sayin' you find it humiliatin' and frustratin' to have needed someone else to rescue you when you would normally be perfectly able to rescue yourself?" The quiet question had come from Vallant, who made no effort to avoid Tamrissa's blazing gaze. "If so, the situation sounds familiar for some reason—And you're very welcome. I didn't mind helpin' out in the least, not when I knew how graciously I would be thanked."

Tamrissa, still furious, parted her lips to say something, then changed her mind and simply stalked away to stand alone. Naran exchanged a pained glance with Rion before going over to join Tamrissa, and Rion decided it might be best to change the topic of conversation.

"It seems, Grath, that you were having trouble of some sort taking rooms for us," he said rather hastily. "If it happens to be a matter of cost, let's disregard the added expense. If it became necessary for me to climb back into that coach tonight, I'd very likely turn violent."

"You'd certainly have *my* company in that violence," Grath commented wryly, then shook his head. "But the problem isn't cost, it's a matter of available space. This inn has become a very popular place in the area since they brought in a troupe of what the boy called exotic dancers. The girls each do their dance, and then they spend the night with the man who bids highest for their company. I've heard about troupes such as this one, and keeping them here for a week or two will bring in enough gold to let the landlord completely renovate this place.''

"I'm pleased for the man, but certainly not to the point of being willing to give up a night's sleep," Rion returned. "Just how short of space are they?"

"There are only two small rooms still available," Grath answered with a sigh. "I've already taken the two, of course, and then tried to offer a bit of a bonus for two more. The boy refuses even to discuss the possibility, and claims the landlord will feel the same way. The man is currently engaged in overseeing the dancing and auctions, but I mean to speak to him as soon as he's free. In the meanwhile we can go into the dining room and have our dinner.''

"We ought to arrange for the drawin' of lots for one of the two rooms just in case," Vallant put in blandly. "Naran should certainly have one of the two, but I'm not in the mood to give up a possible claim to the second for Tamrissa. She seems to think that the rules applyin' to me can't also be applied to her, and I've decided not to stand for that kind of behavior. She'll learn to act properly, or she can sleep in the stable for all of me.''

Rion felt the urge to protest, but the steely look in Vallant's eyes caused him to change his mind. The disagreement between his two groupmates had changed somehow, and something told Rion that he would be much better off staying out of the matter. As long as humanly possible, that is. . . .

The five of them retired to the dining room then, finding it empty except for two lone travelers who each sat alone eating. They chose one large table and sat down at it, but the icy, deliberate silence coming from both Tamrissa and Vallant put a damper on casual conversation among the other three. Naran looked at Rion as though she expected him to do something to change the heavy, chilly atmosphere, but Rion had already decided on the better part of valor. He took Naran's hand and squeezed it gently, then simply sat and waited for a serving person to appear.

The servant arrived in only a few minutes, and shortly thereafter they had something to do with their mouths other than converse. The food came rather more quickly than expected, and Rion discovered that that was because it was rewarmed rather than freshly made. At another time he would certainly have sent it back with his indignation ringing in the servingman's ears, but tonight Rion was too hungry. He therefore attacked the roast beef and boiled potatoes rather than the man who brought them, and the others silently followed his example.

Silently. By meal's end the silence had long since grown grating, with both Tamrissa and Vallant pretending that they were alone at the table. After spending his eating time thinking about it, Rion was quickly coming to the conclusion that the better part of valor wasn't *always* better. Those two hardheaded groupmates of his needed a good talking to, and he was just about to begin giving them one when Alsin Meerk walked into the dining room.

"Alsin, you're back!" Grath exclaimed, blurting the obvious. "Since you probably don't need me, I'll go and check on my horse. I want him to know how much I missed him."

Grath was on his feet and heading out of the room by then, obviously having no intention of waiting to see if Alsin disagreed. The newcomer, brows raised high, watched Grath disappear, then he came to the table and took his associate's abandoned chair.

"What's wrong with *him?*" Alsin asked, still looking puzzled. "He didn't seem to be in love with his horse when I took it this morning."

"A day can sometimes make a lot of difference," Vallant remarked, leaning forward to rest his forearms on the table. "To tell the truth, I'm hopin' you can say the same. What did you find out?"

"I found out that they're using lethe on their . . . guests," Alsin replied, lowering his voice a bit. "It's a gentle sedative that can usually be used for quite a long time without it doing any harm, and they administer it three times a day. That means the captives will come awake in a matter of hours once they stop taking it, although they *will* be a bit confused and disoriented at first. I've also thought of a way to make use of the information—if it turns out to be possible."

"What way is that?" Rion asked, also leaning his arms on the table. "I've got to tell you, Alsin, that the rest of us are agreed: we have to do something *now* to free our groupmates. If you don't agree with that as well, we'll simply have to go forward without you."

"All right, just calm down," Alsin replied soothingly after glancing at Tamrissa and Vallant. Their concurrence was obvious enough that the man had no need to confirm Rion's claim in words. "I said that I might have a plan, but it all depends on just how strong and versatile a High talent is. My idea is that we remove most of the lethe from its various barrels and make up the difference with plain water. The water will be taken from the barrels used by the guardsmen and drivers, and *it* will be replaced with the lethe. If we can do that, your people will be awake and their guards ready to fall asleep by lunchtime tomorrow."

"Won't someone notice the difference in color and taste?" Naran asked while Rion and the others sat silent. "And how would the substitution be made? By some of us sneaking into their camp and changing things around?"

"Lethe is a pale yellow in color, and only has a faintly noticeable taste," Alsin replied with a smile. "The water in the drinking barrels has been in there too long to still be clear, and I noticed that almost every driver and guardsman flavored their ration in some way before drinking it. Not stopping for fresh water must be a standing order, but no, there won't be any sneaking into the camp. I'm hoping that a High talent in Water magic will be able to handle both the water *and* the lethe."

And with that he looked toward Vallant, his expression frankly demanding an answer to his question. Rion would have enjoyed being able to say something, but once again his mind had gone blank. A glance at Tamrissa suggested that she found herself in the same quandary, and then Vallant saved them both the trouble of racking their brains.

"I find this really fascinatin'," he commented, sounding as though he were extremely pleased about something. "If you can suggest that, then my private life *hasn't* been made completely public. With that in mind, it will be my pleasure to try movin' that lethe around as well as the water."

"What?" Rion yelped, finding he had company in voicing the exclamation. Tamrissa had said almost the same thing at almost the same time, and Naran joined them in staring at Vallant in disbelief.

"Why are all of you looking at him like that?" Alsin demanded softly with a frown. "He *is* a High talent, isn't he? I didn't know if he could handle a liquid other than water, but if he says he can, then he should be able to. Shouldn't he?"

"That's not quite the question," Tamrissa ground out, her stare at Vallant beginning to smolder again. "You *should* be asking how he's suddenly able to do anything at all, when he told *us* that his talent was gone. I'd like to know if he was lying then or if he's lying now."

"You can tell her that I don't believe in lyin'," Vallant said at once, giving Alsin no chance to reply or comment. "Not unless it's absolutely necessary, that is, and the lyin' won't cause actual harm. When I said my talent was gone I believed it, but our first mornin' on the road I woke up to find it had returned. It took a while before I understood what had happened, and your answer to the question I asked confirmed my guess."

"You asked me about the man who had brought your breakfast back in the warehouse," Alsin remembered aloud, his frown still in place. "He told you that his brother had the same problem you do about closed in places, and you asked if the man had ever done anything to help his brother when the brother had to stay in the dormitory. I answered—"

"You answered yes, the man usually put a mild sedative in his brother's food," Vallant said, finishing the story when Alsin's words ended abruptly. "None of us realized it at the time, but the man must have done the same with *my* food. Normally it wouldn't have mattered, but with the hilsom powder still lingerin' a bit in my blood, it was like druggin' me all over again."

"But why didn't you tell us you were all right again?" Tamrissa took her turn to demand, the words almost blurted. "You didn't say a single word, letting us spend our time—"

She, too, stopped speaking abruptly, just short of the word "worrying," Rion thought. She clearly wasn't about to admit that, though, and Vallant acted as if he had no idea what she'd been about to say.

"Why would I waste my time tellin' things to people who only care about their *own* feelin's?" he countered bluntly.

''They don't care anythin' about *me*, not when I'm never allowed to be human around them. Human bein's make mistakes and sometimes act emotionally, but my mistakes are always considered unforgivable outrages, and so are any shows of emotion. It's been that way more than once before, but now I find myself sick of it. From now on I mean to talk only to people who understand how human I am, and who are prepared to accept that terrible failin'. Everyone else can find perfect people to associate with, which I'll *never* be. You get somethin' to eat, Meerk, and I'll wait for you outside.''

Rion joined everyone else in silently watching Vallant leave, and once again he had no idea of what to say. Tamrissa sat unmoving as she stared sightlessly down at the table, and Rion's heart went out to her. Vallant had been incredibly harsh with her, and his tirade had strongly suggested that he no longer had any interest in courting her acceptance. Things were now worse than they had ever been between the two, and Rion was certain about one thing only:

If Jovvi wasn't returned to their midst soon, there might not *be* a midst for her to be returned to!

TWENTY-ONE

Vallant strode out of the inn and closed the door behind him, then he moved more slowly toward the stable. It had grown rather cool out, but even if it had been downright cold he would have preferred being outside to remaining with the others. And for once being closed in had nothing to do with the preference.

The ground under his feet was hard-packed earth, dry from all the days it hadn't rained. Vallant paced it in a deliberate way, trying to use his awareness of rain to come to blot out memory of what he'd said to Tamrissa. He hadn't known he was going to say that, it had just come boiling out all on its own. Obviously things had been building toward the outburst ever since that first morning. . . .

Vallant sighed as he remembered how delighted he'd been, waking up alert and strong and realizing that he was whole again. His first thought had been to tell Tamrissa, so that any worry she might be feeling would be laid to rest. He'd dressed quickly and had gone down to the inn's dining room where she and the others were breakfasting—only to have her raise that brick wall again. She'd made it perfectly clear that she wanted nothing more to do with him, and all because of *her* interpretation of what had happened between them.

Scuffing at the dirt with the toe of one shoe, Vallant remembered again how he'd felt. As he'd sat down to breakfast he'd recalled his intention to win her over again—and at that point had wondered why he ought to bother. Because he loved her? Yes, he certainly did still love her, but he wasn't also a lover of pain. And that was all he seemed to get from her on a regular basis, the pain of accusation.

Leaning a shoulder against the wall of the inn, Vallant felt that pain all over again. Ever since he'd met Tamrissa he'd been guilty of *something* in her eyes, and he no longer felt willing to accept the accusation. It was true that he had his problems, but she had problems of her own that she made no effort to solve. Her lack of trust had her constantly challenging his intentions and actions, with everything being interpreted from *her* point of view.

The unfairness of that had obviously been eating away at him, until it built to the explosion of a few minutes earlier. It had been something that had had to be said, but that didn't make the memory of it easier to live with. He'd deliberately given Tamrissa pain after he'd sworn he'd never do that, but sometimes the truth *was* more painful than abuse. And we all owed ourselves and others the truth—didn't we?

Vallant hadn't quite answered that final question to his own satisfaction when the door to the inn opened. Meerk appeared, and after closing the door behind himself he walked over to Vallant.

"I've hired two of the inn's horses, and they're being saddled now," Meerk told him in a soft voice, clearly staring at Vallant through the darkness. "We've got better than an hour's ride ahead of us, and then however long it takes you to do what you're going to do. We ought to get back here in time to get a *few* hours sleep."

"If I don't end up fallin' off the horse and killin' myself," Vallant returned with a weary nod. "Growin' up, I spent most of my time in or on the water. The few times I was forced onto horseback, I didn't exactly cover myself with glory."

"It just takes practice," Meerk assured him, clearly trying to be supportive. "There are also some tricks to make the time a bit easier, and since I need you alive I'll just have to share them. I'd let you practice some around here—if we had the time. Unfortunately, I don't think we do."

"You've changed your mind?" Vallant asked, suddenly very intent on the conversation. "Did something happen to cause that?"

"You might say so," Meerk agreed with a judicious nod. "After I discovered that it was lethe which they were giving to the captives, I had the time to look around a bit, so to speak. I'd had to wait until they'd made camp before I was able to get close enough, and a single piece of information seemed too little for the amount of time I'd spent trailing after them."

Vallant nodded his understanding, at the same time encouraging the man to continue, which he did.

"It suddenly came to me to wonder just how much they carried in the way of supplies," Meerk said, glancing around every now and again in an obvious effort to make certain they weren't being overheard. "It's been clear that they're under orders not to come in contact with any towns or villages or even inns or roadhouses. This road trends westward without going through any towns, and that's probably why they're using it. When I checked, they only had another three or so days of supplies left."

"Which means they expect to get where they're goin' in less time than that," Vallant said, understanding at once. "You never take *exactly* enough supplies, not unless you have no choice. Unexpected delays are always croppin' up, so you're best off plannin' for them from the beginnin'. I'd just like to know how much overage they allowed for: a single day, a day and a half, *two* days?"

"That's the question that changed my mind," Meerk said with another nod. "They *probably* don't have more than a single day's extra rations, not when they can always find a place to buy supplies in a real emergency, but I can't quite make myself count on that. If the guess turns out to be wrong, we could lose every captive in the convoy."

"Where are those horses?" Vallant asked, abruptly turning toward the stable. More urgency filled him now than ever before, and the need to be on his way rose up and held him with a heavy hand.

It wasn't really long before a stableboy led out two mounts, but to Vallant it almost felt like hours. Meerk tossed the boy a couple of coppers, joining Vallant in ignoring the stablehand's very obvious curiosity. People rarely hired horses from an inn in the dead of night, and not to be returned in just a few hours. It wasn't as if the inn didn't have females available if that was what they were after. . . .

Vallant could almost hear the boy's thoughts, but he pushed away everything but the need to remember the little he knew about riding horses. Mounting was no problem, and it was pleasant to find that the stirrups were the proper length, but that was the last of Vallant's pleasure for a while. When Meerk urged his horse into motion Vallant's mount followed, almost unseating Vallant with the unexpected motion.

Hanging on with knees and fists kept Vallant seated until they moved a short way down the road, and then Meerk took some time to offer the help he'd promised. It didn't magically make Vallant a master rider, but also being told that Meerk's talent had a light hold on both horses to keep them under control at least let Vallant relax a bit. The horse couldn't possibly run away with him, a comforting thought he really needed.

It was closer to an hour and a half before they reached

the vicinity of the convoy. Vallant happily joined Meerk in dismounting and tying his horse, then followed the man through the sparse woods to the camp. They had to silently skirt a bored sentry, but that turned out to be no trouble at all. A pair of moments later they stopped near some bushes, just beyond the clearing the convoy had camped in.

"There's another clearing a short distance away from this one with a corral built in it," Meerk said in an almost soundless whisper. "All the horses are in it, with guards around its perimeter."

Vallant nodded as he studied the ten large wagons which had been drawn up in a half circle around the clearing. The canvas enclosing each of them made it impossible to see what they contained, but Vallant's ability told him there were human beings inside. That particular arrangement and amount of water could mean nothing else, but that was all he got. Nothing in the way of an awareness of Jovvi and Lorand came, and that set Vallant to worrying. What if Meerk's information was wrong, and their groupmates were somewhere else entirely . . . ?

Taking a deep breath, Vallant forced himself back to calm. There might not be evidence that Jovvi and Lorand really were there, but there also wasn't proof that they were elsewhere. The only thing to do was to go ahead as planned and hope they weren't wasting their time. If he hadn't been so agitated, he would have thought to ask Rion to accompany them. If the two of them linked up, they might have had more success in searching for their groupmates.

But that was no longer possible, and Vallant realized he'd better hurry. The coming rain was no longer as far off as it had been, and it would be best to get through and away before it arrived. Some of the guardsmen had rolled up in the their blankets near the dying fire rather than finding places under the wagons. Once the rain started, they would surely be awake and trying to find a place to keep dry.

So Vallant opened wide to the power, then reached out to look around with something other than his eyes. A large water barrel was tied to each of the wagons, and inside each wagon was a smaller keg containing something other than water. The liquid in the smaller keg was oily to Vallant's senses, slick and denser than water. A part of the liquid *was* water, but certainly not all of it.

Never before had Vallant tried to use his magic on a liquid other than water, and he frankly didn't even know if it was supposed to be possible. What he did know, however, was that he had to try, and not only try but succeed. Jovvi and Lorand's safety was at stake, and in that particular circumstance there was nothing he would refuse to try.

Spreading out fingers of talent, he began to examine the oily liquid more closely. Removing the water from it would have been simplicity itself, but that wasn't what he had to do. His aim was to move the entire volume of liquid to the large water barrel, and then replace it with undiluted water. But he first had to get a *grip* on the liquid, and the oiliness was making that difficult. His mental fingers kept sliding off . . .

Vallant usually pushed hard when he had a problem, but suddenly something told him to ease off instead. Pushing works to free a wagon stuck in the mud, but not all by itself. The best idea is to combine pushing and pulling, the two actions producing what both individually cannot. Pushing combined with pulling . . . and the memory of plaited patterns done with ropes of water . . .

And that was the key he needed. Those patterns he'd been taught . . . the fools using them thought of them as nothing but exercises, completely missing the fact that they were the means of reaching higher and more distant levels of ability. It was something Vallant wanted to look into more thoroughly, but right now there was something more pressing which had to be done.

Using a variation of one of the patterns, Vallant was able to get a grip on the oily liquid. Transferring it to the companion water barrel on the outside, then returning pure water, took very little time, but the process had to be repeated ten times. Then Vallant checked the entire camp for other containers which might hold water, and found more than a dozen waterskins. Most of them were either attached to saddles or stowed under wagon seats, and Vallant quickly exchanged their contents as well.

"What's wrong?" Meerk suddenly asked in a whisper. "It's taking so long . . . aren't you able to find a way to do it? We've got to get out of here before the rain starts.''

"We can leave right now," Vallant whispered back, feeling more exhilarated than tired. "It's all done, except for those waterskins containin' alcohol rather than water. There were just a few of them, and hopefully their owners don't start to drain them first thing in the mornin'.''

"You did the waterskins too?" Meerk asked, looking startled. "I hadn't expected—Well, that was really good work. Let's get back now.''

Vallant nodded and carefully followed Meerk back toward the horses, all the while wondering why the man had been surprised. He'd made a point of saying that Vallant was supposed to be a High talent, and shouldn't a High talent be *expected* to do a thorough job? Unless Meerk had had something else in mind ...

Like hoping that Vallant would fail when they needed him the most. Vallant untied his horse and mounted silently, doing nothing to show the agitation suddenly in his thoughts. Their aim all along had been to free Lorand and Jovvi, but suddenly Meerk appeared to have an objective of his own. And, since he seemed to have been hoping for Vallant's failure, that objective could only have Tamrissa at its center.

While their horses picked a careful way through the woods and back to the road, Vallant deliberately kept himself from glancing at Meerk. He'd been fully aware of the burly man's attraction to Tamrissa, but since nothing overt had been said or done, Vallant had let the matter ride. Now ...

Now it was time to wonder if Meerk hadn't decided to sacrifice Lorand and Jovvi, which could very well make Tamrissa more available. If there was no Blending for Tamrissa to be a part of, and if Vallant were exposed as less than what he was supposed to be ... But there had been those words between him and Tamrissa, and he *hadn't* been exposed as less, so what would the plan be now?

And just how reliable would Meerk be tomorrow, when they made the real effort to free their groupmates ... ?

TWENTY-TWO

"My lords and ladies, thank you for coming to this meeting," Kambil said, smiling gravely at the assembled throng. "If you've all gotten refreshments, we can move on to the reason why you're here."

Kambil paused to look around, but no one jumped up to refill a teacup or snatch a finger cake. In point of fact most of his audience looked as though they would be happier with a drink a good deal stronger than tea. The rest looked as though they would be happiest away from the palace completely, but that desire they weren't about to be granted. They all currently sat in a medium-sized audience room, with guest chairs arranged more or less casually across the floor. Seating for the Five was on a slightly raised dais, and just now only two of those seats were filled.

"Lord Bron and I are meeting with all of you today because of the disturbing news which has been coming to us over the last few days," Kambil continued. "Our public Seating ceremony was sparsely attended as far as Advisory representation—your superiors—was concerned, and at first we felt hurt. Then, when we discovered that those who were missing were missing from their homes and offices as well, we grew concerned. Does anyone here have any idea what could have become of them?"

Quite a lot of shifting and throat-clearing went on at that point, but the congregation of secretaries and assistants to the former Advisors seemed to have nothing to say. Kambil exchanged a glance with Bron, who showed the same sober visage that Kambil did, then he sighed audibly.

"At this point, I don't think I'd mind hearing that they were all off picnicking somewhere," he commented, making no effort to control anyone in the group. There were other Spirit magic users present, some of them fairly strong Middles. . . . "You don't happen to think that that's where they are?"

A large number of heads shook in response to that, some with smiles, but still no words. Most of them were terrified for one reason or another, and Kambil had to bring them past that.

"It pains me to tell you this, but three of the missing *have* been located," he announced, putting as much sympathy and personal angst into the words as possible. "One was murdered in front of witnesses and under rather bizarre circumstances, and the other two were victims of ordinary accidents. I'll tell you frankly that we don't like the sound of any of it, and we've sent representatives out to investigate."

"If we're going to be frank, let's be blunt as well," Bron put in, also looking around at the group seated with them. "We expected to lean rather heavily on the advice of those long experienced men, but suddenly they're gone and *we're* left twisting in the wind. If someone considered it a good idea to do away with all those innocent people just to make *us* look bad, they won't think as much of the idea once we catch up to them—and that I promise you."

"Surely no one here could be part of something like that, Bron," Kambil said once the muttering comments had died down a bit. The combination of the suggestion and Bron's grim attitude concerning it had affected their audience positively, the first step past their resistance that Kambil had been trying for.

"There may or may not be someone out to do *us* harm," Kambil went on, "but nevertheless people are being hurt and killed. I agree that we have to get to the bottom of the mystery, and that's one of the main reasons we asked you here. You people are the ones who worked most closely with the men who are missing and dead. Isn't there *anything* any of you can tell us to make the search a bit easier? If what you say points us in the right direction, please be assured that our gratitude will be golden and weighty.''

That caused even more muttered comments, so Kambil left his seat on the dais and went to the tea service to refill his cup. Giving their audience a chance to think things over and find what to tell them about would only be an unimportant beginning. If someone powerful and dangerous was named as a suspect and it became necessary to remove that person, finding ''evidence'' implicating him in one or more deaths or disappearances would not be difficult.

But the search for the supposed guilty was only an excuse for bringing in these people. Before the meeting ended he and Bron and Selendi and Homin would have private meetings scheduled with each of them, firstly to find out what their employers were involved in, and secondly to choose those who would continue the work. The ideal candidate would be capable of handling matters alone, but not so ambitious that he or she would put private concerns before those of the Five. *He* would have to make the final selections, Kambil knew, but first the others would help with the weeding out.

Once his cup was refilled, Kambil turned and walked slowly back to his place on the dais. Some of those in the audience seemed ready to make ''helpful'' suggestions, and he was more than ready to listen. Bron, too, had noticed the change in attitude, and he therefore exchanged a satisfied glance with Kambil as Kambil resumed his seat.

For the next hour he and Bron listened attentively as more and more suspicions and accusations were voiced, but there was no need to try to remember all of it. Kambil had arranged for transcribers to listen in to what was said, and a complete and accurate report of the meeting would be available later. But each new person or subject mentioned brought comments from some of those who hadn't yet spoken, until at the end of the hour the entire group was almost to the point of fighting for the chance to speak.

''My lords and ladies, please!'' Kambil was finally forced to interrupt, holding up a soothing hand. ''You'll all have the chance to tell us everything you think we should know, but this isn't the best way of doing it. You'll all be given appointments with one of our Five for later today or tomorrow, and if more time is required than we've scheduled, we'll simply *re*schedule. I'll call the clerks in now, and those of you on the list for this afternoon will remain. The rest of you can return home, until the messengers come with the times of your appointments. Thank you for—"

"Excellency, please excuse my interrupting, but I believe I have information you should be given right now."

The man who had stood to speak looked determined, but his mind quivered with nervousness. Kambil felt tempted to dismiss him with a reprimand, but the man's thoughts said he believed he spoke the truth.

"I'm afraid I don't place you, sir," Kambil said after a moment, feeling the man's immediate extreme relief. "Please introduce yourself and tell us what you consider so important."

"Thank you, Excellency," he said with a bow, forcibly keeping himself from babbling. "I am Lord Rimen Howser, and I'm in charge of certain . . . delicate matters for Lord Embisson Ruhl. Have you been told that Lord Embisson was viciously attacked by thieves, and now lies badly hurt at home?"

"No, we weren't," Kambil replied with complete honesty, frowning as he exchanged another glance with Bron. "We were so preoccupied with the Advisors . . . Did I say that this has definitely gotten out of hand? Do go on."

"Excellency, I would be pleased to, but I feel that this topic should be reserved for your ears alone," Rimen replied at once. "With your permission, of course."

"We'll rely on your judgment, Lord Rimen," Kambil agreed, deciding that privacy could only be a small wasted effort if the man exaggerated. "Please remain here after the others leave. As for the rest of you, thank you again for your cooperation."

That was a dismissal none of them could ignore, so they rose, bowed or curtsied, then headed for the door. The clerks would separate out those who were on the schedule for that afternoon, but the first of the interviews would have to wait.

"All right, Lord Rimen, we're alone now," Kambil pointed out once the door was closed behind the last of the others. "Just what delicate matters are you in charge of for Lord Embisson?"

"It's my responsibility, Excellency, to arrange the transportation out of Gan Garee for those candidates for High practitioner who pass the tests." Rimen now spoke without circumlocution, and Kambil was able to appreciate his earlier reticence. "Not everyone is aware of this practice, you understand, nor do they question the absence of such hopefuls except for when and where they're needed. Starting speculation about where they're sent would be completely contrary to everyone's best interests."

"That's quite true, Lord Rimen," Kambil agreed, wondering if the man would prove to be someone he could use to good purpose—without being controlled. "And what have you learned in the course of this task that you feel we should know?"

"Allow me to begin the tale from the beginning," he said, coming forward to take one of the chairs closest to the dais. "Some days ago I sent out our last convoy, but had to do so with one of its scheduled passengers missing. One of the fools charged with seeing to the segments until the time of their departure had 'misplaced' one of them, but he insisted that it wasn't his fault. Lady Eltrina Razas had taken a fancy to the man, and once he was drugged she insisted on 'borrowing' the segment until it was time for him to leave."

"Lady Eltrina Razas," Bron interrupted in a musing tone. "For some reason her name sounds familiar, and I have the oddest conviction that it has something to do with the competitions."

"It does," Rimen agreed with a cool smile. "Lady Eltrina was in charge of the challenging Blendings which the animals formed, and that was where she saw the one named Ro. He apparently impressed her so greatly that—"

"Just a moment!" Kambil said sharply, no longer worrying about the length of the tale Rimen meant to tell. "Did you say Ro, as in Vallant Ro? One of the five who faced us in the final competition?"

"Well . . . yes," Rimen acknowledged, suddenly looking less sure of himself. "You have my word that everything was perfectly in order, just as it was with the other two members of his group who were already in the wagons. I—"

"I don't believe this," Bron said, turning his head to

Kambil. "When they were carried off the sands I assumed it was to have their throats cut in private. It was difficult to imagine anyone not knowing how dangerous they were, but apparently I overestimated the intelligence of those who were in charge. They actually let those people live!"

"I know exactly how you feel," Kambil said, furious anger beginning to rise inside him as he turned back to Rimen. "Give us the details quickly, and without extraneous comment!"

"I went to Lady Eltrina's house, and forced her to admit that Ro was no longer in her possession," Rimen said immediately in obedience, the words falling over one another. "She said it was the female claimed by Lord Lanir who had stolen Ro, so I went to Lord Lanir's secondary estate and found him mindless from burnout. After that I went to Lady Hallina Mardimil's town house, and found that she'd left for Haven Wraithside—but without her son, whom she, too, had claimed. I came to the conclusion that all three of them had escaped restraint, but could not find anyone to report to. Please forgive me, Excellency—!"

By then Kambil was on his feet, turning the air blue with the foulest curses he could put tongue to. Three of the five members of the Blending stronger than theirs were free, when all the time he'd imagined them safely dead.

"What about the other two?" Bron demanded harshly when Kambil paused for breath. "You said they were already in that convoy of yours, but are you certain? Could they have been carried off without your knowledge?"

"Absolutely not," Rimen denied, his mind confirming the assertion. "I sent the convoy on its way before going after Ro, and all the other segments were precisely where they were supposed to be."

"That means the three on the loose could be following the convoy," Bron said, also now on his feet. "I have no idea how they would have found out about it, but we can't assume they didn't. If they aren't hiding out somewhere in the city, they could be following the convoy. Where is it headed, and what sort of place is it?"

"I—I have no idea," Rimen stuttered, now even more frightened. "I send the convoys off in the direction I'm told to, but only the captains of the escorts know the location of their final destinations. This one headed west . . .''

"Turn out every member of the guard,'' Kambil growled to Bron, trying to ignore the chill which threatened to spread along his intestines. ''I want the entire city searched, but I also want guardsmen sent after that convoy. Those people *have* to be found!''

Bron nodded curtly and headed for the door, and after a moment Kambil strode after him. This couldn't be happening, not *now*! Not when they were just about to make everything turn out right! Curse those five, curse them! They might still be living now, but once the guard caught up to them it would be with orders to destroy them on sight!

TWENTY-THREE

It was raining the next morning, but Rion used his Air magic to put up a shield for all of us until we climbed into the coach. Alsin and Vallant Ro had returned somewhat late the night before, and now Alsin was off again with Grath. Buying a horse for Alsin had depleted our funds even more, but they couldn't very well ride double. Aside from the fact that Grath's horse would have been too overburdened, someone would surely have noticed.

I settled myself on the coach seat, trying to think about nothing but what was ahead of us, but the turmoil in my mind refused to allow that. Last night . . . last night Vallant had said things I couldn't just dismiss or forget, and even my dreams had been filled with uncertainty and distress. Vallant *had* acted badly toward me after I'd gotten him out of Eltrina Razas's house, but—was that really the same as the way *I'd* treated *him* after he'd taken care of that drunk . . . ?

I looked out at the rain while everyone else took their places in the coach, listening to the silent argument in my head. That argument had been going on since last night, but neither side could be considered being even close to winning. Had I really been insisting that Vallant be perfect? I couldn't remember doing that, but I *could* remember all the times he'd treated me as though I were helpless. If I'd managed to give that back to him for once, was it really the terrible thing he'd made it out to be?

"Alsin said he would have Lidris increase the pace of the horses," Rion told us as the coach began to move. "By noon we want to be as close as possible to the convoy without being discovered, so we can take advantage of the situation if the guards begin to doze. They'll stop for the noon meal and to dose their captives, and by then we may even have help from the captives themselves."

"But we'd better not count on that help," Vallant said, looking out of his own window. "Even if the lingerin' effects of the lethe doesn't keep them from touchin' the power, their minds may be too scattered for them to be effective."

"Then we'll accomplish their rescue by ourselves," Rion said, clearly refusing to lose his determination. "No matter what happens or what anyone does to try to prevent it, our groupmates will be free again by tonight."

"Rion, what will you do if the guardsmen aren't as sleepy as they should be?" Naran suddenly asked, the question casual in an odd sort of way. "I mean, what if they've been drinking the sedative the way we want them to, but something has happened to make them more alert than usual? How will you get around that?"

"It could happen," I said, interrupting Rion's gentle pooh-poohing of the idea. "If this is an area where they've learned they have to be especially alert, or if some wild animal's tracks have been discovered, or if any one of another dozen things has happened, they may not be as sleepy as we expect. So Naran's question is worth repeating: what will we do if that's what we find?"

"All right, we'll do the only thing we can," Rion said,

now conceding the need to make an alternate plan. "I'll render any patrolling guards unconscious by taking away most of their air, and then do the same to any others who require a similar treatment. Beyond that, it's up to you two."

"I think . . . *maybe* . . . I can do somethin' more effective than druggin' their water," Vallant said slowly, now looking at Rion. "I've been thinkin' about it, and it might not have been necessary to play with their drinkin' water. That testin' had me puttin' water into really small containers, and last night I learned how to move the lethe around as easily as water. I don't know if it's possible, but maybe I can put the sedative directly *into* their bodies . . ."

"Without having to wait for them to drink it!" Rion said in delighted surprise. "What a marvelous idea! It *is* too bad that you didn't think of it last night, but then you and Alsin would have had to take care of the captives all alone. Now that the rest of us are here to help . . . And what will *you* do, Tamrissa?"

"The only thing I *can* do," I replied with a shrug. "I may have to spread myself a bit thin, but I'll keep the guardsmen and drivers away from the wagons. We don't want them threatening to kill our people to get *us* to surrender, so that means we'll have to make our move only after all the wagons are empty of guardsmen and drivers."

"It may not be too easy tellin' that," Vallant said with a frown. "If we miss seein' one of them enterin' a wagon, how will we know that he's in there?"

"I've been thinking about that, and I may have an answer," I replied, trying to fight off the urge to speak diffidently. "People who are awake and active should have a higher body temperature than those who are unconscious, so I ought to be able to tell that way. Once we get there and I can look around I'll know better."

"We all need that look around," Rion said with a nod, taking Naran's hand in order to stroke it. "And if we're prepared against an eventuality that happens to come about, we'll have Naran to thank for warning us."

"No, silly, *I* didn't do anything," Naran protested with a pleased laugh. "I'm just used to thinking about the possibility of the worst thing happening, because it so often does.

You three will be the ones to free the others, and I'm more than happy to just sit and watch you do it.''

They exchanged a brief kiss then, which immediately made me look out the window again. It wasn't that I begrudged the happiness that Rion and Naran had together, it was simply that I couldn't bear to watch it. *I'd* had something like that once, and I didn't like to think that I might be responsible for having lost it.

Most of the morning disappeared behind the distraction of rampaging thoughts, and the silence in the coach did nothing to dispel those thoughts. The rain continued to fall in a way that said it would probably keep up for the rest of the day, and our more-rapid-than-usual progress along the road sent water sheeting up and away from us. We should have been damp and miserable because of the glassless windows of the coach, but I had the feeling that Rion was blocking out the rain. So that means we were simply not-damp and miserable, at least as far as I was concerned. . . .

"That's Alsin just ahead," Vallant said suddenly as the coach abruptly began to slow. "He's wavin', so he probably wants to talk to us."

The prospect of finally getting down to it made my heart pound a bit faster, but with anticipation rather than fear. If I'd had to sit there thinking for much longer, I probably would have ended up screaming in frustrated insanity. As it was the coach slowed to a stop, and Alsin rode up on Rion and Vallant's side of the coach.

"We have a problem," he announced without preamble, his face looking drawn as well as wet. "The guardsmen and drivers should be ready to nod off by now, but they're not. In fact they look more wide-awake than ever, as if they're expecting some sort of attack. If we go up against them now, there's no telling *what* will happen."

"Yes there is," I said at once, before any of the others could comment. "If we go up against them now, we'll win the way we're supposed to. If we don't even try, I'll probably be dead of old age before we do get around to it."

"In other words, we're goin' ahead with it," Vallant said as Rion's expression told us he agreed with me. "We can't afford to wait for a time when they'll be less alert, because they may get to their destination before that happens. You do remember our discussin' the matter last night?''

"Yes, I remember," Alsin conceded with a sigh. "I'm sure you're right, but I'd be happier if we at least waited until tonight. Will waiting another half day make that much of a difference?''

"You tell us," Rion put frankly, gazing calmly at Alsin. "Can you guarantee that they won't reach their destination before tonight? If so, I'm sure we'll agree to wait. If not . . .''

"All right, you've made your point," Alsin grumbled, now looking even more unhappy than he had. "The attack goes ahead as planned, even if it isn't the best of times. The coach can take you a little closer to where the convoy has pulled off the road, but after that you'll have to walk.''

He turned his horse around and moved toward the front of the coach, and we could hear him saying something to our driver. After that we began to move again, and the four of us inside the coach exchanged glances. We really were about to do it, and once started there would be no turning back.

After about another half mile, the coach pulled to a stop again. Alsin was right there, and he dismounted as we all got out. I'd spoken quietly to Rion, so what we got out into was the pouring rain. Rion might need every bit of his strength for the coming confrontation, so wasting it on shielding us from the rain could end up being fatal instead of just silly. It would hardly kill us to get wet, not when we'd have no trouble drying off again—if we won.

Alsin tied his horse to the coach, then he led off into the woods. Just a short distance up the road it was possible to see the disturbance of the mud where a large number of wagons had turned off, so we followed silently into the trees. Letting them know we were there would have been stupid—assuming they didn't already know. If I'd put people out on guard, they would have been people with the ability to know what the approach of other human beings felt or looked like. Naran had made no effort to go along with us, not when we might be needing to defend ourselves in just a few short minutes. Having someone else to protect in addition to ourselves could mean the difference between victory and defeat.

It had been raining too long for it to be any drier under the trees. The grass under my feet kept trying to sink my shoes into the mud beneath, the bushes showered my clothes with water as I passed, and the leaves overhead dripped, dripped, dripped. It was the most exciting and enlivening time I'd ever had, which means I really had to work hard to control my excitement. I needed to be calm and in possession of myself. . . .

And then it came to me that I might be able to help us get closer without the sentries noticing us. In this weather the best sentries would have Fire magic as well as Earth magic, but there was nothing I could do about those with Earth magic. Fire magic, though, was another story. . . .

"Hold up a minute," I whispered to Alsin, causing him to pause in the cautious way he'd been advancing. We'd just passed Grath's horse, tied to a tree, so the convoy couldn't be all that far ahead. "Just how close are we now?"

"We're almost there," he answered in a return whisper, his face creased into a frown. "If you'll just be patient—"

"No, no, I'm not being impatient," I interrupted, wiping my face with one hand. "If we're almost close enough to be detected, I think I can arrange a distraction."

"Then go to it," he said, losing the frown. "We're almost close enough to step on them."

I nodded to acknowledge that, then took a better grip on the power before sending out my ability. What I now used was the fingers of my talent, trying to touch with them what I couldn't yet see. I didn't know if it would work, but it couldn't really hurt to try . . . especially if I . . . diffused the strength I used, making it hard to tell from which direction it came. . . .

All these new ideas were something I wanted to think about, but right now there wasn't time. My searching fingers of talent had found something, and it took no more than a moment to understand what. There were a large number of sources of heat, the stronger sources undoubtedly horses. The lesser ones had to be the guardsmen and drivers, and the least were surely the captives. There was also a pattern of sorts to their placement, especially the one lesser source of heat closest to us. That must be Grath, watching them while Alsin brought us back.

There were other individual sources of heat ranged around the area where all the others were, and those must be the sentries. I could tell just where they were, so I picked two places, one on each of the far sides of the camp, and heated patches of air in those places. The patches ought to be obvious to anyone with Fire magic, even Low talents, and also ought to distract those talents from our approach.

"All right, let's continue on now," I whispered once it was done. "And since the distraction won't be good for more than a few minutes, let's hurry."

"What did you do?" Alsin asked, his expression more than curious. "I think I hear some shouting . . . No, never mind. You can tell me later, once this is behind us."

He turned and hurried on then, and in another moment we reached Grath where he stood and watched the camp. The scout turned to look at us, his expression almost a match to the one Alsin had worn.

"Is one of you responsible for that minor riot?" he asked, gesturing toward the camp we could just see through the trees. "They were alert but quiet a minute ago, and now they're all running around because someone shouted an alarm."

"Yes, Dama Domon supplied a distraction," Alsin answered softly with his own distraction in his voice. "If none of them are coming our way, this may be the best time to do whatever it is you three mean to do."

"None of them *are* coming this way," I confirmed, able to tell that easily. "The only problem is, three of the wagons have people in them who aren't captives. And now that I'm really looking, I can see that the captives' body temperatures aren't as low as sleeping peoples' should be. Some of the captives are apparently coming out of it more rapidly than others, but they all seem to be coming out of it."

"We should have thought of that," Vallant said, speaking primarily to Alsin. "By takin' them off the sedative and lettin' them come awake, we've brought attention to them. Those who give them the sedatives *have* to have noticed, and that may be why they aren't fallin' asleep. Their victims aren't being good, docile captives, and they're worried."

"Then we'd better get to it," Rion said, straightening where he stood. "Tamrissa, can you direct me to the wagons which have other than captives in them?"

"Good idea," I said, knowing immediately what he meant. "If you put those guardsmen out first, we won't have to worry about what they're doing when we go after their friends. The wagons they're in are the third, seventh, and ninth ones, counting from the first in line."

Rion nodded and looked toward the wagons, and three minutes later the sources of body heat that had to mean guardsmen were horizontal instead of vertical. All three of them had gone down together, which means I was impressed.

"All right, it's done," Rion said once the bodies had been down for an additional minute. "Please keep a watch on them if you can, Tamrissa, to see if they come awake again too quickly. If they do and we haven't won yet, I'll have to put them down a second time. What do we do next?"

"Next it's my turn," Vallant said, also drawing himself up. "If Tamrissa will guard the wagons against anyone doin' anythin' foolish with the last of their strength, we'll see if it works."

Alsin and Grath exchanged a glance filled with nervous curiosity, but neither of them asked Vallant what he meant. And Vallant was too absorbed in gazing toward the wagons to notice them. We could now see quite a number of men in uniforms—and men in ordinary clothes—running about around the wagons, mostly shouting and pointing in the direction of my distraction. I watched those men, some of them having begun to look in other directions as well—and then many of them began to stagger! It was as if something had hit all of them at the same time, as if they were puppets and someone had begun to cut their strings.

Most of the men in view sat or fell to the ground, and so did the heat sources I was still able to detect on the far side of the camp. Vallant was putting the lethe directly into them, into their blood, probably, and the idea of that was rather startling. It's one thing to put a liquid into a small jar, quite another to put it into the tiny channels which carry our blood around our bodies. But he seemed to be doing it, and the guardsmen and drivers were responding by falling over.

But not all of them. When I found myself moving toward the line of wagons Rion and Vallant were right with me, and Vallant still wore that look of concentration. Probably because some of the men were still fighting to stay on their feet, struggling to keep awake despite the sedative being put into them. They were the only ones still between us and our Blendingmates so we didn't let their stubbornness keep us away, but we did watch them.

And that turned out to be a very wise decision. I suppose there are always people around who don't react to things the way everyone else does, and three of those guardsmen refused to fall over. They were big men, taller and huskier than those around them, and when they saw us coming toward them they drew long, ugly-looking knives, and one led the other two in attacking us.

If you've ever been attacked by screaming, wild-looking men coming toward you at a shambling run, you may be able to understand how I felt. That sort of thing has to be terrifying even if you're used to it, although I can't imagine how anyone might get used to it. The part of me not touching the power wanted to scream and run in the other direction, away from the madmen who were clearly ready to end my life.

But the part of me which did touch the power reacted differently to that sort of thing. One of the three came directly toward me, and he was the one given full attention. I stopped to regard him calmly while he came near enough to slash down at me with that long knife, and then—and then his knife moved through a flash of flame so intense that most of the blade vaporized as it passed through. Lack of balance caused him to stumble when the downward arc of his swing found him left with little more than a hilt, and he stood gawking stupidly between me and what was left of his weapon.

Rion stood to my left, and out of the corner of my eyes I'd been able to see that the man who swung his knife at *him* had also not reached his target. The knife came to a jarring stop in front of and above Rion's head, probably because of a shield of hardened air. Fear paled the man's face, just as it did with the man in front of Vallant, who stood to my right. That time it was a thick layer of ice which stopped the knife, and all three men were clearly shaken. Then they were choking and falling to their knees, which obviously meant that Rion had taken away their air. They might have resisted the sedative, but lack of air to breathe can't be resisted.

As soon as the three stopped moving, Rion, Vallant, and I continued toward the wagons with Alsin and Grath trailing along behind. I'd expected to have to look through all of them, but now that Rion and Vallant stood so close to me, something about the sixth and ninth wagons seemed to draw me. And I wasn't the only one who felt that, as Vallant gestured toward the ninth wagon.

"Let's start with that one," he suggested, staring at it in the same way I did. "I have this feelin' . . ."

"And so do I," Rion agreed after glancing at me. "It seems to be drawing me in some way, and I'd say that Tamrissa also feels it. Are either of you getting anything from that wagon three places ahead?"

"You mean the sixth wagon," I said as Vallant simply nodded. "Yes, it's just the same. But this one is closer, so let's start here."

"Wait just a minute," Alsin called from behind us as we began to move again. "What about the rest of the guardsmen and drivers? I don't see more than half of them scattered around on the ground here."

"The rest are scattered around on the ground beyond the wagons," I replied, smiling over my shoulder in order to soothe his nervousness. "Aren't you close enough to them to tell?"

"Only just barely," he said after a second's worth of hesitation, his brow wrinkled with effort. "And yes, you're right, they *are* all out of it. If you three are starting with the ninth wagon, Grath and I will start with the tenth."

"Good idea," Vallant told him, an odd . . . reserve of sorts in his voice. "Just keep half a talented eye open in case some of these guardsmen start comin' around too soon. If you find one that does, just give us a shout."

Alsin nodded, and he and a disturbed-looking Grath headed for the wagon behind the one *we* had the most interest in. . . .

TWENTY-FOUR

Rion helped Tamrissa into the wagon, then followed with Vallant close behind. It was dim inside the wagon with the canvas closed tight all around, but Tamrissa took care of that by creating a ball of brightness which she hung in the air above them. That let them look around, to see the six pallets on which six people lay, the pallets arranged three to each side of the wagon. The people, men and women both, were moving in discomfort, as though they were getting ready to awaken. In the middle of the wagon a guardsman lay slumped in unconsciousness, one of those Rion had put down earlier. And at the front of the wagon, moving even more than the others, was—

"Jovvi!" Tamrissa cried, stepping quickly over the unconscious guardsman to rush to their sister's side. She knelt and raised Jovvi with an arm around her shoulders, then smoothed the tangle of her once-beautiful hair. "Jovvi, it's Tamrissa. Can you hear me? Can you wake up all the way?"

"Tam-ma . . ." The word was slurred and garbled and very soft, but Jovvi was actually trying to speak! "Too . . . much . . . floating . . . Help . . . wake up . . ."

"I think she means she needs help to wake up," Tamrissa said, looking up at them with distress. "*We* can't do anything to help, but maybe Alsin can. Rion, please go and call him in here."

"I don't think that will do it," Vallant said, putting a hand to Rion's arm to keep him from leaving. "Now that I've got the feel of that sedative, I can tell it's in Jovvi's

199

blood—but it's too spread out for me to remove it. Meerk's just a Middle, so it's probably beyond *him* to remove it as well. We'll just have to wait until the lethe is washed out of their systems by their own bodies.''

''Lorand could probably filter it out, but Alsin's not Lorand,'' Rion was forced to agree when Tamrissa looked as though she might argue with what Vallant had said. ''Most likely they'll all have to come out of it on their own, which might actually be for the best. We should prepare for their awakening, and do something permanent about the guardsmen and drivers.''

''And while we're at it, let's get Lorand and put him in here with Jovvi,'' Vallant said with a nod. ''That way Tamrissa can be guardin' the two of them together while we take care of the ones who kept them like this.''

Tamrissa's nod showed she'd changed her mind about arguing, and she went back to paying attention to Jovvi while Rion and Vallant gave their own attention to the unconscious guardsman. The two of them carried the man out of the wagon and put him on the ground near his companions, then Rion followed Vallant to the sixth wagon. They climbed inside and peered through the dimness, and sure enough, the middle pallet on the left-hand side held Lorand's feebly struggling body. Once they found him, Vallant went to one knee beside the pallet.

''It's Vallant and Rion, Lorand,'' Vallant said slowly and clearly, a hand on their brother's shoulder. ''You keep tryin' to wake up, but don't worry about what's happenin'. They had you for a while, but we've got you back now.''

''Val-nt,'' Lorand croaked, obviously trying to open his eyes. ''Where . . .'m I?''

''Right now you're in a wagon,'' Vallant answered, ''but in a few minutes you'll be in a different wagon. I'm goin' to carry you to where Jovvi and Tamrissa are, and Tamrissa will keep you both company until you wake up. You won't be worryin', will you?''

''No . . . won't . . . worry,'' Lorand mumbled, his agitation eased quite a bit. ''Need . . . t'wake . . . up.''

''That's right, you concentrate on wakin' up,'' Vallant agreed, then looked up at Rion. ''I'll pick him up, then you ought to take that pallet so we'll have somethin' to put him on in the other wagon. But I'll need help gettin' him out of here without droppin' him.''

''Helping is my specialty,'' Rion answered with a smile. ''I'll climb out with the pallet, and then I'll take half his weight. That ought to let you get out easily enough.''

Vallant nodded his agreement, then reached down to pick up Lorand. Rion used his ability to help with that, too, as Lorand was far from being a small man. After that it was simply a matter of taking the pallet out and giving the same kind of help with Lorand a second time, which let Vallant just slide out of the wagon. Then they carried their burdens back to the wagon Jovvi was in, and in another few moments Lorand was settled right beside Jovvi.

''You two and Alsin and Grath had better get on with doing something about those guardsmen,'' Tamrissa said once she had settled herself between their groupmates. ''Some of them are beginning to stir, especially the ones you put out first, Rion.''

''Then we'll take care of them first,'' Rion said, his agreement more grim and merciless than his feelings had ever been before. He'd had no idea that he had it in him to be so hard and harsh, but these people deserved nothing better. Even if they weren't privy to what would be done with their captives, they still had to know that they were taking innocent people to what might just be their doom. Claiming they were simply following orders was an excuse Rion was unwilling to accept.

The guardsmen he'd put out first were indeed stirring, so he simply put them out again—along with the others who were trying to fight against the sedative. Alsin and Grath had come out of the tenth wagon by then, and Alsin admitted that there was nothing he might do to hurry along the process of waking. With that in mind they all put their backs into carrying the guardsmen and drivers to the middle of the camp, where they lined them up in easy-to-see rows. Tying them with rope would have been a waste of time, of course, since anyone with even a Low talent in Fire magic could have gotten themselves and the rest of their friends loose with very little effort.

But chains were another matter, and it was Alsin who discovered that each guardsman had a set of fetters in his saddlebags. That meant there weren't quite enough to chain the guardsmen and drivers both, at least not individually. It did prove possible, though, to chain their prisoners wrist to ankle in the row, one man's wrist chained to the next man's ankle, and that man's ankle chained to the next man's wrist.

It took quite a while to get all that done, and once they were through Rion quieted everyone who was beginning to stir again. Then they began to look for the convoy's supplies, as they were now hungry enough to eat some of the surrounding trees. That, at least, was the way Rion felt, but the quick way the others agreed to look for food suggested that they felt the same. They'd decided against buying their lunch at the inn in which they'd spent the night, contrary to what had become their habit with other inns.

The previous night had seen them squeezed into three small rooms—the third grudgingly supplied by the landlord—and breakfast that morning had actually been reheated rather than freshly made. Rion had accepted that with dinner the night before, but a breakfast done the same was inexcusable. So they hadn't bought any lunch, and now needed something to remove the memory of their terrible breakfast.

The supplies carried by the convoy were surprisingly lavish, and Grath took over preparing the meal while the others looked on. The scout insisted on doing so, and simply glanced at Rion and the others.

"You three don't have to stand there watching me," he said with a look of amusement. "I promise not to eat it all myself, and I'll even call you when it's ready."

"What else have we got to do?" Alsin asked as he stretched a large tarpaulin across a section of the wet grass. At least it had stopped raining, for the moment, anyway. "Everything else is taken care of, and now all we can do is wait for the captives to wake up."

"You might try getting some of them up and walking," Grath suggested as he added wood to the sheltered fire which had been built by the convoy people. "I'm told that sedatives wear off more quickly like that, and the sooner they're all awake and alert, the sooner we can be on our way."

"There must be sixty people in those wagons," Vallant pointed out as Alsin's expression said he was in the midst of considering the suggestion. "Since it will take two of us to walk one of them around, we'll still be here next week if walkin' is the only way to wake them. I'm for waitin' and lettin' them do it by themselves."

Rion saw a flash of frustration in Grath's expression, but it wasn't possible to argue the logic of what Vallant had said. Grath was apparently even more eager than they were to leave that area, and Rion couldn't really blame him. But instead of arguing in a lost cause the man went back to giving all his attention to fixing them a meal, and it wasn't long before the food was ready to eat. Rion got up and went to call Tamrissa to join them, and when she left the wagon she did so with a smile.

"They actually each sat up for a few minutes," she said, relief clear in her lovely eyes. "They're pulling out of it more and more rapidly, so in a few hours they ought to be back with us. But what about Naran and our driver? They ought to be just as hungry as we are."

"I'm certain they are, which is why I mean to call them next," Rion assured her with his own smile. "I'll be back with them in just a little while."

"At least the rain has stopped for now," Tamrissa said, looking up at the sky. "It doesn't appear ready to be stopped for good, but it's nice not to need a canopy to stand under. We'll probably have to put one up when it's time to feed the captives. I'm sure they'll wake up ravenous."

"It will probably prove easier to feed them in their wagons," Rion said, considering the logistics of the thing. "They'll surely want to walk around even if the rain starts again, but eating will be more easily accomplished inside the wagons."

"You're probably right," Tamrissa agreed, her attention more on the food than on the conversation. "Let's discuss it later."

That was the most sensible suggestion Rion had heard in a long while, so he quickly agreed and then headed for where the coach had been left. Getting back to it was faster than leaving it had been, as he no longer had to worry about making noise. Naran and Lidris, the driver, stood together beside the coach, and answered his smile with ones of their own.

"Your expression says you were successful," Naran offered as soon as she saw him, her own face lighting up. "I knew you would be, but I can't seem to get out of the habit of worrying anyway."

"There's nothing left to worry about, my love," Rion told her as he folded her in his arms. "The guardsmen and drivers are all subdued, and the captives are beginning to wake up. We should have just enough time to take a meal of our own before we need to see about theirs, and ours is already prepared. If Lidris will pull the coach off the road and into the trees, we can all go back and eat."

"If'n th' horses don' wanna pull, I'll do 'er m'self," Lidris said with enthusiasm, obviously as hungry as Rion. "Gimme a quick minnit."

The man climbed up onto the box in what must have been record time, then the coach was moving through the wet grass and into the trees. Rion hoped they'd be able to free the coach again from the mud as he and Naran followed, but there was no help for it. Leaving the coach where it could be easily seen would be like posting a sign announcing their whereabouts.

As soon as the coach was taken care of, Rion led the two people back to where the convoy had camped. He used Air magic to keep the dripping trees from soaking the three of them, even though he hadn't really dried off from the first time. Now that the confrontation was over, he'd have to speak to Vallant or Tamrissa about ridding him of the dampness. It was deuced uncomfortable, one of the few new experiences Rion had had that he had no interest in experiencing again—or even longer this first time.

When they reached the others, he discovered that they'd waited their own meal until everyone might eat. That had been thoughtful of them but completely unnecessary, a fact he mentioned even as he joined Naran in filling metal plates. The others, seated on the tarpaulin which Alsin had spread, had already filled their plates and were now digging in rather than answering his protest. He quickly did the same, reflecting that he'd never known how good fried beefcakes and potatoes and biscuits could taste.

"I've had a thought," Tamrissa leaned over to murmur to Rion once they'd all sat back with what was left of their tea. "It's possible that if you and I and Vallant link up with Lorand, we can lend him the lucidity and strength to clear his own system of the lethe. We can't include Jovvi because two cloudy minds might throw the rest of us off, but once Lorand is back he can do the same for her."

"And you're not mentioning this aloud because we still don't know exactly how our friends will react to *actually* being with a functioning Blending," Rion returned in the same murmur. "I agree with your caution, and also applaud your idea. Once you return to the wagon, I'll tell Vallant and then he and I will 'stroll over' to see how our group-mates are doing."

She smiled and nodded to that, then finished her tea and arose from the tarpaulin. After thanking Grath for the won-derful meal, she mentioned her intention to return to Lorand and Jovvi, then did so. Rion had, in the interim, whispered to Naran what they were going to do, so she made no effort to join him when he got to his own feet and approached Vallant.

"Tamrissa has had a rather good idea," Rion murmured after crouching beside his groupmate. "We're going to try to link up in order to free Lorand of the lethe, and then Lorand can do the same for Jovvi. But let's not mention it aloud, as we have no idea how our companions will take to seeing us work as a Blending."

Vallant, who had been sipping his tea, simply nodded, and after draining his cup and putting it aside, arose to stand next to Rion.

"Rion has just been sayin' how unfair we're bein', leavin' Tamrissa to tend to Jovvi and Lorand alone," he announced wryly. "I'm ashamed to admit it, but the thought never occurred to me despite the fact that he's right. If you'll excuse us for a short while, we'll go and give her a hand and some company."

Everyone immediately agreed that that was what they should do, so they were able to leave the eating area and walk toward the wagon where their groupmates were. Rion marveled at Vallant's ability to come up with a plausible excuse for their going on such short notice, and decided he needed to learn that trick. It was bound to come in handy many times during his life from now on.

"Grath almost made a really bad mistake," Vallant commented once they were out of easy earshot of the others. "When he started makin' our tea, he used water with a really high concentration of that lethe in it. If I hadn't noticed and removed the sedative, we might be needin' clearin' up ourselves about now."

"That's a serious blunder," Rion said, feeling the frown creasing his face. "Doesn't he know about what you did last night?"

"Apparently he didn't know until this mornin'," Vallant replied. "Meerk said somethin' about how surprised Grath was when he found out once the two of them got here. He hadn't known doin' what I did was possible, and for some reason it unsettled him."

"I think we need to discuss this with Tamrissa," Rion decided aloud. "I've noticed something myself that doesn't sit quite right, and we could conceivably be in danger."

Vallant raised his brows at that, but since they were just approaching the wagon he didn't ask for any details. That was just as well, as repeating himself wasn't one of Rion's favorite doings. They climbed inside, walked to where Tamrissa waited with Jovvi and Lorand, sat down near her, then told her what Vallant had been involved with. Once he'd finished repeating his story, Rion took his turn.

"Our coach has been left out in plain view at every inn which we've stopped at," he said, speaking to the both of them. Jovvi and Lorand were apparently drifting in and out of sleep, just as the others in the wagon were. "As you may know, it's rather unique in style and color and therefore easily recognizable. Since we've been moving at a set pace all along and there's been only one inn we would likely be at, why do you think that was necessary?"

"Obviously it was for the convenience of someone other than our own party," Tamrissa replied angrily. "Alsin told me that he's absolutely certain about the loyalty of all of his members, but now I'm starting to believe that that's wishful thinking. It looks like the nobility planted an informer in his group, so now they probably know exactly where we are. What can we do about it?"

"There's nothin' we can do until Jovvi and Lorand are

back to the way they're supposed to be," Vallant answered, straightening where he sat. "That means we need to try your idea as quickly as possible."

There was no arguing with *that*, so Rion also straightened and prepared himself. Joining together without Jovvi as the center of their group would be difficult, he thought, and was therefore surprised when he and Tamrissa and Vallant immediately linked up with Lorand with no trouble at all. Lorand had had to be *brought* to the power, so to speak, but once he had been, there was nothing to stop an entity from forming.

But not the sort of entity they were accustomed to. This entity was lacking in depth and ability, but the entity was able to know that part of its problem was caused by one of its members. That one had something dragging at its system and talent, a circumstance which could not be allowed to continue, of course. The entity used that member's ability on itself, letting the member's own talent direct the operation, and in moments the member was as it should be. Now the entity was prepared to continue on to other things, but the withdrawal of part of itself brought Rion back to his own awareness.

"What's going on here?" Lorand asked, sounding confused but no longer drugged as he looked around. "Where are we, and what are we supposed to be doing?"

"We're supposed to be rescuing you and Jovvi," Tamrissa said with a big smile, then continued on with the rest of the tale. By the time Lorand had been completely filled in, he'd taken Jovvi's hand to hold and now shook his head.

"So the nobility might catch up to us at any time?" he said, obviously as disturbed by the idea as the rest of them. "Then why are we just sitting here? We need Jovvi back, too, as fast as we can get her."

Rion joined his agreement to that of the others, but not simply for the sake of their safety and completeness and a need for Jovvi herself, as a person. All thoughts of danger aside, Tamrissa and Vallant had been acting perfectly polite with each other. Rion wasn't certain, but that might be worse than their previous wrangling. At the very least, it made *him* incredibly nervous. . . .

TWENTY-FIVE

Jovvi listened with one hand to her head and her eyes closed, trying to assimilate everything the others were telling her. The last few days were nothing but a blur of confusion, of course, and that confusion kept trying to spread out to everything else. And on top of that she felt absolutely filthy, which, apparently, she was. Those miserable people had done the absolute minimum when it came to keeping them clean, and the only thing to be thankful for about the whole business was that she had no memory of the time.

"So now that Lorand and I are back to the way we were, we all have to decide what to do next," she said once the others had finished filling her in. "Am I mistaken in thinking that you all believe we ought to find out how soon to expect the guardsmen the nobles have surely sent after us?"

"It won't help to start clearing the minds of the others if we're going to be interrupted at any minute," Tamrissa said in agreement, smiling when Jovvi opened her eyes to look at her. "We'll have the Blending to defend us, of course, but letting ourselves be surprised doesn't make much sense."

"And if we're right about Grath, he should be able to tell us what we need to know," Rion put in with his own smile. "If we aren't right, however, we ought to know as soon as possible so as not to believe the worst of an innocent man."

"We also need to keep in mind that Meerk may not be what he claims," Vallant said, his own smile looking a bit strained. "We ought to do some checkin' of *his* story, since he let that puttin' the coach out where it can be seen business pass by without sayin' anythin'."

"I can't see Alsin being in league with our enemies," Tamma said with a headshake, her smile having disappeared. "They're his enemies, too, even though the aims of his organization are a bit too innocent to accomplish anything. If Grath turns out to be working for the nobility, that may be why his superiors haven't done anything to break up the organization. Its aims aren't really a threat to the nobility, and it gives its members the feeling that they're fighting against their oppressors even though they aren't. Grath would just be there to make sure none of that changed."

"That part I agree with," Vallant responded, an odd tension between him and Tamma suddenly clear to Jovvi. "They really expect to bring the nobility down without usin' force or spillin' blood, so the nobility must love havin' people join up. But it's always possible that the nobility started the organization in the first place, which would mean that Meerk actually does work for them."

"It shouldn't be hard to find out the truth," Jovvi said quickly before Tamma could disagree with Vallant again. "But first I would enjoy getting something to eat, and also getting some air. I've just noticed how it stinks in here."

"I hate to say it, but *we're* the ones who stink," Lorand said, giving her a supporting smile. "I do, however, agree with the rest of what you said, since my insides feel as though they're rubbing together. Is there anything handy that we can just . . . pounce on?"

"There are fried beefcakes and potatoes left over from our lunch," Tamma said with a grin while the others laughed. Jovvi had expected Lorand to be circumspect about his hunger, but being asleep for days hadn't ruined his tendency to be direct. "I'd just suggest that you check it over before you and Jovvi eat any of it, Lorand. Since we haven't been watching, there's no telling what Grath might have put in it."

"You can bet your last copper I'll check," Lorand said as he began to struggle to his feet. "I've had enough of unconsciousness to last me for the next year."

Jovvi felt exactly the same, especially since she found that although she was able to get to her feet with just a little help, walking wasn't as easy as it used to be. She felt stiff and weak both at the same time, and had to accept Vallant's help while Rion helped Lorand. But at least they were able to leave that wagon, and the poor, confused people who were in the midst of trying to wake up all the way.

Outside the air felt damp and a bit on the cool side, as though a rainstorm were taking its own lunch break. What Jovvi really wanted was a bath house and a lot of soap, but considering what they were in the midst of, bathing would have to wait. She looked around at the rather large clearing, where ten wagons had been stopped in a semicircle, and a large number of men now lay unconscious on the wet ground. Some of them seemed close to waking, but Lorand must have noticed that as well. The next instant they were out again, which had to mean he'd touched them. Happily they were all chained, but there was no sense in taking chances.

A man straightened away from the fire in the middle of the campsite, and Jovvi noticed him immediately. He was also a user of Spirit magic, and interestingly enough was now touching the power. He also tried to hide his emotions at seeing the five of them, but wasn't quite as successful as he clearly thought he was being. If that was the man Grath, then her groupmates hadn't been imagining things.

"Well, I'm glad to see that my business is growing," the man said in an easy, casual voice as they approached him. "Two more customers for lunch, brought here by previous satisfied customers."

"Actually, we've come to eat you *out* of business," Lorand replied in a light tone that didn't match what he felt on the inside. Apparently Lorand had also picked up the false note in the man's supposed friendliness, but had decided against letting him know about it.

"I can understand why," the man said, now trying to project a sympathetic concern. "If you two will find places on the tarpaulin, I'll fill some plates for you right away."

"No, I don't think that's a very good idea," Jovvi said at once, reaching out with her ability to take the man's mind and hold it. "You made a fast decision that pleased you, but it's hardly likely to please us as well. I'd guess that the leftovers are perfectly edible and untainted, but you were about to change that.''

''I—don't know what you're talking about,'' the man choked out, rigid with fear that approached terror. ''Let go of me, please, I really must insist that you let me go. I haven't done anything, you're just imagining enemies because of what the nobles did to you. Please, one of you tell her I'm a friend so she'll let me go!''

''Just calm down,'' Jovvi soothed with both voice and mind as Vallant helped her to sit on the tarpaulin. Part of the man's terror was from the ease with which her strength had brushed aside his own, as though he were a Low rather than a fairly strong Middle. ''There's nothing to be afraid of, so you needn't worry.''

''All right,'' the man replied equably, no longer on the verge of panic. Jovvi had merely overwhelmed him at first, the rest of her ability apparently still partially asleep. As soon as she realized her mistake, however, she had worked immediately to correct it. He was now docile and unafraid, and would answer truthfully any question put to him.

''I'll get the food for you two,'' Tamma announced as she glared at the man Jovvi held. ''And while I'm doing it, why don't the rest of you find another chore for Grath to see to.''

''That will be our pleasure,'' Rion growled, having done no more than glance at Naran, who had hurried over to help Jovvi and Lorand settle themselves. ''It seems our suspicions were correct after all, Grath. You work for the nobility rather than for the organization.''

''Of course,'' Grath replied easily and pleasantly, smiling at Rion. ''Surely you don't imagine that a group like this would be allowed to exist without someone being there to make sure nothing was accomplished?''

''What's going on?'' a strange voice interrupted, and suddenly two more men, who had appeared from around the other side of one of the wagons, joined them. One of the men was large and somehow familiar, the other hanging back as though he felt his presence would be an intrusion. ''Say, you've gotten Dom Coll and Dama Hafford back to themselves.''

''We've done a bit more than that, Meerk,'' Vallant said,

his voice a good deal colder than the other man's had been. "We've also just listened to Grath admit that he's workin' for the nobility. Is there anythin' *you'd* like to add concernin' your own position?"

"Are you crazy?" the man Meerk demanded, his face paling as he turned to look at Grath. "Grath *can't* be working for the nobility, not when he passed our entrance test. Tell him, Tamrissa, tell him it just isn't possible."

"Listen for yourself, Alsin," Tamma said without looking at the man, using the plates she brought to Jovvi and Lorand as the supposed reason for not meeting his gaze. "Tell Alsin who you really work for, Grath."

"I work for the nobility," Grath obliged, smiling at Meerk in the same way he'd smiled at Rion. "Passing your test wasn't hard, Alsin, not when I'm stronger than the Spirit magic user who questioned me, and not when I've also had training which she hasn't had. You were a fool to think your system was proof against invasion, but we were glad to put that foolishness to our own use."

"I don't believe it," Meerk whispered, his face even more pale now. "If the nobility knew about us, why weren't we arrested and dispersed?"

"Why would we break up an organization that was keeping you hotheads quiet?" Grath asked very reasonably. "As long as you thought you were getting away with something, you made no trouble yourselves and kept the others from making any. I was sent to make sure that your very pure aims weren't tarnished by those who would want to use force to overthrow the nobility rather than the law. As long as you continued to insist that things be done *your* way, you were no threat whatsoever."

Jovvi had to block out the very heavy illness filling Meerk's mind, that and a terrible sense of humiliation. The man now knew he had been used by the very people he'd dedicated himself to besting, and it was perfectly clear that he wasn't pretending.

"He didn't know about any of this," Jovvi said, mostly to Vallant. "That means you can go back to questioning Grath while I fight to keep myself from swallowing this food whole."

Lorand had already started on his portion, but Jovvi had

had to pay attention to what was being said. Now that she had one of the answers they needed, she was free to fill the void inside her own middle.

"Were the men of this convoy alert because of something *you* did, Grath?" Rion asked, his thoughts seething. "If so, why did they drink the contaminated water?"

"They drank it because I didn't know it was contaminated," Grath answered at once. "Those two men in the dining room at the inn last night were my contacts, and I took the first opportunity to separate myself from the rest of you so that I could speak with them. If I'd known Alsin would devise a plan like this, I would have stayed to hear the details of it. As it was, I decided that Alsin's learning what the sedative was couldn't possibly do any real harm, and I needed to pass on certain things very badly."

"Like the fact that we were followin'?" Vallant put in, just as angry as Rion. "It looks like you sent one of those contacts here, to the convoy, but where did you send the other one?"

"Back toward the city, and the contingent of guardsmen who are following *us*, of course" he said. "They aren't as close as I would have liked, but you caught me by surprise when you left the city so quickly. I only had time to signal one of my men to follow, and then had to wait until he caught up with us and I could speak to him alone. He passed the word on to his own contact, picked up another of my people, and rode hard to get back here. Yesterday they passed us on the road and were waiting when we reached the inn."

"And what happened to the one you sent here?" Tamma asked, her own anger more than a match to the men's. "I don't see anyone in that chained group except guardsmen and drivers."

"Oh, he's gone back toward the city as well," Grath said. "I made sure he went around your coach, and now he's riding to meet the guardsmen. When he reaches them, he'll be able to direct them to the exact place where we are."

"Just how close to us are they?" Vallant asked after exchanging a glance with Rion. "A day behind? Less?"

"They *were* more than two days behind, but hopefully they've made up a good deal of the time," Grath replied.

"There was a delay in getting them started after us, something about my men not knowing who to report to. Then the Five became involved, and things began to move more smoothly. I'm hoping they'll be here in no more than another day or so."

"The Five," Vallant growled. "Copper to gold he's talkin' about the new Five, so I'll also bet we don't have to worry about bein' taken prisoner again. They'd be fools to want us kept alive, and I don't believe they're fools of that sort."

"And there's almost certainly more than a single contingent of them," Rion put in. "So we're caught between those following and those ahead. Just how far ahead is the destination of this convoy, Grath?"

"I have no idea," Grath responded with a small shrug. "I got the impression from my man that we aren't too far away, but its exact location is something only the leader of the convoy knows."

"And he's unconscious along with the rest," Tamma said, looking at Rion and Vallant. "We'll certainly have to question the man, but first I think we ought to concentrate on getting the rest of the prisoners clear of the lethe. We'll have to find someplace other than here to stay for a while, and getting there will be easier if everyone can move by him- or herself."

"But we'll have to rouse them only a few at a time," Lorand put in, the first words he'd spoken in a while. "They'll certainly be as hungry and as eager to get out of those wagons as we were, and there aren't enough of us to see to all of them at once. The weakness of not having moved in days doesn't wear off very quickly even if you want it to."

"We'll probably do best working out a routine," Jovvi said in support of Lorand's comments. "Some of us can be preparing food while the Blending wakes a certain number of people, then we can all help to get them out here. While they're eating we'll split up again to make more food and wake more people, and then we'll take some time to help the first group begin to move around on their own. After that the ones we've roused can help with the others, so the process ought to speed up with every group we wake."

"I certainly hope it does," Tamma said, her mind even more grim than it had been earlier. "If those guardsmen get here before we're through bringing everyone back, you know we'll have to fight. With that in mind, we'd better not put everything we have into waking people up. I still don't want to have to kill anyone, but those guardsmen won't have orders to hand us visiting cards or courting gifts."

"We might get lucky and have a large number of members from my organization among them," Meerk put in diffidently. "If that happens, we may be able to talk sense to them. You know, tell them to step out of our way to keep from getting hurt. It would be better than just attacking them without warning, without giving them a chance to do what we want them to without trouble."

"Let's ask Grath what he thinks of that plan," Tamma said, interrupting what looked to be a tirade in the making from Vallant. "Since he has no choice about speaking the truth, you won't have to wonder how far to trust what he says."

"That's a good idea," Meerk quickly agreed, beginning to lose the diffidence. "Then we'll all know. Grath, if you were in that group of guardsmen following us or were leading it and some of your men insisted on talking to us rather than simply attacking, you'd bow to that sensible a course of action, wouldn't you?"

"When I'm in charge, my men don't dictate my course of action," Grath said at once, this time without a smile. "If my orders were to destroy the lot of you, that's what would be done—without any mindless discussions first. Do you think my superiors would be interested in what you had to say? Or in any excuses I might make for not having followed my orders? You don't maintain yourself in power by compromise or shilly-shallying around. You do it by acting decisively when the situation calls for it, and this one is that sort beyond all doubt."

"So now we know," Tamma said to Meerk more gently, as the man stood staring at his former follower. "If we expect to stay alive in this . . . game we've fallen into, we have to be just as ruthless as the nobles will be. Worrying about obeying the law is idiotic when your opponents use the law rather than obey it themselves. You can see that now, can't you?''

"All I can see is this empire falling apart because of what we all do," Meerk replied, illness clearly filling him again. "I didn't want it to be this way, but somewhere along the line I lost the choice. And I used to think I knew what it felt like to be helpless. . . ."

The man's words trailed off as he shook his head, then he moved a few steps away just to stand and stare at nothing. Jovvi could feel his pain and dismay clearly, but there was nothing she could do to ease it. Only time and an acceptance of the inevitable would aid the man now, assuming he didn't simply walk away from the whole situation. That was perfectly possible, and the decision to go or stay had to be his alone.

"I think we'd better get started now," Jovvi said after putting aside the plate of food she hadn't been able to come close to finishing. Naran had brought cups of tea to her and Lorand, and that she did need to finish. Going along with the others physically wasn't necessary in order to have the Blending do what it had to, but it *was* necessary if she were ever going to move normally again. She and Lorand, that was . . . especially if they were able to snatch some time to be alone . . .

TWENTY-SIX

Lorand found that he just had to sit down for a while, but not because the Blending had spent too much of its strength. He was the one with the problem in his body, he and Jovvi both. He'd pushed himself more than she had in order to get over the weakness sooner, but there was a point beyond which it simply wasn't smart to go. He'd extended himself as far as possible, and now he just had to sit down for a while.

Everyone else was busy with explanations and food preparation and helping people to get around, so Lorand went to the edge of the eating tarpaulin and eased himself into a sitting position. A canopy of canvas had been erected over the tarpaulin because of the light rain which had started, but feeling the light drops on his face actually made Lorand feel better all over. He was alive again after days of nonlife that somehow felt longer in memory, although not being conscious was supposed to make time pass faster. It hadn't felt that way to *him*, though, and being back felt like he'd escaped a smothering, unpleasant death.

"You're looking a little better," a voice offered, the words on the hesitant side. "If you're not in the mood for conversation just say so, and I'll take my rest period from cooking somewhere else."

"No, I've had my fill of silence," Lorand replied, looking up at the man who now stood near him. "Conversation is more than welcome ... You *are* Meerk, aren't you? You don't sound like the man I knew, but you certainly look like him."

"Alsin Meerk," he replied with a nod and a faint smile as he sat beside Lorand. "Tamrissa said almost the same thing, and I had to explain that my former mode of speech was in the way of a disguise. People pay less attention to those who sound uneducated, which is a prejudice most of us suffer from. As though the uneducated are less able to do us real good or real harm."

"With a basic education free for the taking, anyone who refuses to take advantage of it *is* less able to do good or harm," Lorand pointed out. "And that goes for themselves as well as for others. Are *you* feeling any better now?"

"Not really," Meerk answered with a sigh, picking up a twig to toy with. "First I find out that the nobility *likes* the ideas of my organization, and then I discover that the basic philosophy of my life is wrong. It still doesn't actually *feel* wrong, but with so many people supporting the opposite point of view, it has to be."

"There's nothing wrong with your philosophy, just with the place you're trying to apply it," Lorand replied, understanding the man's depression. "I've always preferred the peaceful way of doing things, but some things can't be accomplished unless you're willing to take a stronger stance. I had the best talent in my family, and my father didn't like the idea of losing that talent for his farm. Since he enjoyed his life he decided that it would also be best for *me*, which was a horribly selfish way to look at it. *He* wanted something, so *I* was supposed to want it, too. When it was time for me to leave I tried to keep things peaceful, but he refused to let me do it."

"My father was a farrier," Meerk said, still paying most of his attention to the twig in his hands. "I was supposed to be the same, and I probably would have been if my father had lived. It just wasn't possible to say no to the man, and that made me detest all those who simply gave orders without caring about the people who were getting those orders. Being pushed around by someone bigger also made me swear that I would never do the same. And that's what using force to depose the nobles feels like, pushing around people who can't stand up to you."

"That's where the misapplication comes in," Lorand pointed out, giving most of his own attention to the delight of feeling the rain on his face. "Since it's the nobility who are and have been doing the pushing around, you're the one who's wrong by telling them that they *should* be doing things *your* way. Instead of acting like both our fathers and trying to tell them how to behave, you should simply be agreeing to use the method *they* prefer. What else could be more fair?"

"You're making excuses," Meerk returned with a snort that wasn't quite laughter. "If we condemn them for the methods they use, we'd have to condemn ourselves if we used them as well. Two groups of people doing wrong has never been able to make a situation right."

"Now you're the one making excuses," Lorand said, turning his head to inspect the man. "If you find it easier to watch peoples' lives being destroyed than to have someone call you a dirty name, you're not being noble, you're rationalizing. Why don't you just simply say it isn't in you to fight no matter what the provocation? That isn't as noble as having 'principles,' but at least it's the truth.''

"So I'm less of a man because I don't believe in fighting?" Meerk demanded, also turning his head. "That seems to be everyone's opinion, everyone's but mine! Why is a man always defined by how willing he is to fight?"

"Only someone who's ashamed of what he is looks at it that way," Lorand said slowly and clearly, trying to make the man believe him. "If you're not a fighter there's nothing to be ashamed of, since it's the nonfighters who hold our civilization together. But by the same token it's the fighters who carve out that civilization to begin with, so if you want people to stop giving you a hard time for being a nonfighter, stop giving *them* a hard time for not sharing your point of view."

Meerk stared at Lorand, his expression saying there was more to argue about but he didn't quite know where to begin. Then an interruption came which ended the conversation for a time.

"I don't believe those people," Tamrissa muttered as she came over to seat herself under the canopy near them. She carried a cup of tea and was being careful not to spill it. "Do you believe that some of them are demanding to be taken back to Gan Garee? They've decided that this all has to be some sort of mistake, and they want to go back to get it straightened out."

"That doesn't surprise me," Meerk said, now sounding distracted. "I've heard of people who were arrested and tried and sentenced to the deep mines who refused to believe that it was actually happening to them. Those people were awake through the whole process, and they still refused to believe. What can you expect of people who were put to sleep without warning and are only now waking up?"

"I expect them to take the word of the people who are trying to save them," Tamrissa replied, the statement slow and cold. "I also expect them to pitch in and help with those who aren't yet awake, not sit there and demand to be taken care of. Jovvi and I just walked away, because Rion and Vallant's patient explanations—*repeated* patient explanations—were getting on our nerves."

"Maybe it's time to do something else for a while," Lorand mused, his attention having been taken by one of their sleeping prisoners. "That guardsman over there is beginning to wake up, so why don't we ask who the leader of this convoy is? Then we can wake *that* one up, and ask a few other questions."

"Let me get Jovvi before you do that," Tamrissa said, starting to get to her feet. "With Grath having been put to sleep to save her the trouble of keeping him under control, she can take control of the convoy leader instead."

"There, you see what I mean?" Meerk said after letting out a sharp breath, his accusing gaze on Lorand again. "None of *us* likes the idea of being controlled, but we don't hesitate to do it to others. If that isn't wrong, I don't know what is."

"Then let me tell you what is," Tamrissa said to Meerk just as sharply before Lorand could reply. "Wrong is taking innocent people and destroying their lives because you're afraid of them. Wrong is keeping everything good for yourself and your friends, and leaving nothing for the people who work hardest to produce that good. Wrong is refusing to do whatever it takes to change that horrible condition, simply because you're too *good* to fight fire with fire. I'll live with being called bad, if that's the terrible price I have to pay to save people from having to go through what we suffered. If you *can't* live with it, I just feel sorry for you."

Meerk stared up at her for a moment, his expression wounded and vulnerable, then he was on his feet and striding away. Lorand briefly looked after him, then shook his head.

"I think friend Meerk is feeling outnumbered," he said to Tamrissa, who was also watching Meerk's disappearance. "He and I were having the same sort of argument just before you got here, but I don't expect that either of us changed his mind. If you feel guilty about not being willing to fight, you seem to be compelled to find reasons why fighting is wrong for everyone else as well. Why can't people just pay attention to their own lives, and leave everyone else's alone?"

"They say misery loves company, so possibly *that's* the reason," Tamrissa replied after taking a deep breath. "I think I'm getting to the point where I don't know *anything* for certain any longer . . . I'll go get Jovvi.''

Lorand nodded, then watched her walk away toward the third wagon, still carrying her cup of tea. She paid no attention at all to the rain, even though it was getting closer to sundown. It would soon be too chilly to enjoy being damp, even just on faces and hands. But there were only the people in the last two wagons who still had to be cleared of the lethe, and some of them were already sitting up and trying to come out of it on their own. Once that major chore was done, they could see about setting up rainproof accommodations for everyone.

Jovvi came out of the wagon slowly and carefully, but she seemed to be doing at least as well as Lorand was if not better. There was joy for Lorand in just sitting and watching her, though he would have enjoyed a few minutes of privacy with her even more. He couldn't yet think about how close he'd come to losing her to some horrible, nameless fate, not without being filled with the most terrible rage. What had been done to *him* might eventually be overlooked and forgotten about, but what they'd almost done to the woman he loved . . . No, Lorand wasn't about to come around to Meerk's way of looking at things.

''Well, don't just sit there being lazy,'' Jovvi said to him with a smile when she and Tamrissa stopped near him. ''If we're going to do some questioning, let's do it.''

''At your service, dama,'' he replied with a grin, then patted the tarpaulin to his left. ''Sit and join me, and we can have the ones we question come to *us*. It's the least they can do, since they're the ones responsible for making us feel like this.''

''That's a good idea,'' she agreed with a small laugh. ''Except for one thing: they're all chained in place. If we have one of them come over, the rest have to come with him.''

''All right, then I suppose *we'll* have to do the going,'' Lorand pretended to complain as he levered himself to his feet. ''Let's get it over with, so we can come back and sit down again.''

Jovvi nodded with complete understanding and agreement, and also took his hand as they walked toward the unconscious guardsmen. Tamrissa walked with them, of course, still holding her cup of tea. The guardsman who was struggling to awaken was in the far row in the center, so Lorand stopped and prodded at him just a little with his talent.

"This is the one we want to ask the first question of," he said. "Did you catch his reaction?"

"I certainly did," she agreed, then turned her head to look over at Tamrissa. "Tamma, dear, would you be so kind as to ask the questions once I have him and the next one under control? I'm really too tired to do it myself, and I think Lorand is in the same condition."

"I'll also try to make it as short as possible, so you two can rest for a while," Tamrissa agreed, putting her hand briefly to Jovvi's arm. "Go ahead and get started, so we can be finished faster."

Jovvi smiled her agreement, and a moment later they had the identity of the leader of the convoy. Lorand put the guardsman back to sleep, and they all walked the five feet to where the leader lay. There was a difference in the collar decorations of his uniform, which was obviously supposed to tell people that he was in charge, but Lorand and the others hadn't the least idea of what any of the insignia meant. This man was one of those whom Lorand had had to put more deeply asleep, so now he reversed the process and then Jovvi took over. That became clear when the man sat up, looking at Tamrissa expectantly.

"You were in charge of this convoy?" Tamrissa started with, returning the man's gaze coolly. "If so, tell me where it was going."

"Yes, I *am* in charge," the man corrected at once, very little friendliness to be seen in his manner. "Our destination was and still is Quellin."

"What's at Quellin?" Tamrissa asked next, apparently having no interest in arguing with the man. "And I'm also curious about where it is, so tell me everything you know about the place."

"Quellin is a small town built up around the depot we're taking these segments to," the man replied with a nod. "It lies less than a full day's travel from here, along the north-west fork. The Rolris Fork, as you ought to know, is about four hours up the road, and it branches southwest and north-west for a while before both roads turn westerly again.''

"I know the Rolris Fork!" Lorand exclaimed, interrupting the narration. "I came to Gan Garee from along the southwest branch, which isn't more than two days from my home district.''

"It's the northwest fork I've been asked about," the convoy leader said with mild reproof in his voice. "Quellin is the main depot from which our army has segments supplied, and where they're sent from there depends on where they're needed the most.''

"I thought the empire didn't have an army," Tamrissa said, abruptly forgetting about the sip of tea she'd been about to take. "If we do and it needs . . . segments, what is it using them for?''

"It's using them for the purpose of extending our borders, of course," the man replied, making it sound as though Tamrissa were totally ignorant and innocent. "The barbarians of Astinda, our neighboring realm to the west, are trying to resist becoming civilized, and we certainly can't allow *that*. So our army takes their realm a few miles and acres at a time, and soon there won't be anything left that isn't part of our empire.''

"Are they doing the same with Gracely to the east?" Jovvi put in, apparently forgetting about how tired she was supposed to be.

"Of course," the man answered, still using that same superior tone of voice. "No empire that intends to survive will allow itself to be surrounded by barbarians. Once they're all under our control, our safety will be assured.''

"Is that the way you make what our people are doing a good and acceptable thing?" Tamrissa asked, anger clear in her voice. "By calling anyone who isn't part of our empire a barbarian? Just how barbaric are they supposed to be? What do they *do* to earn the name of barbarian?''

"That isn't any of my concern," the man returned, the expression on his middle-aged face totally uncaring. "My superiors tell me they're barbarians in those places, and I have no reason to doubt that. I only care about what's best for my own country, and leaving potential enemies free to cause trouble isn't in my country's best interests.''

"How do you know they'd become our enemies?" Lorand was forced to put in himself, just as disturbed as the women were. "And how do you know that they'd make trouble? No, don't bother answering me, I already know what the real answer is. Your . . . superiors want to take over their countries, and as the people there probably tried to resist, that makes them enemies. So what are we going to do about all this? Just because they won't have *this* group of us to fight for them, that won't do anything to stop them from using the people they've already taken control of."

"We'll have to have a talk with the others," Jovvi said, she and Tamrissa both knowing that the last of his words had been addressed to them. "In fact, we'll probably do best having a general meeting. If you'll put this one back to sleep, we can see about arranging it right now."

Lorand nodded and put the convoy leader back to sleep as requested, then he followed Tamrissa and Jovvi as they went to speak to Rion and Vallant. It would have felt better to go back and sit down, but Lorand had the feeling that none of them were going to be sitting around relaxing for quite some time. . . .

TWENTY-SEVEN

Our proposed meeting was delayed when it began to rain hard again. Most of the newly awakened—which meant almost all of the former prisoners—were having trouble getting around, and there wasn't anything like a tarpaulin big enough to make a reasonably dry meeting area. Lorand finally came up with the idea of rearranging the entire camp, since the guardsmen and drivers—our new prisoners—had to be sheltered from the weather along with everyone else. Leaving those particular prisoners to drown wouldn't have bothered *too* many people, but if you're going to kill someone it ought to be on purpose, not by accident.

So we moved all the wagons around until they were backed into a semicircle, as close a one as we could manage, and used the single tarpaulin over our sleeping prisoners. Everyone attending the meeting clustered around the opening in the back of their respective wagons, and we five stood in the open space in the middle. Or at least Rion, Vallant, and I stood. Jovvi and Lorand sat on wooden crates we'd found in the supply wagon, and Rion thickened the air above us to keep us dry.

"All right, people, we have two decisions that need makin' right now," Vallant said loudly enough for everyone to hear. He had the loudest voice among us, so he was the natural choice to run the meeting. "We know there's pursuit comin' from Gan Garee, and because of a spy in our midst, they know where this place is. We have to leave as soon as possible and find a safer place to rest for a while, so that's the first of your decisions. Who's comin' with us, and who's goin' back to give them a second chance to make the slavery work this time?"

A lot of voices spoke at the same time, much of it in protest, and then one voice rose above the rest.

"You're just trying to frighten us!" that voice, coming from a thin, balding man, insisted. "We have nothing but the claims of a group of strangers to say that that was what the officials were doing, and nothing at all to show that our being here isn't a mistake. I say we all have to go back and ask someone to straighten out the mistake."

"All right, let's say it *was* a mistake," Vallant granted, but not in a gentle, friendly tone. "Someone somewhere made a big mistake, and if you go back they'll fall all over themselves fixin' it. But on the other hand—What do you plan to do if it *wasn't* a mistake, and they tell you to drink what they give you and then lie down like a good slave?"

"That can't happen," the man persisted, his own tone completely inflexible. "This is the capital and our government we're talking about, not some group of rabble. It *has* to be a mistake, and if we go back they'll straighten it out.''

"In other words, you're not capable of imaginin' anythin' that doesn't fit into the idea you've already made up your mind about," Vallant told him very flatly, without the least bit of gentleness. "In that event I suppose you *should* go back, and they'll make sure you don't pass on that very dangerous trait to any children. Is there anyone else foolish enough to go along with this man? If there is, I suggest you all get together in the same wagon."

"He isn't foolish, and there are too many of us for just one wagon," a woman said stiffly, a woman who looked young but had an air of command about her. "We aren't just anyone, we're *important*, so they aren't about to just ignore what was done to us. The empire needs us, and just because some fool made a stupid error is no reason not to let his superiors correct it. They'll be very relieved when we get back safely, and we'll be comfortable while the rest of you run and hide like mindless animals."

"Ah, so it's a mistake because you're *important*," Vallant said, looking at her in the same way he'd looked at the man. "If you really were all that important, you would have noticed by now that the 'stupid mistake' happened to an awful lot of people. But you aren't important, not really, not to the nobility in Gan Garee. What you are is a High talent, and they're afraid of Highs, so they deliberately got rid of you. If that's what you want to go back to, be my guest. Just don't try lyin' to yourself out where I can hear it. I spent too long a time there not to know the truth."

The woman clamped her lips together stubbornly, the thin man beside her showing the same expression, but some of the others were looking less certain. Three of them, a woman and two men, had been whispering together, and now the woman stepped forward.

"They won't need quite as many wagons as they think," she said, only glancing at the stubborn two. "Some of us have been talking over what you said, and it might have been a mistake if only a few of us were Highs. But with every one of us the same, it can't possibly be the fault of one ignorant underling. Our being here is deliberate, and we're not about to give them a second chance at us."

Quite a few mutters of agreement came after her words,

and the first couple looked offended and affronted. They seemed to be the sort who *had* to be right all the time, no matter how ridiculous a stance they'd taken. They glared around at some of the others, apparently trying to get people to back down and change their minds, but the tactic didn't work.

"Now I'm hearin' some common sense," Vallant said after the second woman had finished speaking, giving her a supporting smile as well. "At one time or another everyone steps into it accidentally, but only a damn' fool does it on purpose. But here with us, you two and anyone else has the right to be as big a bunch of fools as you like, so I suggest you get goin' back to Gan Garee right now. How many wagons will you be needin'?"

"I'll let you know as soon as I see how many are going to be smart and return with us," the woman said, her tone still stiff as she turned to look around at everyone. "I need a show of hands, please, to get an accurate count."

The thin man beside her raised his hand deliberately, but he turned out to be the only one who did. Some avoided meeting the woman's gaze and some stared straight at her, but no one else raised a hand.

"Looks like there are fewer fools here than either of us thought," Vallant drawled, not quite showing his amusement. "Since there are only two of you, you can have one wagon. And since we'll be discussin' things we don't want passed on to the guardsmen who'll be greetin' you soon, you'd better take the wagon and leave now."

"But how are we supposed to handle a wagon this size all alone?" the thin man complained, righteous anger mixed in with dismay. "I've never driven myself anywhere in my life, and Galeen here certainly can't manage it. You'll have to send someone with us to do the driving."

"If any of these people were foolish enough to let me send them anywhere, they'd already be goin' with you," Vallant pointed out. "If you don't think you can handle a wagon, you can take the coach some of us came here in. Or you can have a couple of the saddle horses those guardsmen were usin'. Just make up your minds and get goin', so the rest of us can finish this meetin' and get on our own way."

"A coach would be just as bad as a wagon, and I can't

ride a horse,'' the woman, Galeen, announced very flatly
and angrily. "You're doing all you can to keep us here, and
I, for one, resent it furiously. You have no right to—''

"Stop right there," Vallant interrupted, even more flatly
than she'd spoken. "I've given you all sorts of options to
let you leave us, but you've found somethin' wrong with
all of them. That means you know how stupid your idea of
goin' back is, but you refuse to admit it. We have no time
to deal with spiteful little children, so either grow up and
start actin' responsibly, or walk away and let *us* do it alone.
Whichever, it has to be done *now*.''

Once again the woman's lips tightened, but this time she
said nothing. The anger in her eyes had been joined by disturbance that looked out of place, as though no one had ever
made her be responsible for her own actions before. The
thin man glanced at her in uncertainty, but when she failed
to return that glance he shifted his gaze to the bottom of the
wagon he stood in and didn't say another word.

"I'm goin' to assume that that topic of goin' back to Gan
Garee is now closed," Vallant said after a moment. "If I'm
wrong and someone has decided to take a wagon or a horse
anyway, just say so . . . No one? All right, then we can go
on to the next topic. Do any of you want to go back to your
own homes instead?''

That brought out a large number of surprised exclamations, as none of them seemed to have thought that going
home would be possible. A lot of rapid conversation was
exchanged in low voices, and then the second woman who
had spoken earlier stepped forward again.

"Going home won't be like going back to Gan Garee at
all," she said. "My friends and I *know* we'll be safe at
home, even if they try to come after us. Our families will
see to it that we are, and everyone ought to know what
we've just found out the hard way. If we spread the word,
there shouldn't be any other unsuspecting Highs being piled
into wagons.''

"That's a good idea," Vallant said, adding his own nod
to the large number of signs of agreement coming from the
others. "We do need to start spreadin' the word, somethin'
they've been workin' real hard to keep from happenin'. So
how many are goin' home?''

This time there were quite a number of hands raised, with a few extra added when people looked around to see how many there already were. At least half of the nearly sixty people seemed to be ready to go home, so Lorand stood up.

"The best thing you people can do from here is to continue on to the Rolris Fork, which is just a few hours ahead," he said in a voice loud enough to carry. "You'll take the southwest fork, that's the left-hand one, and a few hours after that you'll come to the Wenstad Road. At that point you'll see signs pointing the way to various parts of the empire, and you just have to follow the direction of the signs. But not those of you who live to the east. That sign just sends you back in this direction, so head north instead and wait for the next major road before you go east."

"And now's the time to get started," Vallant said over the babble of discussion that arose from that bit of information. "You'll have five of the wagons at least, so if the people from one particular area outnumber the others, that's the area which will have the extra wagon. If two extra wagons are needed, then you'll have that instead. Let's get it movin'."

I suppose they would have stood around talking about it until the guardsmen from Gan Garee rode in, but Vallant refused to allow that. He pointed to four wagons, designating them in turn as north, east, south, and west, and as an afterthought pointed to a fifth and called it Gan Garee. There was a lot of moving around as people went from the wagon they were in to the one they needed to be in, and once the confusion was over Vallant inspected how the numbers had settled out.

"Well, it looks like the north wins," he observed, since there were twice as many people in that one wagon. "They get the extra, and you others can make do with one. The three of you from Gan Garee itself need to think about what *you'll* do, either get dropped off by the wagon headin' east, or go elsewhere with some of the others. But whatever decision you make, do it while the wagons are on the road. The rest of us can't leave until you do."

That statement stopped most of the protests that were being made over the way he all but pushed them out of camp physically, but it wasn't the end of all argument. The woman

Galeen and her male friend hadn't moved to any of the designated wagons, silently insisting that they would stay with the rest of us. I wasn't terribly happy about that, but Vallant went further by refusing to allow it.

"You two aren't stayin' with us," he said in cold, commanding tones that brooked no contradiction. "We won't have time to look after and train small children, so get into one of the wagons that are goin' in another direction. And don't try arguin', because it won't do you any good."

"Going home without the High positions we meant to earn will make us laughingstocks," Galeen snarled while the man with her looked ready to cry. "If arguing with you won't do any good, let's try *this*."

I knew it immediately when she reached for the power, confirming my guess that she was probably a user of Fire magic. She was also rather strong, in point of fact stronger than Beldara Lant, who had been so smugly certain of her superiority. But just as I was stronger than Beldara, I also had no trouble matching and bettering Galeen. The curtain of flames which tried to sweep over and through the five of us stopped dead when I interposed my ability between it and us, and then one large, definite section of the flame curtain died because of the touch of water. Galeen paled when these things happened, and Vallant gave her a smile without any humor in it whatsoever.

"In case we haven't mentioned it before, we're the five people who should now be Seated on the Fivefold Throne," he drawled. "That means we're stronger than everyone here, so flexin' your power won't do you any good either. Get into the proper wagon *now*."

Galeen swallowed hard, but nothing in the way of words came from her as she did as she was told. Amusingly enough it was the wagon heading south that she went to, the part of the empire that Vallant himself came from. Her male companion, though, scurried to the wagon heading east, looking as though he hoped to make it before Galeen noticed. He did, and once some of the provisions had been hastily transferred to each of the departing wagons, they did finally depart.

"All right, now for the last major decision," Vallant announced once the creaking of the last wagon had died away.

"We learned from the leader of this convoy that there's a depot ahead, a place where kidnapped Highs are taken. It's come to us that we know some of the people who must have been sent there, since I'm talkin' about people who survived the competitions we were just in but who didn't win. But even if we didn't know any of them, we'd still have to do somethin' about *our* kind of people bein' made into slaves. That wagon right there is the one you should be in if you don't want to join us in doin' somethin' about that depot."

Rather than a babble of conversation growing up, it became so quiet that it was possible to hear the rain pattering against the trees, and the tarpaulin, and Rion's rain shield. I have no idea what the people who had stayed thought they would be doing, but clearly a number of them hadn't envisioned doing anything as foolish as attacking a depot full of guardsmen. That number hesitated for a long moment, but once the first of them started for the designated wagon, the rest followed. They made up about a third of our remaining total, and after they'd taken their provisions—and another wagon—and had left, there were about twenty people and three wagons remaining.

"I don't want anyone thinkin' they're trapped now that the last wagon has left," Vallant said at that point. "There's still the coach some of us got here in, so anyone changin' his or her mind before we get to Quellin, the depot town, still has a way out. Right now I think we need to get movin' ourselves, to find a place where we can safely spend the night. How many of you can ride a horse instead of ridin' in a wagon?"

Most of the men and two of the women assured him that they would be much happier on horseback than in a jouncing wagon, even in the rain. Some of them must have had Air or Water magic to protect themselves from the rain, and the rest most likely had Earth magic. The idea of riding a horse at any time wasn't one that appealed to me much to begin with, but then I began to think about it. Being dependent on others to get you from place to place put you at their mercy, but if you were able to go and do all by yourself . . .

But that was something to think about at another time. Right now it was time for us to leave, with only two of the three remaining wagons filled with what was left of the provisions along with those who couldn't or didn't care to ride horses. Jovvi, Lorand, Naran, and I would be using the coach, as Rion had been one of those who had opted for a horse. We intended to take extra mounts with us, and turn loose all those horses we didn't want or need. Once our current captives were found and roused, if they wanted to come after us they would have to do so on foot.

Rion walked us to the coach while the very last of the preparations were being made, his magic still keeping the rain off us. He walked with Lorand while Naran and I helped Jovvi, and once we were in the coach he gave Naran a parting kiss and left. I suppose I looked away from that again, and Jovvi wasn't so tired or distracted that she didn't notice.

"All right, now that it's no one but us, tell me what's wrong between you and Vallant this time," she said, clearly trying not to sound weary. "I noticed the distance between you two almost as soon as I opened my eyes, and the passing time has only added to the impression. Is it a simple disagreement, or something more involved?"

"I'd say . . . a lot more involved," I admitted with reluctance, trying not to see Naran's look of concerned support. "I . . . got Vallant away from Eltrina Razas and he was really beastly toward me, so I . . . decided our relationship had come to an end. I refused to listen when he tried to say that it hadn't, but then he . . . stopped apologizing. He . . . made certain statements I couldn't completely argue with, and then he said that now *he* was the one who was unwilling to listen. I've . . . been trying to decide if he was right about the things he accused me of."

"If you've been thinking about it and don't know for certain yet, chances are you're just trying to avoid admitting that he *was* right," she said, leaning forward to touch my hand. "It's possible I'm mistaken about that, but it's something to keep in mind while you do your thinking. Along with deciding what you'll do if it turns out that he was right beyond all doubt."

I distractedly returned the touch she'd given me, having already come to the same conclusion myself. Chances were excellent that Vallant had told the absolute truth, so what *was* I going to do about it? Our relationship had ended because of *me*, so how was I going to correct the error?

As our coach wheels reluctantly pulled free of the mud trying to hold them, I realized I hadn't the faintest idea. I'd have to start with trying to apologize, of course, but something told me that that wasn't going to work. And if it didn't, *then* what . . . ?

TWENTY-EIGHT

Delin came awake slowly, noticing first that the others were all there in the room with him. Then he realized that the room was in his own wing of the palace, and all the rest of his memories came flooding back. They'd won the final competition and they were now the new Seated Five, a fact which brought a thrill of delight. But then other, different memories came, and the delight disappeared as though it had never been.

"That's right, you now know everything that's happened to and around you," Kambil's voice came, bringing Delin's gaze up and to him where he sat. All the others, Bron and Selendi and Homin, sat around Kambil, all of them looking at *him* with chilling amusement.

"I . . . remember hearing you swear that you would never turn me loose again," Delin managed to get out despite those stares. "Why have you changed your mind?"

"What makes you think I've turned you loose?" Kambil countered, his amusement the strongest of all. "My aim was to give you as much grief as you and your madness have given *us,* and now I've thought of the way to do that. You'll be awake and aware of everything happening around you, but you've been given certain orders under Puredan that you won't be able to disobey.''

"What sort of orders?" Delin asked, although he would have much preferred not to say a word. The four were enjoying themselves at *his* expense, the four people who were supposed to be part of him and entirely his.

"The first one was my idea," Selendi said with a light laugh. "You have this entire wing of the palace that's supposed to be yours, but you'll only be allowed to live in one room of it—this one. You'll eat in here, sleep in here on a cot you'll have brought in, and generally spend all the time you're not required to be elsewhere right here in this one room. The rest of the wing is off-limits to you, so you won't use any part of it.''

"And don't expect to enjoy the meals you have in here," Homin said, taking up after Selendi while Delin's mind reeled in shock. "Your food will be very plain, the absolute least you can have and still remain healthy, with no seasoning or sweetening to increase its flavor. You'll insist on that, no matter what your servants do to try to change your mind.''

"And when we're all together you'll walk or stand behind the rest of us, generally behaving like a servant," Bron said, obviously enjoying enormously Delin's being so stunned that he was openmouthed. "You went ahead and did as you pleased about matters which concerned all of us, making decisions alone instead of talking to the rest of us about them. We won't be free of the chaos *that* caused for quite some time, so it's only right that you forfeit your former place among us.''

"Bron's right when he says you have no grounds for complaint," Kambil said, interrupting Delin's wildly babbling protests. "We all know you're insane, Delin, but that doesn't also have to mean that you're stupid. The stupidity seems to be an added bonus that's thrown in, and one you refuse to acknowledge and take into consideration. Are you able to see *yet* how much damage you've done?''

"All I did was make an effort to protect us all!" Delin choked out, having no real idea what they were talking about. "How can you say that protecting us is doing damage?"

"Think, Delin!" Kambil snapped, almost making Delin jump. "I told you that you now know everything that's happened, so try to remember what I said about our interviews with the assistants and secretaries to the Advisors *you* had killed. Only some of them know everything their superiors were involved in, and the rest are just as much in the dark as we are! It's hardly likely that the men who are gone did more than give orders on the important matters, but now we have to search around to find out who they gave their orders *to*!"

"And it's not proving easy," Bron growled, staring at Delin with all amusement gone. "Not only that, but for some reason there are now lapses in shipments that should be coming from all over the empire. The remaining Advisors are getting complaints by the dozen, but they have no idea about what to do. These things were all taken care of by those Advisors who are now gone, specifically the ones *you* had destroyed. The only Advisors left are either very new to their places or entirely useless for any purpose beyond strutting around showing off their rings."

"Do you understand *now*?" Kambil said, the words more of a demand than a question. "Say something to make me believe that you understand."

"I understand that you're having problems that you choose to blame on *me*," Delin returned, his head spinning so wildly that he barely knew what it was that he said. "You saw to the removal of five of the Advisors yourselves. Do you expect me to believe that that has no bearing at all on the trouble you're having now?"

"I told you he'd say that," Selendi put in after making a rude sound. "He's never been able to accept responsibility for his actions, no matter how often he pretended that he did. It isn't the ten people *he* had put out of the way that's causing turmoil, just the five who never would have dirtied their hands on any of the piddling details of running the empire. Our five were only concerned with major efforts, but that means nothing."

"Say something, Delin," Kambil prodded, anger clear in his eyes. "Tell me how much of the mess we now have on our hands is all *your* fault. Prove to me that something of what we've said has gotten through to you."

"Of course, Kambil," Delin acquiesced, forcing his voice to be even and relatively calm. "Everything that's happened is my fault, and I'll be the first to admit it. It was my actions alone that brought about every bit of the difficulty."

"I think I've suddenly developed Spirit magic," Homin said, his tone very dry. "He's said exactly what he thinks we want to hear, but doesn't believe a word of it himself. Am I wrong, Kambil?"

"Hardly," Kambil replied, just as dryly. "He hasn't learned a thing from what we said, but I never really expected him to. So when you start to look around for reasons why this is happening to you, Delin, start with this reason: your stubborn stupidity refuses to learn. If that ever changes I'll know about it, but until then you can see if suffering truly gains us understanding. And now we have several interviews to conduct. Come along."

Delin was appalled by how quickly and obediently he rose to his feet, the others standing in their own good time. It wasn't a joke or a threat, he really had been enslaved, and his numbed mind refused even to search for a means of escape. But that would pass, and once it did . . .

"Oh, by the way," Kambil said as he led the way out of the room. "If you aren't having any luck thinking of a way out of your dilemma, don't be surprised. You've been ordered not to do anything to change your current situation and status, and as the order most strongly reinforced, it should be the one most strongly obeyed. If I'm wrong about that, please let me know."

The sense of shock was more brief this time, a surge of anger rudely displacing it. Delin had nodded his agreement to obey this newest command, and he knew he certainly would. He'd been given no choice but to obey completely, just as though he really were a slave! Fury came at that thought, but at the moment there was nothing Delin could do to change it.

They all walked through the apartment and wing that was supposed to be his, then out into the common hall which led to various interview and meeting rooms in the public wing. The public wing had mostly been used by the Advisors, a properly impressive place to conduct their official business, but Delin now remembered that Kambil had changed all that. The remaining Advisors had each been assigned small meeting rooms, but those rooms couldn't be used without the prior approval of the Five. The power which had previously rested in Advisory hands was now returned to the Five, and Kambil meant to do everything in his power to be certain it never left again.

"Tomorrow we'll begin to conduct interviews to fill some of the empty Advisory seats," Bron commented over his shoulder to Delin, who trailed along behind the others. "Right now we have a more important matter to see to, a mess you happen to be innocent of creating. For a wonder."

Selendi and Homin made low-class sounds of agreement, the humiliation of which nearly distracted Delin. To think that *those* two would dare to mock *him* . . . But then he realized he knew what Bron had been talking about, and the matter really was serious. Those five peasants they'd faced in the final competition, the ones who had nearly overcome them . . . They were not only still alive, but had apparently escaped from the city. Things had been happening with the pursuit, and they had to be updated as to the latest. And they had to institute even greater effort to find and destroy them.

Delin blamed Kambil for that particular mess, and stared at the man's back as he followed the others into a fairly ornate interview room. If *he* had been in charge the way he should have been, those responsible for keeping the five peasants alive would have paid for the incredible stupidity with their own lives. It was only fitting, but Kambil was too soft to do what was proper. He would be their downfall, Delin knew it with utter certainty, but as long as the man had control of the rest of their Five—which he obviously still did—Delin's hands were chained rather than simply tied.

"As soon as we're seated, you may bring in Captain Althers," Kambil said to the servant who awaited them in the room. "You're to stay just outside while we interview him, and when we're done you'll show in the next person we wish to speak to. Is that clear?"

"Completely, Your Excellency," the servant acknowledged with a bow as Delin and the others took their places on the two-stepped dais holding their chairs. Delin's place became the end one on the extreme left, and his humiliation over that was very painful. The last time an interview was conducted like that, his place had been the one Kambil now occupied in the very center. . . .

"Your Excellencies, Captain Althers," the servant announced after he'd gone to the far door of the room and gestured to someone in the room beyond. The man who entered was stocky and older than Delin and the others, but not as much older as the Advisors were. The newcomer bowed while the servant silently left the room and closed the door behind him, and Kambil gestured the man closer.

"Tell us what you've learned, Captain Althers," he said. "You have word from the command sent after the escaped criminals?"

"A number of pigeons flew in together, Excellency," the man replied after having walked nearer. "Considering the weather and how long it took to get them on the road, they made very good time. It wasn't good enough, however, as they reached the convoy far too late for them to prevent the escape of those criminals as well. The ones the command is following somehow ambushed the convoy and made prisoners of the guard members and drivers, and escaped into the countryside. The guardsmen and drivers were all asleep when the command reached them, so they were unable to say whether the criminals left together or separately."

"What about the spy in their midst?" Selendi demanded. "Surely *he* found a way to leave word as to where they were all going?"

"Unfortunately, Excellency, he was found among the sleeping guardsmen," Captain Althers admitted with reluctance. "He was furious over having been discovered, as now there's no one left to keep track of the criminals and pass on their whereabouts."

"This is worse than simply not good," Kambil said in a tone that made the nervous Captain Althers even more nervous. "What does the command intend to do next? Return here with nothing to show for their efforts?"

"Not at all, Excellency," the captain protested, beads of sweat clear on his brow. "Wagons and horses were taken from the convoy, so they mean to cast about for a trail to follow. They won't return empty-handed as long as there's the slightest chance of finding those miscreants.''

"Let's hope for all our sakes that they're successful," Kambil said, the frigid words adding a tremor to the captain's hands. "You're able to send a message by pigeon to them as well?"

"Not directly to *them,* Excellency," Althers corrected carefully. "The town of Quellin, not too far ahead of them, has a facility for receiving pigeon messages, and they'll send someone ahead to see what your orders are now." ·

"Our orders are what they were to begin with," Kambil said in the same chilly tones. "Those people are to be found and executed, since criminals of their sort always make people regret any leniency they've shown. Once executed, the bodies are to be brought back here to Gan Garee, or the heads alone if the rest is too unwieldy to handle. That command is not to return without the results we demand, be sure you make that clear to them. If they do . . . we'll be extremely unhappy."

Delin saw Althers swallow hard before bowing in preparation to take his leave, but there was still quite a lot which *hadn't* been said. If the man knew the exact fate he and the others faced he would be a good deal more earnest in his efforts, so Delin meant to add to what Althers had been told. He started to open his mouth . . . *tried* to open his mouth . . . sat there silently struggling while the man backed away toward the door . . .

"Don't bother, Delin," Bron, who sat next to him, said in a very soft voice. "No one is interested in anything *you* might have to say, so you've been ordered not to say it. Just sit there and listen and think about the freedom your stupidity has cost you."

Delin would have snarled and screamed if he'd been able to, but even that had been denied him. Rather than do anything which might draw attention to him, he had no choice but to simply sit there and accept that raging horror. Kambil chuckled and leaned forward to glance at him briefly, the glance saying Kambil knew exactly how Delin felt and was glad of it. That made it worse, of course, but in a strange, distant way it also made things better. Delin's father had always ruled him with a hand of iron, never allowing him to speak of or show any evidence of what was being done to him. This was a familiar situation, then, and one he had managed to get around . . . in a way . . .

"Excellencies, Lady Hallina Mardimil," the servant announced, then stepped out of the way of the woman. She stalked in with blood in her eye, as far from the fear of the previous interviewee as it's possible to get, and her tirade barely waited until the servant had closed the door again.

"How *dare* you send guardsmen to drag me back here to Gan Garee?" she demanded as she advanced on them, her tone nearly a growl. "Have you any idea of what my standing truly is, that you dare to treat me as though I were a common peasant? You're all mere children, and I know well enough how thoughtless children usually are—and how insolent they can be with their elders. You will *immediately* give orders to—"

"That's enough!" Kambil snapped, interrupting the fool of a woman as the other three on the dais stirred with annoyance. "If you think we don't know that you were related to three members of the previous Five, you ridiculous harridan, you're actually as stupid as you behave. What *you* seem to be overlooking is the fact that it was the *previous* Five you had connections to. To the people who have taken their place, you're less than nothing. Am I speaking slowly and clearly enough for your limited intelligence to take it all in?"

The woman's face had first gone crimson with anger and humiliation, but then it had paled with the realization that she was far from being untouchable in their eyes. Delin could see that although she really was a rather stupid woman—as everyone who had ever come across her knew—she was intelligent enough to be aware of where the true power lay. She'd seemed ready to add to what she'd already said, but instead simply raised her chin in silent defiance of Kambil's tongue-lashing.

"Well, at least we've achieved a somewhat polite silence from you," Kambil observed, leaning back in his chair again, the words just as hard as his previous ones. "Now that we have, we can get to the purpose of this interview. You were stupid enough to flex your influence and reclaim that ridiculous son of yours, and then you were incompetent enough to lose him again. For that, Madam, you will pay hard, because if he isn't recaptured it will be *you* who gives up her life in his place. Are you willing to do that to protect him?''

"Give up my life for *that* ingrate?'' she demanded, her skin now pale as milk. "Surely you're joking. He threw my love and concern back in my face, and I'll never forgive him for that. If it's my permission you want—''

"Wake up, Lady Fool!'' Selendi took her turn to interrupt, the words dripping with scathing contempt. "No one needs *your* permission for anything, least of all *us*. Keep your mouth closed unless you're answering a question you've been asked, and listen to what you're about to be told.''

"I couldn't have put that better myself,'' Kambil added with an approving smile for Selendi, then the smile died when he turned his attention back to the Mardimil woman. "What we want from you is an expenditure of gold and effort, a private attempt to locate what was lost because of your negligence. We have our own people out searching, but we want yours added to them—and we want daily reports on what your people are doing and what they're finding out. If *you* manage to recover your son and hand him— or his body—over to us, you'll be allowed to keep most of what you have. If you leave it to *us* to find him . . . Does the word 'pauper' paint any pictures for you?''

The woman's shock caused her mouth to drop open, and for a moment Delin thought she would fall in a faint. If her skin had been pale before, now it was chalk white. It took her a long moment to recover herself, but then she nodded jerkily. She understood perfectly what had been told to her, and now would surely spare no effort to repair the error she'd made. She curtsied low—and shakily—before beginning to back to the door, not at all the same person who had entered. Delin found that to be very much a relief, and then the servant was entering the room again in her place.

"Lady Eltrina Razas,'' the servant announced, but it wasn't a woman alone who entered. A square-faced, middle-aged man came in with her, a man whose skin was ruddy with embarrassment. Delin didn't know why that was, but once the servant was gone and the two people had bowed, he quickly found out.

"Lady Eltrina Razas and the man she's supposed to be married to," Kambil drawled as he gestured for the two to come closer. "You may be wondering why only your wife was announced, Lord Grall, but that's easily explained. You've made a habit of allowing the female to run around doing as she pleased, just as though she *had* no husband to teach her better. With that in mind, we had you treated as the nonentity you've chosen to be."

The man's jaw clenched hard as he gave the trembling woman a long glance, but he made no effort to deny the charge leveled against him. Delin knew Lord Grall was a man who had fingers in a large number of pies, and was also the sort who had to preside over his holdings and business interests himself. That was why his wife had been free to do as she pleased, but chances were excellent that that would no longer be the case.

"Your lack of puerile excuses impresses us, Lord Grall," Kambil said after a moment, the words sounding sincere. "There are too few people in this empire who take responsibility for the things they should, and I, personally, am pleased that we seem to have found one. You've been informed of what that female has caused to happen?"

"Yes, Your Excellency," the man replied in a deep and gravelly voice. "Her itch to squirm made her claim the use of a condemned criminal, which gave his accomplices the chance to free him. What may I do to help repair that disgusting situation?"

"I'm afraid we'll have to insist that you finance a private search for the criminal, to add to the resources already expended by our own people," Kambil responded with a small nod of approval. "If your forces succeed before our own, you'll find yourself rewarded in a way that should please you. If you fail, well, it's my sad duty to inform you that your wife's life will be forfeit. And that will be so even if you haven't decided to repudiate your marriage and toss her out into the street."

"Those terms are completely acceptable, Excellency," Lord Grall responded, again looking at the trembling woman who now stood with her eyes closed and her face as chalk white as the previous woman's had been. "Although I should say that I've decided against throwing her out for the moment. I haven't had nearly as much use from her as I should have had, but she'll make that up to me while she still lives. It would be unfair to other men if I let her go off on her own to find a fool she can manipulate into acting on her behalf."

"A decision I quite agree with, Lord Grall," Kambil said, again sounding very approving. "We'll expect daily reports on the progress—or lack thereof—of your searchers, and we'll have our own people coordinate with yours to save the duplication of effort. You and your property are now excused."

A grimly satisfied look briefly touched Lord Grall's face at that, and the woman began to sob soundlessly. Kambil had just declared Eltrina a slave where Lord Grall was concerned, and chances were excellent that he would treat her as one from now on. The man took the woman's arm and bowed his way out dragging her along, and Kambil took the opportunity to glance at those sitting around him.

"He wasn't putting on a charade for our benefit," he murmured to his groupmates. "He meant everything he said, so we'd do well to keep him in mind. There are any number of places where he'll be more than useful to us."

Bron and the other two nodded, but Delin didn't bother. He wasn't one of those Kambil had been speaking to, a truth he had no trouble keeping in mind. Lord Grall pulled Eltrina out of the room with a jerk, and the servant appeared again with another bow.

"High Lord Embisson Ruhl," the servant announced this time, then stepped aside to hold the door wide, something he hadn't done the previous times. The reason for that became clear in a moment, when four men carried in a litter which contained Lord Embisson. The High Lord was so clearly in pain that Delin had no trouble noticing—although, come to think of it, Delin hadn't been noticing much at all with his talent lately....

"Set the litter down there and then leave us," Kambil ordered the bearers, pointing to a spot only a few feet from the dais. "You'll be sent for again when the time comes for Lord Embisson to depart."

The four men did as they were told, and once the door closed behind them Delin gave his full attention to Lord Embisson. The man was propped up a bit on pillows, and lingering bruises on his face suggested why he'd had to be carried in. An accident of some sort had obviously befallen the man, and he hadn't yet recovered from it.

"I find myself surprised at your appearance, Lord Embisson," Kambil said in a musing tone. "I'd heard that you were set upon by thieves and beaten, but I thought you would surely be over the thing by now."

"I'm told . . . I won't be over it . . . for some time," Ruhl forced himself to say, his face nearly as pale as those of the two previous women. "More than . . . casual damage was . . . done to me, and . . . my innards . . . require more healing time . . . than my outer self."

"That's interesting," Kambil said, still in that musing tone. "If I were into speculating, I would guess that the thieves were more interested in hurting you than in robbing you. But there's no point in building guesswork in a matter that will never see it proved or disproved, not when the guilty haven't yet been caught. Tell me, Lord Embisson, do you enjoy being a High Lord?"

"I . . . beg your pardon?" Ruhl forced out, confusion now clearly touching him. "Certainly I . . . enjoy my position. Have I . . . misheard or misunderstood your question, Excellency?"

"Not at all," Kambil denied with a small headshake as he sat back in his chair. "I asked simply because I wanted to gauge your reaction more accurately when you learned that you will no longer have the privilege of calling yourself High Lord. Ah, the news is devastating to you, so you did more than simply enjoy your position. It was your greatest delight, which means your punishment is completely appropriate."

"Punishment . . . for what?" Ruhl came close to demanding, the shock holding him so strongly. "What have I done . . . to merit such a terrible fate?"

"We've learned that it was your orders which kept our former opponents alive," Kambil answered, no longer laconic. "It was *you*, you fool, who also allowed the late Lord Lanir to take the girl of Fire magic for his own purposes!

Hasn't anyone told you that Lanir had to be put down after he burned himself out? Circumstances would suggest that he did that trying to match the girl's strength when he discovered that she was no longer under his control. The incompetent idiot *couldn't* match her, of course, and after she dealt with him she left his house and promptly freed two others of her Blending. After that the three of them went after the convoy containing the last two members, and now the five are together again!''

"No!" Ruhl whispered, horror twisting his features. "That can't be true! . . . They can't be free . . . and together again!"

"But they are, and all of that is thanks to you," Kambil contradicted, his tone cold and unforgiving. "Right now we've simply taken away the privilege of calling yourself High Lord. For every three days they remain uncaught, another level of nobility will be stripped from you. If they continue uncaught long enough, you'll find yourself lower than the lowliest peasant. At that point you'll be thrown into the street to beg for whatever you need to keep yourself alive, and the district you'll be begging in will be one of the ones which were part of your former holdings. Your people will be called to carry you out again now, but you'll return here in three days to find out just what your new status is. Do you understand me?"

Ruhl's nod was as jerky as the Mardimil woman's had been, but it was a good deal more brief. The man now *looked* devastated, and when Kambil rang for his bearers he just lay on the litter without moving. Once he was removed Delin expected the next person to be brought in, but the servant didn't reappear and Kambil and the others stood and stretched.

"That's it for now, but we'll have to discuss possible future moves in addition to those already set in motion," Kambil said to the three people near him. "You, Delin, aren't included in that, so you have my permission to return to your wing. When we want you again we'll send for you."

The others smiled with clear amusement as Delin obediently got to his feet and headed out of the room, going back to his wing as he'd been ordered to do. His inside self raged with impotent anger over being treated like this, but that was perfectly all right. Kambil would expect him to react that way, and above all else he needed to act the way he was expected to.

Just as he had when he'd been in his father's complete power. He'd always acted just the way he was supposed to, and his father had never discovered the tiny, private part of his mind that planned and plotted a fitting revenge. That tiny part was now alive again, and somehow, some way, it would find the path to freedom for him just as it had before. And, as he had with his father, Delin now lived for the time when vengeance would be his. . . .

TWENTY-NINE

Lorand sat on the coach seat, Jovvi's sleeping head against his shoulder, wishing he, too, could be asleep. He wasn't far from total exhaustion, but right now there was something required of him that had to be done. They'd been driving for two hours at least, but still hadn't found a safe place to stop and rest.

To Lorand's extended talent, the night was far from quiet. Even in the rain life continued its cycle, as those who prowled the night did so with mild complaint rather than with gusto. Every life-form out there was busy, either hunting, or growing, or warning of danger, or simply healing in sleep. Sleep . . . that would have been nice . . . the way Naran had also fallen asleep . . . and the way Tamrissa was fighting not to. . . .

Suddenly Lorand's head snapped up, sleep no longer the foremost thing in his thoughts. The area they'd just reached

. . . the feelings of the animals around here were just that much different from normal, the normal of empty woods and nothing of human habitation. Here the prowling or resting animals were uneasy and cautious, which ought to mean—

"Rion, tell Lidris to stop the coach," Lorand said out his window, the words Rion had probably been waiting for. The other man had been riding his horse close to the coach, using his Air magic talent to keep himself dry. "I think there may be a farm or something around here, but I don't know exactly where."

"There should be a way to find out," Rion responded, then called to the coach driver to stop. Alsin Meerk also rode on the coach, Lorand knew, his horse tied to the back of it. The man had continued to look disturbed and deep in thought, and it was possible that he rode on the coach with his man so that the two could talk. Lorand wasn't much of a judge, but Alsin Meerk seemed to need someone friendly to talk to very badly.

When the coach stopped, the following wagon naturally did the same. Those on horseback had been riding in various positions, either near the wagon, behind it, or ahead of the coach. Now everyone came together, and Lorand put his head outside the window.

"There should be some sort of human habitation on the right side of the road," he told everyone. "The problem will be finding the way to get to it in this darkness, so I'd like to try an experiment. If those of you with Earth magic will try to link with me, we can search for what would be an unnatural opening in the trees. I take it you all understand what that would feel like?"

"I do," Meerk said as he climbed down from the box, his words joining the agreement of three others on horseback. "How do you want to do this?"

"Open yourself to the power, then reach out with it in my direction," Lorand said, speaking to all of them. "I have no idea whether or not the link will work, but we should try it before we do something else."

Lorand didn't mention that the only something else would be his Blending with his groupmates. Blending was extremely draining, and afterward most of them would be good for nothing but falling down and sleeping. This way something might be accomplished without leaving their strongest protection weak and useless.

It was obvious when the four other users of Earth magic opened to the power, just as obvious as the fact that Meerk was the weakest of the group. The other three really were Highs, and briefly Lorand wondered if their relatively fresh strength would overwhelm him when they tried to link—or if his weariness would be the reason the experiment didn't work. And then their power and talent touched him, and more than new strength flooded into him. His own talent was magnified in some way, at the very least twice as great as it was normally. . . .

"There it is," Lorand said, distantly aware of the same words coming from the other four people in the link. "A crude road cut into the woods about a hundred yards ahead, but more overgrown than a road that's used should be."

They broke the link then so that those on horseback could ride to where the road began, and Lorand had another surprise. The new strength he'd been given had ebbed only a little with the breaking of the link, which meant he'd now have less trouble doing what was needed to make them safe.

Meerk went to his horse rather than climbing back up on the coach, and then their little convoy followed those on horseback. The road they'd found would have been passed without the least notice, thanks to the darkness surrounding it and the fact that it had begun to be overgrown. Other riders came up to join those with Earth magic, and the way light flared in the darkness and rain said that those others had Fire magic. When they turned off onto the road, they would not be traveling blind.

It took quite a few minutes of cautious traveling before they came to an area that had once been cleared for cultivation, and then another stretch of time before they reached buildings. Somewhere in the darkness Lorand could tell that there was a small herd of cattle, but the feel of pigs and chickens was scattered all over the place rather than centered in specific spots.

And the buildings themselves . . . there seemed to be three houses on each side of a larger-than-usual barn, but none of them showed a light. At that time of night the occupants should be asleep, of course, but their arrival was really too noisy to be slept through. And then Lorand realized that there was nothing in the way of indications of living beings inside those houses. . . .

"I think this place is deserted," Jovvi said, obviously having seen the same thing Lorand had. "I wonder why they didn't take their livestock with them."

"*I* wonder why they would build six houses and a barn, then turn around and abandon it all," Lorand countered. "Something about this place just doesn't feel right. . . ."

Shouts came from up ahead, and Lorand had the distinct impression that something had been found. A rider came galloping past the coach to stop at the wagon, the woman on the horse riding with one hand to her mouth. That confirmed the uneasy feeling Lorand had, and Jovvi looked positively alarmed. But they didn't find out what was causing the uproar until Rion came riding back.

"Until a few moments ago, I had convinced myself that I was no longer innocent," Rion said in a wooden voice, his face pale in the glow of the small ball of flame which Tamrissa had set in the air beside him. "Now . . . now I wish I truly were still innocent, as the price of worldliness is at times much too high."

"Rion, what is it?" Jovvi asked very gently, and Lorand had the impression that she touched Rion with soothing and loving concern. "What did you find that caused such an uproar?"

"The people in this place . . . they didn't leave," Rion answered, his voice now filled with pain. "Alsin Meerk suggested that this farm was established so far away from everything else because the people were tired of working just to provide the nobility with more income. So they decided to take unclaimed land and work only for themselves, but clearly the nobility found where they were. They . . ."

Rion's voice faltered as he shook his head, very clearly unable to go on. But by then Vallant had joined him, and their groupmate's face wore an expression of furious and unrestrained rage.

"Those animals couldn't allow six families to escape from them and set up on their own," Vallant growled, not quite looking at anyone. "It would have given other people ideas, and that they certainly didn't want. So they made an example of these people, hangin' each family from crude gibbets put up outside their houses. Men, women, and children, even two infants. They've been hangin' there for some little time, certainly as a warnin' to anyone who came to see how the 'escapees' were doin'. One look tells it all."

Lorand felt shock so great that he couldn't speak, simply holding to Jovvi as she shuddered against him. Tamrissa had one hand to her mouth, as though to hold back physical illness, and Naran wept silently. What Vallant and Rion had just said was beyond belief, far too savage and inhuman for it to be real. There had to be a mistake of some kind. . . .

"My father's farm," he found himself saying. "Could that be the real reason he didn't want me to leave? Because he had to produce a certain amount in order to keep the nobility happy? And to let the rest of us live? But he never said that the farm wasn't his alone . . ."

"We've got to destroy them," Tamrissa's voice came then, calmly reasonable with only a hint of hysteria to it. "The entire world changes with every day and everything new we learn, and every change makes things worse. They kill and maim and destroy and enslave, and no one does anything to stop them. *We* have to do something, or we're no better than those butchers are."

"We *will* do somethin'," Vallant assured her, but his voice was too grim and hard to be soothing. "Right now we've got to take those bodies down, then we'll all spend the night in that barn. In the mornin' we can have a mass cremation, and then talk about the details of what we'll do. This is more than the last straw . . ."

Lorand nodded and began to leave the coach to join them, but Rion quietly told him to stay where he was before turning his horse to follow Vallant's already retreating mount. The new strength that Lorand had found was now drained out of him, so he made no attempt to argue about staying in the coach. He simply felt a vague sort of impatience, wanting his full strength back so that they could begin to avenge six families of people who had sought for nothing but their freedom. . . .

Lidris climbed down from the coach and more of the men and some women came from the wagon, and even Tamrissa and Naran went to join the grisly cleanup effort. Even so it took quite some time, but finally Lidris returned to mount the coach box again and urge the horses forward. They were brought to the front of the barn, where Rion waited to open the coach door.

"The coach and wagon will be put behind the barn, and the horses stabled in the back half," Rion informed them as he helped Jovvi out then turned to give Lorand a hand. "That leaves an adequate amount of space for us humans in the front half, thank whatever Highest Aspect there might be. If we had to stay in any of those houses, I think most of us would have elected to sleep in the rain."

"I know I would have," Lorand said as he turned to close the coach door. "Staying in one of those houses would be an inexcusable intrusion, considering that the owners of those houses were brutally murdered. Is there anything left that Jovvi and I can help with?"

"No," Rion began with a faint smile and a headshake, but his gentle denial was overridden by someone else's much stronger opinion.

"Yes, there *is* something the lady can do," Meerk said as he strode over, his expression totally unlike anything Lorand had ever seen on the man before. "Once everyone is in the barn, she can make certain that there are no more spies among us. Once that's taken care of, I'll describe what I've been thinking about to everyone together."

"What sort of thing have you been thinking about, Alsin?" Jovvi asked, a faint frown line between her brows. "I can see that it's caused you a good deal of pain, but that's all I can see."

"I've come to the conclusion that I deserve the pain," Meerk said, apparently forcing himself to discuss something he hadn't been able to before. "Everyone kept telling me that I was being a backward fool, seeing myself as more noble than the nobility because I refused to use their methods to defeat them. And that *was* the way I saw myself, as someone too nobly upright to lower himself. I was even willing to have people believe me too frightened to fight, rather than letting them know that I was really too good a person to indulge in such bestial tactics. I've now discovered that I've been lying to myself."

"So you've reversed your former position," Jovvi said with a nod, leading them all into the barn and out of the rain. "Are you sure that that's what you really want to do?"

"I've known it's what I *should* do for hours, only I kept finding excuses not to," he replied, looking down at his feet rather than at them. "I even tried to get Lidris to remind me what I believed our aims *ought* to be, but Lidris has been doing his own thinking. We assured each other that we would continue to do things the *right* way, and then we got *here* . . ."

"And the right way became something else entirely," Jovvi finished for him with another nod. "Yes, I not only understand completely, I feel the same way. Everyone here is filled with thoughts of vengeance and violence, and rather than trying to soothe those feelings away, I'm joining in feeling them with everything inside me. Tomorrow we *will* make plans, but frankly I have no idea what they should be beyond freeing any of our people who are still in Quellin."

They were interrupted by sounds of satisfaction coming from all around, and Lorand suddenly realized that the dampness he'd been feeling for hours and had stopped noticing had abruptly disappeared. Then he saw Vallant standing with two other people, all three of them glancing around in the same direction, and thought he knew what had been done. Vallant had linked with others having Water magic, and together they'd removed every bit of moisture from the clothing of their group.

"Bless that man," Jovvi said with a satisfied sigh of her own. "That wasn't anything like being able to use a bath house, but somehow I now feel a bit cleaner. In the morning, when we've all regained our strength, we've *got* to see about getting a bath."

"There's something we have to see about before that," Meerk said, not so much disagreeing as speaking what was uppermost in his mind. "We'll have to put sentries out close to the road, to let us know the minute our pursuers come in range of their talent."

"So that we can hide all traces of where we are," Jovvi said, a faint dissatisfaction now touching her. "It's too bad there isn't something else we can do. . . ."

"But there is, and not only *can* we, but we *must*," Meerk

said, drawing himself up straighter. "Going up against Quellin is all well and good, but not while a large number of guardsmen are coming up behind us. Before we turn our attention to the enemy ahead of us, we have to completely eliminate the enemy at our backs. No one who knows anything at all about warfare would consider any other course of action."

Hearing that, Lorand stared at Meerk with an expression that must have suggested the man had two heads. He'd said warfare, as though the word meant more to him than just another word for large-scale fighting. Was it possible that the man actually *knew* something about it, which the rest of them didn't? If so, the knowledge might actually make the difference between their winning a battle or two, and their eventually standing victorious over *all* their enemies. . . .

THIRTY

Jovvi wasn't sure about how to respond to what Alsin had said, not when his thoughts were so grimly hard. What had happened to the man was something Jovvi had seen twice before, both times in the presence of some sort of traumatic incident. The person involved had usually had many private doubts about what he or she was doing, and the shock of whatever incident reached them was so strong that they began to blame themselves for what had happened. And they accepted that blame without argument, thinking that if they hadn't clung to their previous opinions then the incident might not have taken place.

In some cases the change was a good thing, but in most

it produced a strong fanaticism in the reverse stance which the person adopted. Their previously rejected ideas were now the only thing possible for them to do, and they began to pursue the completion of those ideas no matter who tried to stand in their way. It was true that they all needed to be strong and hard right now, but fanaticism was something else entirely. . . .

"I hadn't realized that you knew so much about warfare, Alsin," Jovvi hedged, trying to get a clearer reading of the man. "While we were looking for a safe place to rest, Tamrissa told me that you'd mentioned how unfortunate it was that we had no one who could be considered experienced in actual warfare. We all agreed that that was because the empire wasn't even supposed to have an army, although now we know it does."

"I've suspected the existence of an army for some time," Alsin responded, his tone of voice and the tenor of his mind saying again that he now confessed the terrible things he'd done before. "I . . . happen to be a student of history, military history in particular, and one of the books I read said that no political entity like our empire ever existed in the world without an army, unless it existed alone. And even then there would probably be at least the remnants of the army which caused them to *be* alone in the world."

"That makes sense," Lorand put in with a nod, and Jovvi was glad to see that he sounded supportive and cautiously enthusiastic. "Now that you've made the point, I agree that we need to do something about the guardsmen who are coming after us. Even if they simply passed us by and continued on to Quellin, that would do nothing more than reinforce the people we need to go up against."

"Exactly," Alsin said with his own nod, now warming to his subject a bit more. "So we have to set up an ambush, and make sure they don't ever reinforce anyone ever again."

"You want us to kill them all?" Lorand blurted, and Jovvi could feel the shock in him that the concept had been put that baldly. "But didn't you say some of *your* people might be with them? How can you suggest killing your own people?"

"Any guardsman who's a member of my organization will stand back and refuse to participate in a fight," Alsin stated, the words very flat. "At least that's what they all swore to do, just as Grath swore to be loyal to us. If they break their sworn word the way he did, they deserve whatever happens to them."

"I . . . see," Lorand muttered, still taken aback, but Alsin Meerk noticed nothing of that. He clapped Lorand on the shoulder, then looked around.

"People are beginning to bring the blankets and things out of the wagon," he said, nodding toward the men walking from the back of the barn with their arms full. "That means they're in the process of stabling the horses, and they'll need help with that. You and I will have to talk again later."

Jovvi watched Lorand smile and nod before Alsin turned away, knowing well enough how he really felt. Once Alsin strode off, Lorand put an arm around her and drew her close.

"This isn't something I have to *pretend* to be enjoying," he murmured, looking down into her eyes with a smile. "I've needed this since the time *before* I woke up, but before we go any farther with our personal lives—such as they are—we need to talk. Is he really as bad off as he seems?"

"Alsin is a very disturbed man," Jovvi replied with a sigh, raising one hand to touch Lorand's cheek. "I intend to work with him to see if I can help him to pull out of it, but if I can't we'll have to be very careful. He isn't far from suspecting everyone around him of being in league with 'the enemy,' and that will come to mean everyone who disagrees with him."

"Are you really going to check everyone's true feelings tonight?" Lorand asked, now looking concerned. "I can see how tired you are, which means it might be best to save it for the morning."

"I wish I could," Jovvi said, automatically soothing his concern for her. "It isn't very likely that any of the people with us are really on the opposite side of this, but considering the ruthlessness of the nobility, we can't afford to take any chances. Let's find a comfortable place to sit, and I'll get it over with."

When he simply nodded and began to look for the place she wanted, Jovvi realized that she loved him more than ever. Another man would have added to her burden by trying to "protect" her, but Lorand simply helped her do what she needed to. There was no certainty that they would survive the coming confrontations with their enemies, but if they did Jovvi knew she would never let Lorand out of her sight and reach again.

An abandoned bale of hay near one of the stalls made a good place to sit down, and Jovvi noticed that others of the group were similarly seated on other bales. After looking at those who were sitting down and those who were up and helping to get them settled, it became clear that those who had been roused first were running out of strength first. Those who hadn't been awake as long were moving with difficulty, but they were still moving.

Without the Blending entity to help her, Jovvi was only able to do a surface scan of their companions. Those who were Highs in Spirit magic were the hardest, of course, but it quickly became clear that they hadn't had her training or practice in using their talent. Duplicity, marked by nervousness or smugness, was easy to see, so that was what she searched for. Once she had touched everyone and hadn't found anything suspicious, she turned her head to Lorand again.

"There isn't anything overt to find, so that should do it for tonight," she reported. "Some of them have reservations about being involved in this, but that's natural enough. Tomorrow we can use the Blending entity to check more deeply, but I've had a thought. Are we going to urge these people to form their own fives, and then teach them how to Blend?"

"If you're worried that giving them the information will put them in jeopardy, don't forget that they're already in it," Lorand pointed out. "If you think instead that they might run wild, I'll agree that that's a possibility—if *you'll* agree that the choice and opportunity is rightfully theirs. Keeping things from people because they *might* not handle the information properly is living their lives for them, and no one has the right to live someone else's life."

"Not unless they want to end up being just like the nobility, even if only in a small way," Jovvi agreed. "No, running wild wasn't what I was thinking about. Training was my concern, as it's fairly obvious that these people haven't had much. Well, tomorrow we can discuss it with the others and find out what they think.''

Jovvi had shortened the discussion because she saw Tamma, Rion, and Naran approaching with blankets and waterskins. The three looked almost as tired as Jovvi felt, but their smiles of greeting were warm.

''We've taken possession of this big box stall over here,'' Tamma said, gesturing with her head as she and the others stopped a few feet short of where Jovvi and Lorand sat. ''If you'll give us a couple of minutes, we'll have your beds all laid out and ready to get into.''

''Just ours?'' Lorand asked, helping Jovvi up before moving forward to give Tamma a hand with her burdens. ''What about the rest of you? Unless you've found some deep, mystical secret, you need sleep as badly as we do.''

''Oh, we'll certainly be joining you,'' Naran said with a smile and a headshake as Lorand tried to take her blankets as well. ''No, thank you, my dear, but these aren't so heavy that I can't take them the rest of the way. And you can be certain that Rion and Tamrissa will be using their own beds. Vallant is taking charge of the first watch, Rion will have the second, and Tamrissa the third.''

''Having third watch was my own idea,'' Tamma said over her shoulder as she took one of the blankets from Lorand and began to spread it over the relatively clean straw in the stall. ''There are two bath houses a short distance behind this barn, equally distant from both rows of three houses, and we're going to assume that one is for men and one for women. While the Water people are on watch they'll purify the water as best they can, so that when I and other Fire magic users come on, we can heat it for bathing. If we don't find those following guardsmen in our laps first thing tomorrow morning, I'm going to have a bath.''

''And I'll be right there with you,'' Jovvi assured her. ''We don't, by any chance, have any clean clothes available, do we?''

Jovvi knew her voice had been wistful, but having clean clothes handy wasn't very likely. She knew better than most what it was like to be on the run from those who wanted to hurt you, and cleanliness showed up in a very minor position on the list of absolute necessities.

"Our associates don't have any, of course, but it so happens that we do," Tamma answered, then laughed at Jovvi's expression of delighted surprise. "You can thank Naran for that, because she's the one who packed them while there was still time to do things like that."

"Don't thank me until you see what I chose," Naran denied with a small laugh as Jovvi went over to hug the girl. "I grabbed whatever happened to be handy, so we'll all probably end up looking as though we were dressed by the color-blind."

"That's better than having people think we were dressed by someone without a sense of smell," Jovvi retorted with her own laugh. "But why are we all standing around here? Let's everyone make his or her own bed and then lie in them, because come morning we get to bathe!"

Everyone joined the laughter then, but they also did as she'd suggested. The beds were made up rather rapidly with room to spare, then Rion looked around.

"I'm going to speak with Vallant one last time before I retire," he said, his hand touching Naran's arm gently and briefly. "It shouldn't take more than a moment or two, and then I'll be back."

"Rion, wait," Lorand said softly, then turned to Jovvi. "Is *he* anywhere close enough to hear me?"

"No," Jovvi replied after a quick look around with her talent, knowing Lorand referred to Alsin Meerk. "He's still busy with getting all the horses settled in."

"Good," Lorand said, then returned his attention to Rion but included Tamma and Naran in on the conversation. "All of you—and Vallant—should know what happened with Alsin Meerk just a little while ago. We may end up having trouble with the man."

Lorand repeated the discussion as briefly as possible, and when he was through Tamma shook her head while Rion and Naran simply looked disturbed.

"I really hope Jovvi can pull him out of it," Tamma said, a large portion of her weariness showing through. "I understand that we have to do something about the guardsmen coming behind us, but to think that we should just kill them . . . I don't know if I can agree with that. If they were the ones who hanged these families it would be different, but just because they probably wear the same uniforms . . ."

"I'm forced to agree with Tamrissa," Rion said, still held by disturbance. "We must consider all our options carefully before we do something rash, and killing without much prior thought is about as rash as it comes. But I'll take Vallant aside and warn him, and tomorrow we can all discuss it with clear heads."

After touching Naran's arm again Rion left, and the rest of them went to the blanket-beds they'd prepared. Lorand had put his right next to Jovvi's, of course, but the satisfaction of that was dimmed by the thought of what tomorrow might conceivably bring. Jovvi had been able to feel what her groupmates had at the thought of killing, but she remembered something they apparently didn't: they'd already killed without regret, in that first competition. Being part of the Blending entity seemed to change all of them. . . .

And, if it became necessary, they would certainly kill again. It just remained to be seen how everyone would take mass slaughter of the helpless, if it came down to that. . . .

THIRTY-ONE

Rion stretched when he awoke and reached to where Naran had slept, but only to discover that she was no longer there. Deep breathing said that he wasn't alone in the box stall, but sitting up and looking around showed only a sleeping Vallant. Everyone else was gone, including the woman of Rion's heart. That probably meant she was off in the bath house, which made Rion chuckle. His greatest rival for Naran's affections was a pool full of warm water.

Although he would have welcomed a few more hours of sleep, Rion decided it was time to start the new day. He, too, would enjoy being able to take a bath, and having clean clothing available was the result of a joint effort. They'd gotten into the habit of washing their worn clothing in the face basins of their inn rooms, and then Vallant would remove most of the water from the freshened clothing. Then Tamrissa would use heat to remove the rest, at the same time taking many of the wrinkles from the clothing as well. The last of it had been *his* chore, unnecessary but nevertheless rather pleasurable: he would bring air scented with fresh forest odors, and pass that through the washed clothing.

Rion smiled wryly at that as he stepped quietly out of the box stall, still rather shocked that he took such things in stride. He should have been bewailing the loss of servants to do the work, the fact that he'd been reduced to sleeping in a *barn*, the truth that he was now a hunted criminal. But none of that seemed to matter, and in point of fact he'd never been so happy in his life. Now *there* was something Mother would have loved to hear. . . .

Here and there there were people still asleep in various box stalls, but the horses seemed to have been taken out and turned loose in a large paddock. Rion stopped at the coach to get the only set of clothing that was really his—the outfit he'd been wearing when Tamrissa had rescued him. What he now wore was Vallant's clothing, which fit surprisingly well. But clothing wasn't his real immediate problem; finding out which of the set of bath houses was being used by the men was.

So he walked away from the coach and the barn heading for both of them, then got the luck he'd been hoping for when he saw one of the men coming out of the bath house to the right. The man nodded to him pleasantly, a combined greeting and confirmation that that was the men's bath house, so Rion returned the nod and entered the house.

"Rion, why are you up so early?" Lorand's voice came, drawing Rion's attention to those in the water. "After the hours you spent on watch, you should still be sleeping."

"I'll sleep longer once we have all the nastiness behind us," Rion replied as he headed for a bench where he might leave all his clothing. "How's the water?"

"Lifesaving," Lorand responded, causing the other five men in the bath with him to chuckle. "And as soon as we finish washing, we have a good breakfast to look forward to. Our coach driver Lidris's main occupation isn't driving a coach, it seems. He's really an experienced chef, and that's the way he earns his silver when he isn't working for Meerk's organization. He's taken over the chore of feeding us, and everyone else will take turns helping him."

"I wonder if *I* have any talent for cooking," Rion mused aloud as he undressed. "I certainly have an interest in eating, but I understand that the two don't necessarily go together."

"No, they don't," Lorand agreed, laughing along with the others again. "I'm living proof of *that*. . . ."

Rion wondered why Lorand's comments seem to simply trail off, and then he wondered if he were only imagining things. That was an excellent possibility—until he entered the bath and Lorand came up to him after he'd been given the time to wet himself thoroughly.

"We have to talk," he said softly, as though he merely inquired again about the enjoyability of the water. "We have to decide about sharing our knowledge with the people around us."

"I hadn't realized there was a question about that," Rion replied in tones equally as soft, this time seriously surprised. "Aren't there too many people around who are keeping secrets as it is? Why would we want to join their number? And if this is truly war which we face, anything we hold back could conceivably be the one thing which gives victory to our enemies."

"You misunderstand me," Lorand said with a wry smile. "I've already listed all the reasons why we *should* share what we know, so you don't have to do it all over again. What I meant was decide about *how* to share the knowledge. These people have only had a very small amount of instruction in using their talents, about as much as we got in the beginning in those qualifying classes. Should we begin by putting them through those exercises until they're good at them, or should we go straight to having them make up Blendings?"

"There are about twenty of them, I think," Rion said,

automatically wetting his arms and shoulders and chest. "Is there an even division of talents in that twenty? If not, there might be a problem about forming Blendings."

"There might be a problem even if there is," Lorand said with a thoughtful frown. "If some of them don't get along with the others, no one will want to be in a Blending with them. And if all the rejects end up in the same Blending, either they won't be able to make it work, or they'll be constantly starting up with the other Blendings rather than waiting to use their ability on the enemy. We'll have to talk to the others about this, but I think we'll have to go with training them first. That way we can get to know them as they get to know each other."

"You make it sound as though we have all the time in the world," Rion remarked, looking around for the jar of soap he'd seen at the bath's edge before entering the water. "I seriously doubt if that's true, and there's another problem you seem to have overlooked. We also have to decide what to do with Alsin Meerk, even if he returns to his original self and stops being so intense. He and Lidris are the only two people among us who aren't High talents, and that's bound to make trouble no matter what any of us do."

"That's something else I hadn't thought about, and I should have," Lorand said, running both hands through his wet hair. "I'll go and talk to Jovvi and Tamrissa, and when Vallant wakes up we can have a meeting. Meanwhile, I think we'll do well to set up a practice schedule for our companions. If they don't overdo it, the workout will help them no matter what we decide to start with."

Rion nodded his agreement, then went for the soap while Lorand headed out of the bath. He used the soap to wash first his hair and then his body, and when he'd rinsed off completely, one of the other men in the bath approached him.

"I'm Torbin Lohl, Air magic," the man said by way of introduction, his smile somewhat on the tentative side. "Do you mind if I ask you something?"

"Not at all," Rion replied as pleasantly as possible. He still felt a bit of reserve with strangers, but nothing like what he used to. "And I'm Rion Mardimil, also Air magic."

"I know," Torbin Lohl replied, his manner still tentative.

He was a tall, thin man with a long face, approximately the same age as Rion and his Blendingmates, but with a bit less self-possession. "Since we're both Air magic users, I decided that you're the one I should ask. Did I hear you and the other man say something about training us?"

"That's Lorand Coll, Earth magic, and yes, you certainly did," Rion responded. "Our five went through rather intense sessions of training, which improved our handling of our various talents. We know you'll all benefit from the same, but *what* we teach you and when depends on how long we have until the pursuing guardsmen catch up to us. It won't help to form you into Blendings if you don't have time to practice as Blendings."

"You . . . want us to become Blendings?" the man asked, now looking disturbed as he glanced back at the others in the water. "But that's against the law. If they catch us, we'll be executed on the spot."

"My dear man, what do you expect will happen anyway?" Rion said, trying to hold back his sudden annoyance. "The nobility got rid of you people in the first place because you're much too dangerous to have around, and that, by the way, is the reason for the law you just mentioned. The nobility is *afraid* to have anyone know too much about their ability, for fear that someone will find out that their Seated Blendings aren't really what they're supposed to be. My groupmates and I have decided not to let that continue, and we thought you all chose to join us in our endeavors. Were we wrong?"

"Very frankly, I have no idea," the man said, sounding as bewildered as the other three looked. "We all woke up to find ourselves in a situation we never imagined, and for one reason or another decided against going home. We also decided to throw in our lot with *your* group, but I never thought—Well, I don't know *what* I never thought, but it looks like I have to do some thinking now."

The other three men murmured their agreement, and Rion suddenly realized how . . . disoriented and lost they must feel. One minute they were being tested as potential Highs who might have careers with the empire, and the next they awoke to find themselves hunted criminals. It was a terrible thing to have happen, even to people who were more or less prepared for it.

"You might also want to discuss it with the others," Rion suggested after a moment, now speaking a good deal more gently. "You're all entitled to make your own decisions just as we did, so don't be afraid that you'll be forced to do anything you don't want to. Think about it, talk it over with the others, and then we'll all have a meeting."

Lohl and the others nodded, but not with very much enthusiasm. That couldn't be helped, of course, but one thing could be: his presence was now an intrusion, keeping the four men from speaking their mind to each other. For that reason Rion rinsed off one more time, then left the bath. The four men would appreciate the privacy, and hopefully use it to settle all their qualms.

Once dressed again and outside, Rion discovered that the temporary kitchen had been set up at the back of the wagon, which stood on the opposite side of the barn doors from the coach. Interesting aromas wafted to him from the large cookfire, and made him glad that the sun was trying to come out. The lack of rain would make their eating outdoors seem almost like a picnic—unless the pursuing ants swooped down at just the wrong time. For their own sake, Rion hoped they didn't. If his meal was interrupted before his hunger was assuaged, he would take his crossness out on those who caused the interruption.

Naran greeted him with a radiant smile and a tasty kiss, the tastiness coming from the food she'd been in the process of eating. There were eggs on the metallic plate she ate from, but there was also chicken and ham. Not exactly the most usual of breakfasts, but apparently a hearty one.

"You look troubled, my love," she said after a moment, her smile fading. "Is something wrong?"

"Only in a manner of speaking," he replied, smoothing her hair back with one hand as he tried to use his own smile to restore hers. "Some of our companions are . . . confused about what they might be asked to do, and we need to have a general meeting. But first the others and I should talk."

"Jovvi and Tamrissa are over there," Naran said with an understanding nod, indicating the two women Rion had already noticed. "Lorand has gone to bring food to the men on watch, and should be returning any moment. I'm not certain, but I think Vallant is still asleep.''

"He was when I left the stall," Rion agreed, then touched her arm gently. "I'm going to get something to eat myself, then I'll talk to Jovvi and Tamrissa. Will you do me the honor of staying by my side?"

"Forever," she replied with that dear smile curving her lips again, but then it was lost for the second time. "But I have the definite feeling that we'd do best not spending too much time in discussion. Those guardsmen who are coming after us . . . I can almost feel them breathing down the back of my neck."

Rion experienced a chill at those words, so closely did they match his own feelings. They weren't going to be allowed much time at all, so they had to do as well as they could with what they had. After that . . . well, that all depended on what happened *before* the afterward came. . . .

THIRTY-TWO

By the time Lorand came back from bringing food to the people on watch, Vallant had come out for his own breakfast. He'd also taken a quick—cold—bath before lying down for a few hours of sleep, so once he and Lorand finished eating we were able to have our meeting—which Lorand opened.

"We all agree we don't have much time, so let's get to the most important topic first," he said as he looked around at us. "Rion told us that some of our companions here might not be ready to commit themselves to our plans yet, and that despite the fact that they've come along with us. Should we simply get them started on practice exercises, or get the question of commitment settled first?''

"Why don't we start by asking them if they've made up their minds yet?'' Jovvi suggested. We stood by ourselves to one side of the back of the barn, and the others seemed to be deliberately giving us privacy. "If they *have* made up their minds, then that part of it is out of the way. If they haven't, they can practice while they're thinking about what to do.''

Everyone liked that suggestion, so Rion partially changed the subject by asking how we were going to train the Air magic users once we got past the initial exercises. The building he'd been trained in had been sealable, but we had nothing like that at our disposal. It was a definite problem, but rather than try to think of a solution, my mind insisted on returning to the problem that was mine to solve. I'd already done more thinking about it than I'd found comfortable, but the conclusion was unavoidable. I had to apologize to Vallant.

I glanced at him where he stood sipping tea, more than aware of how far away from me he'd kept himself. I suppose I'd even half expected *him* to apologize, but an awful lot of time had passed since he'd spoken his mind. If he were going to regret what he'd said he would have already done so, so that meant it was up to me. Which it really should be, I admitted to myself with an inner sigh. He'd done more than his share trying to make a relationship between us work, so now it had to be my turn.

The others didn't take very long to decide that nothing could be done about Rion's problem at the moment, so all we could do was keep it in mind in case a solution presented itself at some future time. We were one step away from ending the meeting and calling the others together—in between which times I'd girded myself to speak to Vallant—when an unexpected interruption came.

"The six of you are off here all by yourselves," Alsin's voice suddenly came as he appeared almost out of nowhere. "Would you like to tell the rest of us what you're talking about?"

"You could have joined us and found out firsthand,"

Jovvi said at once before anyone else could speak, giving him the sort of smile I didn't know if *I* would have been able to show. "We discovered that some of the people here aren't quite sure about committing themselves completely to our efforts, so we're going to give them a chance to think about it and let us know when they make up their minds. We've also decided to get started right away with showing them the first of the exercises they need to do to increase their talents, and Rion has pointed out a problem we'll be having with Air magic training. After that, we decided it was time to call a general meeting."

"And you needed to be off by yourselves for *that*?" he asked with a snort, making his disbelief very clear. "Somehow I don't think so, but we can discuss what you really talked about later. Right now I want to hear about the people you say have decided not to join us. They *can't* not join us, and we have to make that clear to them."

"Alsin, I said they hadn't yet made up their minds," Jovvi corrected gently but firmly. "But even if some of them *have* decided not to participate in whatever we do, there won't be any question about forcing them. If we start out right from the beginning doing things the way the nobles do, what's the sense in our bothering to displace them? There's a big difference between using their own methods against them to defend ourselves, and using their methods to control the people supporting us."

"But didn't you just say they weren't *going* to support us?" he countered, obviously hearing only what he cared to. "If we're going to win this thing, we have to understand that anyone not with us is against us. We—"

"No," Lorand denied, interrupting immediately. "That doesn't happen to be true, so don't even think it, let alone say it. There *is* such a thing as being neutral, since not everyone can handle the idea of a fight. We won't be forcing anyone to do what they don't decide on their own to do."

"Is that your way of saying I'll be standing alone?" Alsin demanded, his craggy face twisted into something that wasn't very nice to see. "That even *your* group has decided to abandon me? If that's the case, then—"

Suddenly his words broke off, and he simply stood staring into space. He'd obviously been working himself up into a true rage, so I had no idea what was happening until Jovvi spoke.

"I have him under control now, and not a minute too soon," she said, her voice the least bit uneven. "His mind has really buckled under the strain, and he was about to become totally irrational. I think I might be able to bring him back, but I've got to work on him *now*. Lorand, please help me take him into the barn, then keep everyone else out for a while."

The rest of us stood there watching as Lorand took Alsin's arm and gently began to guide him into the barn behind Jovvi. The man moved as though he were asleep, jerkily and slowly, and I thought that Jovvi needed Lorand's presence for something other than help. If she had Alsin under control, he would have followed her without protest to wherever she wanted him to go. Rion and Naran moved closer to the barn doors, obviously ready to keep others out, so I took the opportunity to grab my courage with both hands and turn to Vallant.

"Guilt can do some really terrible things to a person," I commented, holding back on the shiver I felt on the inside. "And speaking of guilt, I'm forced to admit that it's become my turn to apologize. I . . . *was* seeing things from only my own point of view, and I *have* blamed you for things that weren't really your fault. You were right about everything you said the other day, and I . . . apologize."

"Apology accepted," he said, but he still sipped at his tea and gazed at something other than at me. "Don't let it bother you anymore."

"Don't let it bother me," I echoed, having no idea what was wrong. "Is that all you're going to say? I thought . . . After I made myself do the right thing . . ."

My limping protest ended rather abruptly, since I had no idea what might be added to it. I suppose—no, I *know*—I expected everything to be all right between us again, but there he stood, barely paying even half attention to me. But then he seemed to draw himself together again, and that very light gaze fell on *me*.

"What else do you *want* me to say?" he asked, his voice containing echoes of that commanding tone he'd been using so much lately. "You apologized to me and I appreciate that, but it isn't really *you* doin' the apologizin'. You're usin' the power to help you do what you think is fair, but I'll wager that the little girl inside you still believes everythin' was *my* fault. You're gettin' really good at forcin' yourself to do what you think you should, but that still isn't *you* doin' it. *You* still want someone who's perfect, and that isn't me.''

''Where do you get off telling me what I do and don't want?'' I demanded, suddenly so outraged that I could barely contain the anger. ''It nearly *killed* me to apologize to you, and now you're saying it doesn't count? Who in chaos do you think you are to tell *me* what I want?''

''I'm someone fairly personally involved,'' he countered, a gleam in those very light eyes that wasn't *quite* amusement. ''Right from the beginnin' I spent my time tryin' to force myself on you, and I've finally learned that that kind of thing never works. Now you're the one doin' the forcin', so I'm tryin' to save you some trouble. When you *really* want somethin' to grow between us it will, but until then you're wastin' both our time.''

''Why, you stiff-necked, opinionated—'' My words broke off, but not because I thought I might offend him. I simply couldn't think of anything vile enough to call him, not after he'd told me that I didn't know my own mind! ''How dare you treat me as though I were a giggling, mindless child? I *do* know what I want, and I don't need *you* to tell me what that is! If I've decided there should be something between us, who are *you* to tell me I'm wrong?''

It actually took a couple of minutes before I realized what I'd just said, but I was so angry that I didn't care. And the fact that his amusement suddenly became more obvious didn't help in the least. I was absolutely furious, and I might have lost my temper completely if Rion and Lorand hadn't suddenly appeared between us.

''Tamrissa, take it easy,'' Lorand soothed, his gentle hand to my face almost more than I could bear. ''You can't afford to kill him the way he so richly deserves, not now. We need everyone available to fight against the real enemy, but as soon as we take care of *them*, he's all yours. Jovvi said to tell everyone that she was able to reach Alsin Meerk's problem more easily than she'd dared to hope, and is now in the process of helping him to heal himself. As soon as she's through, we'll—''

This time it was Lorand's words which broke off abruptly, and the way he looked away from me and into the far distance was disturbing enough to reach through my anger. I was about to ask him what was wrong, when his answer came before the question.

''They're starting to surround us,'' he said, his tone perfectly reasonable and matter-of-fact. ''Our sentries are busy watching the road, but they aren't *coming* along the road. They've taken to the woods to approach, and there must be at least a hundred of them. We've got to do something, or we'll all be taken.''

''Naran, tell Jovvi!'' Vallant snapped, tossing away his teacup as though it were an unimportant piece of paper. ''Have her make the sentries pull back, and then get ready to Blend. Rion, tell the others what's happenin'. Lorand, how far away are they? How much time do we have until they're close enough to attack?''

''We have no more than twenty minutes to half an hour until they're completely in position,'' Lorand replied, no longer sounding as though he were half-asleep. ''Chaos rot those sentries! I told them to use their talent rather than their eyesight, but they weren't even touching the power when I brought them their food. Everyone is too well trained *not* to touch the power, and they haven't overcome the habit yet.''

''If they don't learn to adapt, they won't live *to* overcome it,'' Vallant said shortly as he looked around. ''And so much for trainin' the others to use their talent. We'll have to do what we can with what we've got, but we need an organized plan of defense. Is Meerk likely to be in shape to help us?''

''I seriously doubt it,'' Lorand said with a headshake. ''Jovvi told me he'd be confused, disoriented, and unsure of himself for a while after she released him. It looks like we're on our own.''

''But our own is a good deal better than nothing,'' I pointed out, taking a deep breath as I straightened up. ''Someday I might tell you what being alone can be like, rather than being one of a group. Since we *are* a group, I'm not worried about what will happen. Whatever they try, we'll be able to handle it.''

"That's the way I feel," Lorand agreed with a small but actual smile, looking first at me and then at Vallant. "Well, we've all been wondering what our Blending might be able to do against more than just another Blending, and now we're about to find out. If we end up disappointed, it won't be for long."

Vallant made a sound of distracted but amused agreement, and I also felt the same. Those guardsmen in the process of surrounding us weren't likely to let us live if they won, so our losing would definitely not be a disappointment to us for long. I realized I ought to be upset over the possibility that I might die soon, but I wasn't. Living or dying would be done with my groupmates, and that made whatever came perfectly acceptable.

People were already running over to join us, with Rion striding along behind. It looked like he'd wisely handed over the job of alerting everyone to someone else, and now returned to be with us. The babble of questions was rather intense, but Vallant simply waved their questions away with a distracted air. Everyone would be told what was happening at the same time, his refusal suggested, and Lorand was unavailable to ask as he had gone back toward the barn to see about Jovvi.

One of the new arrivals had the bad judgment to grab *my* arm in a demand to know what was happening, but he snatched his hand back quickly enough when I put a few flames under it. Then he had the nerve to look shocked, so I shook my head at him.

"Are you really too stupid to understand that we're all getting ready for a fight?" I asked, annoyed over how wounded he looked. "You don't touch people in that sort of frame of mind, not unless you don't mind getting hurt. You already know everything we do, so just stand there and keep quiet. Once everyone is together, we'll decide what to do first."

More than that one man heard what I said, so they busied themselves pestering each other with questions rather than bothering us. People were still running over when Lorand and Jovvi came out of the barn, and when they reached us Jovvi shook her head in answer to Vallant's unasked question.

"Alsin will be all right, but he can't help us now," she said with a sigh. "His mind is busy healing itself and re-arranging the ideas which had begun to obsess him, so his military knowledge is out of reach. I touched our sentries and made them hurry back here, so they'll be with us in just a few minutes. Is anyone else missing?"

We all looked around to check on that, but even Lidris had left his cooking fire to find out what was going on. Once the sentries got back we would all be there, to discuss what to do against the people who were after us. My touch on the power fought to keep my mind and thoughts hardened, but one of the things Lorand had said kept ringing in my head: there were at least a hundred of them. All told, our side had barely more than twenty-five. If those hundred or so linked up, would that make up for their not being High talents?

And how much help would our twenty be to *us*? Enough to let us win against four times our number? The day was becoming really nice and warm and sunny, but a sudden, invisible cloud brought a definite chill with it. . . .

THIRTY-THREE

"We won't wait for the sentries," Vallant suddenly decided aloud, quieting the babble of voices with the tone he some-times used to use aboard ship. "Even on horseback it will take them a few minutes to get here, and those are minutes we can't spare. As all of you should know by now, the guardsmen who were chasin' after us are now tryin' to sneak up on us. There are about a hundred of them, and they'll be here in about twenty minutes. Does anyone have a plan of defense they'd like to suggest?''

"We have to talk to them," a man in the back of the crowd said in a very . . . assured tone of voice. "We're all High talents here, after all. Once we explain that and they understand clearly what they'd be facing, they're certain to change their minds. They aren't stupid, after all."

"No, stupid isn't the proper word for them, just as it isn't for you," Vallant said, again overriding the babble. "You don't want to fight, so you're searchin' for reasons why *they* won't fight. What you're not takin' into consideration is the fact that their *wants* aren't at all important, not when they have their *orders*. They're supposed to capture or kill us, and if we don't surrender that's exactly what they'll try to make happen."

"Then we have to surrender," a woman said, also sounding completely reasonable. "If we don't give them a reason to kill us, they'll have to take us back for a trial or something. That's better than trying to resist uselessly, so—"

"Woman, *you* are stupid," another male voice interrupted, sounding completely out of patience. "Have you already forgotten those bodies we found hanging when we first got here? What do you imagine those small children and infants did to cause themselves to be killed? This probably won't be the same group coming after us who did that to the farm families, but they *are* being sent by the same people. If you want to bet your life on their being reasonable, I don't."

"All right, no personalities," Vallant ordered as people began to argue more than discuss. "I don't want to hear anyone callin' anyone else names, not when we have more than enough enemies comin' through the woods. I take it that no one has an actual plan, otherwise they would have already said so. Am I right?''

He looked around slowly enough to give everyone a chance to disagree with him, but unfortunately no one did. That meant just one thing, so he got right to it.

"Then the only thing we can do is play it by ear," he said, trying to keep all feelings of impending defeat out of his tone. "We'll have a general plan, but one with enough flexibility to let us adapt it to whatever happens. The first thing I want you to do is to get into groups along with the others of your aspect. When the time comes you'll all link up, but until then save your strength.''

No one was particularly happy with that, but not even the sentries, who had ridden up by now and dismounted in a cloud of dust, could suggest anything better. Trying to put those people into Blendings would have been a waste of time they didn't have, since the pressure of the coming attack could well work against the Blendings forming. He hadn't wanted to say so out loud, but mostly it would be up to their own Blending to make sure everyone survived.

"Lorand, how close have they gotten?" Vallant asked softly, so as not to rattle their companions needlessly. "And does anyone have any idea what their attack may consist of? Our defense will be a lot more effective if we know in advance what to expect."

"They're still about fifteen minutes away from surrounding us," Lorand reported, staring off briefly into unseen distances. "Possibly more, if they continue to be as cautious as they're being. And as far as what they'll do goes, quite a large number of them are Earth magic users. I can tell because they're touching the power, of course, and the rest must be doing the same even though they're of different aspects."

"That obviously means they can do almost anything in attack," Rion pointed out needlessly, his arm tightly around Naran's shoulders. "They can cut the ground out from under us, pelt us with rocks and stones, possibly even drop a tree on us. What they cannot do, however, is put us to sleep or even stop the hearts of one or more of us. We should all be a good deal stronger than they are, at least individually."

"Does anyone remember hearin' anythin' about how many people of the same aspect can link up?" Vallant asked, looking through the barn to its far side. That would be the way the major part of the attack would come, once the rest of the force had them surrounded. They would attack from one side, hoping to stampede them into running— and then would stand there and let their quarry stampede into the waiting arms of the rest of their force.

"I've never heard of more than three or four trying it," Jovvi said, her voice calm but her expression fighting worry.

"Those who do try it usually only boast about it when they're drunk, assuming they mention it at all. It *is* very much against the law, after all."

"I'll bet it's not against the law for those guardsmen," Tamrissa said, her voice tight and angry. "They probably practice linking all the time, and know just what they can do with it. Only a few days ago I said I couldn't see myself simply killing so many innocent people, but at the time I wasn't quite picturing a hundred of them. Now, when it's a question of them or us, I certainly want it to be them. The only question I have is: *can* we handle that many? They won't be coming at us as a single entity."

"Not even if they link," Lorand said in agreement, sounding disturbed. "Their ability will be merged and enhanced, but they'll still be individuals. And that, I'm afraid, is how we'll probably have to handle them: as individuals."

"And since they're individuals, they're very much a danger to you," Naran said suddenly, her voice trembling. "Oh, I know that sounds silly, but I'm not explaining what I mean. I meant to say that with individuals, some of them can sneak up really close and hurt your bodies while you're Blended and fighting the rest. That's the way you lost that final competition, isn't it? Because they did something to your bodies that your Blending entity didn't notice?"

"That's exactly the way we lost the competition," Vallant said slowly, turning to look at her with new respect. "And thank you for pointin' that out, because it passed me by completely. We're so strong and capable when we're Blended, I forgot that that doesn't include our physical forms. Now I know what our companions will be doin' most durin' the fight."

"Protecting our bodies," Rion said with a loving smile for his woman as he briefly tightened the arm he had around her. "And protecting Naran at the same time. How many times does that make now, the times you've been invaluable to us, my love? I think I'm beginning to lose count."

"Of course she's invaluable to us," Jovvi said with a warm smile for the other girl. "She *is* one of us, after all. And that's the point at the back of my mind that I couldn't quite bring into the open, the one that's been bothering me. We do have to protect our bodies, and now that we know

it, I suggest we get started. It makes very little sense just to
stand here and wait for them to start the fireworks.''

"I'll get the others and explain what they have to do,"
Lorand volunteered. "But I don't think I'll explain precisely
why they're doing it. Somehow I'll feel better if they think
they'll be forming up for mutual protection or something,
rather than just protecting us. Am I catching whatever it was
Meerk had?''

"Personally I think you're just being sensibly cautious,"
Naran said before Jovvi could answer, then she smiled shyly
at Jovvi. "But excuse me for butting in."

"Butt in any time you like," Jovvi replied with a small,
amused laugh. "You said just what I was about to, but in
a much nicer way."

Lorand smiled and headed for the people in their groups,
and the two women actually began to chat a bit. Vallant
wondered how they could be so cool as to do that, since he
himself was wound up as tight as a spring. Things would
start to happen any time now, and he could never just let
his mind wander. . . .

Even though it did want to wander, and to the same subject that had been giving him such a hard time for so long.
Tamrissa, the woman he would probably be best off avoid-
ing for the rest of his life, but also the woman he couldn't
get out of his head and heart. He'd come close to needing
to ask someone to chain him up, just to keep him from going
to her and apologizing for what he'd said. Only stubbornness had kept him away from her, and now . . .

And now *she'd* come to *him*. He hadn't really believed
she would ever do it, and then he hadn't believed the words
coming out of his own mouth after *she* apologized. He'd
told her the truth about how a large part of him still felt,
the part that didn't want to say to chaos with it all and then
take her in his arms. *All* of him wanted to hold her, and
show her how much he loved her, but he simply couldn't
do it. That would only set the scene for the same thing
happening again between them, at some time in the future.
They would both be better off if he refused to allow that to
happen. . . .

"Okay, we're all set," Lorand said, pulling Vallant out
of his brown study. "Our new friends will form up around

us, like aspect standing near like. That way if it comes to a final defense, we won't have to have everyone running and pushing and shoving.''

Lorand hadn't kept his voice down, obviously so that the people he'd brought over with him would hear and believe the explanation he'd come up with. For that reason Vallant nodded absently, as though he were hearing something he already knew, and then he looked at Jovvi.

''The five of us will probably be best off standing in a circle for this, with Naran on the inside,'' she said, doing no more than simply glancing at the rest of their group-mates. ''That way we can all be near each other, without anyone being in the way. Are we ready to take a preliminary look around?''

Vallant added his nod to everyone else's, so the group was ready. The High talents they'd rescued were arranging themselves in a thin protective circle facing outward from their center five, the nervousness and tension of the five's ''protectors'' so strong that a dead man would have been able to feel it. He looked at Jovvi again and she nodded once, showing that she knew what he was thinking. Once they'd Blended, their first chore would be to calm the people they'd made responsible for the safety of their bodies. If any of those people gave way to panic, it would be all over for everyone.

Vallant felt it when Jovvi's mind reached out to him, but that was the last individual sensation he had. The Blending came into existence so quickly that he nearly gasped, then it was no longer him alone. The entity was born again, complete and ready for the first time since it had been ended so suddenly during the final competition.

And the entity was vastly annoyed that it had been treated in so high-handed a fashion. True emotion was almost alien to it, just as it should be, but somehow it felt that what it experienced was proper. Those it sprang from were responsible for what the entity was, and arguing with what *is* is nothing more than foolish.

Therefore the entity got immediately to work. The first task to its immaterial hand was assuring the safety of the bodies of those it was born from, which meant calming and centering those individuals who stood about the five bodies.

The minds of the nearly two dozen people were strong, but the entity was far stronger. It did what was necessary to ensure its future safety, then it floated away to see what the approaching enemy was up to.

Floating could be fast or slow, just as it wished, and this time the entity wished speed. Those approaching life-forms, easily noticeable by the use of Earth magic, fairly shouted to the Spirit magic part of it that they meant to cause great harm. These were life-forms who cared very little about others, their major concern being only with themselves. For that reason they would do just as they were told to by their superiors, and in that way earn more than just silver. They were a specially gathered group, and had proven their value to their employers more than once.

Or so said the individual whom the entity took and questioned. The individual was one toward the back of the horde, in his mind and the minds of others the leader of the group. The man's thoughts were oddly twisted, for he very much enjoyed sending his hardened murderers against others.

"They deserve whatever is done to them," the man whispered in answer to the entity's inquiry, whispering so as not to alarm any of his men. "Those people in there, I mean. I learned the hard way not to argue with those stronger than me, and then I was put through pain and humiliation for even trying. The same lesson must be taught to *those* criminals, and then the next ones to come along won't even try."

—And that will keep *your* defeat from humiliating you even further,—the entity commented, knowing it for the truth.—But tell me now what your intentions are. Are those people to be captured, or simply put out of the way?—

"They're to be killed, of course," the individual replied, faint surprise behind the words. "My men are aspect-linked into groups of five, which makes them stronger than anything they're likely to come across. The males will be killed at once, the females after they give pleasure to those of my force who wish it from them. When we bring back all the heads, we'll collect a bonus in gold."

—What of those like you who are ahead, in the town called Quellin?—the entity put next.—Are some of them to come and assist you if assistance is necessary?—

"We don't need *their* help," the individual replied with

a snort of ridicule. "They're ordinary, and we're not. Besides, they want this dross for their own purposes, so we've been ordered not to let them know who we're hunting. They're in touch with Gan Garee by carrier pigeon, just as we are, but they're just supposed to hold our messages and pass them on when we get there."

—Tell me what will happen if you recall your force,—the entity directed, its thoughts rather full.—They will obey you, will they not? If you then return with them to Gan Garee—

"You have to be joking," the individual said with another snort of ridicule, actually interrupting the entity. "If I tried to call them off now, I'd be mobbed if I couldn't produce a damned good reason for doing it. Like having the Five standing next to me, rescinding the orders they gave which sent us here. Nothing less will stop them, so even the freaks among the dross will be helpless. My men can't be stopped, and they certainly can't be resisted."

So they *had* been told something about its five, the entity mused. Not enough to really prepare these people, but enough to bring them a small amount of caution. And yet it wasn't caution which moved them ahead so slowly, the individual explained. They fully expected their prey to know they were here by now, and their advance was leisurely rather than careful. They meant to produce terror in the victims they stalked, which they would enjoy to the full before they ended the lives of those victims.

And that, the entity decided, meant the hunters must all be destroyed. But they moved through the woods linked by fives in their various aspects, and testing the strength of one of those links showed the entity that although it had greater strength, overcoming the link would be far too time-consuming. The entity would be able to reach and stop no more than half their number before the rest attacked with full viciousness and twisted delight. Those who awaited them *were* stronger, but the larger number of the attackers and their positive attitude would overcome that greater strength. . . .

The entity reflected for quite some time, nearly a full minute, before deciding to take the only possible course of action. The ploy it had decided on was amusing in a distant sort of way, but it would not be fully and totally effective. The entity itself would have to stand before the intended victims, sheltering and protecting them against those links which managed to approach too closely. Well, so be it. The fact that in battle the attacking links would have no chance against it meant nothing. Those who attacked could hardly complain when their attack was resisted.

Wasting any further time would be completely nonproductive, so the entity began to put its ploy into effect at once. Moving itself to the nearest groups of links, the entity began to convince those links that the enemy was not ahead, but advancing through the woods and fields on the far side of their position. The links had to be touched one at a time, but soon the entire group of them had turned their attention to the real enemy. And the enemy was extremely dangerous, so it had to be attacked at once.

Sounds of aspect battle erupted behind the entity as it floated swiftly back to where its own people were. Those with Earth magic tore up sections of the landscape, those with Fire magic set fire to it, those with Water magic drowned or desiccated it, and those with Air magic made breathing difficult. Only a single link had been capable of Spirit magic, and they worked to convince their enemies that resisting was unnecessary and undesirable.

The entity managed to station itself before its flesh forms just in time. The links which had circled around behind the houses on the left had no idea why battle raged on the far side of the barn, nor did they care. Their objective lay before them, and they clearly believed that those who actually attained it would surely be rewarded while the others might be penalized instead. So they came ahead, and suddenly four of the five aspects were attacking at once.

Those who protected the entity's flesh forms were ordered to link, which produced a protective wall of sorts consisting of all of the aspects. This . . . separation of the aspects disturbed the entity in some strange and unexplained way, but there was scarcely time to dwell on the matter. Defense does nothing to halt an attack, and halting it was the only thing which would save them all. Therefore the entity moved forward, and began to oppose what was being sent.

Countering each aspect separately was obviously a poor

tactic, so the entity used a more effective ploy. The wall of flame produced by the Fire link was redirected toward the Earth link, which quickly eliminated the Earth link. The envelope of airlessness from the Air link was forced around those with Fire magic, and they clawed at their throats and died while those with Water magic produced the globes of water which began to drown those with Air magic. That left those with Water magic to be seen to, and the entity didn't hesitate.

Removing all the moisture from the bodies of those men allowed them to scream only briefly before they were no longer *able* to scream. Then the powdered remains of their former bodies sifted down to the ground, and that part of the attack was over.

But *only* that part. More than half the attacking force fought against itself and another segment had just been wiped out, but that still left the final portion of the hunters. Another four link groups came from behind the houses on the right, and they, too, cared nothing about the battle going on in the distance. The idea of gaining an advantage over their fellows brought them eagerly forward, ready to destroy anything in their path to success.

And as they advanced the entity paused for a moment, assessing its own strength—which suddenly seemed much less than it had been. Quite a lot of effort had been expended, and its automatic reaching for more of the power was halted in mid stride, so to speak. To take in more of the power was certainly possible, but for some reason was less than desirable. Could it be . . . was it possible . . . Yes, that was it. The strain on its flesh forms had been too great, and if the entity took in more of the power it would simply damage its own components, possibly beyond repair.

And that realization left the entity in something of a quandary. The coming attack needed to be countered if its group was to survive, and yet a counterattack could well cause the destruction of its flesh forms. One choice was equally as bad as the other, and yet one of them must be accepted. There *were* no other choices . . . it *seemed* as though there were no other choices . . . Wait, a faint and distant memory . . . Not *its* memory, and yet available and unmistakably relevant. Yes, *that* was what had to be done!

With the speed of thought, the entity gathered in the linked talents ranged about its flesh forms. Those talents tapped the raw power directly, and the entity tapped them. It was the third choice it had been seeking, a way to gain strength without endangering itself. And what strength! Linked High talents, all pouring their ability and mettle into the entity, who knew exactly what to do with the gifts.

The four attacking links, poor, pitiful creatures that they were, died together almost in mid stride. Their hearts were stopped, their lungs denied air, their flesh denied moisture, and their remains vaporized in a funeral pyre so intense that to look upon it was to lose bodily vision for a time. In the next heartbeat the entity turned that incredible ferocity on the rest of the attacking force, touching those who still lived and snuffing out those lives. The last to die was the leader of the horde, ending his howl of agony at the realization that his irresistible force had been defeated.

A quick sweep which ranged across miles showed that no other of the enemy remained, and that was definitely that.

THIRTY-FOUR

"What do you mean, Captain Althers has disappeared?" Kambil demanded of the brawny, stolid guardsman who had come with the news. "He was supposed to be getting information for us, important information!"

"Don't know nothin' about it, Excellency," the guardsman repeated, just as he'd *been* repeating those same words ever since he got there. "All they told me was t'tell ya— oh, an' give ya this here batch a papers. Almos' forgot."

The brawny man reached into the scrip at his waist and awkwardly drew out a sheaf of papers which had obviously been stuffed into the scrip. He offered them as though they were so much straw to be thrown into a stall, and all Kambil could do was grab the papers with a curse. The man who had been sent to give them the news about Althers knew nothing about the entire affair, so striking him dead would have done nothing more than set a bad precedent. Aside from how good it would have made Kambil feel.

"You go back to your superiors now and give them a message from the five of us," Kambil said as he worked to straighten the papers into some semblance of neatness. "Tell them that the next time someone like you is sent in place of one of *them*, being at a distance from us won't save them. I want Althers's replacement here tomorrow without fail, along with his two immediate commanding officers. Do you understand all that well enough to repeat it to the people who have to hear it?"

"Sure, Excellency, I'm real good at rememberin' stuff like that," the brawny man acknowledged with a nod. "I'll tell 'em just what you said."

Rather than bowing, the brawny man came to attention, threw his arm across his chest in a salute, then turned and marched out. Kambil felt the urge to close his eyes and scream, but that would have done as much good as trying to tell the fool of a guardsman what he'd done wrong.

"I can't understand why they sent *that* thing rather than coming to us themselves," Homin said once the door of the meeting room had closed behind the guardsman. "It really isn't their fault that Althers decided on an informal, permanent leave, after all, so why would they—"

"Chaos take them!" Kambil snarled, interrupting Homin with no more than a passing awareness of having done it. He'd glanced through the pages given him, bothered by what he *didn't* see, and then he'd come to the final message. "I don't believe this! No wonder Althers decided to disappear. He must have thought he would never survive the delivering of this message, and he was probably right!"

"Why?" Bron asked, clearly speaking for all of the others. "What does it say?"

"It says that the command sent after those five peasants

has completely disappeared,'' Kambil replied, looking bleakly from one face to the next. ''The group leader sent one of his men ahead to Quellin with orders to collect any messages sent to them, and to pass on the word that a definite trail left by the fugitives had been found. When the man returned to where the command should have been, he found them and all traces of them gone.''

''Then they must still be following that trail,'' Selendi said with a frown. ''What else could have happened to that many men?''

''Our erstwhile opponents happened to them,'' Kambil stated, having not the least doubt that he spoke the truth. ''If the command was simply following a trail, they would have left signs for the man sent to Quellin. The absence of those signs leaves only the other possibility.''

''But how could they have defeated a hundred men?'' Bron demanded, and Kambil was able to feel how rattled the man was. ''Even using our Blending entity, I'd hate to have to do the same thing! Tell me how *they* could have done it!''

''How am I supposed to know that?'' Kambil countered, feeling more than a bit unbalanced himself. ''I'm just certain that they did, and now I have a more disturbing question than 'how.' Tell me what they intend to do next.''

Bron parted his lips, but nothing in the way of words came out. His complexion had gone almost as pale as Selendi's and Homin's, and those two had nothing in the way of an answer either.

''So you see our most pressing dilemma,'' Kambil said, glancing at the ever-silent Delin. The man was just as disturbed as the rest of the Five, but he'd been forbidden to speak unless spoken to. ''Does anyone think it's possible that they'll be returning *here*? Or should I have said likely? Everything is possible, but how *likely* is their immediate return?''

''I'd say very likely,'' Selendi put forward when the two men remained as silent as Delin, stirring where she sat. ''If it were me and I'd found a way to destroy a hundred men without leaving a sign of them, I'd turn right around and march back to the place I'd just run away from.''

''I'm not sure *I* would,'' Homin ventured, giving Selendi

a small shrug of apology for disagreeing with her. "I'd probably prefer to find a place of my own to get comfortable, and would spend my strength defending that place. After all, what is there *here* for them?"

"Do you mean aside from this palace and our places on the Fivefold Throne?" Bron said with heavy sarcasm. "Not a thing that *I* can think of. How about you, Kambil?"

"Let's not start to bicker among ourselves," Kambil said sharply, blaming himself for losing control to so great an extent. "The problem is that all of you are right, since your views depend on your own way of looking at things. The peasants are also individuals, and they may not find it possible to agree on a course of action. That would be completely to our benefit, but we can't count on it. We'll have to set up outposts along the road to the city, so that if the peasants do decide to return we'll know about it before they get here."

"And meanwhile we'll have to try to figure out what they did," Bron muttered, less emotional now after having been rebuked. "If we don't, we won't dare to face them."

"We'd be fools to face them anyway," Homin said with a headshake. "We can't afford to forget that they're stronger than we are, and not only because of whatever they just learned to do."

"I want all of you to understand one thing very clearly," Kambil said, giving his groupmates a taste of his unbending resolve along with the words. "I did *not* go through all that trouble to gain the Throne just to lose it again to a bunch of peasants. And we don't *have* to face them again, not when everyone believes that we bested them the first time. If necessary we'll throw a *thousand* guardsmen in their path, and then we'll see how well they do. In the meanwhile, I don't want to hear another word about how strong they are or how afraid we are of them. Is that clear?"

The three nodded, with Delin simply sitting and staring as always. Kambil stared at the man in return, finding a good deal less pleasure in his awakened presence than he had. Delin often raged inwardly over his captivity, but there was also something disturbing inside him. It was probably the man's insanity, which meant Kambil could ignore it and concentrate on more important matters.

"Let's spend the rest of this morning thinking, and this afternoon we'll have a meeting and make suggestions," Kambil said after a brief pause. "And let's bear in mind that the peasants may have *left* the city by the west road, but they don't necessarily have to use it to return. I'll want lists of everything you can think of that we can do to protect ourselves, as well as suggestions as to how we can do it all without letting people know what's happening. If anyone finds out the details of what's going on, we'll have to eliminate them before they can tell anyone else."

Kambil began to leave the room as he spoke, and Bron and Selendi and Homin immediately walked along with him. Delin trailed along behind, of course, but Delin no longer mattered. What did matter was those peasants, and a way to make very sure that they stopped being a problem ever again. . . .

Delin walked behind the others, his mind mulling over everything he'd heard. On the one hand he was delighted that Kambil was having difficulty, but on the other he, Delin, was in that difficulty with him. But at least they couldn't blame *this* on him, not that they wouldn't try. It would probably turn out that he'd done something that caused something else to happen and that something else caused this. In a distant way, of course, but without the least doubt.

Delin snorted to himself, realizing he was in the process of losing every scrap of the small amount of respect he'd ever had for Kambil. Things around them got worse with every passing day, and all their supposed leader could do was send threatening messages. He *should* have sent that guardsman back with his throat opened, to show how displeased they were with the ploy the man's superiors had used. He should also have given orders to have those superiors put down, and then their replacements would have done the job properly right from the first.

But the high-and-mighty leader of the Seated Five was too softhearted to do what he should, so things would continue to go from bad to worse. Kambil had been just as frightened as the others had obviously been, and because of that he'd made a bad mistake. He'd told everyone what he wanted them to do, and he hadn't excluded Delin from the command. That meant he *had* to obey, and for the first time he truly looked forward to doing it. That tiny part of his mind . . .

That tiny part of his mind was composed of all the strength and cunning and rebellion that his father had never allowed a very young Delin to show. It was smarter and even more ruthless than the rest of the man named Delin, and many years ago it had . . . almost separated itself from him. At times it whispered to him, usually when things were going worst, telling him that *it* would make sure that everything turned out all right. It had whispered to him again only a few minutes ago, and this time it had sounded gleeful.

Kambil wanted lists of things they could do to protect themselves, and also wanted to keep people from knowing what was going on. Those two things were commands to Delin, and even as he trailed along behind everyone else, his inner companion explained how they would take advantage of those commands. Someone without Delin's experience in controlling his reactions might have laughed out loud, but Delin simply put his unending, simmering anger to the front of his mind and did his laughing behind it.

Soon, very soon, he would be able to take his revenge, and then—then!—

Hallina Mardimil was furious, and she made sure to let everyone around her know it—especially the fool of a man who now stood before her.

"How dare you come to me with nothing to show for all the gold I've spent?" she spat, sending her venom full force at the man she spoke to. "You can't tell me that that ingrate simply disappeared from the face of the world! He must have gone *somewhere*, and I want to know where that is."

"My own men have been coordinating the search with the groups assigned to the matter by the Five," the man, named Ravence, replied wearily. He was a short and pudgy man, but the look in his eyes was anything but soft. "We have our own sources of information to tell us about the things they're holding back on, and we've learned that your son and his friends were taken in temporarily by a bunch of supposed conspirators. They're firm believers in nonviolence, so the powers that be allow them to continue with their plotting—with suitable watchers keeping an eye on them. They—''

"I don't care about a handful of stupid peasants!" Hallina interrupted, her small amount of patience long since exhausted. "If my son is among them, why haven't you gotten him out and brought him to me?"

"I said he was with them *temporarily*," Ravence corrected, the look in his eyes sharpening. "He and the others left rather quickly, and the fact that they're gone entirely from Gan Garee has been confimed. And if you're dissatisfied with the way I'm handling this, Lady Hallina, do feel free to find someone else."

"Don't be insolent!" Hallina snapped, hating the need to associate with a peasant. But more than one person had assured her that Ravence was the best to be had, so she had to put up with his irritating presence. It was a pity that no one of her own class would even dream of doing such menial work. . . .

"It isn't insolent to expect common courtesy from people," the man dared to say, looking her straight in the eye. "I know that your sort detests all things common, but in this one instance you *will* comply, otherwise you'll *have* to find someone else. That means I'm not above getting up and walking out, so watch your tone when you speak to me. Now, do you want me to continue?"

What Hallina *wanted* was to see the man beaten before her eyes, but that couldn't be done right now. Once she no longer required his services it would be another story, but for now all she could do was nod without speaking.

"Very well," he said, obviously knowing that he'd gotten all the concessions he would out of her. "Once I knew that your son had definitely left the city, I sent men out along all the major roads to find out which direction he took. They were supposed to stop at both the first and second inns along the way, but the man I sent west got lucky rather quickly. The landlord in the first inn claimed to remember nothing, but one of the serving girls was glad to take my man's silver. Your son was there with two other men and two women, and they continued on the next morning."

"So now he's with two sluts," Hallina muttered, fury rising in her again. "I kept him pure for so long, and everything was marvelous between us. Then those sluts got their hooks into him, and now he prefers *them* to me! But once I catch up to them I'll make them *all* sorry, you wait and see if I don't.''

"I now have four of my best people following their trail,'' Ravence continued. ''They have remounts and pigeons with them, so they can travel fast and keep in touch. When they locate your son and his friends they'll send me that location, and then I'll pass it on to you. Is there anything else you want to know?''

"Not at the moment,'' Hallina replied, her heart beating excitedly at the thought of being able to give those five vicious children the location. She would throw it in their faces and then march out, and there would be nothing they could do to her after that. Her power and position rested on more than her kinship with three of the former Five, and that those children would eventually learn.

And after her ingrate of a son and his filthy friends were gone, when the Five were least expecting it, Hallina Mardimil would have her revenge against *them*. . . .

Embisson Ruhl sat leaning on pillows in his bed, still aching from the latest forced trip to the palace. Those people were impossible, now insisting that he wasn't even allowed to call himself an ordinary lord. Just because those peasants were still on the loose, as though the whole thing really *were* his fault. This time he'd pointed out that he'd had his orders from Zolind Maylock, but they hadn't cared. Zolind was dead and so couldn't be punished, but *he* remained alive. It had also made no difference that his people were hot on the trail of the fugitives. As long as they remained at large, Embisson would, little by little, lose everything he had.

Or so they thought. A knock came at the door, a knock he'd been waiting for, and when he called out the order to enter, his caller did. Edmin Ruhl, Embisson's eldest son, closed the door behind himself then walked closer to the bed.

"How are you feeling today, Father?'' Edmin asked, his concern most likely real. Embisson had been very close to Edmin while the boy grew up, finding in his first son a kindred spirit. They still enjoyed each other's company from time to time, and when Embisson's ills had first begun, Edmin had immediately shown up to help.

"The pain leaves me no more than slowly, and being dragged to the palace helps not at all," Embisson replied. "I certainly hope you've had more success than I have."

"I made the effort to see how your searchers were doing, and I've satisfied myself that they're overlooking nothing," Edmin said with a faint smile. "They'll find those fugitives if it's humanly possible, but in the interim I've done some finding myself. When you spread bribes lavishly in the right quarter, people fall all over themselves trying to earn more. In this case they earned more by supplying the identities of two of your attackers, and my people took the two last night."

"Those pigs would sell their own mothers for gold," Embisson said with all the disgust he felt, then he smiled at Edmin. "But you, my son, would make even the most exacting father proud. And you must have gotten an answer, otherwise you would not have come. Tell me who paid for all the pain I've had to suffer."

"The fools tried to insist that they had no idea of the identity of the person who hired them," Edmin said with a wider smile. "A masked agent hired and paid them, so how were *they* supposed to know who stood behind the agent? It took a while to make them admit that they'd followed the agent after he'd left, to find out who the man reported to. They had blackmail in mind, of course, and were almost ready to make their demands—of Lady Hallina Mardimil."

"Her!" Embisson blurted, scarcely believing his ears. "That stupid slut, how dare she!"

"I'd say she discovered that it was you who refused to include her 'son' as an entrant from the nobility," Edmin responded with a small shrug. "You had no choice, of course, but obviously she refuses to see it like that."

"Anyone but an utter fool would understand how ridiculous she was to even suggest it," Embisson said, nearly huffing with outrage. "Just because she's always insisted to everyone that she bore the boy, that doesn't change the fact that it was one of her maids who was the child's real mother. When the girl died, Hallina took the infant away from its father, dismissed the man from her service, and raised the brat herself. There *are* a few of us who know that, so how was I supposed to pretend that the boy was anything but the peasant he is?''

''You couldn't have, but the woman is much too self-centered to allow anyone to cross her,'' Edmin said. ''She obviously considers the action a humiliation, and made the effort to return pain for it. What would you like me to do now?''

''Make suitable arrangements to repay her for her gift to me,'' Embisson said, speaking the words Edmin clearly expected—and anticipated with enjoyment. ''I want her to suffer just as I have, you understand, not escape retribution in death. I leave it to you to decide what her punishment ought to be—but there's something more important—and more dangerous—that I must also ask you to do.''

''You needn't speak the words aloud,'' Edmin said at once, deliberately glancing around. ''Too often the walls have ears, and we would *not* want this particular subject to get out. Don't worry, Father, your enemies are my enemies, and I've already begun to look into a way to solve your biggest problem.''

''My son,'' Embisson managed to get out, holding out his hand so that Edmin might grasp it in both of his. Pride choked him so badly that he was quite unable to speak, but as his son had said, words were unnecessary. They still thought so very much alike, that Edmin had already begun what Embisson had hesitated to ask of him.

Embisson smiled, pleased and satisfied. Edmin was incredibly good at making plans and seeing them to fruition, at times being even more inventive than his father. Once he felt better Embisson would add his own expertise to the matter, and then, hopefully, the new Seated Five would no longer be in a position to give trouble to anyone!

Eltrina Razas moaned softly, the pain in her wrists so great that it nearly overcame the rest of the pain of her body. Her wrists were fastened with rough rope which was anchored to the wall above the pallet she lay on, a position she'd been in for at least three hours. This was Grall's latest effort in his campaign to punish and humiliate her, and the fact that the pallet had been put in the main sitting room of

the house—with her being absolutely naked on it—made
the effort a successful one.

"Ah, there she is," Grall's voice came suddenly as he
entered the room. "For once right where she's supposed to
be. I hadn't realized that regular whippings did so well with
a woman, or I would have begun the practice a good deal
sooner."

"You should have asked me," another male voice replied
lightly, one Eltrina didn't recognize. "I've always disci-
plined my wife on a regular basis, and for that reason have
never had a moment's trouble with her."

The two men came to stare down at Eltrina where she
lay, and she couldn't keep from flinching when she saw that
Grall carried the switch he'd been using on her so often
lately. Her entire body ached from the beatings, but none of
them had been so bad that she was in danger of dying from
it. Unfortunately. The thought of death had frightened her
at one time, but now she knew there really were things a
good deal worse.

"You've never met her, I know," Grall continued to his
male companion, "but I'm sure you understand that I'm no
longer introducing her to people. She's here to keep me
amused in various ways while I struggle to keep what she
nearly caused me to lose, and I'm making appreciable head-
way. If the Five don't end up taking her life to pay for her
stupidity, that's all she'll ever be allowed to do for the rest
of that life. What do you think?"

"You were completely correct," the stranger, a tall, lean,
handsome man, said as he stared down at her. "She does
have a fairly good body and a certain appeal, so I'll be
pleased to accept your offer. Would you like to remain?"

"If you don't mind," Grall answered with a smile, one
which made Eltrina's heart beat harder with sudden fear.
"This is the first time I'm requiring this of her, and I'd like
to see her reaction to it."

"Then let's by all means elicit that reaction," the stranger
said with his own smile, and then it started. He knelt and
began to make free with her body, which caused her pain
as well as blazing humiliation. She wasn't able to respond
to him, not with the way she felt, but that was clearly of no
concern to him. After a few moments of toying with her

breasts and poking at her womanhood, he opened his trousers and took her use. She screamed when he forced himself into her, struggling to escape such debasing insult, but the effort was useless. He had his way with her to pleasurable completion, and all the while Grall stood there watching and chuckling.

"That was rather entertaining, and I thank you for the opportunity to indulge," the stranger said to Grall once he had finished and was again on his feet. "What did you think of her reactions?"

"They came as no surprise," Grall said, disgust clear in his voice even as he avoided looking at her. "She had no desire to squirm for you, but you caused her to do so anyway. She's nothing but a slut, and fit for nothing but serving men on her back—which she'll begin to do more frequently now."

"You sound as though you have definite plans," the stranger commented with faint curiosity. "Plans beyond simply offering her to a chance business acquaintance."

"I do," Grall replied with that same smile as he put a hand to the stranger's arm, urging the man to walk with him. "There are a large number of men in my employ in just this house alone, and I mean to make her available to all of them. I've been taking my own entertainment elsewhere for quite some time, so there's no reason not to return to that practice. Having her knees spread so often should please her, considering what her habits were. . . ."

Grall's voice trailed off as the two men left the room, but Eltrina was already weeping silently. He hadn't just been threatening, she knew; her own husband was actually going to let their servants do as they pleased with her! The peasants would be using *her*, not the other way about, and the shame of it would come close to killing her. But Grall would make sure she survived, to be certain that she continued to be punished.

Sobs racked Eltrina's aching body, but even as they did, her mind raged against what was being done to her. It wasn't *fair*, not any of it, especially not when she'd been so close to being rid of Grall forever! It was all the fault of those filthy peasants, but even if they were caught she would have no chance to wreak her vengeance on them. She was a prisoner, a slave to the man she detested the most. . . .

So she'd have to find a way to do something about that. Her sobs eased off a bit as the decision was made, a decision she had no idea how she would implement. But she would find a way, by the Highest Aspect she *would* find a way, and then . . . !

THIRTY-FIVE

When Jovvi withdrew from the Blending, she staggered and nearly fell. Only Lorand's arm coming around her shoulders as fast as thought kept her on her feet, and it was clear that Lorand was in the midst of having his own trouble standing. As was Rion, and Tamma, and even Vallant. It felt just like the time of that very first test. . . .

"I'm not sure I understand what happened," Lorand said, sounding as tired as Jovvi felt. "And for that matter, I'm not sure I *want* to understand."

"What happened to them all?" Tamma asked in a whisper, clinging automatically to a Vallant who had stepped closer to hold her erect. "One minute they were there and alive, and the next—And why did the same thing have to be done to their horses?"

"We obviously wanted to remove all traces of them," Vallant said, his own mind a bit numb with shock. "What's gettin' me is the fact that nothin' else is damaged or burned. It's as though we pointed at them and they simply disappeared."

"Why should anything else be damaged or burned?" Tamma asked, and Jovvi could tell that the girl was still in shock. "I never burn anything by accident, only the things I want to—"

"No, Tamma, it wasn't your doing alone," Jovvi said quickly when Tamma's words abruptly ended with a sob. "It was just your ability which was used. It hurts to admit it, but the *decision* to do it came from all of us."

"Yes, it must have," Rion agreed quickly, Lorand and Vallant joining his agreement. "No one of us directs the entity, after all, so the blame—or credit—belongs to us all. And there is surely credit as well as blame, since we and these other people are no longer in danger of being murdered. Which would have happened if we hadn't stopped those guardsmen."

"It was a very real possibility," Naran agreed gently from the circle of Rion's arms, gazing at Tamma with compassion. "There were so many of them that there was always the possibility that your Blending would find it impossible to defend us. And if you'd gone down, the rest of us would have quickly followed you."

"Speaking of the rest of us, what's wrong with those people?" Lorand asked, looking around at the former captives, who still stood in a protective ring around them. "The attack is completely over, but they haven't moved or relaxed in any way."

"Oh, dear," Jovvi said, knowing immediately what was wrong. "The entity set them to defend our bodies, but we dissolved the Blending without canceling that order. And it *has* to be canceled, or they'll defend us from now on for the rest of their lives."

"Well, I don't know about you, but I don't have the strength left to Blend again," Lorand said with a sigh. "What I need to do is collapse and sleep, and then maybe I'll be able to function again. You can't bring them back to normal alone?"

"Not even if I weren't half-dead," Jovvi admitted ruefully. "And you're not the only one who can't Blend again right now. So what will we do? Leave these poor people to stand here guarding an empty circle?"

"What other choice do we have?" Vallant asked, adding a sigh of his own. "I'll be joinin' Lorand in that collapsin' business, and the sooner the better. We'll have to apologize to them later, but right now we need to sleep.''

"I don't, so I'll be glad to keep an eye on them," Naran offered with a smile. "That is, if all of you don't mind."

"You really are a lifesaver, Naran," Jovvi said with as good a smile as she was able to manage, patting the girl's arm as she began to make her way toward the barn. "I'm going to lie down now, and if anything happens you can wake me up. Later I'll thank you in more detail."

Everyone agreed with that as they also began to make their way through the ranked ex-captives, but then an odd thing happened. The people who had been ranged around them outside the barn didn't hesitate to follow, and when Jovvi and the others reached their stall, *it* became surrounded.

"It looks like we're going to be safe while we sleep," Tamma said, still extremely disturbed but beginning to pull out of it. "And if anyone cares, I'm glad we are."

"Take my word that all the rest of us feel exactly the same," Jovvi assured her as she moved toward her blanket-bed. "It will hopefully save us some bad dreams."

None of them took their time lying down, not when they were so very drained, but Vallant took a moment to pull his blankets closer to Tamma's. That was because Tamma had released him only reluctantly, Jovvi knew, and he obviously knew it as well. Well, *that* was a step in the right direction, she thought before falling asleep still holding Lorand's hand.

When Jovvi awoke again, she and Tamma were the only ones left in the stall, and Tamma was already awake. She sat up and rubbed her eyes, feeling decently rested, and then heard Tamma stir a bit.

"Naran was here a couple of minutes ago," Tamma informed her, happily sounding more like her usual self. "She said we've been asleep about six hours, which leads me to believe that we're a lot stronger than we used to be. The men woke up a short while before us, probably because their talents weren't used as much as ours by the entity, and three-fifths of our guard force went with them when they left. Our three groupmates are right now in the midst of making something for all of us to eat, and I have a problem."

"What sort of problem?" Jovvi asked at once, turning to

look at her. "Your mind feels perfectly normal and strong, and—Oh."

"Yes, oh," Tamma agreed glumly, still looking at Vallant's blankets, which had been moved back to where they'd been originally. "He wouldn't have bothered with those blankets if he hadn't been trying to send me a message, but it's not one I want to hear. When we came out of the Blending I was absolutely shredded, and he didn't hesitate to be there for me. Now he's gone back to keeping his distance until, I suppose, the 'inner me' wants the same thing as the outer. How do I convince him that that's already happened?"

"What's wrong with simply telling him?" Jovvi ventured, privately deciding that being attacked again by guardsmen would probably be safer than getting in the middle between Tamma and Vallant. "He does speak the language, after all, and that's probably all he's waiting for."

"Take another look at those blankets, and *then* say that," Tamma disagreed with a headshake, raising her skirt-covered knees a bit so that she might circle them with her arms. "He's obviously announced that he wants to be convinced, and the way I tried earlier—sort of—yelling—didn't do the job. But he got me so angry when he insisted he didn't believe I meant what I said."

"That sounds like a woman's objection," Jovvi commented, faintly amused. "It's usually the woman who doesn't believe that the man's intentions are honorable, especially if they've already been intimate. You ought to know yourself how hard that is to get around, since that's the treatment you gave Vallant in the beginning. In order to counter it, he had to—Hey, maybe that's it!"

"What's it?" Tamma asked, looking as wide-eyed and happily expectant as a trusting child. "You've thought of something I can do?"

"Ah . . . maybe," Jovvi hedged, suddenly seeing all the possible ramifications. "In order to get around *your* doubt, Vallant had to actively court you. Do you think . . . *that* would work the other way around?"

"You're telling me to court him?" Tamma asked, now looking at her blankly. "How am I supposed to do that? What do *I* know about courting someone?"

"Well, you know what *you* would like, so why can't you reverse that?" Jovvi said, beginning to warm to the subject. "Even if it turns out to be something other than what he wants, at least it's something to *do*. Aside from 'yelling' and giving up entirely."

"Well, I won't give up," she muttered, "at least not until I've made *some* effort, so I might as well start with this one. If it doesn't work, we can always try to think of something else."

That "we" made Jovvi wince a bit, but outwardly all she did was smile encouragingly and nod. If you thought of something for people to do and it didn't work, all too often *you* were the one who was blamed for the failure. But Tamma was closer even than a blood relation, and hopefully would not be that narrowminded. In any event, Jovvi did want to do all she could for Tamma and Vallant . . . as long as they continued to consider it help rather than interference. . . .

Jovvi got to her feet at that point with Tamma doing the same, and the two of them left the stall and then the barn. Their protectors followed along behind, like so many flesh puppets on attached strings, and that really disturbed Jovvi. No one should be made to behave like that, but at the time their Blending entity knew it was necessary. Now, happily, it no longer was.

"Excuse me, but what's going on?" a voice asked as Jovvi and Tamma approached the barn exit. They turned to see Alsin Meerk coming out of the stall where Jovvi had worked with him, and the man looked terribly confused and a bit uncertain.

"It's all right, Alsin," Jovvi said at once, reaching out with her ability to soothe his confusion. "While you were healing, the guardsmen following us attacked. With the help of the others we were able to defend ourselves, but it took all the strength we had. We needed to sleep for a while, and now that we have we can finish up what we couldn't do earlier."

"We were attacked?" Alsin echoed, self-annoyance clear in his voice as he walked along with them. "And I wasn't there to help even a little? Isn't it a lucky thing I came along with you."

"It *is* a lucky thing, which you'll find out as soon as we begin to pester you for planning," Tamma told him, her tone sure and firm. "Everything isn't over, it's only just starting."

"Don't forget that we'll be going on to Quellin after this," Jovvi added to clarify the matter. "They weren't told what our attackers were up to, so hopefully they won't be expecting us. Does that make things easier for you?"

"It should, but it isn't wise to count on that sort of edge," Alsin replied, now sounding thoughtful. "People learn about things they aren't supposed to know all the time, and there's no reason to believe that those in Quellin are any different. We'll plan a surprise attack just in case it does turn out to be a surprise, but we'll make sure it's something that will work even if it's expected."

"That sounds good," Tamma said warmly, then turned her attention to something Jovvi had already noticed—and was salivating over. "I'm starving, and that chicken smells delicious. Let's take care of that little chore we couldn't do earlier, and then dig in."

Jovvi agreed completely, and since they'd left the barn and the men had seen them, she was able to initiate the Blending. The entity came into being briefly, removed the protection command from the ex-captives—after telling them that their behavior had been perfectly normal—and then Jovvi was back to being an individual again. Almost everyone around them was stretching and chuckling and delighting in the idea of being safe again, including the man Lidris. He, however, hadn't simply been standing around, and Lorand came over to explain what he *had* been doing.

"Obviously, the idea of blanket protection covers a lot of territory," Lorand said after giving her a brief but very sweet kiss. "Lidris was in the group which came with us, and when he saw that we meant to cook for ourselves, he immediately pushed forward and took over. To keep us from poisoning ourselves, is my guess."

"I'd have to agree, and I'm duly grateful," Jovvi said with a small laugh. "I haven't had much experience with cooking, and I get the impression that Tamma is in the same position. That makes five of us in the group who can't cook, and maybe even six if Naran shares our lack. Do you think there's some honorable way we can keep Lidris from ever leaving us?''

''I'm fully prepared to try begging,'' Lorand suggested with a grin, leading her closer to the cooking fire with an arm around her shoulders. ''Maybe if Rion and Vallant and I beg while you and Tamrissa cry . . . No, making someone feel guilty isn't really what can be considered honorable. We'll have to put some thought into it.''

Jovvi nodded her agreement, but most of her attention was on the serving of fried chicken Lidris now handed to her. He had a similar plate filled for Tamma, along with fried potatoes mixed with green beans. Jovvi had no idea how Lidris had managed to collect all that food, but that didn't keep her from immediately falling on it and devouring it to the last crumb.

Everyone else was almost as hungry, and with the five fed it became the turn of the others to collect their own meals. Fresh tea was also available, and once everyone sat with filled bellies and refilled cups, Vallant stood up to look around.

''It's time to ask the question that's been waitin' for an answer,'' he said in a voice loud enough to carry to the entire group. ''And since we haven't replaced our sentries yet, it's the perfect time to get that answer from everyone. Jovvi, Tamrissa, Rion, Lorand, and I mean to go on to Quellin to free whatever captives they happen to have there, people who are captives because they're like all of *us*. After that, well, we don't quite know yet, but at some time we'll be goin' back to Gan Garee to face the people who stole the Fivefold Throne from us. Are any of you interested in goin' along for any of that?''

''Are you trying to say we have a choice?'' a man asked, his tone more disturbed than accusing. ''We stayed in the first place because we had nowhere else to go, so aren't we committed to you now?''

''We don't believe in associatin' with slaves, which is what you would be if we took your presence for granted,'' Vallant replied, the words calm and unaccusing. ''It really wasn't your choice to become mixed up with us, which means it now has to be *made* your choice. If we took over your lives and ran them to suit ourselves, we'd be no better than the people we mean to fight and replace. We do want all of you to come with us, but only if that's what *you* want as well. If you decide to leave, we'll do our best to help you safely on your way.''

"But on our way to *where*?" a woman begged rather than demanded, looking as though she were about to cry. "We can't go back to our former lives, not when *they* know where we come from and can follow us there. My father has always been willing to believe the worst about his children, so he'd never even *try* to keep them from taking me again ... I have nowhere to go, but I'm ... afraid to stay with *you* ...''

"Let *me* answer her," Tamma said to a suddenly uncomfortable Vallant, then she turned to the woman. "A lot of us go through life being pushed around by every circumstance we come across, but the day comes when we reach a fork in the road. One of those forks lets us continue on the same way we've *been* going, allowing everyone but us to be in charge of our lives, but the second fork offers the opportunity for change. It gives us the chance to take charge of our own lives no matter how scary that sounds, so that we'll learn how to cope with things *without* fear. Whether you decide to stay or decide to go after all, you first have to choose one of those forks. You haven't been abandoned by circumstance, you've been given an opportunity—but only if *you* make it one. All anyone else can do is wish you luck, which I now do.''

The woman stared at Tamma with desperation in her eyes, but her mind was actually beginning to think about what she'd been told. The idea of change is always painful and hard, Jovvi knew, not to mention frightening, but if more people tried to embrace it they would certainly surprise themselves. The woman might be able to do it, but that remained to be seen.

"The five of us, along with anyone who cares to come, will be leavin' first thing in the mornin'," Vallant said into the following silence. "That means you have until then to make up your minds, unless you already have. For those who have, we'll be havin' a meetin' later to discuss our plans, and we'll announce when as soon as we decide about it. For those of you who decide to leave, we wish you all the best.''

And then Vallant went back to rejoin Rion and Lorand, having no idea that he'd put Jovvi on the verge of having a terrible headache. All those emotions flying every which way . . . Jovvi erected what barriers she could, then hoped very hard that everyone made up their minds as quickly as possible. . . .

THIRTY-SIX

When Vallant closed the door on any more open discussion, everyone started to talk to the people around them. Or almost everyone. Some of them looked as though they'd already made up their minds, and I would have enjoyed knowing in which direction. It did matter, I told myself, but then I had to admit that I was so very interested in how people would decide because that kept me from trying out Jovvi's idea. I was supposed to court Vallant the way he'd courted me, trying to get him to change his mind the gentle way. When I discovered myself thinking that I'd rather yell and shout, I felt not only disgusted but ashamed. If he'd made the effort for me, and he had, how could I refuse to do the same for him?

I took a deep breath after silently admitting that I couldn't, and finally looked over at him where he stood drinking his tea. Rion and Lorand had gotten into a conversation and Naran stood listening to them, so the opportunity I'd spoken about earlier couldn't be ignored. I stood up clutching my own cup of tea, and forced myself to walk over to him.

"I think you were wise not to let a debate get started," I began, wishing I'd taken a deeper breath before beginning. "No matter what anyone says, some of them may not even have their minds made up by tomorrow morning."

"Well, they can't stay here," Vallant responded, only giving me a quick glance. "Meerk pointed out that this is the first place the next group of guardsmen will check, and anyone left behind here will be retaken. I'll be mentionin' that later, so they'll know they *have* to make up their minds by the mornin' . . . Tamrissa, I don't want you gettin' the wrong idea. What I did before we slept had nothin' to do with the decision I told you about. Just because you needed someone—and I did, too—doesn't mean I've changed my mind."

"Oh, I know that," I told him with a small laugh, taking the first step to calm his fears. "There's no need to worry about it. I just wanted you to know I thought you did a marvelous job, guiding everyone in the direction they have to go in. You always look so handsome that they couldn't help but be impressed, especially in the shirt and trousers you're now wearing. All colors suit you, but these most of all."

"Blue and white with touches of gray," he said, sounding as though he mentioned the colors because he couldn't think of anything else to say. He also looked suddenly worried. . . . "Tamrissa, what are you doin'?"

"Oh, nothing," I responded with a smile I hoped was appropriate. "I just thought it would be pleasant if I were nice to you for a change. I mean, you were really nice to me just a little while ago, and it's only right to show how much I appreciated it. I hope it doesn't embarrass you, or make you uncomfortable . . . ?"

I let my words trail off into a question, ignoring the way he looked even more worried now. I would *not* let myself get annoyed over the fact that the imminent attack of a hundred guardsmen had fazed him not at all, but *my* being nice got him worried. . . .

"I . . . suppose it just takes some gettin' used to," he finally responded, his tone and expression both extremely cautious. "But I'm afraid you'll have to excuse me now. There's somethin' I've been needin' to ask Meerk."

"Of course," I made myself answer with the same smile, holding tight to the power to keep from losing my temper. "You and I can talk again later."

"Later, right," he muttered with that same expression, then he hurried off to where Meerk was talking to Lidris. I watched him for no more than another moment, then turned and walked over to Jovvi.

"So how do *you* think it went?" I asked her, very aware of her strange expression as she tried not to glance at Vallant. "My own opinion is that he may very well leave with those who decide against joining us."

"Oh, it isn't *that* bad," she hastened to assure me, sounding about as convincing as someone speaking to a dying person and telling them that they're going to live. "I'll admit he was a bit . . . taken aback, but didn't *you* feel the same when he started to court *you*?"

"I was nervous, not panic-stricken," I pointed out, trying to get rid of the dryness my voice had taken on. "If the next time I go to talk to him he turns to run, would it be more polite to trip him, or simply run along behind? Talking all the while, of course, in an effort to calm him down."

"All right, I'll admit it didn't go very well at all," she said, finally letting out the soft laugh she'd been choking on. "You did make him extremely nervous, because he doesn't understand what you're up to. Men are like that sometimes, so maybe you ought to tell him what you're doing. It would be easier than tripping him or chasing along behind."

"Easier, but not quite as fair," I mused. "After all, you have to remember that he didn't tell *me* what he was doing when he decided to court me. He pretended it was just some innocent conversation he was after, that and a bit of time in my company. If I'm supposed to do things the way he did, wouldn't explanations be out of order?"

"I suppose that depends on whether you're trying to get him back or trying to get even," she replied, her smile now on the wry side. "When you make up your mind, you'll be able to answer your own question. And while you're thinking about it, let's help with the preparations for tonight's mass cremation. We can't leave here without giving those people a proper send-off.''

That was something I didn't even want to argue, so I followed her while my mind worked on the last question she'd put. It was fair to ask whether I was interested in getting back the man who meant so much to me, or whether I was simply interested in getting even with him. If I hadn't been touching the power, the answer would have been easy.

But I *was* touching the power and couldn't *stop* touching it, so my reactions were almost alien to what I used to consider normal. The way Vallant looked down at me so warily, almost as though he were afraid of me, was hilarious to my current mood once I thought about it for a while. It wasn't my talent that caused his reaction, but small, helpless, little me. At one time I would have been horribly upset at the thought, that *I* could make a man his size want to run.

Now I just wanted to laugh in delight, enjoying the pure silliness of the situation. I had no idea what he imagined I would—or could—do to him, but the urge to chortle over possible future scenes was definitely there. That wasn't to say that I didn't seriously want him back, but maybe I could keep the silliness going a *little* longer . . . ?

It took all the rest of the afternoon to prepare for the mass cremation, and by the time everything was ready I no longer wanted to laugh. Those poor people had been murdered in cold blood, and I couldn't help wondering if they'd known their children would be killed along with them. Knowing that would have been harder than the awareness of their own coming deaths, and I no longer felt queasy over what we'd done to those attacking guardsmen. They may or may not have been the actual ones who'd killed all those people, but they were certainly of the same type. They'd been ready to kill *us* without giving us the least chance, counting on their greater numbers to let them do it in safety.

But they hadn't been quite as safe as they thought, and as I ranged myself along with the other Fire magic users in our group, I found that a satisfying memory. If you only pick on people you know you can best you're a coward, and cowards deserve everything that happens to them.

Our group of Fire magic users linked in order to set flame to all the bodies at the same time, something I could have done alone if I'd had to. But this send-off was important to everyone there, and by letting it be a group effort we were including even those who didn't have Fire magic. We all watched the flames consume those poor, pathetic bodies, and when there was nothing left but ash, Vallant stepped forward.

"Everyone should know by now that it won't be possible for anyone to stay here after the rest of us leave," he announced. "There will be more guardsmen comin' after that first group, and this is the first place they'll check. Those of us goin' to Quellin will be havin' a short meetin' now, and anyone who's decided to come along with us should join the meetin'. The rest of you can have your own meetin', to decide where you're goin' from here. Just know that you'll be takin' our good wishes with you."

He began to walk toward the cooking fire near the barn, and the first tentative stirring of the crowd turned into a stream of people who followed him. After the stream ended there were four people who hadn't gone with the rest, three men and a woman. They looked longingly after everyone else, but ended up turning and walking in the other direction. The woman with them was the one who had spoken earlier about being afraid, and I couldn't decide whether or not to feel sorry for her. If *she'd* made the decision not to stay, that was all right. But if she'd let her fear make the decision for her . . .

But all *I* could do was shrug and follow along after everyone else. I'd wanted to see how many had decided not to go with us, and now I had. I'd also wanted to see if any of them would turn out to have Fire magic, but none of the four did. I suppose the talent does affect a person's nature to some extent, but when I reached our meeting and heard Alsin talking, I forgot about everything else.

". . . have to get a look at the place first, but I seriously doubt that it's a fortress," he was in the midst of saying. "Our general plan will be to cause a distraction designed to draw away whatever guards are nearest our people, and then to release our people. Once our numbers are increased, our position will be a good deal stronger."

"What will we do if our people are drugged, the way we were?" one man asked. "We won't be able to simply release them then, not when they can't run with us.''

"Chances are good that they *won't* be drugged, but they might well be conditioned," Alsin responded. "If they are, then it's up to our Blending to uncondition them. They think they can do that, and it will be done before we stage our distraction. But please keep in mind that this is a general outline, which will almost certainly be changed once we see what Quellin is like. If their garrison isn't very big, we can take them over instead of having to distract them. After that we can take more time getting our people back to themselves, but not too much time. The pursuit from Gan Garee will certainly continue, and we have to keep that firmly in mind."

"Is that what we'll be doing once we free those people in Quellin?" someone else asked. "Spending the rest of our lives running away from pursuit? That's not my idea of a very satisfactory life."

"It isn't ours either," Vallant stepped forward to say when Alsin hesitated. "But it also wasn't our idea to have the nobility cheat us of what we'd earned, then set guardsmen after us to take our lives. The rest of you weren't meant to be killed, just enslaved in some way, but now they won't be takin' any chances. You've all found out about their cheatin', and they'll also be afraid that we told you about Blendin'. And we *will* tell you all about it, but we urge you not to try it until you've had a bit more practice with your talent. And until we can find a place for you to practice without anyone noticin'.''

That sent a ripple of surprised exclamations through the crowd, possibly because none of them believed that we *would* share the way to Blend. Some of them might decide that they didn't want to know, but the rest would listen with both ears. . . .

And listen they did. Someone stood up and asked if they could hear the details right now, and when Vallant agreed at once, no one got up and left. He described the proper way to stand and how the Spirit magic member had to start things by reaching out to everyone else, then talked about the need for everyone to reach toward the other members of their group. It didn't take very long, and once he was through explaining, the meeting was obviously over. Our companions were too eager to discuss what they'd just learned to want to sit and listen to anything else. Our own group moved off to one side, and no one noticed that we were gone.

"We're going to have to find a place for them to practice rather quickly," Jovvi told us in a soft voice once we all stood together. "Caution will keep them from trying to Blend for a short while, but once that caution fades . . ."

"They'll try it just the way we did," Lorand finished when she didn't. "No one can blame them, but we also don't want them to get hurt. Yes, I agree that we'll have to find a practice place for them."

"But that's for another time," Vallant said with a nod to show that he nevertheless agreed. "Right now we need to get some sleep, so we can be out of here bright and early. We don't know how much time we have until the next group of guardsmen catch up to us, so we can't afford to waste any."

"And I really do need to get a good look at Quellin," Alsin agreed in turn. "If they have some unexpected defenses against invasion, I'll need some of the time we don't have to figure out a way around those defenses."

"Then let's all go to bed," Rion said, Naran under his arm at his side. "The more quickly we take care of all the petty annoyances which lie ahead of us, the more quickly we'll be able to begin our own normal lives. And we *will* be able to begin them, I'm completely determined on that point."

Jovvi and Lorand glanced at each other with smiles before quickly supporting Rion's point of view, and I chimed in right after Vallant. But I didn't look at him, as I was a bit too tired to do any running. Although I did mean to have a word or two with him once the meeting was over. He needed to be assured that I meant him no harm, and maybe then his nerves would relax a bit. The group began to break up then, but before I could make my way over to Vallant, Alsin Meerk stepped in front of me.

"Tamrissa, I wonder if I might have a moment of your time," he said, sounding downright shy. "I've been trying for days to get up the nerve to speak to you, and now I finally have."

"Speak to me about what?" I asked, puzzled as to what he might mean. "And why would you need to get up your nerve? I don't bite people who talk to me all *that* often."

"Well, since we've talked so often, I thought it might be my turn to be bitten," he came back with a grin. "In any event, ever since Jovvi helped me to straighten out the mess in my head, I decided I had to put myself on record. If I don't and I lose out, I'll have no one but myself to blame."

"What are you putting yourself on record about?" I asked, trying not to feel as though I were repeating myself. Alsin had had a hard time, and until he was completely over it he'd need the help of all of us.

"I'm making an official announcement that I intend to court you," he said, sending my jaw down toward the ground and making me wish I hadn't asked. "I know you and Vallant had something between you, but it's perfectly obvious that that something no longer exists. That means the way is clear for *me* to give it a try, so please be warned. If you see me staring at you with cow eyes, or find me bringing you bunches of wildflowers for no reason, there *is* a reason."

"But Alsin, you can't!" I protested, now trying not to sound frantic. "There *was* something between Vallant and me and there will be again, so I don't want to see you hurt. I'm really not interested in—"

"Hush, little one, and listen to me for a moment," he interrupted gently as he took my hand. "I saw the way Ro was treating you, and that's no way to behave with a woman you have feelings for. All I'm going to do is show you how *I* treat that sort of woman, and leave you to make the comparison. If, after you have, you decide you're not interested in me, well, at least I tried. But you can't in all good conscience deny me the chance to try, can you?"

"Why not?" I countered weakly, but all that got me was a chuckle from him. Then he kissed my hand and walked away, leaving me to wonder how I always seemed to manage to get into that kind of position. I'd told the man the truth about how I felt, just as I'd told Vallant, but neither of them had believed me. Could I somehow be *saying* it wrong . . . ?

Taking a deep breath made me feel only fractionally bet-

ter, especially since I suddenly remembered that Naran had
warned me about Alsin's feelings. He'd been interested for
more than a couple of days, then, which made the situation
worse. I could see it now, me chasing after a fleeing Vallant,
with Alsin chasing me in turn. All we needed now was
someone for Vallant to chase, who could then chase Alsin
while he chased me—

I had to close my eyes for a moment to drive away the
picture I'd inadvertently painted, and then I was able to
make my way toward the box stall that was our group bed-
room. If we Blended again before we slept and checked the
area for enemies as far as we could reach, we should be
able to eliminate the need for people to stand watch. It
hadn't done any good to have people on watch earlier, so it
just made sense to do something else. And once again it was
obvious that I had no wish to think about anything really
relevant, so I'd found something else to take my attention.

I paused to pick a straw out of a handy bale, and took it
with me to the box stall. Tomorrow I would speak to Jovvi
again, and if what I held didn't turn out to be the *last* straw,
I was afraid to consider what *would* be. . . .

THIRTY-SEVEN

Lorand stood among the trees not far from the road, waiting
for Alsin Meerk to reach him. The man was on his way
back from Quellin after looking the town over, and should
get to where Lorand waited in just a few minutes. Meerk
had insisted that the Blending remove all memory from him
of where their camp was, so that if he happened to be taken

he would not be able to betray them. Lorand had worried that Meerk's paranoia was returning, but Jovvi had assured him that it was just a commonsense precaution. Meerk *could* have been caught, and they were camped less than an hour away from Quellin.

It had been Meerk's suggestion that they set up camp on the far side of the town, to keep from boxing themselves in between the forces in Quellin and the next group of pursuing guardsmen. They'd all considered that a good idea, but it had taken time to work their way around the town without being detected. But at least they hadn't had any trouble finding a good place to camp. Less than an hour beyond the town there was a very pleasant glade near a fast-running stream, with small stands of trees separating the glade into what could almost be considered private rooms. Between that and the supply wagon, they were more comfortable than they'd expected to be.

And he and Jovvi had actually had some privacy the night before. The men had strung rope between some of the trees and then had hung blankets on the rope, providing separate accommodations for the women among them. Jovvi hadn't hesitated to share hers, and he'd made love to her for a very long time before falling asleep while holding her in his arms. And their lovemaking had been more confident than desperate, showing that they both believed that things would work out for them. They still didn't know exactly how, but simply being together made the details something they would find out about later.

Lorand sent his talent out along the road, only to discover that Meerk was still a few minutes away. The man had ridden out of town toward Gan Garee, and then had circled around to reach the road he was now on. But he expected to soon find something to tell him it was time to turn around again, to circle back a second time to the road on the far side. He believed that that was where the group had camped, on the road leading back to Gan Garee, and he was simply making sure that he wasn't being followed. Once he was certain he'd gone far enough, he would turn around and really go in the proper direction.

But speaking about being followed, Lorand suddenly had the strangest feeling. He extended his talent again, finding

Meerk easily—and then he found the rider a short distance behind Meerk. The second man wore nothing in the way of a uniform, but there wasn't much doubt that he followed rather than simply rode. It was something the group had been hoping would happen, and they were prepared to make use of the break.

Reaching out toward Jovvi with his mind had become as easy as breathing for Lorand, so he did it now as they'd agreed he would. She responded immediately by forming the Blending, and then it was the entity which found the second rider. The man's thoughts were smug and unconcerned until the entity took control of them, and then they were merely obedient. The entity withdrew again and disappeared when they severed the Blending, and Lorand stood alone again to wait until Meerk rode into sight.

When he did so, Lorand stepped out of the trees and waved his hand, signaling the man to stop. Meerk was surprised, of course, which his first words confirmed.

"Lorand, what are you doing *here*?" he demanded. "Is everything all right? I hope you haven't come with bad news . . ."

"Relax, Alsin, everything is fine," Lorand hastened to assure him. "I'm here to tell you that you don't have to turn around again, because *this* is where we're camped. You had us take our true location from your mind, just in case you were captured by our enemies."

"Yes, that sounds like something I would suggest," Meerk agreed with a grin. "And all this time I thought I was just trying to find out if anyone was following me—which they aren't."

"Ah . . . as a matter of fact, someone is," Lorand said as tactfully as possible under the circumstances. "You probably didn't notice him because he has Spirit magic, and has learned how to make himself all but invisible. If I'd been as close to him physically as you were, I probably wouldn't have noticed him either."

"I didn't know it was possible to do that with Spirit magic," Meerk responded, more startled than embarrassed. "It looks like we'll be learning a lot of new things before this is all over."

"And everything we learn adds to our strength," Lorand

said, echoing what Meerk himself had been saying since they left the hidden farm. "While we're waiting for your shadow to get here, tell me what Quellin is like."

"It's like your average small town," Meerk replied with a shrug before beginning to dismount. "It has shops and a tavern and a smithy, with people going about their own business. The only obvious difference is the stockade on the south side of town, along with the number of uniformed men you see everywhere on the streets. And there seems to be a lot of wagon traffic going in and out of the stockade. The main street leading from the place has been lined with stone, which is a dead giveaway."

"Well, we know what's in *some* of those wagons," Lorand said, a part of his attention on the road again. "Hopefully we'll know more before too long, and then we'll be able to firm up our plans."

"Are you just going to stand here until the man following me sees you?" Meerk asked, pausing in the act of leading his horse into the trees. "If we just let him ride on past, he'll never know at which point he lost me."

"He won't be going past," Lorand said, glancing at the man he spoke to. "We used our Blending, and once he gets to the camp with us he'll tell us everything he knows. That information I mentioned—remember?"

"Yes, of course," Meerk said with a sigh. "Things like this still disturb my sense of the proper, but my opinions have become a bit more flexible. When you're dealing with people who are willing to do anything necessary to destroy you, worrying about infringing on their rights as human beings is childish. If they really were human beings, you would not have the problem in the first place."

"You're using the term 'human being' in a way most people don't," Lorand observed as he kept one eye on the road. "Are you suggesting that the title should be earned, rather than bestowed on anyone who happens to be born of human parents?"

"Why not?" Meerk countered, now also watching the road. "If your actions earn you the title of 'good' or 'bad,' why shouldn't the same thing be true of 'human being'? Was it human beings who hanged every member of those farm families, including small children and infants? If so, then I want to be called something else—so *no* one ever confuses me with *that* sort.''

"You and me both," Lorand muttered, then he stepped forward to gesture and say in a raised voice, "Over here, friend. Just ride up and dismount."

Meerk's shadow had ridden into view, and when he saw Lorand he came over as ordered. His dismounting showed him to be of average height, which meant both Lorand and Meerk were larger. He was also of average appearance with brown hair and eyes, and even his horse was brown and nondescript.

"For some reason I had the impression that you were . . . more imposing, I suppose," Lorand said to him. "By your looks you would be lost in a crowd, but your thoughts don't reflect that."

"Of course not," the man answered with a small laugh. "I *am* imposing, as my position makes me more than a little important. You people don't realize it, I know, but my being here is a very great compliment to you."

"Let's find out just how great a compliment," Lorand said as Meerk simply made a rude sound. "Come this way."

The man nodded pleasantly and followed after Lorand, leaving Meerk to bring up the rear. As they went, Lorand was able to hear the small sounds made by the linked Air magic and Earth magic people. That particular link was brushing away the horses' hoofprints and the men's footprints, leaving nothing that even the best tracker in the world would be able to follow. Once the ground was taken care of, fresh air would be brought down from high up to disperse the scent of man and animal alike. They'd captured this man from Quellin very easily, which meant the whole thing might be some sort of trap.

Everyone in camp stood waiting when Lorand and the others walked in, as nothing the five did was being kept secret from the people who had joined forces with them. The least those people were owed was honesty, as some of them might not survive to see the end of the fight. And their numbers included two more than they'd expected it to, since only two people had gone their own way instead of four. The woman and one of the three men had changed their minds and stayed, a decision they still seemed pleased with.

It remained to be seen how long they *stayed* pleased.

"Just leave your horse there, where he can graze," Vallant said to their visitor as he looked the man up and down, gesturing to the edge of the glade. "You yourself can come over here and sit down."

Once again the man obeyed without hesitation, and soon everyone had taken a place either on the ground or on the edge of a blanket. No one spoke, of course, as everyone wanted to hear what their visitor had to say.

"You can start by tellin' us who you are," Vallant said to him, using that commanding tone that seemed so natural to him. "After that we'll want to know why you were followin' Meerk."

"I'm Fladir Sord," the man answered smoothly. "My actual rank is colonel, but most people think I'm no more than a corporal or a private. It's my job to know exactly what's going on around Quellin, and to make sure nothing interrupts the smooth flow of segments to where they're needed. I followed your friend there because I was certain he was one of those all those messages from Gan Garee spoke about."

"You know about the messages?" Vallant put next, his eyes narrowing. "We had the impression that no one from Quellin was supposed to know anythin' about them."

"Oh, I knew about them even before that fool came racing back in hysterics," Sord replied with a laugh. "For a supposedly tough guardsman, the man was closer to tears than I like to think about. All his people were gone, he kept saying, gone without a trace. My nominal superior tried to calm him by pointing out that they'd probably gone off in an unexpected direction after the fugitives, but he refused to accept that. They finally had to put him to sleep and sedate him to keep him under."

"And is that all they did?" Vallant pursued. "Didn't they also send word about his claims to Gan Garee?"

"Well, of course they did, but only to cover themselves in case something actually came of his raving," Sord answered. "They didn't believe him for a moment, and I certainly didn't. Those fools from the city most likely lost track of their fugitives, so they arranged to 'disappear' for a while. It's hardly likely that anything else happened to them, not against what reason says has to be a rather tiny force. If even half the segments they 'rescued' stayed with them, I'll eat my horse.''

"You seem very familiar with what you call segments," Jovvi put in, speaking more softly than the look in her eyes would suggest. "Just what do you mean by that? What *are* segments?''

"Segments of our army, of course," Sord responded with a faint sound of exasperation. "How could you not know that? Do you think the backward fools in Astinda have been just *giving* us parts of their country for the last three years? A year ago we began to move seriously against Gracely to the east as well, so even more segments were needed. When they find out how many segments you people are responsible for stealing, they'll probably kill you very slowly indeed.''

"Whoever *they* are, they're welcome to try," Jovvi responded, not the least bit of warmth in her voice. "So they *are* using our people to extend the empire by force. Tell me how they control the Highs they drug and enslave.''

"They use Puredan, of course, but the segments aren't just Highs," Sord said with a small shrug of unconcern. "Every once in a while the shipments include a few strong Middles, ones who for one reason or another weren't sent back home. After that the segments *have* to obey orders, and there's never any trouble.''

"That should have changed with some of the last people brought in here," Vallant said, exchanging a glance with Jovvi. "If I'm not mistaken, our friends in the other challengin' Blendin's were sent here when they lost in the competitions. Do you happen to know if the last shipments have been sent anywhere yet? And why don't your bosses use Puredan right from the beginnin', instead of sendin' the people here unconscious?''

"We've learned that there's a difference in *attitude* when people suddenly wake up in a place they can't remember coming to," Sord told them. "It disconnects them from their past lives in some way, and it makes it easier for us to adapt them to the new one. Obedience all by itself doesn't do the job, you know, not when you're dealing with humans. You can order them to be calm and to keep up their strength with the food they're given, but then they have hysterics on the inside, and the food ends up doing nothing to keep them healthy. You'd be surprised at how many link segments we used to lose, just because they were homesick or some such nonsense."

"Nonsense," Jovvi echoed with a growl which would have sounded more fitting coming from any of the others of them. "You call it nonsense because you don't *have* any place to be homesick for. But that's beside the point. You avoided answering the first part of the question put to you, which you shouldn't have been able to do. Answer it now, and then tell me why you avoided it."

"How can you be so obscenely strong?" Sord complained even as he colored a bit. "You're a nothing, and a woman besides ... All right, the answer to your question about the last shipment we got is that I don't know. I'm *entitled* to know, but those fools running the place consider me less than they are because I'm just an illegitimate son of nobility. But that still makes me nobility, so they have no *right* to keep things from me! I usually find out on my own, but this time there were ... distractions."

"He probably means us," Vallant said to Jovvi, then turned his attention back to Sord. "How many people man that stockade? And for that matter, how many men will they be bringin' against us when we attack? And is there any way they *expect* us to attack?"

"Don't be ridiculous," Sord replied with a snort. "Attacking the stockade is out of the question, so how could they be expecting it? They have more than three hundred and fifty men to oppose anyone trying, and that doesn't count the segments—which they'll use to add to their defenses. You fools don't stand a chance, and they know it even if you don't."

"They say you can teach people who *don't* know, but not people who *know*," Tamrissa commented with what struck Lorand as a very ... feral expression. "I think we're about to change that, in the only way it *can* be changed—by force. Especially since we'll have help on the inside."

"You mean me," Sord said with a nod. "Yes, with me helping you, your chances are much improved. Those fools don't know the half of what I'm capable of . . . What will you want me to do?"

"We'll tell you that after you give us every detail about the stockade," Vallant responded, this time exchanging a quick glance with Tamrissa. "But before we go into that, I'll ask if anyone else here has any questions. Don't be shy and hang back because you have no experience with this sort of thing. None of us has experience, and you could well think of somethin' we're missin'."

"My question won't help in that particular way, but I'd like to ask it anyway," Meerk said, speaking up for the first time. "I'm the one you were following, you sludge, and I'd like to know how you spotted me—and what you meant to do when you finally caught up to me."

"Spotting you wasn't hard," Sord said with a ridiculing smirk. "You came into town claiming you were heading to Gan Garee, and were looking for some work to add to your stake. You sounded too stupid for anyone to want to hire you, but the way you looked at everything said you weren't as stupid as you pretended to be. And that accent you used—it's typically poor-section Gan Garee, but you claimed you'd never been to the city. Careless of you, *I'd* say."

"Yes, very," Meerk agreed dryly. "And what about your intentions?"

"Obviously I meant to follow you back to this camp," Sord continued with the smirk increased. "At that point I meant to decide whether to return to Quellin to get help to take all of you, or to do the thing myself. I'm really very strong in Spirit magic, and I've learned how to make most people do everything I want them to. But quietly, of course, so no one gets suspicious."

"And that's how you got to be so *important*," Jovvi said with a sound of disdain. "By manipulating people, instead of earning what you were given. Yes, I can believe you come from nobility stock. That's exactly the way *they* do it."

"Well, why shouldn't I?" Sord countered calmly. "And for that matter, why shouldn't *they?* We have exactly what we want, while you people have nothing—and you won't have even that much once we get through with you. It's fairly obvious that our way is better than yours.''

"You should have used the word 'simple' somewhere in there, because that's what your outlook is," Jovvi returned at once. "When you get what you want using unfair means, you do two things at once: first, you admit to the world that you're too incompetent to get those things fairly, and second, you encourage those who are better than you to use the same means to defend themselves. The result of that second point is that you lose what you should never have had in the first place, so you find yourself regretting the loss for the rest of your life. And you *will* lose it, you have my word on that."

All traces of the smirk had vanished from Sord's face by then, replaced by a look of uncertainty that Lorand was able to understand. It hadn't been possible to doubt Jovvi, who seemed furious because the man had Spirit magic. Lorand understood that as well, not to mention a third thing: with both Tamrissa and Jovvi as angry as they were, he would not have wanted to be on the receiving end of their next Blending efforts himself!

THIRTY-EIGHT

By the time they had all the information the man Sord could give, Vallant felt almost as tired as physical labor would have made him. Somehow Sord was actually resisting the commands he'd been given by their Blending entity, not completely but enough so that they'd had to be very careful with the questions they put and the answers they'd been given. If no one pressed the point, Sord ignored certain questions and gave less than full answers to others. They'd had to constantly repeat the demand that he tell all he knew about something, otherwise the man would have held back on half of what they needed to know.

"Now *that* was a workout," Jovvi said as she pushed back her hair with both hands. "I had no idea it would work like that, but obviously it does."

"You had no idea *what* would work like *what?*" Tamrissa asked, looking just as draggled. "And I still think we would have avoided a lot of that if you'd have let me . . . persuade him a bit."

"You could have fried him for breakfast for all of me, but it wouldn't have done any good, Tamma," Jovvi said with a sigh. "The man is a conscienceless liar, meaning that he says anything he pleases or has to in order to get what he wants. It doesn't bother him the least bit when he lies, because it's so much a part of his nature. His true self and feelings are always in reserve, so to speak, and that's why he's partially able to resist the order we gave. It isn't in him to be completely truthful."

"Unless he's forced to it, the way we did it," Vallant said with a weary nod. "Do you think he's still holdin' somethin' back?"

She turned to look at Sord, where he now sat leaning against a tree, and slowly shook her head.

"No, he's too unhappy and downright distressed to have held anything back," she decided. "If he'd been able to slide over or ignore even one item we need, he would be feeling fulfilled and satisfied. It seems to be part of his very essence to keep the truth to himself and from the world."

"That sounds like someone who's had nothing but pain and betrayal all his life," Lorand commented, also studying Sord. "Or someone who's always been desperately lonely. But that has nothing to do with what we're here for. Do we really have a chance against them, Alsin?"

"More than a chance, *I'd* say," Meerk replied, sounding and looking thoughtful. "They have about three hundred and fifty men to defend the stockade, men who have trained in link-groups. They also have their captive Highs, who will have long since been given the Puredan. If we can somehow eliminate the threat of the Highs, we might be able to take out the rest of them piecemeal.''

"But not without their noticing," Rion pointed out. "What good will it do to drop groups of them in their tracks, if the rest are left awake and alert and able to harm the very people we've come to rescue?"

"They won't do anything to their captives except as a last resort," Meerk assured him soberly. "They'll want to *use* the ability of the Highs, remember, which they can't do if they kill them. And since we have the advantage of surprise on our side, it would be foolish not to use it. No one will notice if their friend or coworker is put down if they themselves are asleep for the night.''

"And that way we can take care of them a few at a time!" Lorand exclaimed, obviously pleased with the idea. "Once that's done Sord opens the gate and lets us in, and the stockade is ours without the least amount of fuss."

"Don't you believe it," Meerk disagreed, but with a sigh. "Only rarely do things work out the way they're supposed to in war, all the books agree on that. And if you think this isn't war, you're in for a nasty surprise."

"I'm hopin' that they're the ones who will get the surprise," Vallant said when Lorand simply nodded wry capitulation. "If Pagin Holter and his Blendin' are still in the stockade, they won't be under the influence of the Puredan. That means they'll be free to help *us*, which ought to make things go more smoothly.''

"Only if they *are* still there," Meerk felt it necessary to point out, then he stretched widely. "I'm going to see if Lidris will fix me something to eat, and then I'll sit down and begin to sketch out the moves we'll be making. And you'll all have to decide if we're going tonight, or if there's a reason you want to wait. If you're thinking about waiting, please bear in mind that we're rapidly running out of time."

None of them really had to be reminded of that, least of all Vallant. He knew there were scores or hundreds of guardsmen who were on their way from Gan Garee to search for them, and only the constant checking the Blending did let him fall asleep at night. But he didn't sleep well or soundly, not the way he used to. It would take that horror being completely over to return him to his old habits, and that would be . . . how long?

"Don't worry, everything will work just the way it's supposed to," a voice said, drawing him out of distraction. All the others had gone with Meerk to the cooking fire, all except—

"Tamrissa, you—startled me," Vallant said, to cover the way he'd jumped when he'd realized it was she. The woman was slowly turning him into a nervous wreck, or maybe not so slowly. She never actually *did* or *said* anything out of the way, but her new habit of smiling and complimenting him made him feel like a calf being fattened for slaughter. And the way she looked at him . . . She seemed to be trying to decide which garnish would go best with his coloring.

"Oh, I'm sorry," she apologized at once, another new thing she'd taken to doing. "I didn't realize I was sneaking up on you, not since I approached you directly. Have you decided yet which side of the question you're on? The one about attacking immediately or waiting, I mean."

"I'm for movin' as soon as possible," he replied, feeling the definite urge to take a big step backward. She'd come up so *close* to him, and although he really meant to keep his word about not becoming involved with her again, being this close to her made it damned hard. Somehow her hair still smelled faintly of wildflowers, and he kept picturing himself burying his face in it . . .

"Yes, I agree," she said, now sounding as though she'd soberly considered the matter. "The longer we wait, the more of a chance there is that we'll be interrupted by the new group of guardsmen. Or that something will go wrong, and the people in the stockade will be warned. I'm fairly certain that everyone else also feels the same, so does that mean we'll be doing it tonight?"

"I would say so, yes," he allowed, now fighting the urge to loosen his collar. The fact that he wore an open shirt meant nothing; he definitely needed to loosen his collar. "And since we probably *will* be doin' it tonight, you might want to get a nap now while you can. Once we start, we'll need all our strength to finish it on *our* terms."

"That's an excellent suggestion, so I think I'll accept it," she said lightly, giving him nothing of the argument he'd expected. "I'm really glad that you've taken charge of things. You do it so . . . *well*. We'll speak again later."

Those beautiful eyes of hers held to his almost longer than Vallant could stand, but then she swung away and strolled off—and he actually took one step after her before finding it possible to bring himself up short. If he didn't know better, he would have sworn the woman had found a new kind of magic, a kind he seemed to be helpless against. She'd really begun to frighten him, but strangely enough the fright itself was somehow a draw rather than an aversion. What in the name of chaos was she doing to him . . . ?

Vallant couldn't answer that, but then he saw something that drove the question out of his mind. As Tamrissa moved along past the cooking fire, Meerk left it to intercept her. He stopped her and said something, and then he handed her a tiny bunch of flowers. She said something in return and left the man, but she still took the flowers. And the way Meerk stared after her . . . If that had been nothing but casual conversation, Vallant was a cross-eyed sea monster.

Instant, towering anger filled Vallant's mind, pure emotion with nothing of calm, rational thought behind it. He'd known all along that Meerk was more than slightly interested in Tamrissa, but until now the man hadn't done anything overt to show it. Obviously that had changed, and Vallant discovered that he didn't care for it one little bit. Even though there was no longer anything between him and Tamrissa . . .

"At the moment," he growled under his breath, watching Meerk return to the fire to accept a plate of food from Lidris. "If she does come around to wantin' the same thing I do in the same way, that's goin' to change really fast. And since it can happen at any time, I'll have to be sayin' somethin' to Dom Meerk. . . ."

But not now. Vallant blew out a breath of exasperation, but the decision had to stand. Making an issue of the man's actions toward Tamrissa just before they attacked the stockade would be stupid, an act that would affect everyone there. He'd have to wait until the trouble and danger were behind them, but then he'd take Meerk aside. And maybe even speak to Tamrissa on his own behalf. But no, he couldn't do that. Saying anything at all to Tamrissa would probably turn her even more strange than she was right now, and Vallant simply didn't have the nerve to face that possibility. If anything real was to develop between them, they *couldn't* rush a relationship again. . . .

Taking a very deep breath helped Vallant only a little, but that little allowed him to walk toward where Jovvi and Lorand and Rion and Naran stood while pretending nothing had happened. They had to make a decision about tonight, and if they were agreed they all needed to nap the way Tamrissa was already on the way to doing. It took only a minute or two to discover that the others did agree, and that included a worried but definite Naran. She held tightly to Rion's hand while stressing how much danger there would be for them, but was forced to admit that they had no other choice.

So, with no other choice, they gave Meerk their decision to pass on to everyone else, then they went to take their naps—after stopping near Tamrissa's area and Blending again. There continued to be nothing but usual signs of life as far as the Blending entity could reach, but right at the edge of its perception, toward Gan Garee, there was something like a roiling smudge. . . .

"That's going to turn out to be the next stage of pursuit," Jovvi guessed once they had withdrawn from the Blending. "Coming from the city, it's hardly likely to be anything else."

"And at most they're two days' travel away," Lorand said in agreement. "Two days under normal circumstances, but they're not likely to be taking their time. They're probably pushing their mounts and allowing only minimal time for sleep and rest, which means they could be here in as little as another day and a half—or less."

"Which means our decision was a sound one," Rion added his own agreement. "We must strike now, while we can, but what will we do then? Leave this area as quickly as possible, or stay and face the pursuit?"

"I'm for staying," Tamrissa said, but thoughtfully rather than belligerently. "If we leave they'll just continue to follow us, and then we'll have to worry that they might catch up to us at the worst time possible. Taking care of them here and now is a much better idea."

"That all depends on what kind of shape we're in after takin' the stockade," Vallant pointed out as most of the group nodded to what Tamrissa had said. "That pursuit won't have just a few men in it, so we'll have to wait and see. But if we *are* forced to run, we'd better spend some time decidin' on where to go."

"There won't be a whole lot of choice in *that*," Lorand said, now looking troubled. "I've never been to this particular area before, but I know *about* it because it isn't far from where I used to live. This road heads west again in a couple of miles, and after that about three days' normal travel takes you to the border with Astinda. Is that someplace we really want to go?"

"When we're likely to run into the army trying to take Astinda?" Jovvi said, making a small sound of gentle ridicule. "I really don't think so, my dear. But since you're the only one who knows this area, why don't you mull over where we *can* go. We can all discuss your suggestions once we've taken the stockade."

"Maybe one or two of the captives we free will have a suggestion as well," Naran ventured, sweetly eager to be part of the discussion. "But in any event, we'll have to consider how fast we can all travel in so large a group. Because most of those captives will want to stay with us, I know they will."

Everyone nodded absently, knowing that that aspect of the logistics would play an important part in their planning, and then they separated to get what rest they could. For Vallant it wouldn't have been much, not when there were so many things for him to think about, but once again Jovvi came to their rescue. This time she linked with Lorand to help them all get to sleep, the last realization Vallant had before consciousness faded.

Vallant awoke again at sundown, and after washing the sleep out of his eyes he discovered that just about everyone in camp had also slept. They all felt strong and rested, and as Vallant walked among their companions he learned from their conversations and comments that they were eager to get to the attack. They all expected their small group to win against the defenders of the stockade, but Vallant wasn't quite as uncritically certain. Too many things could go wrong, no matter how well they planned and prepared. . . .

Lidris had made an excellent meal around the deer one of the Earth magic people had caught, and everyone ate well while being bathed in the general atmosphere of assured excitement. Meerk seemed more . . . suppressed than usual, Vallant felt, the man apparently wrapped up in his thoughts to the point where he didn't even seem to notice Tamrissa. Most likely he was immersed in going over the plans he'd made, checking and rechecking them for flaws.

After the meal, Meerk got up and began to tell them what he'd worked out. They would send Sord back to the stockade as late as possible, under orders, of course, to say nothing about what had happened to him. After that they would wait for everyone to go to bed and fall deeply asleep, then they would put the gate sentries to sleep forcibly. Sord would then let them into the stockade, and they would find the commandant and have the man tell them the new keying phrase used on the captive Highs. After that the Highs could be freed and taken out of the stockade, with no one the wiser. Anyone waking up or stumbling across them would be put to sleep by the Blending or *their* linked Highs in Earth or Spirit magic, and their aim would be achieved without the least fuss or fury.

A small number of people in the group seemed disappointed that there would be no real attack against the stockade, but the rest took to the idea at once. Vallant saw that Meerk had no real concept of what the Blending could do or at what distance from its objective, but there was no need to go into that kind of detail at the moment. He exchanged glances with his Blendingmates, knowing from their wry expressions that they knew and felt the same. They would have to explain matters to Meerk more clearly, but there was time for that later, once their "attack" was under way.

They waited until full dark before they released the man Sord, who assured them that he would return to the stockade in plenty of time to be admitted for the night. Fifteen minutes after Sord left, the rest of them followed him onto the road. They would find a place to wait right outside the fringes of Quellin, and would therefore be close enough to notice any alarms raised or any furor there shouldn't be. Only horses were used by their group, which meant a number of the ladies among them—and two of the men—received their first lessons in riding.

Experienced riders were paired with the novices, and Vallant discovered that Meerk had assigned *himself* to look after Tamrissa. Once again Vallant wanted to protest, but once again he had to bite his tongue. Meerk did know more about riding than Vallant did, and Vallant *wanted* Tamrissa to have the best instruction possible. The two conflicting desires, wanting Tamrissa to have the best and wanting to be the one to supply that best, set Vallant into a foul mood he had to fight to overcome.

It took the entire ride to the outskirts of Quellin for Vallant to push away rumbling anger and stomach-upsetting indecision. It occurred to him that he might be wrong in believing that Tamrissa wasn't ready for a real relationship yet, so he decided to speak to her after the rescue and find out for certain. If he had to continue on with his thoughts driving him crazy, he would certainly negate any benefit his ability brought to the group.

Lorand and the other Earth magic users found an abandoned shack beyond the town that was just large enough to shield the group's presence from the road. The darkness was deep and complete enough, but the moon was almost full and it was a clear night. One glimmer of light from the harness of just one of their horses could betray them, Meerk had pointed out, if the wrong people came up the road at the wrong time. There was no sense in taking that sort of chance, so they hid the horses behind the shack and then got down to it.

The Blending formed instantly once everyone had dismounted, and the first thing the entity did was arrange everyone else, aspect-linked, in defensive positions around the five. Then the entity floated rapidly toward the stockade, intending to see how the man Sord was making out. Sord puzzled the entity a bit, as the man should never have been able to resist the commands he'd been given. Possibly, if there was time, the entity meant to investigate the matter.

No one noticed when the entity floated into the stockade, of course, but it was impossible to miss the fact that there were more people moving about than seemed proper for that time of night. It felt as though everyone in the entire stock-

ade was awake and doing, which puzzled the entity even
more than the man Sord. And speaking of Sord, just where
was he . . . ?

The now-familiar thought patterns of the man drew the
entity to a large room toward the center of the stockade.
Quite a few men stood in that room, and one of them spoke
harshly to Sord.

". . . know you never just ride off without reason, so tell
me now what you were after," the large, red-faced man
demanded in a growly voice. "You've found that group of
fugitives, haven't you, and now you intend to contact the
Five and claim the reward for yourself. Tell me the truth!"

"I really have no idea what you're talking about, sir,"
Sord replied, managing to look puzzled as well as faintly
hurt. "If I'd found any trace of those supposed fugitives, I
would certainly have come straight to you with it. My guess
is that they've left this area entirely, and anyone who goes
searching for them is wasting his time."

"Really," the heavy man growled very flatly. "And *my*
guess is that you know exactly where those people are, and
may even have thrown in with them. We've been warned
that they may try to free the segments we have here the way
they freed the last batch which was supposed to be sent to
us, so I've put everyone in the stockade on the alert. If they
don't come at us tonight or early tomorrow, they won't have
the chance to come at us at all. A force of two hundred is
on its way from Gan Garee, and we were told to expect
them sometime tomorrow night. Take him away and lock
him up. I'm told there are people who are experts at questioning among those who are coming, so after giving some
of our own people the first chance to get answers, I'll leave
him for *them* to see to if he decides to be too foolishly
stubborn."

Sord's mind jumped about wildly as he fought to keep
his protests mild as two big men took his arms and began
to drag him out of the room. Things weren't going exactly
as expected, the entity realized, not in any way at all. . . .

THIRTY-NINE

When the Blending dissolved, Rion heard Alsin Meerk saying, "... people shouldn't be doing that now. You should be sitting down and resting, because the five will need you later. Do you people hear me? What's wrong?"

"There's nothing wrong, Alsin," Jovvi hurried to assure him, undoubtedly feeling the beginnings of panic that even Rion was able to see in the man. "We Blended to have a preliminary look around in the stockade, and our companions are simply protecting us."

"Meanin' nothin' is wrong *here*," Vallant clarified, sounding as disturbed as Rion felt. "Inside the stockade is another matter entirely, since every man available has been put on the alert."

"What?" Meerk yelped, now looking even closer to panic. "How can that possibly be? I thought Sord was given unbreakable orders about not telling his people anything."

"It wasn't something Sord said or did," Jovvi explained, her distant expression suggesting she now examined the scene again. "Those men were alerted even before he returned to the stockade, so my guess would be that someone warned that commandant that the disappearance of the first guard pursuit was nothing to ignore or dismiss. And the commandant clearly hates and distrusts Sord, so his late return to the stockade simply made the man suspicious of what Sord might have been doing."

"Which leaves us where?" Tamrissa asked, her own disturbance colored with frustrated annoyance. "We can't wait for them to fall asleep because they're not *going* to sleep, so what do we do now? Attack anyway, and hope we have enough strength to overcome that many men?''

"No, no, no, there's no such thing as 'hope' in warfare," Meerk said with a dismissive gesture, his head down as he obviously considered the problem. "We have to find something that *will* work, with no hoping about it. But first explain what was going on with your Blending. I was under the impression that you had to be a lot closer than this to whatever you were Blending against.''

"That's right, you missed the first battle," Lorand recalled aloud. "Then we'd better tell you what you need to know.''

They all took turns describing what their Blending entity was capable of—as far as they knew—and Meerk stood listening to most of it with his mouth open. By the end of the explanation he was merely shaking his head, most of his wide-eyed expression having disappeared.

"No wonder you didn't want any of the others practicing exercises in camp," he said then. "If they had and there'd been a working Blending in the stockade, we would have been spotted. Is it likely there *is* another working Blending there?''

"No," Vallant answered, the words morose. "If there was we would have known about it, and I, personally, would have recognized Pagin Holter's talent. He and his Blendin' must have already been sent to wherever they send their 'segments.' ''

"So much for us having allies inside the walls," Meerk muttered, then he looked around at the five. "All right, we'll have to do this in steps. Step one will be to neutralize the High talents they have in there, otherwise we're probably beaten before we start. And we might be best off waiting until tomorrow night after all, to take the edge off their alertness.''

"I knew we forgot to mention something," Rion exclaimed, annoyed with himself for not having been able to pinpoint the thing which had been nagging at him. "We found out that waiting is out of the question, as they're expecting another two hundred guardsmen by tomorrow night. We have to free their captives and then we must leave, but to go where we still have no idea.''

"And there probably won't be any question about our having the strength to face those two hundred newcomers," Tamrissa said with a sigh. "If we don't end up expending everything we have on getting the captives freed, wishes will start to come true on a regular basis."

"Is there any other good news you haven't yet passed on?" Meerk asked, his tone more depressed than sarcastic. "If there is, please tell me now; there's still one small patch of belief inside me that says we do have a chance to be successful. If it's going to be wiped out completely, I'd rather have it done before I grow too fond of it."

"Personally, I'd rather *not* have any more good news of that sort," Jovvi said, putting a hand to his arm in gentle support. "If our first step is to neutralize the captives, you can consider the matter taken care of. We shouldn't have any trouble with *that* part of it, but we still need to know about step two."

"Step two will probably end up being the guiding of the captives to a back way out, as well as the total destruction of anyone who notices or gets in the way." Meerk's tone had now gone grim, a fitting match to his faintly haggard expression. "That is, if you can *find* a back way out. I would imagine that a stockade is usually considered a place which doesn't need one."

"We'll probably have to make our own back way out," Tamrissa said, clearly considering that part of it in *her* province. "But if we do, we'll certainly attract more attention than we like. If so, what do we do then?"

"Anythin' we have to," Vallant said, looking around at all of them. "Does anyone disagree?"

Rion felt no happier than the others looked, but he also joined them in shaking his head. If it became necessary they would destroy anyone and everyone they could, no matter how ill the memory of it made them later on. Rion glanced down at Naran, concerned that she would be even more deeply bothered than the rest of them, but strangely enough she seemed serenely content. She smiled at Rion and gently squeezed the hand holding hers, as if to say that nothing he did would ruin her love for him. That was comforting to know—even though the point had as yet to be proven.

"Then let's get to it," Meerk said, obviously forcing himself to briskness. "Where does your five have to be for you to reach the captives and neutralize them?"

"We could do it from here, but I'd rather not," Jovvi said, looking around at the rest of them to see if they agreed. "The closer we are the less our strength will be drained, so why don't we try to find a place at least as good as this one, but closer to the stockade?"

"We'll have to use the Blending," Lorand said, also looking at his groupmates. "Sneaking around physically and checking out neighborhoods in a strange town takes too much time, not to mention increasing the risk of our being seen by the wrong people. We'll do it from here, then we can go there a few at a time."

"I have a different suggestion," Vallant said, interrupting Rion and Tamrissa's nods of agreement. "Let's use the entity to question someone who *does* know this town, which ought to do the findin' easier and faster. Then we all go together, but with our Spirit magic people usin' that 'I'm invisible' trick of Sord's. If we separate, it just increases the chance that one of our groups will be seen."

"I like your idea better than mine," Lorand said at once, giving Vallant an amused smile. "As a matter of fact, I like anything that means less work and less danger. Does anyone else have a better idea? No? Then let's get to it."

As soon as Jovvi reached to them they Blended, and a moment later the entity floated through the town, seeking the someone who was most familiar with it. That someone turned out to be a staggering drunk, who ceased being drunk when all the alcohol was removed from his system. By then the man was under the control of the entity, and he did indeed know the perfect place for its flesh forms. A large, in-town estate was situated not far from the stockade, only two streets separating the two locations. Even more, the estate had its own exit to a private road which led to the road outside of town. The owners of the estate had left two days earlier for a long stay in Gan Garee, and all their servants had gone with them.

"Obviously lesser members of the nobility," Rion said once the Blending had dissolved after wiping the former drunk's memory of the interview. "If they were really important, they would maintain a staff here no matter how long they stayed in the city."

"Let's be glad they are," Jovvi said with a chuckle. "And if I had to guess, I'd say we had our ... 'friends' in the city to thank for that house. Someone must have warned those people that they might be in a dangerous position, so they packed up fast and left."

"I consider that extremely accommodating of them," Tamrissa said, also amused. "Let's get on the road and find that back gate, and maybe we can take a couple of minutes to bathe before we start our war. We'll probably need a bath more *afterward*, but I doubt if we'll have the time."

"Let's get there first, and then we can discuss making use of the place's amenities," Lorand said, interrupting Jovvi's—and even Naran's—enthusiastic agreement with Tamrissa. "And even if we *can* take the time to bathe, don't forget that we can't take the time or use the strength to reheat the water. Are you ladies all that eager to take a *cold* bath?"

"Talk about throwin' cold water on an idea," Vallant said with a grin for the expressions of distaste the women now wore. "I think bathin' will probably wait for a time when they'll get a ... warmer reception."

Rion joined Lorand in laughing and booing that terrible statement, but their banter was interrupted by a clearly annoyed Meerk.

"I do hate to intrude on your good time, but would the bunch of you mind sharing with the rest of us what you're talking about?" he said tightly. "You were only ... away ten minutes or so, and most of us expected it to take longer. Are you trying to say that you've found a better place for us *already*?"

This time Rion joined the others in quickly apologizing for their thoughtlessness, then kept silent while Vallant described what they'd found. Everyone in the group was delighted with their good fortune, and they all made their way to their mounts in better spirits. Having an actual roof over their heads was far better than standing around in the dark behind a shack, even if they would not have the roof for long.

Rion rode close beside Naran after helping her into the saddle, fully aware of the easy, familiar way she handled her mount but nevertheless unwilling to take chances with her safety. They used the left-hand branch of the main road to circle the town rather than ride through it, and about two-thirds of the way around they came to the gate the former drunk had visualized. The heavy wooden bar on the inside was chained and locked, they discovered, but their Water magic members took care of the problem. They flooded the lock with water then instantly froze it, and after a loud cracking sound, everyone could hear the pieces of broken lock fall to the ground. Air magic then removed the chain and bar, and they were able to ride through the now-open gate before closing and barring it again behind themselves.

The rest of the ride was along the private road, which led after a while to the house. It was a fairly large house, which was all to the good. Being cramped and uncomfortable would certainly not have helped them, Rion knew, and possibly would have been worse than standing around behind a deserted shack.

They discovered that the estate was completely walled, but that didn't mean they felt they could afford to be sloppy in disguising their presence. The horses were put into the stable even if there weren't stalls enough for all of them, and then they were given liberal helpings of the fine oats they found stored in the feed room. Rion watched that activity for a moment, and then he realized what was bothering him.

"Unless I'm mistaken, we can't simply sneak the captives out of the stockade," he said to Vallant, who stood near him on Naran's other side. "If we bring them out on foot, they'll most likely be forced to stay on foot. We don't have extra mounts for them, we aren't likely to find the necessary mounts in that town, and we certainly can't ride double or triple, depending on how many of them there are."

"I never thought of that," Vallant admitted with a frown. "I wonder if Meerk did, and has somethin' in mind to solve the problem. If not, we'd better do some thinkin' before we get to the attackin' part."

Rion agreed, of course, but discussing the matter with the others didn't occur immediately. Half their number had gone toward the house, and when he and Naran and Vallant followed, they discovered that those with Fire magic were giving separate guided tours. Lighting lamps in every room was not something they were going to do, but kindling small columns of flame to see by was another matter entirely.

"Meerk and the others should be finished with the horses soon, so let's tell the women and Lorand," Vallant suggested. "That way if Meerk is as much at a loss as we are, one of the others might have a suggestion."

Rion considered that course of action sensible, so he and Naran split up from Vallant to search for the others. Rion led the way to the second floor while Vallant searched through the first, and upstairs was where their three groupmates were. Tamrissa lit the way for Jovvi and Lorand as they explored the large, poshly decorated house, but when they heard the question they lost interest in exploring.

"I hope Alsin does have the answer," Jovvi said, and from the various expressions on their faces she obviously spoke for Lorand and Tamrissa as well. "I have no idea how we can get them mounted, not if we don't take the mounts from the stockade as well. But to do that we'd first have to . . . eliminate all those men, which we're all still reluctant to do—even assuming we have the strength."

"So let's see what Alsin has to say," Tamrissa suggested, then led the way back downstairs. By then Meerk had come in from the stable and Vallant had spoken to him, and unfortunately his reaction was a perfect match to theirs.

"I don't understand how I could have missed that," he muttered, now looking more haggard than ever. "And I thought I was doing so well with all this military nonsense . . . So does *anybody* have a suggestion?"

"I suggest we ask the rest of our group," Naran said when no one else spoke up. "If they don't have any immediate ideas, they may be able to think of something."

Since that was the most practical next step, that was what they did. Rion watched their companions while Vallant made the announcement about their dilemma, but no one's face lit up with the answer. The dimness of the sitting room they'd all gathered in accounted only partially for that; the rest was deep perplexity.

"It's a good thing you were bright enough to bring up

the point, Rion," Tamrissa murmured to him while a mutter of comments and exclamations went through the group. "Otherwise we'd be standing there with all these freed captives, and no way to get them out of this town."

"I think . . . our main difficulty is that none of us has experience or familiarity with situations such as this," Rion answered slowly, his thoughts . . . stretching in an odd direction. "I was in that very position myself when I first joined the rest of you, and what I needed to do was ask for guidance from those who did have the experience. We need to speak to the commandant of the stockade about the keying phrase for his captives and about where the other challenging Blendings have been sent, so why not ask him about this as well?"

"What if *he* doesn't have the answer either?" Meerk put flatly, obviously having overheard the exchange. "You'll then be left in the middle of the stockade with a large group of people you can't move out quickly, and no easy answer to changing the situation."

"Actually, *we* won't be in the stockade at all," Tamrissa corrected gently as annoyance flared in Rion over Meerk's new tendency toward defeatism. "Our Blending entity will be there, and it's even possible *it* may find the answer we individuals can't. It's either go ahead and take the chance that we'll work something out, or just sit here until that new contingent of guardsmen comes and wipes us out. Which option would *you* prefer to take, Alsin?"

"As if we had a choice," Meerk muttered in answer, then he struggled to put a smile on his face. "But you're absolutely right, Tamrissa, so don't mind me. Someone must have chosen me as designated pessimist of the group while I wasn't looking, and now I can't resign from the position. When do the five of you plan to start?"

"I think we all ought to have some tea first," Jovvi suggested immediately before anyone could say something else. "I know *I* need a cup, and the longer we wait, the less alert those people will be. It's certain to be a very long night, so let's get as comfortable as possible before we begin it."

Everyone was enthusiastic in their support of that idea, but when a search for Lidris began, it was discovered that the man had anticipated the request. A large quantity of tea was already steeping, so it wasn't long before they all had refreshments. There had been many tins of small cakes among the stores in the convoy, and Lidris had brought along a number of the tins, which he opened to go with the tea. They all had their snack, took turns in the comfort facilities of the house, then were ready to begin.

The Blending entity, already knowing the general layout of the stockade, went directly to the room where the one called commandant had been the last time. The flesh form was still there, only now there were no others in the room with him. The remnants of a meal sat abandoned on a tray to one side of the man's desk, and the man himself sat with feet stretched out and a cup of tea in his hands. His thoughts were tinged with satisfaction, and the entity found itself curious.

—Something fills you with satisfaction,—the entity put once it had the man in its control.—What would that something be?—

"I've taken the opportunity to teach that wretch Sord some manners," the man replied, a smile curving his thick lips. "I had him put to the question rather harshly, and even though I learned nothing, there will be no repercussions from any of his—acquaintances. The emergency we are now in the midst of will excuse whatever was done."

—Why do you loathe the man so?—the entity inquired, still curious.—What has he done to deserve your hatred?—

"He presumes, and the fool who fathered him has once or twice supported the bastard," the man returned, a snarl now twisting his pudgy face. "For that reason Sord comes and goes just as he pleases, laughing all the while and thinking that I don't dare oppose him. His sire may not come to his rescue, but then again, he might. Uncertainty has stayed my hand until now, but the commands of the Five have freed me to do what should have been done long ago."

—And what commands are those?—the entity put next, dismissing the unimportant point about the man Sord. —What information have you been given, and what were you told to do about it?—

"I've been officially informed that dangerous fugitives are in this area," the man replied promptly. "They somehow managed to ambush more than thirty guardsmen who

were following them from Gan Garee, and it's thought that
they may well try to free the segments I still have here in
camp. The miscreants also ambushed the convoy I was expecting and stole the segments that are so badly needed at
the front. My men and I are ordered to destroy them utterly,
and when reinforcements arrive I'm to get the remaining
segments sent on their way—under guard—as quickly as
possible.''

—More than thirty guardsmen,—the entity mused.—Was
the number put just that way? And just how dangerous *are*
the dangerous fugitives?—

"Yes, the number was put that way," the man responded,
now sounding faintly annoyed. "That's enough, I think, to
make anyone nervous. And we were told that they were *very*
dangerous, so they're not to be given the chance to pretend
to surrender. We're to destroy them utterly, but preferably
leave enough to send back to Gan Garee as proof of their
death. But if a choice has to be made, complete destruction
is the top priority.''

—So if you were told that the number of the guardsmen
killed was more like one hundred than thirty, that might
affect your eagerness to face the fugitives?—the entity
asked, pursuing its line of curiosity.—What of your men?
Would they feel the same?—

"If they ever learned that a hundred guardsmen were
killed rather than thirty, half of them would probably de-
sert," the man said with a snort of ridicule. "They're mostly
Low talents with a smattering of Middles, after all, so what
else would you expect? I, myself, would ride out with my
personal guard to meet and warn the contingent coming
from Gan Garee, and as soon as my back was turned I would
lose half the men now here. But since the number *isn't* a
hundred, I won't be turning my back and my men won't be
deserting.''

—No, not yet,—the entity agreed, filing the information
away for use at another time.—Now you may explain why
the . . . segments are so vitally important at what you called
the front. What *is* a front, and why is there a rush to get the
segments there?—

"You don't know much, do you?" the man replied, now
openly sneering. "I, personally make it my business to

know everything I need to, which any superlative leader would do. The front is where the fighting is going on in Astinda, and the segments are desperately needed because the fighting is suddenly going against us. Those backward fools in Astinda seem to have found a way to counter our attacks, which has stopped our advance rather abruptly. We can't afford to let that continue, of course, so a massive counterthrust is being called for—*before* those in Gan Garee find out what's happening. Our noble superiors aren't known for their patience with failure, but they won't learn the truth from *me*. I would love to be promoted to the place now occupied by those at the front, but not while they're losing."

—Only someone capable of turning the loss around would think differently,—the entity commented, then got on with the primary reason for its being there.—You will now supply the keying phrase used on your captives, and will also detail whatever orders they've already been given. After that you will suggest the best way to get all those captives mounted and out of here.—

"But they can't be mounted and gotten out of here," the man protested with a small laugh of incredulity. "If my men see them trying to leave, they'll attack at once. The segments have been forbidden to harm anyone here, so they won't be able to defend themselves. The keying phrase is, 'I am in command,' but no one but me can use it—unless I'm officially replaced by someone else, and then only that someone else will be able to use it. The segments know well enough who is and isn't in command, and they won't accept orders from someone not authorized to issue them."

—The solution to that dilemma is simple,—the entity remarked, distantly scornful of the feeble attempt to circumvent its desires.—You will now visit those segments and secretly free them, with this entity accompanying you. In the meantime you will consider the best way to secure mounts for the captives, and will suggest that best way as soon as all are free. You may begin right now.—

The man promptly put aside his teacup and got to his feet, then headed out of the room. Once they had left the man's aide behind in the reception room beyond his own, the entity had the man explain where the "front" was in

more precise terms. The man did so, falling silent at any
time someone else would have been able to hear him, and
at last they reached the first of the groups of captives.

"You will hear me and obey, for I am in command," the
man said clearly to the captives once his own men had been
sent away. "You will not be bound by any previous orders
given you, and after this final command, you will never obey
the orders of others against your will again. As you understand, you may now comply."

The five people all began to speak at once, as though they
had just come out of a trance of some sort, and the entity
touched and calmed them. It promised to explain all once
everyone else had also been freed, and ordered the five to
remain where they were until then, pretending that nothing
had changed. The captives had been arranged into a link-
group, of course, and their agreement was filled with confusion but nevertheless unwavering. They would do as
they'd been asked, at least for a short while.

The same scene was repeated over and over again, until
more than sixty captives had been freed. A large dining hall
was designated by the stockade's commandant as the best
meeting place for their purpose, so all the former captives
were gathered together there. Most of them had had the
chance to think over—and to some extent talk over—what
their situation was, and when the last of their number arrived, a slender man with elegant mannerisms stepped forward.

"Whoever you are, are you able to hear me?" he asked,
looking about as though expecting to see the entity. "Can
you show yourself to us?"

—Becoming visible is not presently possible,—the entity
responded, sending the words to everyone there.—This entity is a Blending of a five, and it stands ready to assist you.
You will all require mounts, and then complete freedom will
have been returned to you. From here our flesh forms go to
free others of our own who have also been enslaved, and
all of you are welcome to accompany us.—

"I believe I speak for all of us when I say we would be
delighted to accompany you," the slender man responded,
looking about himself to see the nods of many of the others.
"There is, however, one thing we must do first. The time

we spent here has been an agony of humiliation and pain, for those about us knew we were helpless to defend ourselves against any despicable act they cared to offer. First we will give thanks for that . . . hospitality, then we will be truly free to join you.''

The roar of agreement arising from all those minds nearly staggered the entity with its intensity, then they all began to stream out of the meeting hall. The entity attempted to stop them, attempted to speak reason and caution, but their fury became a shield of sorts, shutting out everything but what they wished to hear. Astonished by its helplessness, the entity hovered in the now-empty room a moment, then hastily followed the throng. A terrible premonition had come to the entity, and it had to find *some* way to avert what promised to be disaster . . . !

FORTY

But averting disaster proved to be impossible. The captives, freed at last from the confines of their own minds, streamed out across the stockade in their link-groups. The military men, already alerted against attack from without, suddenly found themselves under attack from within. A military link-group in Fire magic attempted to defend itself with a wall of fire, but a thicker, heavier wall of flames consumed theirs and left them shocked and shaken. Then all five crumbled to dust which sifted to the ground, mute proof that a link-group in Water magic had made certain that that particular military link-group would never perform again.

All around the entity it was attack and counterattack, with

the former captives as the stronger force. The entity found itself hoping that that would end the battle with the former captives as the victors, but it—and they—had forgotten how many more military men there were. Sixty High practitioners against a like force of Lows and Middles would certainly have prevailed, but against three hundred and fifty Lows and Middles . . .

The surprise of the attack brought the former captives quick successes, but then the tide began to turn. More and more of the military men entered the fray, with screams and shouts and raging and cursing coming from all directions. People staggered as Earth magic raged inside their bodies, and with their dying efforts they took the air from the nearest group of enemies. Some blistered or burned or turned to charred ash; some drowned or turned to dust; some gasped for air or choked on some fetid stench held around their heads; some were pelted by flying stones or had their hearts stop beating; and some lost interest in the battle and in defending themselves. These last were under attack by those with Spirit magic, and in losing interest they also lost their lives.

The entity, usually so dispassionate, felt a definite sense of malaise. It had naturally expected to join in the battle, but the former captives fought with such savagery that they brought the same out in the military groups. This produced physical fighting as well as talent battle, and in many places the two factions flowed together, one group almost indistinguishable from the other.

And the power that was being used! The source of power was like a limitless ocean, and even the entity took little more than a comparative cupful. But those doing battle were, in multiple groups, using it more by the bucketful. The whirling agitation in the power caused an odd humming to force its way into the entity's awareness, something of a staticlike lightning, which threatened to interfere with the entity's own use of the power.

That, of course, was a more-than-serious situation, therefore the entity strove to balance itself in the midst of the storm. Its help was needed by the former captives, but any attempt to interfere now would most likely destroy friend along with enemy. Balance and control . . . balance and control . . . the second was impossible without the first. In the midst of chaos the entity fought its own silent battle, and then . . . just a hint . . .

But a hint which showed the way to the answer. Once again it lay in those woven patterns its flesh forms had been taught, and now only the proper pattern was needed. The entity flashed blindingly fast from one pattern to another, until the proper one was discovered. A complex pattern to be sure, but one which returned both balance and control. The entity wove it about itself, then looked around—

Only to let forth a voiceless wail of horror! Most of the former captives were dead, and even as it watched, the remaining few link-groups were in the midst of being overwhelmed. The entity had come to *help* the captives, and instead had stood uselessly by and watched them being destroyed! Dispassionate the entity had always been, but suddenly it experienced the taste of rage. . . .

And with that rage came action. The storm of power still lingered in the surrounding air like a thick flurry of leaves during a violent rainstorm. The entity captured that power and added it to what power it was able to draw for itself, then sent the combination sheeting over the military groups which had begun to shout in delighted victory. There was still almost a third of its original force left, but only until their shouts turned to screams. And then only echoes of those screams were left, as the living beings who had produced them disappeared completely. . . .

The entity looked about itself with grim pleasure, weary but satisfied with what it had wrought. . . .

And then it was me back to myself again as Jovvi dissolved the Blending. If I hadn't already been sitting down I would certainly have staggered and then fallen, but not from exhaustion. If I hadn't been in shock I would have been violently sick to my stomach, and Jovvi's muffled sob said she felt exactly the same. Lorand and Rion looked pale with a like illness, and even Vallant was clearly shaken.

"What's wrong?" Alsin Meerk asked as soon as he realized that we were no longer Blended. "Weren't you able to get through to the captives? What took so long? Will we have to go into the stockade after all? What—"

"Stop!" Vallant ordered with one hand raised, not quite

able to look at the man. "Stop askin' all those questions. We got the captives free of the orders holdin' them, but they refused to leave until they got some of their own back from the ones who had held them captive. We couldn't stop them, and the battle turned into somethin' . . . horrifyin'. Our entity got tossed around like a feather in a high wind, and by the time it was able to stabilize itself—All the captives are dead, and we accounted for all the link-groups they didn't."

Exclamations of shock and dismay came from the people around us, and even Alsin had gone pale.

"They're all dead?" he asked in a whisper, his expression showing how difficult it was for him to accept that truth. "We came here and risked ourselves for nothing?"

"We came here and risked ourselves to give them freedom," I corrected harshly, helpless to keep the words back. "What they chose to do with it was their decision, but—I *hate* what it did to *us*. Am I the only one who feels . . . twisted?"

"Hardly," Rion responded first, the others adding their own agreement. "I considered the emotionlessness of our entity a disquieting thing—until it ceased to be that. The simple memory of its rage is almost more than I can bear."

"It was a conglomeration and combination and magnification of our own natural anger and distress," Jovvi said, sounding more weary than the rest of us. "Knowing what being angry feels like lets us control the emotion, but the entity is like a child in its level of experience. That terrible storm of power ripped through its protective shield of emotionlessness, and that caused it to lose control."

"Only over its own feelings," Lorand pointed out after taking a deep breath. "It was in complete control of everything else, proven by the fact that those military men just . . . disappeared. And this time it wasn't in a blaze of fire."

"I had the feelin' it used everythin' at once," Vallant said, pushing both hands through his long, pale hair. "The last time it let one or another of our aspects dominate, but this time it blended them all. Or Blended them. Is it just learnin' what it's all about, or has it taken the wrong branch down a dark road?"

When we heard that question we all looked at Jovvi, but

she gave each of us a glance and then made a sound of ridicule.

"Since I was right there along with the rest of you, how do you expect *me* to know when you don't?" she asked, obviously struggling to sound reasonable. "Right now we probably know more about Blending entities than anyone else alive—with the possible exception of the so-called Seated Five—and we know almost nothing. Do we have any choice other than to simply go along, learning by doing? If we do I'd like to hear about it, but right now we have another question to answer: where do we go and what do we do next?"

"With this small a force, what *can* we do?" Alsin asked, more wounded than scornful. "And if things got this badly out of hand here, won't it be worse if we come across an even larger installation?"

"I'm for goin' to that 'front,' " Vallant said, suddenly sitting straighter in his chair. "That's where Pagin Holter and his people have to be, and maybe even your friend Hat, Lorand. Meerk is right in sayin' we don't have a large enough force to do anythin' meaningful, and if we don't get one we might as well wait here and let them kill us. This time there are two hundred guardsmen after us. Next time they'll make it five hundred or more."

"You should tell everyone what a front is," Alsin said, looking around at us. "And then I'd like to hear what we're supposed to do when we get there."

Vallant made the explanations while I, at least, considered my decision, and by the time he was through I'd come to the only conclusion I could.

"So that means we have to go and try to free their 'segments,' " I said while Alsin sat there looking thoughtful. "We can hope that it won't be the same as it was here, since there isn't likely to be all that pent-up rage inside the captives. Unless I've gotten the wrong impression, they'll be spending their rage on those poor, helpless people in Astinda."

"If they're so poor and helpless, why do the commanders of our own forces need so many more segments?" Rion asked, looking disturbed. "That man told us that the war was suddenly going badly, which means our own people are being defeated. Is walking into the middle of that the wisest course of action?''

"It's either that or try to reach the same organization going up against the people of Gracely," Lorand answered for the rest of us. "They've only been at it for a year in Gracely, but these people have been at it for three and now they're losing. Which group do you think will be more likely to notice our arrival, the ones still winning, or the ones losing?''

"Point taken," Rion conceded, holding up one hand. "Going against an alert, well-organized force would be as-inine, not to mention too time consuming. We could end up surrounded by pursuers in all directions before we came within twenty miles of the place.''

"I agree," Jovvi said, also straightening in her chair. "We have only one place to go and one thing to do, so now we can ask who means to go with us. If the answer is every-one, we really should replenish our supplies from what they have stored in the stockade. *They* certainly don't need them any longer.''

Our companions were quick to assure us that they meant to continue in our company, but I think that was only be-cause they experienced nothing of what had happened in the stockade. They still felt safe with us, but I wasn't absolutely sure that *I* did. We should have had complete control over our Blending entity, but now . . . Instead of acting the sav-iors, were we turning something horrible loose on the world?

I nearly refused to Blend again in order to transfer the supplies, but everything went smoothly. The entity found the stockade's stores and used Air magic to lift and transfer what we wanted, drawing heavily on the power of our com-panions when our own began to be drained. After we sep-arated we were tired but not exhausted, though Jovvi still looked troubled.

"I couldn't help noticing that there were two people still left alive in the stockade," she said when Lorand put an arm around her shoulders and asked what was bothering her. "One was that commandant man, and his Low talent wasn't enough to shield him from all that raw power everyone used. He's now a drooling idiot, but the second survivor isn't the same. That man Sord is badly hurt, but his mind is still intact."

"He's hurt because they tortured him," I said, knowing it for a fact. "I also noticed him, but there's nothing we can do for him. He isn't to be trusted even if we keep him under control, which is why the entity released control of both men. But didn't we heal him just a little?"

"Yes, enough so that he won't have any trouble surviving until those guardsmen get here," Lorand confirmed. "Since it's undeniably our fault that he was tortured to begin with, there was nothing else we could do. But you're right about our not being able to take him with us, even if he *is* a really strong Middle talent."

"Assumin' we get to where we're goin' soon enough, we ought to have all the Middle and High talents we need," Vallant said, standing up to stretch. "I'm hopin' Lidris has a meal ready for us, and after I eat I'm gettin' some sleep. We need to be out of here before sunup tomorrow, but until then there are real beds waitin' to be used."

There wasn't anyone in the house foolish enough to argue with *those* suggestions, and we actually all ended up with our own rooms. Some of us doubled up deliberately, of course, but by using fast footwork I was able to keep Alsin from proposing that he share *my* quarters. I'd been careful to treat him with nothing more than pleasant friendliness, but the deliberate distance I'd evoked was being ignored by him. The man really was persistent. . . .

I sighed as I looked around the room I'd chosen, seeing the small sitting area to one side of the sleeping chamber. I *was* tired but not yet ready to get into bed, so I went to the sitting area and took a chair near a small, beautifully carved desk. Since as a child I'd been forbidden to go near my father's desk, that particular piece of furniture had always held a special appeal for me. Hidden treasures, forbidden delights, illicit marvels . . . I *had* to open the drawers, just to see what was inside.

The desk held nothing but a large, ledger-sized book bound in leather, filled completely with blank pages. There were also pens and many inkstones, as though someone had intended to do a lot of writing at some time. I began to put the ledger back into the desk, conceiving of no immediate

use for it, then I changed my mind and took the inkstones
and pens out as well. Having something to write in—or on,
if we tore out a page or two—might well come in handy,
and we also needed to search that house for clothes. My
own outfit was threatening to become threadbare at any moment, and the others' couldn't be in much better condition.

Tomorrow, before we left, we could do the necessary
searching, and once we brought the supply wagon up to the
house, I'd make sure to include the ledger and ink and pens
in what was loaded. Why, one of our people might even
want to write an account of what had happened to us. . . .

FORTY-ONE

Lorand rode slowly back to where the others were camped,
trying to rid himself of the picture of devastation and ruin
that he'd just encountered. It had taken them a bit more than
four days to reach that part of Astinda, and they'd all been
appalled at what they'd found. Destruction and ruin in all
directions, including the pretty little town he remembered
his father taking them to when he was still a boy. It had
been a meeting of border farmers from both countries, and
those attending had been encouraged to bring their families.
The people of that town had fed and housed them and made
them feel like welcome neighbors, and they'd all been sorry
to leave.

And now nothing was left of that town, not buildings and
certainly not people. Fire had touched everything there, and
not particularly recently. What hadn't been burned was ruined by being exposed to the elements, and the soil had an

odd . . . taste/smell to it. Something like that heavy black semiliquid they'd made him use his talent to scatter around during the qualification tests. It had soaked into the soil and ruined the ground for crops, and only a lot of mind-breaking work with Earth magic at some future time would ever make that land viable again.

"And this was done by those who are supposed to be *my* people," Lorand muttered, wavering between crying like a child and screaming out his rage as his talent sought enemies to destroy. "They wanted this land so they killed those who already occupied it, and why not? Haven't they done the same to enough people in their own country?"

Lorand's mount moved skittishly, unsettled by the lack of grazing and pasturage and general unfriendliness of the area they'd passed through. Going farther into Astinda would be hard on all the horses, especially since they no longer had the supply wagon. They'd left it behind in Quellin, after helping themselves to a number of the horses from the stockade. Once Meerk had settled down, he'd mentioned how much they would be slowed up by using the wagon. With pursuit less than a full day behind them—which it would be even if the guardsmen stopped for a while in Quellin—packhorses would be a much better idea.

So they'd used packhorses, and everyone had gotten used to being in a saddle all day. Well, maybe "gotten used to" was too positive a phrase, Lorand admitted privately. All those who were new to riding had been suffering to one degree or another, but none of them really complained aloud. And at least they all had a bit more to wear than previously. Outfits by the dozens had been left in that house they'd spent the night in, and if the clothing didn't fit everyone, at least it was usable by most of the group.

But the time hadn't been easy for anyone, and if tempers were occasionally short it was completely understandable. They'd been able to keep the pursuing guardsmen the same distance behind them, but only by spending all of one night riding. The guardsmen had kept going after sundown so they'd had to do the same, working to ruin the guardsmen's plan to catch them asleep somewhere. At least that's what they thought the plan was, and the guardsmen hadn't tried it again. Happily.

"Lorand, you're back," one of their sentries, Wrixin, said as he stepped out from his place behind a bush in a small stand of trees. "Did you find what you went looking for? You weren't gone very long."

"That's because there was nothing left of what I went looking for," Lorand replied, finding it impossible to put life into his voice. "You'd better pass the word to the other sentries that we'll be moving on again as soon as everyone has rested for a while—and the horses have been allowed to graze. There's nothing for them to graze on up ahead for as far as I went, so we'll just have to keep going until we find someplace decent."

Wrixin nodded in that same sober way they were all starting to use, so Lorand continued on into the copse where everyone else was. As soon as he dismounted he unsaddled his horse, hobbled it, and turned it loose to graze with the others. They could probably spend another hour in that copse, but then they would have to move on.

"Are things any better up ahead?" Jovvi asked as soon as she saw him. Then she held up a hand as she shook her head. "No, don't bother answering that. The tone of your thoughts is answer enough."

"But you do still need an answer in words," Lorand said as he stopped to kiss her grimy but very soft cheek. "It's worse up ahead, and I don't know how far the devastation goes. We'll have to try to get through this area as quickly as possible, otherwise we'll lose the horses. Pushing them hard and starving them on top of it will kill them faster than anything but deliberate slaughter."

"I suppose it's a good thing, then, that we have fewer supplies for the packhorses to carry," Rion said from where he and Naran sat, not far from where Jovvi stood. "Lighter burdens may balance the lack of grazing, at least for a short while."

"What we all need, people and horses alike, is a place to stop and rest for a while," Naran said, sounding almost as weary as Lorand felt. "Not to mention someplace decent to take a bath. If we have to do without for much longer, we won't need your Blending to handle any enemies we come across. All we'll have to do is get upwind of them, and then we can stand there and watch them fall over."

"Now there's a potent weapon in our arsenal we haven't been counting on," Jovvi said with a grin while Lorand and Rion laughed. "Let's mention it to Alsin, and see what tactics he can come up with to use it most effectively."

"Where *is* Meerk?" Lorand asked, taking the cup of tea Jovvi had poured for him before joining her in sitting near Rion and Naran. "I'm used to seeing him somewhere around Tamrissa, but she's over there scribbling in that ledger she found. I'm glad we all talked *her* into doing the writing. I may be mistaken, but since she started that project she's been feeling more . . . balanced."

"She *is* more balanced," Jovvi confirmed with a smile for the way he'd used a word more suited to *her* province. "Writing down what's happened to us seems to be bringing her a focus she lacked before, not to mention greater emotional control. She's already better off than she was, and her inner strength seems to be growing daily."

"And our friend Alsin is taking a nap," Rion put in, answering the rest of Lorand's question. "Since Vallant is now drilling the Water magic people and you won't be starting with the Earth magic people until he's done, Meerk took the opportunity to get some sleep. Once you start to use Earth magic, he'll be wide-awake."

"I have the feeling he'll be waking up to face something more than just the use of magic in his own aspect," Naran said, now looking faintly troubled. "Vallant has been watching Alsin show his interest in Tamrissa, but while she continued to spend a good deal of time smiling at and talking to *him*, he hasn't said anything to Alsin. Now that she's spending so much time with her writing, I think Vallant is about to have words with Alsin. I wish he would talk to *her* instead, but the chances of that are almost nil."

"That's because he's still faintly frightened of her," Jovvi said with a wry smile. "He knows she's ruining his resolve to have nothing more to do with her for a while, so he's afraid to get too close. He won't even admit to himself that his resolve isn't working, not as stubborn as *he* is. He'd rather growl at Alsin than whisper sweetly to Tamrissa— and that was a very astute observation you made, Naran. For someone without Spirit magic, you're very sensitive."

"You're a love for saying that, Jovvi, but the situation is

so clear that even Rion had no trouble noticing," Naran replied with a faint blush and a pleased chuckle. "And do stop looking at me in that wounded way, my love. You know you don't notice a lot of these things until they come up and tap you on the nose."

"That is unfortunately all too true," Rion admitted, apparently giving up on trying to make Naran feel guilty for what she'd said. "I wish it were otherwise, so I've been making the effort to change—myself as well as the subject. Lorand, when do you think we'll reach the place that man called the front?"

"We should get to the area sometime tomorrow night," Lorand said after thinking for a moment. "It isn't really all that far away, but the traveling won't be very easy. When I reached the outskirts of that town I couldn't bear to go any nearer, so I stretched out my perceptions to check beyond it. I may be mistaken, but I think there are some deep, wide holes in the road beyond the place where the town was."

"Then I'm very glad we no longer have the wagon or the carriage with us," Jovvi said. "Getting vehicles past large holes might have delayed us long enough for those guardsmen to catch up. Oh, look, here comes Vallant. It seems to be your turn now with practicing, so you got back just in time."

"I'm taking my tea with me," Lorand stated as he began to get to his feet. "I think that's one of the things *I* miss most: being able to sit down with a cup of tea at regular intervals."

And he also had to gather his people, he said to himself. They'd been teaching their companions the patterns they'd learned and had used to such good—and varied—purpose, and most were doing excellently well with them. Soon, possibly even tomorrow night and before they made contact with the army, they ought to try putting together more Blendings. He'd have to talk to the others about it, once they got back on the road. . . .

Vallant nodded to Lorand as they passed each other, smiled to the others where they sat, then went to pour himself a cup of tea. When he'd first made up his mind about talking to Meerk he'd felt as though he could use something stronger than tea, but that feeling had passed. Right now he was downright eager to get things straightened out about Tamrissa, which he ought to be able to do in just a few minutes. As soon as Lorand got his group started on practicing, Meerk would be up and about again.

And the time came just as quickly as Vallant had been expecting. He still had half the tea in his cup when Meerk appeared, stretching and rubbing sleep from his eyes. The man paused to look around, saw Tamrissa sitting and writing away in her ledger book, and obviously made up his mind to interrupt her. A foolish smile spread across his face as he started in her direction, but since Vallant stood a small distance to Meerk's right and Tamrissa sat the same small distance to Vallant's right, Vallant was able to step out and intercept Meerk.

"You and I need to talk," he said softly to a startled Meerk. "I've been wantin' to get a few things straight between us, and now's as good a time as any."

"As you like," Meerk agreed in a suddenly neutral way. "I've been wondering if you would start a conversation like this, because I have a few things of my own to say. But since this is your idea, you have the right to start things off."

"That's not the only right I have," Vallant retorted, speaking calmly and quietly. "I also have the right to tell you to stop pesterin' Tamrissa. She isn't interested in you, Meerk, so why don't you find a woman who is?"

"I'd say that comes under the heading of *my* business," the man responded, obviously working to match Vallant's calm. "But don't you think it's up to Tamrissa to say whether or not she's interested? She's well enough aware of the fact that I'm courting her, and since I still haven't been turned to ash it's fairly safe to say that she doesn't mind."

"You're missin' the point, Meerk," Vallant said, now finding it harder to hold his temper. "*I'm* the one who minds, which means I'm not tryin' to make Tamrissa's decisions for her. She and I are a part of each other in a way you can't understand, so I'm entitled to mind. Find a different woman and leave *her* alone, or there will be more than just words between us."

"Are you saying you mean to pursue her yourself?" Meerk had the nerve to ask. "I've noticed that you never go near her on your own, unless it has something to do with the Blending. All the rest of the time you avoid her, making *her* come after *you*. It must tickle your vanity to have a woman chasing after you, a woman you push away if she gets too close. But Tamrissa is too wonderful a person to be put through something like that, so I won't allow it. I intend to continue courting her, and if I'm very lucky she'll agree to marry me. If you decide you don't like that idea, go ahead and do whatever you feel you have to."

And with that Meerk turned and went back the way he'd come, leaving Vallant to stare after him. A minute earlier Vallant would have been furious to have the man simply walk away from him, but now it was something of a relief. The accusation Meerk had made was ridiculous, but Vallant didn't quite know how to answer it. Of course he wasn't forcing Tamrissa to chase after him, and vanity had nothing to do with his actions. He was just trying to avoid another shallow, temporary association with a woman he happened to love quite a lot. . . .

But that didn't change the fact that Meerk had refused to agree to Vallant's demands. He had openly admitted he was courting Tamrissa, and with marriage in mind! That part of it had also shaken Vallant, as he'd never expected Meerk to have honorable intentions. It changed things in a vague but definite way, if anything could be both vague and definite at the same time. It also meant that he would have to speak to Tamrissa, something he'd been hoping to avoid. Every time he got close to her and she smiled that beautiful, enticing smile . . .

It took a small effort for Vallant to get control of himself again, but as soon as he did he headed straight for Tamrissa. If he put off talking to her Meerk might come back and say the wrong thing, and that would be worse. Better to get there first and avoid confusion. When he stopped beside her she looked up, then she smiled that smile.

"Well, this is a surprise," she said, actually putting aside the pen she'd been using. "Or is it time for us to Blend again?"

"No, it isn't time to Blend," Vallant answered quickly,

feeling a flush in his cheeks as he crouched beside her. Wasn't that part of what Meerk had said . . . ? "I just wanted to talk to you for a moment, to ask a favor. Will you mind doin' me a favor?"

"Of course not," she answered, looking as though she forcibly kept herself from reaching out to touch him. "What favor would you like me to do for you?"

"I want you to tell Meerk to stop . . . doin' what he's doin'," Vallant said, having more trouble putting the thing into words than he'd expected to. "He isn't part of our group, after all, and it just isn't right."

"What isn't right about it?" she asked after a very brief pause, an odd expression flickering in her lovely eyes. "He isn't doing anything but courting me, and in a most polite way. He isn't by some chance interfering with someone else's intention to court me—is he?"

"Ah . . . no, he isn't," Vallant said through teeth that seemed to want to clench. "It . . . isn't time yet for . . . somethin' like that. But that doesn't make what he's doin' all right. He isn't really one of us, and that makes a big difference."

"It hasn't made a difference for Rion and Naran," she countered, the expression in her eyes having suddenly changed. "Are you saying you consider Naran an outsider because she doesn't Blend with us?"

"No, of course not," Vallant hastened to assure her, beginning to feel that the conversation was getting out of hand. "Naran is one of us without question, but that's completely different. Meerk isn't like Naran, not in any way at all."

"And why would that be?" she demanded, all sweetness and smiles having disappeared. "Tell me, Dom Ro, why is it different? I want to hear a reason for what you're saying."

"It just is, that's all," Vallant muttered, determined not to be stampeded away from the decision he'd previously made. "And it doesn't even matter. You agreed to do me the favor, so I expect you to hold to that."

"I agreed before I understood what the favor was," she stated, showing nothing of the fluster she once would have. "Now that I have all the details, I'm afraid I must decline. I happen to like being courted, since I don't intend to spend the rest of my life alone. If you don't like what you're seeing, my suggestion would be to stop looking.''

And with that she gathered her things together and got up, walking away from him in the same way Meerk had done. Vallant rose to his full height and stared after her, fighting the urge to chase after and stop her. There were so many things he wanted to tell her, but he knew she wasn't ready to hear them. He *knew* that, although he certainly wished he didn't. . . .

FORTY-TWO·

I barely noticed the rest of that day's ride, and didn't sleep very well the following night. Oh, I was certainly tired enough from all the unaccustomed exertions of the trip, and the destruction and desolation we rode through was enough to make anyone want to hide in sleep. But even though Lorand and the other Earth magic people managed to find a corner of land with trees and grass, that didn't help my frame of mind. I spent the night trying to decide whether I felt more hurt or more angry, and even now, after we'd started to move again, I still hadn't decided.

The day was cool but trying to be pretty, which certainly didn't match the torn-up landscape all around. It was almost as though whoever had done the damage had ruined the land deliberately, making it uninhabitable for the people who used to live there. That was a horrible thing to do, destroying a place so that it was no longer able to support the people who used to live there, but it sounded so typical of the nobility. They could afford to wait until the land returned to itself, and it wouldn't have bothered them a bit that the people who had depended on it to survive *couldn't* wait.

"This is really awful, isn't it?" a voice said, and I turned my head to see that Alsin had ridden up beside me. "I've read about things like this, the total destruction of land and the people on it, but I never expected to see it with my own eyes. To tell the truth, I wish I hadn't."

I nodded to show that I understood what he meant, finding it difficult to speak after what we'd passed a little while earlier. The bodies of an entire family had been hung head down near the burned-out remnant of their house, dangled from posts like grisly trophies or sick-minded boasting. They hadn't been hanged like the six farm families we'd found, but I had a terrible suspicion that I needed to have confirmed or erased.

"Alsin, please tell me the truth," I said, not quite looking at him. "I certainly didn't stare at those bodies long, but even a glance made me believe—Please tell me if they were still alive when they were hung up there."

"I was hoping you'd missed that," he answered after a small hesitation and a sigh, sounding as ill as I felt. "Those of us with Earth magic didn't, of course, but we all agreed not to say anything."

"I started out wondering why their hands had been tied behind them," I said, fighting not to become physically ill. "Then I realized that you don't tie dead people, and cursed myself for being so logical-minded. Did they do that just to show what great big marvelous victors they are?"

"They probably did it as a warning to whoever happened to see it," he answered. "The implication is that the same thing can happen to anyone who tries to oppose them, and it's called terror tactics. If people are so afraid of you that they run away before you reach them, it saves you a lot of trouble. Tamrissa . . . I thought you were going to ask about something else when you said you wanted the truth. Do you mind if we talk about *that* instead?"

"I think we may find it easier to discuss conscienceless murder," I responded, only glancing at him. "At the moment I'm still trying to decide whether to be furious or just plain angry."

"Because he tried to tell you what to do with your life,"

Alsin said with a nod. "I know how that feels because I felt exactly the same, but that's not the important thing involved here. What I need to know is . . . Do you intend to obey him?"

"Obedience doesn't enter into the matter," I said a bit more stiffly than I'd intended, thanks to the extreme annoyance filling me. "He asked me to do him a 'favor,' but when I heard what it was I refused. Does that answer your question?"

"To a certain extent," he agreed cautiously. "I now know that you won't be telling me to stop courting you, but—is that because you really don't want me to stop, or because you're in the mood to spite him?"

"Neither," I said at once, refusing to be cornered. "You're both trying to manipulate me into doing things your way, but I refuse to let that happen. I told you in the beginning that I have no real interest in you, but if you want to continue with the courting I still have no objection. And as far as Dom Ro goes, what I have to say to him is between me and him."

"That's fair enough," he assented with another nod. "Just as it's only fair to keep certain things between him and *me*. If it comes down to it, can I count on your staying out of anything which might develop? I'm not asking for your help, only your neutrality."

"I'm going to say this once to each of you, and once only," I stated, deliberately turning my head to look directly at him. "Since I'm the only one who has the final say over my life, a fight between the two of you would not only be pointless but extremely insulting. If it ever happens, I'll make *both* of you regret that insult."

"I'm afraid I'm going to have to take my chances," he replied, looking faintly apologetic but not in the least uncertain. "It's something that happens between men at times, and not a thing easily explained to a woman. If Vallant Ro and I end up facing each other, you'll only be a part of the reason for it. The best I can do is say that I won't force the issue, but if it happens I also won't simply walk away. We'll talk again later."

He turned his horse and touched it with his heels then, returning to the back of our column. I stared after him, hating what I'd heard. Yes, we certainly *would* talk again later. . . .

We stopped at noon to have a meal, but didn't stay in the area long because there was no grazing for the horses. During the meal I caught Vallant staring at me, as though he'd witnessed the talk I'd had with Alsin. He couldn't have known what the topic of discussion was, but I had the definite feeling he now waited to find out if I'd done him that favor. I met the man's gaze then deliberately looked away, hoping to give him an answer to his question. If it didn't work, he'd find out for certain the next time Alsin brought me one of those silly little gifts, like the three wildflowers he'd been producing. . . .

But there weren't any wildflowers in the countryside we rode through, nor much of anything else either. After about an hour of trying not to think, I had to admit that the pain *wanted* me to think about it. Vallant had said that he didn't want Alsin to court me, but when I gave him the chance to say that that was because *he* meant to do some courting, he'd flatly refused to commit himself. No, he wasn't interested in me himself, he just didn't want anyone else to be interested. And I'd tried so *hard* . . .

"Tamma, are you all right?" Jovvi asked as she guided her horse over to walk beside mine. "You've been trying to keep yourself under control, but I'm afraid it isn't working."

"I've decided to start a collection of failures," I told her, even more depressed over the fact that she'd had to be disturbed. "I have so many of them, after all, that it would be a shame to just throw them out. But please don't worry about me. After this is all over I'll probably never associate with another man again, and the thought of that is very soothing right now."

"I can't think of anything short of drugging that would soothe that roiling mess inside you," she said, reaching over to touch my arm briefly and gently. "Would you like to talk about it? I'd offer to calm you down with my talent, but I don't think I can. The strength of your mind has been growing at an enormous rate, possibly because you never release the power. Maybe, if you like, I can try joining the link-group . . ."

"But your expression says you think that would just be another failure to add to my collection," I finished for her. "I appreciate your wanting to help, Jovvi, but I seem to have reached the point of understanding that the only one who can help me is me. Try to block me out for a little while, and I'll see what I can do to change the subject of my thoughts."

"I don't like to feel useless, especially when someone as close as you needs what I can do so easily for others," she complained, making a sour face. "I've been thinking about touching the power all the time myself, and—"

"What is it?" I asked when her words broke off, and her face took on the expression that said she now heard something with her talent. "What's going on? Is something wrong?"

"More unexpected, very much so," she muttered in answer, still listening on the inside. "Do you remember when the Blending checked the distance to the nearest human life this morning? It should be at least another half day's travel away from us, but suddenly I'm picking up something all by myself on the other side of that ruined village just ahead. And not just a few minds, but almost as many as we sensed this morning."

"Well, I know we weren't mistaken this morning," I said, feeling the frown I'd developed. "So now the question is, where did *this* group come from? And what are they doing on the other side of a destroyed village?"

"I don't know, but we'd better tell the others," she said, tightening her grip on the reins and kicking her horse. She took off immediately, of course, but it was another moment before I could do the same. Jovvi had years of experience in a saddle, she'd told me, but usually in a divided riding skirt rather than in an ordinary dress. She found it slightly uncomfortable, but other than that wasn't bothered at all. I, on the other hand, had never ridden a horse in my life, and if my mount hadn't been very patient and almost slow, I probably would have been a nervous wreck. . . .

Not that any of that really distracted me from worrying about what might lie just ahead of us. My first thought was that the guardsmen from Gan Garee had circled around, but that simply wasn't possible. We'd found that they'd gained just a little on us when we'd checked this morning, but aside from that they were right where they'd been all along. No, this had to be something else, but what?

By the time I reached the others, Jovvi had already told them about what she'd sensed. Our column had stopped dead, of course, but Vallant didn't like that idea.

"Let's move up to the edge of that blasted-out village," he said, pointing to the place that lay broken and deserted not far ahead of us. "Those ruined houses and shops won't give us much in the way of shelterin', but they'll be better than nothin'. Pass the word back, then get movin'."

Those of our companions at the head of the column obeyed him immediately about moving, and those behind us passed back the word before quickly following. Alsin was taking his turn leading one of the strings of packhorses toward the rear, I knew, which meant we would reach the village before he'd find it possible to join us. With Vallant leading the way, I discovered that even extremely unpleasant circumstances sometimes have their bright side.

The buildings at the edge of the village were completely destroyed, with nothing but debris left on the ground to show where they'd been standing. A bit farther in there were walls still standing and one or two small houses that seemed intact, but nothing retained a roof. They must have used thatch for roofing, which meant that when it burned it must have collapsed inward, setting fire to whatever the small houses had in the way of furnishings. Not to mention any people who might have taken shelter inside from the attack. . . .

By the time we reached the third or fourth house in the village, I'd pretty much decided not to go into any of those buildings no matter what. Happily, though, I didn't have to. The house we stopped near had a large corral behind it, as though it had been used for the temporary holding of horses and cattle herds. That was where we put the horses, still with their saddles and bridles on, but untied. Grass had begun to grow inside even though the village itself was covered only in weeds, and the horses had earned a bit of a treat.

The rest of us gathered at the side of the house, which had three walls still standing. Two of those three walls stood between us and the people Jovvi had discovered so close to us, which would hopefully help a bit if they came even closer. No one said much of anything as our five stood together in the ring of our link-groups, and once everyone was there and in place we quickly Blended.

The entity was aware of the sense of urgency filling its flesh forms, therefore it lost no time in seeking out those who had come so close to them. There was a very large number of the beings, whose minds all seemed to be filled with turmoil. Fear clearly predominated, with anxiety a close second, and then the entity noticed something odd. The beings were apparently in different relationships to one another, which could be broken down into three groups.

The first and largest group consisted of the most able talents, Highs and strong Middles with, for the most part, anxiety rather than fear filling them. The second largest group, perhaps a tenth in number compared to the first, were lesser talents, Lows with a smattering of ordinary Middles. This group projected much more fear, but not quite as much as the third and smallest. That group numbered no more than half a dozen, were all Low in talent, and most were terrified. One of the half dozen, the one who seemed to be most in charge, was furious, his own fear buried deeply beneath his ranting and raving.

That one was the obvious choice for controlling, but just as the entity decided to touch him it found itself distracted. Another mind trace intruded itself into its awareness, of a pattern and strength which seemed extremely familiar. The entity moved toward that being instead, and rather than take control of it, it made contact.

—You seem to be the being my flesh forms know as Pagin Holter,—the entity said after taking the being's attention.—Are you aware of what this entity is?—

"You bet I am!" the being replied with excitement and delight. "You're Vallant, an' Tamrissa, an' Lorand, an' Rion, an' Jovvi! And you gotta be close, somehow! But don't come *too* close. Most a these here Highs is controlled by th' noble scum, an' there's nothin' they c'n do t'help us. C'n ya get me an' my groupmates away 'thout you gettin' hurt? Us Blendin' don't do no good, 'cause there's too many of 'em who could be turned agin us."

—This entity would prefer to free those others as well as you and your groupmates,—the entity responded.—It would not be practical for your own entity to give assistance, for you seem to be under surveillance by some of your associates. Allow this entity to see to the matter, for it appears to be possible to turn matters completely about.—

The being nodded eager agreement, therefore the entity began the procedure one of its flesh forms had been considering as a possible ploy. Floating to the nearest link-group of Highs, it touched all of their minds together.

—I am in command,—the entity sent, using the word "I" out of necessity.—This fact may be proven by the simple observation that this entity is the strongest and most able among you. You are therefore obligated to acknowledge this truth.—

"We acknowledge that truth," one of the flesh forms in the link-group responded for all of them, its tone of voice completely without inflection. "What would you have us do?"

—The first thing you must do is ignore any previous orders given you,—the entity told them.—The second is that you must stand ready to protect the flesh forms of the being called Pagin Holter and those he calls groupmates. The third is that you must link and begin to draw power into yourselves, so that this entity may share that power. The fourth is that you are not to allow others to become aware of what you are in the midst of, and the fifth is that you are to accept instructions from no one but this entity. Should this entity not command you again within the week, you will thereafter be free to command yourselves. Is all of that clear in your understanding?—

"It's clear," the being acknowledged, now exchanging glances with the others in its link-group. "We stand ready to assist you in any way you consider necessary."

The entity, pleased with the response of the link-group, moved on to the next closest groups. It repeated what it had previously said, and shortly there were six link-groups for it to draw power from. This the entity did, conserving its own strength for an emergency, and little by little all the members of the largest group were taken from the control

of the smallest. When the chore was done, the entity returned to the being called Pagin Holter.

—All those about you are now prepared to protect you,—
the entity informed the being.—Those of lesser talent, however, have not been so commanded, therefore are you to be
alert against them. The flesh forms of this entity are not far
from your present position, therefore they and their companions will soon join you. Be prepared for their arrival.—

"I'm lookin' forward to it," the being replied with a
chuckle, most of the anxiety gone from it. "Whut I most
wanna see is thet there general tryin' t' give 'em orders. But
they better shake a leg. We ain't got a whole lotta time."

That last remark was perplexing to the entity, but questioning could wait for another time. It withdrew back to
where its flesh forms waited, and then we were individuals
again. Tired individuals, but not as tired as all that work
should have made us.

"Rion, that was *your* idea!" Jovvi exclaimed with the
same delight I felt myself. "The one about borrowing
strength *before* we had to, I mean. It was absolutely brilliant,
and is probably the only reason we aren't stretched out on
the ground in exhaustion right now. How many link-groups
did we take over?"

"Fifty at the very least," Lorand offered as he stretched.
"Since the entity didn't bother counting, we won't know
for certain until we get there. Are we going right away?"

"Going where?" Alsin asked just as Vallant was about
to answer. "Who did you find over there, and what did you
do about it?"

"We found a section of our victorious army," Vallant
replied, speaking to everyone rather than just to Alsin. "For
some reason they didn't *look* very victorious, and we were
warned against draggin' our feet in joinin' them. What took
so long was that we turned their Highs and strong Middles
into *our* supporters, so only the nobles leadin' the section
and their pet roaches are left as they were. Anybody interested in goin' straight over there and tellin' them how much
we appreciate what they tried to do to our lives?"

A roar of agreement from our companions answered that
question without any doubt, drowning out anything Alsin
might have said. He hesitated a moment before joining the

rest of us in going for our horses, but it was perfectly clear that the matter wasn't over and done with. Vallant had taken all control right out of his hands, and it wasn't necessary to have Spirit magic to know that he was not prepared to let the matter pass.

If I could have, I think I might have ridden off alone in another direction entirely. At the moment that was impossible, but as I mounted and turned my horse in the direction where Pagin Holter and the others waited for us, I decided to look for a time when it would not be impossible at all. . . .

FORTY-THREE

It didn't take long to reach the place on the far side of the village where Pagin Holter and the others waited, and Jovvi made sure to be right up front with those who rode into the makeshift camp first. The small group of nobles—who were dressed up in uniforms to show how high their rank was— were in the midst of giving some sort of instructions to their cadre of guardsmen-equivalents, and when they saw the newcomers, the one wearing commandant tabs on his collar exploded.

"Who in the name of chaos are *those* peasants?" the man demanded, interrupting his second-in-command's speech to the others. "Never mind, I don't *care* who they are. Have the link-groups destroy them, but not the horses. We can use whatever supplies they have, and the horses themselves will do for remounts for us."

"Link-groups, attention!" one member of the cadre with smaller collar tabs bellowed in a voice that carried easily.

"Destroy the intruders, but not their mounts. That's an order!"

Then the commandant and his friends and followers stood there waiting to be obeyed, smirks of pleased expectation on their faces. It took a moment or two before they realized that the order which had been given wasn't being obeyed, and by then Vallant had reined up in front of them.

"Don't waste *your* breath or our time repeatin' that order," he drawled as he looked down at the group. "You don't have a bunch of slaves to do your dirty work for you anymore, but don't let that keep you from tryin' us yourselves. Go ahead, try us."

A number of the nobles including the commandant seemed to reach out to the power, then they gasped and went pale along with those of the cadre who also had clearly decided to flex their ability.

"You really are a pretty talentless bunch, aren't you?" Tamma said then with a laugh. "I don't know about the other aspects, but as far as Fire magic is concerned none of you could light a stove with a match."

"Or handle more than three grains of dirt," Lorand put in after her with a nod of agreement. "With that in mind, why don't those of you with knives and cudgels and things stack them over there, out of easy reach of your group, and then go back and sit down where you're now standing. We'll get to you after we say hello to some old friends of ours."

Jovvi knew that Lorand meant to search for his friend Hat, although the entity would certainly have found the man if he had been there. But Lorand *needed* to search, so Jovvi simply exchanged a glance with Tamma then dismounted, to help convince their new prisoners not to make a fuss.

"You can't possibly expect to get away with this!" the commandant was sputtering out while his fury raged. "You're a group of peasant nothings, and this section of the army is *mine*!

"Correction," Vallant said as he, too, dismounted and moved forward to face the commandant. "Nothin' here is yours any longer, except the blame for what's been destroyed. And as far as ownin' things goes, you and the rest of the leeches like you won't be doin' *that* for much longer either. Now sit down, or you won't like the way I make you do it.''

The fool of a noble had to look up at Vallant, and that was one of the man's pet hatreds. Jovvi knew he detested people who were taller than he, but that included most of the human race. He snarled something obscene and actually tried to backhand Vallant as he would have done to one of his servants, but Vallant blocked the blow and took the man by the front of his once-fine uniform. A hard shake rattled the noble's teeth in his head, a shove threw him to the ground, and then bedlam of sorts erupted when the former captive Highs all laughed and cheered.

''That applaudin' should tell you who's on which side,'' Vallant said then to the rest of the officers and their minions. ''This is the last time I'll be usin' words: get rid of anythin' that might be considered a weapon, then sit down and do as you're told.''

The officers were furious and those of lower rank sullen, but everyone obeyed the order without further argument. Potential weapons were thrown down out of easy reach, and then they all sat on the ground around their thoroughly humiliated leader.

''All right, people, keep an eye on them, please,'' Lorand said to their own companions, still anxious to get started with his search. ''We're going to have a few words with the newest members of our group, but if you need us, don't hesitate to call. And while you're watching those lowlifes, think about what we can do with them.''

That made their own people chuckle and grin, especially when they looked down at the captives. Jovvi checked the captives herself, to be certain that none of them intended immediate attack, but apparently none of them did. Later on would be another story, of course, but for the moment it was possible to give full attention to the people they had actually managed to rescue.

''. . . don't know where you come from, but we're mighty glad you did,'' Pagin Holter was saying happily to Rion as Jovvi walked over to join them. ''Thought I was dreamin' when thet there entity a yourn talked to me, but then, when it started workin', I could feel it was real. Don't know how much longer we coulda lasted here 'thout this kinda help.''

"Why not?" Jovvi asked as Rion waved away the man's thanks with a smile. "If you and your group were free of the Puredan, and you should have been, why was there a problem? And why are you here in the first place? Couldn't you have done something to escape when you were in the stockade?"

"Weren't in no stockade," Holter replied with a shake of his head. "Thet there noble Blendin' bested us mostly fair, an' ended knockin' us out. It felt like a real long time b'fore I woke up, an' when I did we wus with these here folk. Arinna, you tell 'em, 'cause you talk better'n me."

"You talk just fine, Pagin, but I'll be glad to help out," the woman Arinna said with a smile. She was a small and pretty woman, a bit smaller even than Holter, but the lively look in her eyes said she was much bigger on the inside, where it counts.

"I'm our group's Fire magic user," Arinna continued, also smiling at Vallant and Tamrissa, who had now come over to join the conversation. "As Pagin said, we blacked out during the competition and didn't wake up again until we were with *this* group. They told us they'd given us Puredan and we were bound to obey them the way everyone else did, but we knew better. When we got together we laughed over the secret we had, then we got ready to Blend and get ourselves away. That was when we discovered that it couldn't be done like that."

"Because a fully Blended group doesn't do well moving around," Jovvi said while everyone else made sounds of surprise and questioning. "That's fairly obvious, but you'll notice that some of *our* group overlooked the point, too. You could have defended yourselves as a Blending, but you couldn't have left the area; or you could have left the area, but couldn't have defended yourselves with the strength of a Blending."

"Exactly," Arinna said with a wry expression. "And on top of that, we had no idea where we were. After a little while we discovered that we'd been sent directly to the front, because Lord General Grib over there had run into resistance no one had been expecting. That was when we realized that we were in Astinda, and that most of the destruction we saw was our own empire's doing. We pretended to go along with what they wanted, but none of us actually added strength to the link-groups we were assigned to.''

"Which someone would have noticed fairly quickly,'' Tamma said, nodding her understanding. "Now I see why Pagin was in such a hurry for us to get here.''

"No, actually, that wasn't the reason,'' Arinna denied as she exchanged a disturbed glance with Holter. "Our biggest problem stems from the fact that we're now in retreat. In point of fact we've been running for half the day, trying to put as much distance between us and our former position as possible. People from other sections came streaming into our camp, some of them wounded and some just hysterical. The people of Astinda have been resisting this invasion all along, but now they've apparently managed to put together an army which ours can't stand against. We don't know just how close that army is or what its composition is, but old Gribby over there has been furious over the need to run away.''

"An' his bullies've been takin' it out on us,'' Holter added with a growl. "They're real big men, knowin' nobody c'n do nothin' to 'em no matter whut *they* do. But I'd like t'see 'em try it again *now*.''

"If most of them don't live very long, don't wonder why,'' Arinna said with a tightness to the words. "The army calls the men below the officers prods, meaning their job is to 'prod' the segments and link-groups into doing what the officers want done. Our people had to obey their orders, you see, but none of them were happy about it. The prods would beat them—us—to make us work harder and faster, and at night the women among us were shared around by the officers as well. My groupmates Blended to keep me and Raddia safe, but the same couldn't be done for the others . . .''

Her words ended on a note of inner turmoil, and Jovvi reached out automatically to soothe the woman as best she could. All these people had had a really terrible time, but at least it was over now.

"It might be a good idea for the Blendin' to have a look around before we get to questionin' those officers,'' Vallant said as he fought an inner disturbance of his own. "We need to know what they're runnin' from, but even more we need to know how close that somethin' is. If we have the time, we might want to stay here for a bit. There's grazin' for the horses, and we ought to talk about what we're all goin' to do next.''

Everyone agreed with that, of course, which produced one reaction that was less than positive. Jovvi turned her head in surprise over the flash of heavy anger she felt, and was even more surprised that it came from Alsin Meerk. He now looked at Vallant with a glare of thick resentment, which gave Jovvi a fairly good idea about what the problem was. Alsin was supposed to be in charge of their strategy and tactics, but Vallant hadn't even consulted him before making his suggestion. And Jovvi was fairly certain that the omission had been deliberate on Vallant's part. What in the world was going on between those two?

The next instant Jovvi shook her head at herself, annoyed at having asked so foolish a question. Tamma was what was wrong between Vallant and Alsin, that and the fact that they were both natural leaders. They'd worked together well enough until now, but whatever had gotten Tamma so upset must be at the root of this new hostility. Jovvi decided that she'd have to speak to Lorand and Rion. Possibly the three of them working together could find a solution to the difficulty. . . .

But that would have to wait until later. A disappointed Lorand was walking back toward them, so in another moment they would be able to Blend. Jovvi looked around while she waited, trying to decide whether to hope they could stay there for a while, or hope that they couldn't. There was a . . . heavy, invisible cloud hovering over that entire area, a cloud composed of agony and terror, desolation and despair. And Jovvi wasn't the only one who felt it, she knew. Everyone seemed unhappy there, or at the very least uncomfortable.

And then Lorand joined them, so Jovvi was able to initiate the Blending. The entity formed as quickly as usual, looked about at the flesh forms it had visited earlier, then began to change its focus to find the enemy they had spoken about. It *began* to, then something else, in the opposite direction, took its attention. Those enemy flesh forms who had been following . . .

Intent became action, and the entity floated quickly in the direction its own flesh forms had come from. That morning it had found the enemy a shade closer than they'd been until now, but not close enough to cause worry. This time, however, no more than hours later, the distance between them had closed drastically. It would be only a short while before that particular group of enemies reached them, a disturbing revelation even for the entity.

It flashed back to where its flesh forms waited, then took a quick look in the direction it was to have investigated. Although a large number of beings could be detected in that direction, they were in no wise as close as the first group. That, then, would have to be made the first priority. . . .

"Those miserable sons of chaos," Vallant growled as soon as Jovvi dissolved the Blending. "They must have realized we were checkin' on them only in the mornin' and at night, so they waited until after our mornin' check and then galloped flat out in an effort to catch up before we noticed. And since we've been takin' our time, they can't be more than a couple of hours away."

"This must be what all those remounts were for," Lorand put in, sounding just as angry. "They disguised the two extra horses each guardsman led as pack animals, but they're really remounts. They ran the first set of horses into the ground, and now they're on the second. When these are done, and they're almost to that point now, they'll mount the third and just keep coming."

"But now we have the means to defeat them," Rion pointed out, gesturing to the people they'd freed. "If our new friends are willing to cooperate, we should have no trouble overcoming those louts."

"Are we to understand that the guardsman detachment is almost on top of us?" Alsin interrupted to ask, looking around at everyone but Vallant. "I thought you people were keeping an eye on them."

"They obviously have a better strategist than we do, so the eye did no good," Vallant replied, almost in passing. "But that's beside the point. Right now we have to find out how many of these new people are willin' to fight on our side. We can compel them of course, but I don't believe we should."

"No, of course not," Jovvi began, but Alsin's increased anger forced him to interrupt.

"What do you mean, *ask* these others?" he demanded. "If you can compel them to fight, that's what you have to do. We don't have the chance of a water drop on a hot skillet without them, and for some reason I'm not in the mood to die. Tell me how close that detachment is, and I'll start to make immediate deployment plans."

"Alsin, calm down," Lorand said, overriding the angry response Vallant would have made. "None of us wants to die, but forcing people into fighting for and with us is wrong. We all know you believe the same, and probably more strongly than we do, but right now you're upset. Take a couple of minutes to pull yourself together, then we'll talk about this again."

Jovvi felt Alsin's urge to snap out a refusal and disavowal of what Lorand had said, but since she already touched the man with her talent, that didn't matter. He calmed at once, of course, having no idea that he'd been soothed by her, but the intrusion had been necessary. If there was a worse time to fight among themselves, it could only be when the enemy was actually in sight.

"Let's start asking around," Tamma suggested when Alsin calmly turned away to sit down alone a short distance off. Jovvi knew that the others all realized what she'd done, and only Vallant was faintly disappointed. All the others were more relieved, and they really did have very little time.

They went in separate directions and spread the word, and it took a while but the wait and effort were worth it. Some of the link-groups weren't happy about it, but all of them agreed to fight against the coming guardsmen. Their hatred and resentment of empire authority was intense, representing as it did the instrument by which their lives had been ruined. In contrast to the bold wine red and white uniforms worn by the officers and prods, the "segments" were dressed in clothing that was little more than rags. Most of them were also gaunt from not having been fed very well, and some of them were even in pain from the "discipline" given by the prods. But all of them were willing to give the five and their companions all the help they needed.

"I'm glad I asked Lidris to make a big meal from the

army supplies before we began to talk to those people,'' Lorand said to Jovvi after they'd finished speaking to their new allies. ''They need a solid meal desperately, and now it's just about ready. And our Earth magic people have volunteered to do some healing for those who need it. By the time all that is done those guardsmen will be here, but then our forces will be in better shape to face them.''

''In better shape physically,'' Jovvi corrected with a sigh. ''Their minds are terribly hurt, Lorand, and I'm not sure they'll ever be able to get over this horrible experience. But they *are* ready to fight with us, and at the moment that's what counts. Later we'll have to try to help them forget, but for now . . .''

''For now we none of us have a choice,'' Lorand agreed as he touched her face gently and with love. ''But I meant to ask you: what's going on between Vallant and Alsin? If you and I hadn't interfered, I think they would have been at each other's throats.''

''They seem to have two disagreements,'' Jovvi responded, glancing around to see that the former captives were already lining up for their meal. ''One is Tamma and the other is leadership, and we're going to have to keep them apart until we have the time to sit them both down for a talking-to. We'll also have to tell Rion about what's happening, since I'm certain we'll end up needing his help.''

Lorand nodded, then he led Jovvi over to join the very long lines of those waiting for food. They'd already had their lunch, but with fighting so close on the horizon for them, another meal would do more good than harm.

No one took their time eating, which turned out to be a very good thing. Jovvi and Lorand were able to speak to Rion and Naran and to finish their own meal, and then the link-group acting as sentries alerted them. The guardsmen were only a few minutes away, and they seemed to have already linked up. And it also seemed that they had no intention of stopping and dismounting. Their unslacking rate of speed suggested they meant to gallop into and through the camp, trampling anything and everything unfortunate enough to be in their path.

''So what do *we* do?'' Tamma asked after hurrying over to where Jovvi and Lorand and Rion and Naran now stood.

"If we Blend, our bodies could be trampled. If we don't, our forces will have to do without our entity's strength. There has to be another choice!"

Jovvi shared the frustration filling Tamma and the others, but an answer to the question refused to come—until Naran spoke hesitantly.

"Excuse me, but I have a silly question," she ventured. "If I'm bothering you when I shouldn't I apologize, but I was just wondering . . ."

"Wondering what, love?" Rion asked gently when her voice trailed off. "As you're certainly one of us, no intrusion can be possible. Tell us what has occurred to you."

"All right, if you're sure," Naran agreed, bolstered not only by Rion but by the nods of everyone else. "I just wondered why you needed other people to protect your bodies while you were Blended. Couldn't your—entity—station itself in front of you, and use its strength from there? But you're always talking about how it goes places, so maybe that isn't possible."

Jovvi exchanged silent stares with her groupmates, feeling just as stupid as they now did. Of course their bodies could be trampled if they Blended, but not with their entity standing—or floating—right in front of them. Their protective link-groups might be run down just as easily, but if anything got past their Blending entity, the fight would be completely lost anyway.

"Naran, the next time we forget to consult you about a problem we have, please do us the favor of kicking us hard," Tamma said after a moment. "We've gotten so used to *sending* our entity places, we forgot that we don't have to. We certainly *can* stand it in front of us, since that's what we did only a short while ago, so that's what we'll do again now."

Naran was extremely pleased by Tamma's comment, but not nearly as pleased as Jovvi and the others to have their dilemma solved. They also took a moment to speak to Pagin Holter and *his* group, who were eager to get more experience with their own Blending entity. The two Blendings would be stationed on either side of the rest of the fighting group, hopefully doing their best to save their peoples' lives.

And they had just enough time to set themselves before

the riders came storming through the camp. Everyone was ready and properly linked, not to mention expecting the terror tactics the guardsmen had hoped to rout them with. The element of surprise was turned in the other direction, especially when shallow trenches opened in the earth in front of the leading line of horsemen. The horses stumbled and many of the riders were pitched off, and then the following riders blasted into them before it was possible to slow or stop. Link-group battles were already taking place, and the murdered landscape all around echoed to a renewal of what had killed it in the first place.

The entity hovered in front of its flesh forms, fully determined to keep all harm from them. Some of the enemy jumped their horses over the tangle of men and beasts and continued to come on at top speed, but little good it did them. The men disappeared in a flare of intense brightness, and the now riderless horses were easily turned aside. After the initial attack, most of the enemy concentrated its efforts in the entity's direction, but again to no avail. The entity's allies struck hard again and again, and soon there were very few left of the two hundred men who had attacked.

Then there were none left, none but the trembling officers who were their captives, some of whom had tried to attack at the same time as the guardsmen. That particular treachery had been expected, and those who tried found that they weren't killed out of hand as the guardsmen were. They were struck unconscious instead, so that their punishment could be decided on and meted out at leisure by those they'd wronged. Death would be too merciful, their former captives had decided, and the entity's flesh forms would make no effort to disagree.

With all enemies in sight either down or gone, the entity made a quick check to see if any of them had refrained from joining the attack in order to fall upon them later, when they considered the battle over and won. But that hadn't been done, which meant the danger was completely over. The entity sent a greeting to its brother/sister entity on the opposite side of camp, received an answering greeting, and then Jovvi had dissolved the Blending.

Some of their own people had been hurt a bit during the fight, people who had started out too badly starved or beaten to begin with. Jovvi took a link-group of Spirit magic users to help Lorand and his own link-group of Earth magic users, and they began to soothe and heal their wounded. Happily there weren't that many of them, and they had just finished up when a rider came galloping into camp from the opposite direction from which the guardsmen had attacked.

The man wore a uniform with small collar tabs and looked as sweaty and foam-covered as his horse, and he didn't seem to notice the remains of the battle so recently over. That no link-group had stopped him meant they knew—or suspected—how terrified the man was, and realized they all needed to know what had frightened him. As he pulled his horse to a dirt-scattering stop near the former officers and leaders of the section and half fell to the ground, Jovvi and the others moved closer to hear what he would say.

"Lord General . . . forgive me for . . . taking so long," the man panted out, trying to speak and gasp for breath at the same time. "You must . . . gather your forces and . . . leave here at once, or . . . the section will surely . . . be overrun. All the rest of . . . our army in . . . their path has been . . . destroyed. They're so strong . . . and there are so . . . many of them . . ."

"How many?" Vallant asked, and the newcomer's head snapped around to stare at him. "Don't talk to the leech, man, talk to me. The leech won't be runnin' this section again, not in this lifetime. Tell me who's comin', how many there are of them, and about how strong you think they are."

"The . . . the ones coming are the army Astinda put together to resist us," the man replied haltingly, uncertain about speaking to a stranger but needing to get his warning delivered. "I've never felt such strength or seen such utter destruction, and they're coming so fast . . . I saw one section try to surrender, but they didn't even answer. They just destroyed them, and continued to come on . . ."

"You still haven't given us the most important answers, boy," Alsin growled as he stepped forward. "How many of them are there, and how soon do you expect them to be here?"

"I'm not a boy!" the young man flared, then he shook his head once, dismissingly. "As if that matters. There are ten times the number of them than you, and they're no more than a day's march away. One of *their* day's march, which seems to cover more ground than our own. I think they're headed for the border, and I don't think they mean to stop when they reach it.''

At that point there wasn't a sound to be heard anywhere, not in the midst of all the shock that Jovvi could feel in everyone's mind. Having the empire invaded in retaliation for the invading the empire's forces had done could be considered only fair, but it wouldn't be the nobles who paid for their evil. It would be all the innocent people between here and Gan Garee. . . .

FORTY-FOUR

''That can't possibly be true!'' Kambil snapped at the fool standing like a block of stone in front of him. ''Everyone dead in the stockade in Quellin, and word from the second command of guardsmen too long overdue? Someone must have made a mistake, and I demand that you go back and find out who that is! We're being given a false picture here, and how are we supposed to make proper decisions with false information?''

''Excellency, there's no mistake,'' the fool repeated doggedly, just as he'd been doing for the last ten or fifteen minutes. ''Do you imagine that I would have brought word like this to you without making very sure it was accurate? Three men serving in the Quellin stockade survived because they were on leave and not close enough to be called back, and one of them had experience with the birds. He reported that everyone but the commandant and one private—the private having been in a cell after being . . . questioned about something—were dead, and the commandant's mind was gone. The private insisted that he was unconscious during whatever happened, and so knows nothing about it. We're told that that's very probable.''

"Have him brought here anyway," Kambil ordered in what was almost a snarl. "When *I* get finished with him, we'll know for certain whether or not he's telling the truth. What about the second guard command?"

"Six of the dozen birds they had left have returned here, but they carried no message," the man, Lord Falas Grohl, said with a sigh. "We're forced to believe that they were released accidentally, so for a while it was possible that no message was sent because the command intended to save what birds it had left. Now that's no longer a possibility, not when three reporting times have passed with no word. If we haven't heard from them, it's because they aren't *able* to report."

"Could it be something else in that part of the country which might have . . . sidetracked or delayed them?" Kambil asked, almost desperate for any sort of reassurance. "We were told that the army is operating not far from there in Astinda, so maybe they became involved . . .''

"Excellency, I truly wish it were possible," Lord Falas said stolidly, refusing to offer even the least crumb of hope. "The reports from our army are at least as alarming, screaming for more segments rather than supplying details of their operations. That's when they communicate at all, which they aren't doing nearly as often as they're supposed to. Something is very wrong over there, and I've been asked to . . . request the aid of the Five."

"Request our aid?" Kambil echoed, finding it hard to believe his ears. "Are you asking us to volunteer as segments, or just to take a pleasure trip over there to rescue an *ARMY*! Are you people out of your minds, or just a bit retarded?"

"Excellency, this could very well be the crisis your Five is meant to overcome," Lord Falas said, obviously as thick in the head as in the body, for pressing the point. "Historically, each new Five is called on to face the challenge of crisis, and more than a few people are already saying that yours has come. Even the common folk know there's some kind of trouble in the west, and they're also expecting the Five to respond."

"Are you suggesting that we're answerable to the city's rabble?" Kambil asked, stopping the pacing he'd been doing to stare directly at the man. "Or even to you and your friends? We are the *Seated Five*, and what we do and when we do it is *our* decision! Is that clear enough so that even you can understand it?"

"Excellency, I'm a very unimportant man," Lord Falas said, something odd stirring in his stolid gaze. "I've often had to pretend otherwise, but in my heart I know the truth. You and the rest of the Five, however, are not unimportant. You are vital to the safety and prosperity of the empire. When the crisis comes the Seated Five *must* respond, otherwise all of us are lost. We all rely on your courage and ability and judgment, and we know you won't fail us. There's nothing else I can say."

Kambil parted his lips to retort with something sarcastic, but at the last instant realized that the man was speaking the absolute truth as he saw it. Here was someone who believed everything he'd ever been told about the Five and what they were and weren't supposed to do, and he'd actually made no demands. He'd all but begged for the help of the Five with what he seriously considered a crisis, and because so many people thought the way he did, the man had to be handled carefully.

"What you've already said has made a very great impression on us, Lord Falas," Kambil replied, his tone now as solemn and calm as it should have been all along. "My Blendingmates and I will do some investigating of our own, and then we'll discuss the matter among ourselves. If this *is* our crisis, we'll certainly handle it as promptly and thoroughly as we're expected to. You're excused now, but don't forget to have that private brought here to the palace."

Falas bowed low to acknowledge the command, then backed out of the room still somewhat bowed over. Everyone waited until the door had closed behind the man, then Bron made a sound of scorn that his expression echoed.

"What a fool!" Bron said with ridicule thick in his voice.

"Talking to us about crises and fairy tales like that! Doesn't he know that the last three or four Seated Blendings couldn't possibly have handled any sort of crisis, not when they weren't even Highs? The whole thing was a mockery to fool the commoners, but it seems to have caught a few members of the nobility as well."

"Mockery or not, you're forgetting something," Kambil said, turning to look at him and Selendi and Homin. "Our predecessors may not have had our strength, but what they did have was the help of a group of Advisors who knew what was going on in the empire, people who were in control of most of it. We don't have that sort of help, and it may turn out to be more crippling than a lack of aspect strength."

"Can they possibly be serious about this being a crisis?" Selendi asked with no sign of Bron's skepticism. "I remember that my tutor talked about the crises faced by the various Fives, and there are actual records of the times. Lots of other people witnessed them, so they couldn't have been nothing but complete trickery."

"And if they aren't, then we have a serious problem," Homin put in, his expression faintly worried. "That blasted five seems to have headed straight for whatever trouble is brewing in the west, and I would not put it past them to add to it in some way. Or to be responsible for a good deal of it. But I still can't understand how they could possibly have accounted for two hundred guardsmen."

"Or an entire garrison in the Quellin stockade," Bron added, less mocking but still unconvinced. "Weren't there more than three hundred men there? It's simply and patently impossible."

"It's not impossible if you remember that the segments being held there were dead as well," Kambil countered. "Chances are good that *they're* the ones who accounted for the garrison, working in link-groups. There weren't enough of them to get away unscathed themselves, but they were all Highs or strong Middles. I'd say they took down most of the garrison before they were taken down themselves, and probably finished it with their dying breaths."

"But it had to be our fugitives who freed them to do it," Selendi said with something of a headshake. "They probably wanted to recruit those segments, but had to leave without them when they died. And yet they were able to account for those two hundred guardsmen, and probably with only a handful of Highs from the convoy to help. How *did* they do it?''

"I'm more concerned with what they intend to do now," Kambil retorted, a hand in his hair as he tried to think coolly and logically. "Wherever they are they'll want to make trouble for us, of course, and using the idea of a crisis will come to them eventually if it hasn't already. That means we can't give in to any pressure to travel west, no matter who insists on it."

"I think we'll have to start some counterstories to the effect that the fugitives are trying to trap us," Homin said thoughtfully. "If we claim that they want to lure us away to the west in order to overwhelm us with help that they couldn't bring to the competitions, the pressure should ease off quite a lot. We'll tell everyone that we refuse to let them steal what they couldn't win honestly when they faced us."

"That's really good," Bron said with a grin and a nod of approval for Homin. "People call you sullen and uncooperative when you simply refuse to do what they want you to, but if you calmly give them a reason for the refusal that they can't argue, they call you logically cautious."

"But we still have to do something about those five people," Selendi said, no more satisfied than Kambil himself. "They seem to have found a way to get around the orders given under Puredan, and they've learned how to defeat large numbers of opponents. If we don't go to *them,* they'll probably end up coming back to us."

"Now *that's* something we've discussed before," Kambil said in glum agreement. "If they think they're supported well enough, they'll come back here sooner rather than later. We have to—"

His comments were interrupted by a knock on the door of the small audience room they were using, then one of the servants came in.

"Excellencies, Lord Rimen Howser begs an audience," the man told them very formally. "He has no appointment, but says the matter is extremely urgent."

"Oh, send him in," Kambil agreed crossly. He certainly

was in no mood to hear about things that others considered urgent, but Howser had volunteered to help with the matter of the fugitives. There wasn't much he could have done here in Gan Garee, but considering the information he'd brought the first time . . .

The servant bowed and stepped aside, and Howser came through the doorway without delay. But he was trailed by a raggedy, scruffy-looking specimen, and as soon as the servant closed the door again the man bowed and explained what he was about.

"Excellencies, my investigations may have borne some potentially interesting fruit," he began at once. "I had the idea to look into the doings of the fugitives while they were here in Gan Garee, hoping to find a clue as to where they went. Instead I found that one of them, the Earth magic user, attended the last challenge for Seated High in Earth magic. At first I considered that a matter of simple curiosity on the part of the animal, but my people questioned everyone who was there at the time, and learned that the fugitive spoke to one of the challengers. The way they spoke, the informant concluded that the two were friends."

"Lord Rimen, what point are you trying to make?" Kambil asked, fighting to control impatience. "Losing challengers in the various ceremonies are sent to augment the segments in our army, something you should know well enough yourself. At this point the man could be anywhere."

"Excuse me, Excellency, but that particular animal happens to be right here," Howser replied with cool amusement and a gesture toward the scruffy specimen. "One of our peers was at the challenge for simple amusement, but decided on the spur of the moment to claim this animal. Lord Nombin needed someone with strength to maintain his gardens and lawns, and so he had the animal tamed and put to work. I'm told that it's rather lazy, but Lord Nombin's overseers take care of that swiftly and sternly."

"Yes, I expect they do," Kambil murmured, now staring at the peasant who stood so uncomfortably and unhappily behind Howser. "And do you require a *lot* of correction, peasant?"

"They beat me because they're afraid to face me with talent," the peasant replied sullenly, trying not to show how impressed he was with his surroundings. "I'm better than all the rest and they know it."

"But you can't be better than that friend of yours," Kambil said, digging for the reason behind an odd, disconnected resentment that the man nursed in his private thoughts. "If you were, you would have been made a part of a Blending of your own, just as he was. So between you, he's the better man."

"He's not better in any way at all!" the peasant actually had the nerve to shout, showing that that *was* the basis of the resentment. "If I'd been in his place I would never have left *him* to be made into a slave! But all he did for me was do me *favors*, pretending he cared about our friendship! All he really cared about was playing big man, letting people think of *him* as a High, but me as nothing but a stinking Middle! He could have made things right for me but he couldn't be bothered, and I'll get even for that if it takes me forever!"

"You may have your opportunity sooner than you expect," Kambil said, not in the least disturbed by the peasant's outburst. In point of fact Kambil had been able to tell that the man saw things with the bias of disappointment and disillusion, and the Earth magic user most probably *had* been trying to be a good friend to this sorry example of peasanthood. That could come in handy if the five fugitives did return to the city. . . .

"Lord Rimen, you will certainly be rewarded handsomely for this piece of work," Kambil continued. "You may return the man to Lord Nombin for now, but make certain that Lord Nombin knows how much we value the peasant. He can work the man as he sees fit, but nothing of a permanently damaging nature is to be done to him. Also tell him to be prepared to turn the peasant over to us on very short notice, but not to worry about compensation. We'll see to it that he's repaid for the loss. And while you're at it, see if you can't find something of the same sort to link to the others."

"Excellency, I shall certainly do my best," Howser replied with a courtly bow and a smile of very deep satisfaction curving his lips. "If I learn more, I'll be in touch at once."

Howser bowed his way out, but not before ordering the peasant down on his hands and knees to crawl out of the august presences. The man's hatred of commoners was amusing in some ways, and merely useful in others.

"So we now have a hostage to use against one of the fugitives," Homin commented. "Considering the way they shared the information we gave them with their fellow commoners, the hostage should actually be useful against them. How many more do you think he'll come up with?"

"If he can't *find* any more, he'll probably manufacture one or two," Bron said dryly. "Howser's airs of superiority have always annoyed me, so I don't intend to let him get away with something like that. And simply having hostages won't be enough when those five finally do come back here. What else can we do?"

"There should be quite a lot, but we'll have to discuss it and make a list," Kambil said, deciding against sitting in his chair again. "We were supposed to have done this before, but something always came up to delay it. We'll go to my wing to do the discussing, and have a meal at the same time. I don't want us wasting any time in making these preparations, not when I have the distinct feeling that we don't *have* much time. We have to make sure that when those people come back here, they don't survive setting foot within city limits."

The others all said something to assure him that they'd find a way to do that, all of them, of course, but Delin. Their fifth wasn't looking terribly good, but he was certain to survive long enough for Kambil to find a replacement for him. As soon as they made their preparations against their greatest threat, there would be time to start interviewing potential Highs in Earth magic. . . .

Delin, having been dismissed from joining the others in Kambil's wing, returned to his own as he'd been ordered to do. It became harder and harder for him to bear up under the oppression and humiliation of the situation which had been forced on him, but somehow he kept from going completely insane. Only the thought of escape and eventual retribution had made it possible, but the longer it took, the less possible the idea became . . .

Walking into the small sitting room, the only room Delin was permitted to occupy in his wing, nearly sent him into a fit of suffocation. It had been a cozy room to begin with, and now, with the hard, narrow cot which had been brought in for him to sleep on, there was barely enough room to turn around. But the place was spotlessly clean, thanks to the efforts of the servants he wasn't even permitted to order about.

"Excellency?" a voice said, and Delin turned around to see the servant he'd been hoping for, the one he hadn't been able to expressly request. Gella was an older woman, the kind of woman who usually found him extremely attractive, and who had struck Delin as the sort who was concerned about others to the point of softheadedness. At least she'd shown concern for *him*, and that could possibly be the key to his freedom.

"Excellency, are you all right?" Gella now asked, coming slowly and hesitantly into the room. "Forgive me for saying so, but you look worse than you did the last time I was on duty. May I get you something, like something to eat? The cook would like to make you something marvelous, not what you *have* been eating. Please, may I fetch it?"

It wasn't difficult for Delin to let tears come to his eyes as he slowly sat in the hard wooden chair which had been supplied just for him. Hunger had become his constant companion, and he often dreamed of eating the way he'd always done in the past. The tasteless gruel kept him alive, but there was a very great difference between living and existing.

"By my word, you poor thing!" Gella exclaimed, seeing the tears and quickly coming over to pat his arm. "Something is wrong without doubt, but you aren't saying what it is! Won't you tell me about it so that I can help?"

Delin began to sob just a little, and as he did so he slowly shook his head. He needed the peasant to understand his meaning without hearing the words, but chances were excellent that she just wasn't bright enough.

"You *won't* tell me what's wrong?" she said, naturally giving his actions the wrong interpretation. "I don't understand why not, unless . . . unless you *can't* tell me, rather than won't. Can that be it, that you aren't able to tell me?"

His nodding encouragement must have been pathetic, but

that was exactly what Delin wanted it to be. Without someone's help, he would continue to be as much of a slave as
that peasant who'd been brought by Howser. Gella bright-
ened at seeing his nod, and took one of his hands before
kneeling in front of him.

"So you aren't able to tell me what's wrong," she repeated, probably just to get it straight in her head. "That
must mean you've been ordered by someone not to speak,
which is a vile thing to do to someone. Is there any chance
that they'll change their minds and give you permission to
speak after all?"

Once again Delin shook his head slowly, then pointed to
her. This was the crucial part of his plan, the part that had
to be understood completely, otherwise he was doomed.
She'd done surprisingly well so far, but this time . . .

"Please don't cry even harder," she begged, tears appearing in her own eyes. "You're saying they *won't* change
their minds, and you want *me* to do something about it. Does
that mean you want me to talk to them, to try to get them
to change their minds? We're discussing the other Excellencies, of course, and you think they'll listen to *me?*"

Delin shook his head again but this time almost violently,
panic fleeting across his mind. If this woman let Kambil
know he was trying to escape, he was completely done for.
Only that one small corner of his mind, the corner that
wasn't being controlled by the drug and the orders, had let
him do even as much as he'd done. Kambil would find out
about it and remove it, and then he would be lost forever. . . .

"No, no, of course they would never listen to me," Gella
said quickly, clearly trying to soothe him. "You know that
even better than I do, so you must have meant something
else. What can that something else possibly be?"

The woman began to wrack her brain, which increased
the acid currently consuming Delin's entire stomach. His
fate lay in the hands of an overweight, middle-aged, graying
commoner, and everyone knew how stupid commoners
were. How could he have ever expected that she would understand what was necessary and free him? He must have
been insane to think—

"I know, you want *me* to give you the order to speak!"

Gella suddenly exclaimed, startling Delin nearly out of his shoes. "Is that what you want? Is it really likely to work?"

Delin nodded so hard that his head almost fell off, but he refused to allow relief to touch him. Not until he was back in possession of himself would relief be appropriate. And then there would be other emotions even more appropriate than that. . . .

"All right, then I order you to talk to me," Gella said, sounding odd using so commanding a tone. "I want you to tell me exactly what's troubling you."

"The others all hate me, and this is their idea of a joke," Delin croaked, the first words he'd uttered in too long a time. "I've been given no choice but to obey them, and have even been humiliated to the point of needing to obey everyone else as well. But if you were to order me to forget all previous orders and from now on obey only myself . . . Would you do that for me? Even though it might get you in trouble?"

"You poor, dear man, of course I would," she responded immediately, tightening her grip on the hand she held. "Doing something like that to someone is cruel, not a joke, and I'm not worried about getting into trouble. I now order you to forget all the other orders you've been given, and from now on take orders only from yourself. There. Does that do it?"

"It does indeed, my very dear," Delin said, giving the woman his best smile. "I intend to see you rewarded beyond your wildest dreams, but not immediately, of course. It would never do if my groupmates found out that I'd escaped from their cruelty, so we'll have to pretend that everything remains the same. Or almost everything. Would you do me the very great favor of quietly bringing the marvelous meal you said the cook is ready to prepare? I'm positively famished, and after I've eaten I'll be able to give you *something* of your reward. But please remember: not a word to anyone about this. Tell the cook that you mean to try to talk me into eating the meal, but you don't expect to succeed."

"I'll return as quickly as I can," she promised, giving his hand a last squeeze before releasing it and rising awkwardly to her feet. "And since I haven't really done all that much, don't worry about rewarding me. Seeing you smile is reward enough.''

The look she gave him was ludicrous, trying as it was to be coquettish and sexual. So that was what she wanted, to be considered for his bed so that she might be kept in appropriately high style. He nodded his thanks and hinted at agreement, but the woman really was a fool. Once she'd brought him the meal he needed so desperately, he would send her back to the kitchen on one pretext or another and then cause her to have a fatal heart attack. No one but himself could be trusted to keep this particular secret, and that one meal, which he would claim *she* ate, would have to do him for a while.

"Because, my very *dear* groupmates, you will not know that I'm free again until I want you to know," he whispered aloud after getting to his feet. "And when *that* time comes . . .''

Yes, it would be absolutely marvelous. . . .

Look for Book Five of *The Blending* coming soon.

Discover the secret ways built into the
structure of existence in

KEEPERS OF THE HIDDEN WAYS

by Joel Rosenberg

"Combines a firm, practiced grip on reality with
an effective blend of Irish and Norse mythologies
in a taut, gripping narrative."

Kirkus Reviews

THE FIRE DUKE: Book One
72207-0/$5.99 US/$7.99 Can

THE SILVER STONE: Book Two
72208-9/$5.99 US/$7.99 Can

THE CRIMSON SKY: Book Three
78932-9/$5.99 US/$7.99 Can

Ray Bradbury

SOMETHING WICKED THIS WAY COMES
72940-7/$5.99 US/$7.99 Can

QUICKER THAN THE EYE
78959-0/$5.99 US/$7.99 Can

GOLDEN APPLES OF THE SUN
AND OTHER STORIES
73039-1/$10.00 US/$14.50 Can

A MEDICINE FOR MELANCHOLY
AND OTHER STORIES
73086-3/$10.00 US/$14.50 Can

I SING THE BODY ELECTRIC!
AND OTHER STORIES
78962-0/$10.00 US/$14.50 Can

And in Hardcover

THE MARTIAN CHRONICLES
97383-9/$15.00 US/$20.00 Can

THE ILLUSTRATED MAN
97384-7/$15.00 US/$20.00 Can